THE THIRD SECRET

"*Da Vinci Code* fans will flock to this story. . . . An excellent, tightly plotted thriller."
—*The Roanoake Times*

"A racy read . . . skillfully combines Vatican insights, old-fashioned thrills, intrigue, murder, ambition and retribution."
—*Orlando Sentinel*

THE ROMANOV PROPHECY

"[Berry's] history-based thriller is a coup."
—*The Philadelphia Inquirer*

"Berry uses Russia—past and present—to excellent effect . . . a solid tale a cut above—and then some—many thrillers on the market."
—*Publishers Weekly*

THE AMBER ROOM

"Compelling . . . adventure-filled . . . a fast-moving, globe-hopping tale."
—*San Francisco Chronicle*

"A first thriller that will easily keep you entertained."
—*The Denver Post*

THE VENETIAN BETRAYAL

A Novel

STEVE BERRY

BALLANTINE BOOKS • NEW YORK

2008 Ballantine Books International Edition

Copyright © 2007 by Steve Berry
Excerpt from *The Charlemagne Pursuit* copyright © 2008 by Steve Berry

Published in the United States by Ballantine Books, an imprint of The Random House Publishing Group, a division of Random House, Inc., New York.

BALLANTINE and colophon are registered trademarks of Random House, Inc.

Originally published in hardcover in the United States by Ballantine Books, an imprint of The Random House Publishing Group, a division of Random House, Inc., in 2007.

This book contains an excerpt from the forthcoming hardcover edition of *The Charlemagne Pursuit* by Steve Berry. This excerpt has been set for this edition only and may not reflect the final content of the forthcoming edition.

ISBN 978-0-345-50865-2

Cover photographs: St. Mark's Square © Vladimir Pcholkin/Getty Images; water © Joe Drivas/Getty Images

Printed in the United States of America

www.ballantinebooks.com

OPM 9 8 7 6 5 4 3 2 1

For Karen Elizabeth,
A journey complete

ACKNOWLEDGMENTS

First, Pam Ahearn—and beware, an agent with a new BlackBerry is a dangerous thing. Next, as always, the wonderful folks at Random House: Gina Centrello, my publisher (which I say with great pride); Libby McGuire, for being there with unwavering support; Mark Tavani, who again offered superb editorial insights; Cindy Murray, who takes great joy in sending me away; Kim Hovey, who somehow makes people want me; Rachel Kind, who spreads the books across the globe; Beck Stvan, a cover artist supreme; Carole Lowenstein; and finally all those in Promotions and Sales—absolutely nothing could be achieved without their superior efforts.

A few extra mentions: Vicki Satlow, our Italian literary agent who made the trip to Italy productive; Michele Benzoni and his wife, Leslie, who made us feel welcome in Venice; Cristina Cortese, who showed us St. Mark's basilica and provided invaluable insights; all the folks at Nord publishing in Italy, what a terrific team; and Damaris Corrigan, a brilliant lady who, one evening over dinner, spurred my imagination. My sincere thanks to you all.

For my brother Bob and his wife, Kim; daughter, Lyndsey; and son, Grant; a long overdue special mention. Though it's not said enough, all of you are quite special to me.

Finally, this book is dedicated to my wife of the past few months. She's watched this story grow from a rough idea to words on a page. Along the way she offered guidance, criticism, and encouragement.

Toil and risk are the price of glory, but it is a lovely thing to live with courage and die leaving an everlasting fame.
—ALEXANDER THE GREAT

It is a divine right of madness, not to be able to see the evil which lies just in front.
—UNKNOWN DANISH PLAYWRIGHT

TIMELINE OF RELEVANT EVENTS

JULY 20, 356 BCE	Alexander of Macedonia is born.
336 BCE	Philip II is murdered. Alexander becomes king.
334 BCE	Alexander crosses into Asia Minor and begins his conquests.
SEPTEMBER 326 BCE	The Asia campaign ends in India when Alexander's army revolts. Alexander returns west.
OCTOBER 324 BCE	Hephaestion dies.
JUNE 10, 323 BCE	Alexander dies in Babylon. His generals divide the empire. Ptolemy claims Egypt.
321 BCE	Alexander's funeral cortege leaves for Macedonia. Ptolemy attacks the procession. The body is taken to Egypt.
305 BCE	Ptolemy is crowned pharaoh.
283 BCE	Ptolemy dies.
215 BCE	Ptolemy IV erects the Soma to house Alexander's remains.
100 CE	St. Mark is martyred in Alexandria, his body hidden.

391 CE	The Soma is destroyed and Alexander the Great vanishes.
828 CE	St. Mark's body is stolen from Alexandria by Venetian merchants, taken to Venice, and stored in the Doge's palace, its whereabouts lost over time.
JUNE 1094 CE	Body of St. Mark reappears in Venice.
1835 CE	St. Mark is moved from the crypt to beneath the main altar of the basilica that bears his name.

THE
VENETIAN
BETRAYAL

PROLOGUE

ALEXANDER OF MACEDONIA HAD DECIDED YESTERDAY
to kill the man himself. Usually he delegated such tasks,
but not today. His father had taught him many things
that served him well, but one lesson above all he'd never
forgotten.

Executions were for the living.

Six hundred of his finest guardsmen stood assembled.
Fearless men who, in battle after battle, had surged
head-on into opposing ranks or dutifully protected his
vulnerable flank. Thanks to them the indestructible
Macedonian phalanx had conquered Asia. But there'd
be no fighting today. None of the men carried weapons
or wore armor. Instead, though weary, they'd gathered
in light dress, caps on their heads, eyes focused.

Alexander, too, studied the scene through unusually
tired eyes.

He was leader of Macedonia and Greece, Lord of
Asia, Ruler of Persia. Some called him king of the world.
Others a god. One of his generals once said that he was
the only philosopher ever seen in arms.

But he was also human.

And his beloved Hephaestion lay dead.

The man had been everything to him—confidant, cavalry commander, Grand Vizier, lover. Aristotle had taught

him as a child that a friend was a second self, and that had been Hephaestion. He recalled with amusement how his friend had once been mistaken for him. The error caused a general embarrassment, but Alexander had only smiled and noted that the confusion over Hephaestion was unimportant *for he, too, was Alexander.*

He dismounted his horse. The day was bright and warm. Spring rains from yesterday had passed. An omen? Perhaps.

Twelve years he'd swept east, conquering Asia Minor, Persia, Egypt, and parts of India. His goal now was to advance south and claim Arabia, then west to North Africa, Sicily, and Iberia. Already ships and troops were being amassed. The march would soon begin, but first he had to settle the matter of Hephaestion's untimely death.

He trod across the soft earth, fresh mud sucking at his sandals.

Small in stature, brisk in speech and walk, his fair-skinned, stocky body bore witness to countless wounds. From his Albanian mother he'd inherited a straight nose, a brief chin, and a mouth that could not help but reveal emotion. Like his troops, he was clean shaven, his blond hair unkempt, his eyes—one blue-gray, the other brown—always wary. He prided himself on his patience, but of late he'd found his anger increasingly hard to check. He'd come to enjoy being feared.

"Physician," he said in a low voice, as he approached. "It is said that prophets are best who make the truest guess."

The man did not reply. At least he knew his place.

"From Euripides. A play I much enjoy. But more is expected from a prophet than that, would you not say?"

He doubted Glaucias would reply. The man was wild-eyed with terror.

And he should be scared. Yesterday, during the rain, horses had bent the trunks of two tall palms close to the ground. There they'd been roped, the two lashings intertwined into a single binding, then fastened to another stout palm. Now the physician was tied in the center of the V formed by the trees, each arm secured to a rope, and Alexander held a sword.

"It was your duty to make the truest guess," he said through clenched teeth, his eyes tearing. "Why could you not save him?"

The man's jaw clattered uncontrollably. "I tried."

"How? You did not give him the draught."

Glaucias' head shook in terror. "There was an accident a few days before. Most of the supply spilled. I sent an emissary for more, but he'd not arrived by the time . . . of the final illness."

"Were you not told to always have plenty available?"

"I did, my king. There was an accident." He started to sob.

Alexander ignored the display. "We both agreed that we did not want it to be like the last time."

He knew the physician recalled, from two years past, when Alexander and Hephaestion had both suffered fever. Then, too, the supply had run low, but more had been obtained and the draught relieved them both.

Fear dripped from Glaucias' forehead. Terrified eyes pleaded for mercy. But all Alexander could see was his lover's dead glare. As children, they'd both been students of Aristotle—Alexander the son of a king, Hephaestion the heir of a warrior. They'd bonded thanks to a shared appreciation of Homer and the *Iliad*. Hephaestion had been Patroclus to Alexander's Achilles. Spoiled, spiteful, overbearing, and not all that bright, Hephaestion had still been a wonder. Now he was gone.

"Why did you allow him to die?"

No one but Glaucias could hear him. He'd ordered his troops only close enough to watch. Most of the original Greek warriors who'd crossed with him into Asia were either dead or retired. Persian recruits, conscripted into fighting after he'd conquered their world, now made up the bulk of his force. Good men, every one of them.

"You're my physician," he said in a whisper. "My life is in your hands. The lives of all those I hold dear are in your hands. Yet you failed me." Self-control succumbed to grief and he fought the urge to again weep. "With an accident."

He laid the sword flat across the taut ropes.

"Please, my king. I beg you. It was not my fault. I do not deserve this."

He stared at the man. "Not your fault?" His grief immediately evolved into anger. "How could you say such a thing?" He raised the sword. "It was your duty to help."

"My king. You need me. I am the only one, besides yourself, who knows of the liquid. If it is needed and you are incapable, how would you receive it?" The man was talking fast. Trying whatever might work.

"Others can be taught."

"But it requires skill. Knowledge."

"Your skill was useless for Hephaestion. He did not benefit from your great knowledge." The words formed, but he found them hard to speak. Finally, he summoned his courage and said, more to himself than his victim, "He died."

The time last fall at Ecbatana was to be one of great spectacle—a festival in honor of Dionysius with athletics, music, and three thousand actors and artists, newly arrived from Greece, to entertain the troops. The drinking and merriment should have continued for weeks, but the revelry ended when Hephaestion fell sick.

"I told him not to eat," Glaucias said. "But he ignored me. He ate fowl and drank wine. I told him not to."

"And where were you?" He did not wait for an answer. "At the theater. Watching a performance. While my Hephaestion lay dying."

But Alexander had been in the stadium viewing a race and that guilt amplified his anger.

"The fever, my king. You know its force. It comes quickly and overpowers. No food. You cannot have food. We knew that from last time. Refraining would have provided the time needed for the draught to arrive."

"You should have been there," he screamed, and he saw that his troops heard him. He calmed and said in a near whisper, "The draught should have been available."

He noticed a restlessness among his men. He needed to regain control. What had Aristotle said? *A king speaks only through deeds.* Which was why he'd broken with tradition and ordered Hephaestion's body embalmed. Following more of Homer's prose, as Achilles had done for his fallen Patroclus, he'd commanded the manes and tails of all horses to be severed. He forbade the playing of any musical instrument and sent emissaries to the oracle of Ammon for guidance on how best to remember his beloved. Then, to alleviate his grief, he fell upon the Cossaeans and put the entire nation to the sword—his offering to the evaporating shade of his beloved Hephaestion.

Anger had ruled him.

And still did.

He swung the sword through the air and stopped it close to Glaucias' bearded face. "The fever has again taken me," he whispered.

"Then, my king, you will need me. I can help."

"As you helped Hephaestion?"

He could still see, from three days ago, Hephaestion's funeral pyre. Five stories high, a furlong square at its base, decorated with gilded eagles, ships' prows, lions, bulls, and centaurs. Envoys had come from throughout the Mediterranean world to watch it burn.

And all because of this man's incompetence.

He whirled the sword behind the physician. "I won't require your help."

"No. Please," Glaucias screamed.

Alexander sawed the tight strands of rope with the sharp blade. Each stroke seemed to purge his rage. He plunged the edge into the bundle. Strands released with pops, like bones breaking. One more blow and the sword bit through the remaining restraints. The two palms, freed from their hold, rushed skyward, one left, the other right, Glaucias tied in between.

The man shrieked as his body momentarily stopped the trees' retreat, then his arms ripped from their sockets and his chest exploded in a cascade of crimson.

Palm branches rattled like falling water, and the trunks groaned from their journey back upright.

Glaucias' body thudded to the wet earth, his arms and part of his chest dangling in the branches. Quiet returned as the trees again stood straight. No soldier uttered a sound.

Alexander faced his men and shrieked, *"Alalalalai."*

His men repeated the Macedonian war chant, their cries rumbling across the damp plain and echoing off the fortifications of Babylon. People watching from atop the city walls screamed back. He waited until the sound quieted, then called out, "Never forget him."

He knew they would wonder if he meant Hephaestion or the hapless soul who'd just paid the price of disappointing his king.

But it did not matter.

Not anymore.

He planted the sword into the wet earth and retreated to his horse. What he'd said to the physician was true. The fever was once again upon him.

And he welcomed it.

PART
ONE

ONE

THE SMELL ROUSED COTTON MALONE TO CONSCIOUS-
ness. Sharp, acrid, with a hint of sulfur. And something
else. Sweet and sickening. Like death.

He opened his eyes.

He lay prone on the floor, arms extended, palms to the
hardwood, which he immediately noticed was sticky.

What happened?

He'd attended the April gathering of the Danish Anti-
quarian Booksellers Society a few blocks west of his
bookshop, near the gaiety of Tivoli. He liked the
monthly meetings and this one had been no exception. A
few drinks, some friends, and lots of book chatter. Tomorrow morning he'd agreed to meet Cassiopeia Vitt.
Her call yesterday to arrange the meeting had surprised
him. He'd not heard from her since Christmas, when
she'd spent a few days in Copenhagen. He'd been cruising back home on his bicycle, enjoying the comfortable
spring night, when he'd decided to check out the unusual meeting location she'd chosen, the Museum of
Greco-Roman Culture—a preparatory habit from his
former profession. Cassiopeia rarely did anything on
impulse, so a little advance preparation wasn't a bad
idea.

He'd found the address, which faced the Frederiks-holms canal, and noticed a half-open door to the pitch-dark building—a door that should normally be closed and alarmed. He'd parked his bike. The least he could do was close the door and phone the police when he returned home.

But the last thing he remembered was grasping the doorknob.

He was now inside the museum.

In the ambient light that filtered in through two plate-glass windows, he saw a space decorated in typical Danish style—a sleek mixture of steel, wood, glass, and aluminum. The right side of his head throbbed and he caressed a tender knot.

He shook the fog from his brain and stood.

He'd visited this museum once and had been unimpressed with its collection of Greek and Roman artifacts. Just one of a hundred or more private collections throughout Copenhagen, their subject matter as varied as the city's population.

He steadied himself against a glass display case. His fingertips again came away sticky and smelly, with the same nauseating odor.

He noticed that his shirt and trousers were damp, as were his hair, face, and arms. Whatever covered the museum's interior coated him, too.

He stumbled toward the front entrance and tried the door. Locked. Double dead bolt. A key would be needed to open it from the inside.

He stared back into the interior. The ceiling soared thirty feet. A wood-and-chrome staircase led up to a second floor that dissolved into more darkness, the ground floor extending out beneath.

He found a light switch. Nothing. He lumbered over to a desk phone. No dial tone.

A noise disturbed the silence. Clicks and whines, like gears working. Coming from the second floor.

His training as a Justice Department agent cautioned him to keep quiet, but also urged him to investigate.

So he silently climbed the stairs.

The chrome banister was damp, as were each of the laminated risers. Fifteen steps up, more glass-and-chrome display cases dotted the hardwood floor. Marble reliefs and partial bronzes on pedestals loomed like ghosts. Movement caught his eye twenty feet away. An object rolling across the floor. Maybe two feet wide with rounded sides, pale in color, tight to the ground, like one of those robotic lawn mowers he'd once seen advertised. When a display case or statue was encountered, the thing stopped, retreated, then darted in a different direction. A nozzle extended from its top and every few seconds a burst of aerosol spewed out.

He stepped close.

All movement stopped. As if it sensed his presence. The nozzle swung to face him. A cloud of mist soaked his pants.

What was this?

The machine seemed to lose interest and scooted deeper into the darkness, more odorous mist expelling along the way. He stared down over the railing to the ground floor and spotted another of the contraptions parked beside a display case.

Nothing about this seemed good.

He needed to leave. The stench was beginning to turn his stomach.

The machine ceased its roaming and he heard a new sound.

Two years ago, before his divorce, his retirement from the government, and his abrupt move to Copenhagen, when he'd lived in Atlanta, he'd spent a few hundred dollars on a stainless-steel grill. The unit came with a red button that, when pumped, sparked a gas flame. He recalled the sound the igniter made with each pump of the button.

The same clicking he heard right now.

Sparks flashed.

The floor burst to life, first sun yellow, then burnt orange, finally settling on pale blue as flames radiated outward, consuming the hardwood. Flames simultaneously roared up the walls. The temperature rose swiftly and he raised an arm to shield his face. The ceiling joined the conflagration, and in less than fifteen seconds the second floor was totally ablaze.

Overhead sprinklers sprang to life.

He partially retreated down the staircase and waited for the fire to be doused.

But he noticed something.

The water simply aggravated the flames.

The machine that started the disaster suddenly disintegrated in a muted flash, flames rolling out in all directions, like waves searching for shore.

A fireball drifted to the ceiling and seemed to be welcomed by the spraying water. Steam thickened the air, not with smoke but with a chemical that made his head spin.

He leaped down the stairs two at a time. Another swoosh racked the second floor. Followed by two more. Glass shattered. Something crashed.

He darted to the front of the building.

The other gizmo that had sat dormant sprang to life and started skirting the ground-floor display cases.

More aerosol spewed into the scorching air.

He needed to get out. But the locked front door opened to the inside. Metal frame, thick wood. No way to kick it open. He watched as fire eased down the staircase, consuming each riser, like the devil descending to greet him. Even the chrome was being devoured with a vengeance.

His breaths became labored, thanks to the chemical fog and the rapidly vanishing oxygen. Surely someone would call the fire department, but they'd be no help to him. If a spark touched his soaked clothes . . .

The blaze found the bottom of the staircase.

Ten feet away.

TWO

ENRICO VINCENTI STARED AT THE ACCUSED AND ASKED, "Anything to say to this Council?"

The man from Florence seemed unconcerned by the question. "How about you and your League cram it."

Vincenti was curious. "You apparently think we're to be taken lightly."

"Fat man, I have friends." The Florentine actually seemed proud of the fact. "Lots of them."

He made clear, "Your friends are of no concern to us. But your treachery? That's another matter."

The Florentine had dressed for the occasion, sporting an expensive Zanetti suit, Charvet shirt, Prada tie, and the obligatory Gucci shoes. Vincenti realized that the ensemble cost more than most people earned in a year.

"Tell you what," the Florentine said. "I'll leave and we'll forget all about this . . . whatever this is . . . and you people can go back and do whatever it is you do."

None of the nine seated beside Vincenti said a word. He'd warned them to expect arrogance. The Florentine had been hired to handle a chore in central Asia, a job the Council had deemed vitally important. Unfortunately, the Florentine had modified the assignment to suit his greed. Luckily, the deception had been discovered and countermeasures taken.

"You believe your associates will actually stand with you?" Vincenti asked.

"You're not that naive, are you, fat man? They're the ones who told me to do it."

He again ignored the reference to his girth. "That's not what they said."

Those associates were an international crime syndicate that had many times proven useful to the Council. The Florentine was contracted help and the Council had overlooked the syndicate's deception in order to make a point to the liar standing before them. Which would make a point to the syndicate as well. And it had. Already the fee owed had been waived and the Council's hefty deposit returned. Unlike the Florentine, those associates understood precisely who they were dealing with.

"What do you know of us?" Vincenti asked.

The Italian shrugged. "A bunch of rich people who like to play."

The bravado amused Vincenti. Four men stood behind the Florentine, each armed, which explained why the ingrate thought himself safe. As a condition to his appearing, he'd insisted on them coming.

"Seven hundred years ago," Vincenti said, "a Council of Ten oversaw Venice. They were men supposedly too mature to be swayed by passion or temptation, charged with maintaining public safety and quelling political opposition. And that's precisely what they did. For centuries. They took evidence in secret, pronounced sentences, and carried out executions, all in the name of the Venetian state."

"You think I care about this history lesson?"

Vincenti folded his hands in his lap. "You should care."

"This mausoleum is depressing. It belong to you?"

True, the villa lacked the charm of a house that had once been a family home, but tsars, emperors, archdukes, and crowned heads had all stayed under its roof. Even Napoleon had occupied one of the bedrooms. So he said with pride, "It belongs to us."

"You need a decorator. Are we through here?"

"I'd like to finish what I was explaining."

The Italian gestured with his hands. "Get on with it. I want some sleep."

"We, too, are a Council of Ten. Like the original, we employ Inquisitors to enforce our decisions." He gestured and three men stepped forward from the far side of the salon. "Like the originals, our rule is absolute."

"You're not the government."

"No. We're something else altogether."

Still the Florentine seemed unimpressed. "I came here in the middle of the night because I was ordered to by *my* associates. Not because I'm impressed. I brought these four to protect me. So your Inquisitors might find it difficult to enforce anything."

Vincenti pushed himself up from the chair. "I think something needs to be made clear. You were hired to handle a task. You decided to change that assignment to suit your own purpose."

"Unless all of you intend on leaving here in a box, I'd say we just forget about it."

Vincenti's patience had worn thin. He genuinely disliked this part of his official duties. He gestured and the four men who'd come with the Florentine grabbed the idiot.

A smug look evolved into one of surprise.

The Florentine was disarmed while three of the men restrained him. An Inquisitor approached and, with a roll of thick tape, bound the accused's struggling arms behind his back, his legs and knees together, and wrapped his face, sealing his mouth. The three then released their grip and the Florentine's thick frame thudded to the rug.

"This Council has found you guilty of treason to our League," Vincenti said. He gestured again and a set of double doors swung open. A casket of rich lacquered wood was wheeled in, its lid hinged open. The Florentine's eyes went wide as he apparently realized his fate.

Vincenti stepped close.

"Five hundred years ago traitors to the state were sealed into rooms above the Doge's palace, built of wood and lead, exposed to the elements—they became known as the coffins." He paused and allowed his words to take hold. "Horrible places. Most who entered died. You took our money while, at the same time, trying to make more for yourself." He shook his head. "Not to be. And, by the way, your associates decided *you* were the price they would pay to keep peace with us."

The Florentine fought his restraints with a renewed vigor, his protests stifled by the tape across his mouth. One of the Inquisitors led the four men who'd come with the Florentine from the room. Their job was done. The other two Inquisitors lifted the struggling problem and tossed him into the coffin.

Vincenti stared down into the box and read exactly what the Florentine's eyes were saying. No question he'd betrayed the Council, but he'd only done what Vincenti, not those associates, had ordered him to do. Vincenti was the one who changed the assignment, and the Florentine had only appeared before the Council because Vincenti had privately told him not to worry. Just a dog and pony show. No problem. Play along. It would all be resolved in an hour.

"Fat man?" Vincenti asked. *"Arrivederci."*

And he slammed the lid shut.

THREE

COPENHAGEN

MALONE WATCHED AS THE FLAMES DESCENDING THE staircase stopped three quarters of the way down, showing no signs of advancing farther. He stood before one of the windows and searched for something to hurl through the plate glass. The only chairs he spotted were too close to the fire. The second mechanism continued to prowl the ground floor, exhaling mist. He was hesitant to move. Stripping off his clothes was an option, but his hair and skin also stank with the chemical.

Three thuds on the plate-glass window startled him.

He whirled and, a foot away, a familiar face stared back.

Cassiopeia Vitt.

What was she doing here? His eyes surely betrayed his surprise, but he came straight to the point and yelled, "I need to get out of here."

She pointed to the door.

He intertwined his fingers and signaled that it was locked.

She motioned for him to stand back.

As he did, sparks popped from the underside of the roaming gizmo. He darted straight for the thing and kicked it over. Beneath he spotted wheels and mechanical works.

He heard a pop, then another, and realized what Cassiopeia was doing.

Shooting the window.

Then he saw something he'd not noticed before. Atop the museum's display cases lay sealed plastic bags filled with a clear liquid.

The window fractured.

No choice.

He risked the flames and grabbed one of the chairs he'd earlier noticed, slinging it into the damaged glass. The window shattered as the chair found the street beyond.

The roving mechanism righted itself.

One of the sparks caught and blue flames began to consume the ground floor, advancing in every direction, including straight for him.

He bolted forward and leaped out the open window, landing on his feet.

Cassiopeia stood three feet away.

He'd felt the change in pressure when the window shattered. He knew a little about fires. Right now flames were being supercharged by a rush of new oxygen. Pressure differences were also having an effect. Firefighters called it flashover.

And those plastic bags atop the cases.

He knew what they contained.

He grabbed Cassiopeia's hand and yanked her across the street.

"What are you doing?" she asked.

"Time for a swim."

They leaped from the brick parapet, just as a fireball surged from the museum.

FOUR

Supreme Minister Irina Zovastina stroked the horse and prepared herself for the game. She loved to play, just after dawn, in the breaking light of early morning, on a grassy field damp with dew. She also loved the famed, blood-sweating stallions of Fergana, first prized over a millennia ago when they were traded to the Chinese for silk. Her stables contained over a hundred steeds bred both for pleasure and politics.

"Are the other riders ready?" she asked the attendant.

"Yes, Minister. They await you on the field."

She wore high leather boots and a quilted leather jacket over a long *chapan*. Her short, silver-blond hair was topped by a fur hat fashioned from a wolf she'd taken great pride in killing. "Let's not keep them waiting."

She mounted the horse.

Together, she and the animal had many times won *buzkashi*. An ancient game, once played across the steppe by a people who lived and died in the saddle. Genghis Khan himself had enjoyed it. Then, women were not even allowed to watch, much less participate.

But she'd changed that rule.

The spindly-legged, broad-chested horse stiffened as she caressed his neck. "Patience, Bucephalas."

She'd named him after the animal that had carried Alexander the Great across Asia, into battle after battle. *Buzkashi* horses, though, were special. Before they played a single match years of training accustomed them to the game's chaos. Along with oats and barley, eggs and butter were included in their diet. Eventually, when the animal fattened, he was bridled and saddled and stood in the sun for weeks at a time, not just to burn away excess kilos, but to teach him patience. Even more training came in close-quarter galloping. Aggression was encouraged, but always disciplined so that horse and rider became a team.

"You are prepared?" the attendant asked. He was a Tajik, born among the mountains to the east, and had served her for nearly a decade. He was the only one she allowed to ready her for the game.

She patted her chest. "I believe I'm properly armored."

Her fur-lined leather jacket fit snugly, as did the leather pants. It had served her well that nothing about her stout frame was particularly feminine. Her muscular arms and legs bulged from a meticulous exercise routine and a rigid diet. Her wide face and broad features carried a hint of Mongol, as did her deep-set brown eyes, all thanks to her mother, whose family traced their roots to the far north. Years of self-imposed discipline had left her quick to listen and slow to speak. Energy radiated from her.

Many had said that an Asian federation was impossible, but she'd proven them all wrong. Kazakhstan, Uzbekistan, Kyrgyzstan, Karakalpakstan, Tajikistan, and Turkmenistan were no more. Instead, fifteen years ago, those former Soviet republics, after briefly trying independence, merged into the newly formed Central Asian

Federation. Nine and a half million square kilometers, sixty million people, a massive stretch of territory that rivaled North America and Europe in size, scope, and resources. Her dream. Now a reality.

"Careful, Minister. They like to best you."

She smiled. "Then they better play hard."

They conversed in Russian, though Dari, Kazakh, Tajik, Turkmen, and Kyrgyz together were now the official Federation languages. As a compromise to the many Slavs, Russian remained the language of "interethnic communication."

The stable doors swung open and she gazed out onto a flat field that stretched for over a kilometer. Toward its center, twenty-three mounted horsemen congregated near a shallow pit. Inside lay the *boz*—a goat's carcass, without a head, organs, or legs, soaked in cold water for a day to give it strength for what it was about to endure.

At each end of the field rose a striped post.

The horsemen continued to ride. *Chopenoz*. Players, like herself. Ready for the game.

Her attendant handed her a whip. Centuries ago they were leather thongs tied to balls of lead. They were more benign now, but still used not only to spur a horse but to attack the other players. Hers had been fashioned with a beautiful ivory handle.

She steadied herself in the saddle.

The sun had just topped the forest to the east. Her palace had once been the residence of the khans who ruled the region until the late nineteenth century, when the Russians had invaded. Thirty rooms, rich in Uzbek furniture and Oriental porcelain. What was now the stables had then housed the harem. Thanks to the gods those days were over.

She sucked a deep breath, which carried the sweet scent of a new day.

"Good playing," the attendant said.

She acknowledged his encouragement with a nod and prepared to enter the field.

But she could not help wondering.

What was happening in Denmark?

FIVE

VIKTOR TOMAS STOOD IN THE SHADOWS, ACROSS THE canal, and watched the Greco-Roman museum burn. He turned to his partner but did not speak the obvious.

Problems.

It was Rafael who had attacked the intruder, then dragged the unconscious body into the museum. Somehow, after their surreptitious entrance, the front door had become ajar and, from the second-floor railing, he'd spotted a shadow approaching the stoop. Rafael, working on the ground floor, had instantly reacted, positioning himself just inside. True, he should have simply waited and seen what the visitor's intentions had been. But instead, he'd yanked the shadow inside and popped the side of the man's head with one of the sculptures.

"The woman," Rafael said. "She was waiting, with a gun. That can't be good."

He agreed. Long dark hair, shapely, dressed in a tight-fitting bodysuit. As the building caught fire, she'd emerged from an alley and stood near the canal. When the man appeared in the window, she'd produced a gun and shot out the glass.

The man, too, was a problem.

Fair-haired, tall, sinewy. He'd propelled a chair through the glass then leaped out with surprising agility, as if he'd done that before. He'd instantly grabbed the woman and they'd both plunged into the canal.

The fire department had arrived within minutes, just as the two emerged from the water and blankets were wrapped around them. The turtles had clearly performed their tasks. Rafael had christened them with the label since, in many ways, they resembled turtles, even possessing the ability to right themselves. Thankfully, no remnant of the devices would remain. Each was made of combustible materials that vaporized in the intense heat of their destruction. True, any investigator would quickly label the blaze arson, but proof of the method and mechanism would be impossible to determine.

Except that the man had survived.

"Will he be trouble?" Rafael asked.

Viktor continued to watch the firemen battle the blaze. The man and woman sat on the brick parapet, still wrapped in their blankets.

They seemed to know each other.

That worried him more.

So he answered Rafael's inquiry the only way he could.

"No doubt."

MALONE HAD RECOVERED HIS WITS. CASSIOPEIA HUDdled in a blanket beside him. Only remnants of the museum's walls remained and nothing of its inside. The old building had burned quickly. Firemen continued to mind the blaze, concentrating on confining the destruction. So far, none of the adjacent buildings had been affected.

The night air reeked of soot, along with another smell—bitter, yet sweet—similar to what he'd inhaled while trapped inside. Smoke continued to drift skyward, filtering the bright stars. A stout man in dingy yellow firefighting gear waddled over for the second time. One of the crew chiefs. A city policeman had already taken a statement from both he and Cassiopeia.

"Like you said about the sprinklers," the chief said in Danish. "Our water only seemed to spark it up."

"How'd you finally control it?" Malone asked.

"When the tanker ran out of juice, we dipped our hoses into the canal and pumped straight from it. That worked."

"Salt water?" All of Copenhagen's canals connected to the sea.

The chief nodded. "Stops it cold."

He wanted to know, "Find anything in the building?"

"No little machines, like you told the police. But that place was so hot it melted the marble statues." The chief ran a hand through his wet hair. "That's a powerful fuel. We'll need your clothes. May be the only way to determine its composition."

"Maybe not," he said. "I took a dip in that canal, too."

"Good point." The chief shook his head. "The arson investigators are going to love this one."

As the fireman lumbered off, Malone faced Cassiopeia and plunged into an interrogation. "You want to tell me what's going on?"

"You weren't supposed to be here till tomorrow morning."

"That's not an answer to my question."

Wet tangles of thick dark hair hung past her shoulders and roughly framed her alluring face. She was a Spanish Muslim, living in southern France. Bright, rich, and cocky—an engineer and a historian. But her presence in Copenhagen, a day earlier than she'd told him, meant something. Also, she'd come armed and dressed for battle—dark leather pants and a tight-fitting leather jacket. He wondered if she was going to be difficult or cooperative.

"Lucky I was here to save your hide," she said to him.

He couldn't decide if she was serious or teasing him. "How did you know my hide needed saving?"

"Long story, Cotton."

"I've got the time. I'm retired."

"I'm not."

He heard the bitter edge in her voice and sensed something. "You knew that building was going to burn, didn't you?"

She did not look at him, just stared off across the canal. "I actually wanted it to burn."

"Care to explain that one?"

She sat silently, absorbed in thought. "I was here. Earlier. I watched while two men broke into the museum. I saw them grab you. I needed to follow them, but couldn't." She paused. "Because of you."

"Who were they?"

"The men who left those machines."

She'd listened as he'd given his statement to the police, but he'd sensed the whole time that she already knew the story. "How about we cut the crap and you tell me what's going on. I almost got killed over whatever it is you're doing."

"You should ignore open doors in the night."

"Old habits are hard to break. What's going on?"

"You saw the flames. Felt the heat. Unusual, wouldn't you say?"

He recalled how the fire had descended the stairs then stopped, as if waiting to be invited further. "You could say that."

"In the seventh century, when the Muslim fleets attacked Constantinople, they should have easily routed the city. Better weapons. A mass of forces. But the Byzantines had a surprise. They called it liquid fire, or wild fire, and they unleashed it on the ships, totally destroying the invading fleet." Cassiopeia still wasn't looking at him. "The weapon survived in various forms to the time of the Crusades, and eventually acquired the name Greek fire. The original formula was so secret that it was held personally by each Byzantine emperor. They guarded it so well that, when the empire finally fell, the formula was lost." She breathed deeply as she continued to clutch the blanket. "It's been found."

"You're telling me that I just saw Greek fire?"

"With a twist. This kind hates salt water."

"So why didn't you tell the firemen that when they arrived?"

"I don't want to answer any more questions than I have to."

But he wanted to know. "Why let this museum burn? There's nothing of any consequence there?"

He stared back toward the burned hulk and spotted the charred remains of his bicycle. He sensed something more from Cassiopeia, as she continued to avoid his gaze. Never in all the time he'd known her had he seen any sign of misgiving, nervousness, or dejection. She was tough, eager, disciplined, and smart. But at the moment she seemed troubled.

A car appeared at the far end of the cordoned-off street. He recognized the expensive British sedan and the hunched figure that emerged from its rear seat.

Henrik Thorvaldsen.

Cassiopeia stood. "He's here to talk with us."

"And how did he know we were here?"

"Something's happening, Cotton."

SIX

VINCENTI WAS GLAD THE POTENTIAL DISASTER WITH THE Florentine had been averted. He'd made a mistake. Time was short and he was playing a dangerous game, but it seemed fate had dealt him another chance.

"Is the situation in central Asia under control?" one of the Council of Ten asked him. "Did we halt whatever that fool had tried to do?"

All of the men and women had lingered in the meeting hall after the Florentine, struggling within his coffin, was wheeled away. A bullet to the head should have, by now, ended further resistance.

"We're okay," he said. "I personally handled the matter, but Supreme Minister Zovastina is quite the showgirl. I assume she'll make a spectacle of things."

"She's not to be trusted," another said.

He wondered about the declaration's vehemence considering Zovastina was their ally, but he nonetheless agreed. "Despots are always a problem." He stood and approached a map that hung from one wall. "Damn if she hasn't accomplished a lot, though.

"She managed to merge six corrupt Asian states into a federation that might actually succeed." He pointed. "She's essentially redrawn the world map."

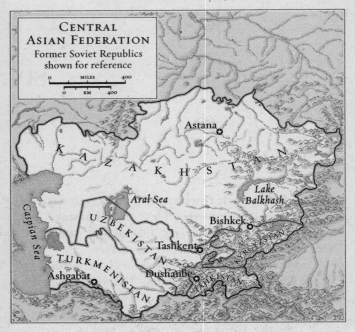

CENTRAL
ASIAN FEDERATION
Former Soviet Republics
shown for reference

0   MILES   400

0   KM   400

K   A   Z   A   K   H   S   T   A   N

Astana

Aral Sea

Lake Balkhash

Caspian Sea

U Z B E K I S T A N

Bishkek

Tashkent

KYRGYZSTAN

T U R K M E N I S T A N

Dushanbe

Ashgabat

TAJIKISTAN

"And how did she do it?" came a question. "Certainly not by diplomacy."

Vincenti knew the official account. After the Soviet Union fell, central Asia suffered civil wars and strife, as each of the emerging "nation-stans" struggled with independence. The so-called Commonwealth of Independent States, which succeeded the USSR, existed in name only. Corruption and incompetence ran rampant. Irina Zovastina had headed local reforms under Gorbachev, championing perestroika and glasnost, spearheading the prosecution of many corrupt bureaucrats. Eventually, though, she led the charge to expel the Russians, reminding the people of Russia's colonial conquest and sounding an environmental alarm, noting that Asians were dying by the thousands from Russian pollution. Ultimately, she stood before Kazakhstan's Assembly of Representatives and helped proclaim the republic.

A year later, she was elected president.

The West welcomed her. She seemed a reformer in a region that rarely reformed. Then, fifteen years ago, she stunned the world with the announcement of the Central Asian Federation.

Six nations, now one.

Yet Vincenti's colleague was right. Not a miracle. More a manipulation. So he answered the inquiry with the obvious. "She achieved it with power."

"And the fortunate demise of political opponents."

"That's always been a way to power," he said. "We can't fault her for that. We do the same." He stared at another of the Council members. "Are the funds in place?"

The treasurer nodded. "Three point six billion, scattered at a variety of banks around the globe, access clean, straight to Samarkand."

"I assume our members are ready?"

"A renewed influx of investment will start immediately. Most of the members are planning major expansions. They've been careful, per our directive, to this point."

Time was short. Just as with the original Council of Ten, half of the current Council would soon rotate off. League bylaws mandated that five members changed every two years. Vincenti's term would expire in less than thirty days.

A blessing and a problem.

Six hundred years ago Venice had been an oligarchical republic, governed by merchants through a complicated political system designed to prevent despotism. Faction and intrigue were thought foiled by processes that relied heavily on chance. No one person ever held sole authority. Always groups advising, deciding, and acting. Groups that changed at regular intervals.

But corruption still crept in. Plots and pet projects flourished. Webs of conspiracy were woven.

Men always found a way.

And so had he.

Thirty days.

More than enough time.

"What of Supreme Minister Zovastina?" one of the Council asked, breaking his thoughts. "Will she be all right?"

"Now that," he said, "may well become the talk of this day."

SEVEN

ZOVASTINA SPURRED HER HORSE. THE OTHER *CHOPENOZ*
whipped their mounts, too. Mud splattered up at her
from wet turf obliterated by hooves. She bit down on
the whip and gripped the reins with both hands. No one
had, as yet, made a move on the goat carcass lying in its
earthen pan.

"Come now, Bucephalas," she said through clenched
teeth into the horse's ear. "Time to show them." She
yanked and the animal bolted right.

The game was simple. Grab the *boz*, ride with it in
hand to the far end of the field, round the pole, then return and deposit the dead goat in the circle of justice,
outlined in lime on the grass. Sounded easy, but the
problem came from the *chopenoz* who were allowed to
do most anything to steal the *boz*.

An invitation to play *buzkashi* with her was considered an honor, and she chose the participants with great
care. Today's were a mixture of her personal guard and
nine invited guests, making for two teams of twelve.

She was the only woman.

And she liked that.

Bucephalas seemed to sense what was expected of him
and closed on the *boz*. Another player slammed into the

horse's right flank. Zovastina retrieved the whip from her mouth and slashed a blow at the other rider, popping the man's face with leather tendrils. He brushed aside her attack and continued his assault, now joined by three other horsemen trying to stop her.

Two of her team closed ranks and battled the three opponents.

A storm of horses and riders orbited the *boz*.

She'd told her team earlier that she wanted to make the first run around the pole and they seemed to be doing their part to accommodate her.

A fourth player from the opposing team drove his horse close.

The world spun around her as all twenty-four *chopenoz* circled. One of her opponents' whips found her chest, but the thick leather jacket deflected the blow. Usually, striking the Supreme Minister was a capital offense, but that rule was waived during *buzkashi*. She wanted players to hold nothing back.

A horseman slipped from his mount and slammed to the ground.

No one stopped to help. Not allowed.

Broken limbs, cuts, and slashes were common. Five men had actually died on this field during the past two years. Death had always been common during *buzkashi*. Even the Federation's criminal code contained an exception to murder that applied only during the game.

She rounded the shallow pit.

Another rider reached for the *boz*, but she pounded his hand with her whip. She then pulled hard on the reins and slowed Bucephalas, whirling them both around and, once again, charging the carcass before the others caught back up with her.

Two more riders plunged to the ground.

Each of her breaths came laced with grass and mud

and she spat out the sediment, but she welcomed the scent of sweating horseflesh.

She stuffed the whip back in her mouth and leaned down, one hand keeping a stranglehold on the saddle, the other yanking up the carcass. Blood squirted from where the goat's hooves and head had been severed. She dragged the dead goat up and held tight, then signaled for Bucephalas to sweep left.

Only three rules now governed.

No tying of the carcass. No striking the hand of the holder. No tripping the horses.

Time for a run at the pole.

She spurred Bucephalas.

The other team closed.

Her teammates galloped to her defense.

The carcass was heavy, maybe thirty kilos, but her strong arms were more than capable of holding on. Blood continued to soak her hand and sleeve.

A blow to her spine caught her attention.

She whirled.

Two opposing horsemen.

More swarmed inward.

Hooves pounded the damp earth like thunder, pierced by the frenzied screams of horses. Her *chopenoz* came to her defense. Blows were exchanged. She held the *boz* in a death grip, her forearms aching.

The pole stood fifty meters away.

The field spread out behind the summer palace on a grassy plain that eventually ended at thick forest. The Soviets had utilized the complex as a retreat for the party elite, which explained how it had survived. She'd changed the layout, but a few aspects of the Russian occupation had been wisely retained.

More riders joined the fray as both teams fought with each other.

Whips snapped.

Men groaned in pain.

Obscenities were exchanged.

She surged into the lead, but only slightly. She'd have to slow to round the pole and begin her return to the circle of justice, which would give them all an opportunity to pounce. Though her team had been accommodating to this point, the rules now allowed anyone to steal the *boz* and make a run of their own.

She decided to catch them all off guard.

Kicking, she directed Bucephalas to angle right.

No out of bounds governed. Riders could, and did, venture anywhere. She arced their galloping path outward, the bulk of the *chopenoz* massed to her left, stretching her advance to the field's fringes where rows of tall trees guarded the perimeter. She could weave between them—she'd done so before—but today she preferred a different route.

Before any of the others could react to her sudden shift, she hooked left and crisscrossed the field, cutting off the main body of galloping riders, causing them all to slow.

Their instant of hesitation allowed her to sweep ahead and loop the pole.

The others followed.

She turned her attention ahead.

One rider waited fifty meters down the field. He was swarthy, bearded, with a stiff face. He sat tall in the saddle and she saw his hand emerge from beneath a leather cape, holding a gun. He kept the weapon close, waiting for her.

"Let's show him, Bucephalas, that we're not afraid."

The horse raced forward.

The man with the gun did not move. Zovastina stared him down. No one would ever cause her to retreat.

The gun came level.

A shot echoed across the field.

The man with the gun teetered, then collapsed to the wet ground. His horse, spooked by the retort, raced away riderless.

She trampled the corpse, Bucephalas' hooves digging into the still-warm flesh, the body swept away in their wake.

She kept riding until the circle of justice came into view. She rode past and tossed the *boz* into its center, then brought Bucephalas to a stop.

The other riders had all halted where the dead man lay.

Shooting a player was absolutely against the rules. But this was not part of any game. Or maybe it was? Just a different contest. With different players and different rules. One none of the men here today would either understand or appreciate.

She yanked on the reins and straightened herself in the saddle, casting a glance toward the palace roof. Inside one of the old Soviet gun stations, her sharpshooter signaled success by waving his rifle.

She returned the gesture by rearing Bucephalas onto his hind legs and the horse whinnied his approval of the kill.

EIGHT

CASSIOPEIA FOLLOWED MALONE AND HENRIK THOR-
valdsen into Malone's bookshop. She was tired. Even
though she'd expected a long night, the past few months
had taken a toll, especially the last few weeks, and the
ordeal seemed far from over.

Malone switched on the lights.

She'd been told about what had happened the previous fall—when Malone's ex-wife had appeared . . . and
the firebombing—but the restorers had done a terrific
job. She noted the workmanship. New, yet made to appear old. "My compliments to the craftsmen."

Thorvaldsen nodded. "I wanted it to look like it once
did. Too much history in this building to be blown away
by fanatics."

"Want to get out of those damp clothes?" Malone
asked her.

"Shouldn't we send Henrik home first?"

Malone grinned. "I hear he likes to watch."

"Sounds intriguing," Thorvaldsen said. "But tonight
I'm not in the mood."

Neither was she. "I'm fine. Leather dries quickly. One
reason I wear it when I'm working."

"And what were you working on tonight?"

"You sure you want to hear this? Like you say all the

time, you're a bookseller, not an operative. Retired, and all those other excuses."

"You sent me an e-mail telling me to meet you at that museum in the morning. With what you said back at the fire, there wouldn't have been any museum there tomorrow."

She sat in one of the club chairs. "Which is why we were going to meet there. Tell him, Henrik."

She liked Malone. He was a smart, confident, handsome man—she'd thought that when they first met last year in France. A uniquely trained lawyer. Twelve years he worked for the U.S. Justice Department in a covert unit known as the Magellan Billet. Then, two years ago, he opted out and bought a bookshop from Thorvaldsen in Copenhagen. He was plain spoken and sometimes rough in manner, just like her, so she couldn't complain. She liked his animated face, that malicious twinkle in his bright green eyes, his sandy-colored hair, and the always-swarthy complexion. She knew his age, mid-forties, and realized that, thanks to a bloom of youth that had yet to fade, he was at the zenith of his charms.

She envied him.

Time.

For her, it seemed in such short supply.

"Cotton," Thorvaldsen said, "across Europe there have been other fires. They started in France, then in Spain, Belgium, and Switzerland. Similar to what you just experienced. The police in each location realized arson but, so far, none of them have been connected. Two of the buildings burned to ash. They were in rural locations and nobody seemed to care. All four were unoccupied private residences. The one here was the first commercial establishment."

"And how did you connect the dots?" Malone asked.

"We know what they're after," she said. "Elephant medallions."

"You know," Malone said, "that's exactly what I was thinking. Five arsons. All across Europe. Has to be elephant medallions. What else could it be?"

"They're real," she said.

"Nice to know, but what the hell is an elephant medallion?"

"Twenty-three hundred years ago," Thorvaldsen said, "after Alexander the Great conquered Asia Minor and Persia, he set his sights on India. But his army quit him before he could take much of that land. He fought several battles in India and, for the first time, encountered war elephants. They crushed the Macedonian lines, wreaked havoc. Alexander's men were terrified of them. Medallions were later struck to commemorate the event, which depicted Alexander facing off with the elephants."

"The medallions," she said, "were minted after Alexander's death. We have no idea how many, but today only eight are known. The four already taken, the one from tonight, two more in private hands, and one on display in the Museum of Cultural History in Samarkand."

"The capital of the Central Asian Federation?" Malone said. "Part of the region Alexander conquered."

Thorvaldsen slouched in one of the club chairs, his crooked spine cocking his neck forward and settling his fleshy chin onto a thin chest. Cassiopeia noticed that her old friend looked worn. He wore his customary baggy sweater and oversized corduroy trousers. A uniform he used, she knew, to conceal the deformity. She regretted involving him, but he'd insisted. He was a good friend. Time to see how good a friend Malone was. "What do you know about the death of Alexander the Great?"

"I've read about it. Lots of myth mixed with conflicting facts."

"That eidetic memory of yours?"

He shrugged. "It came with me out of the womb."

She smiled. "What happened in June 323 BCE made a great deal of difference to the world."

Thorvaldsen gestured with his arm. "Go ahead. Tell him. He needs to know."

So she did.

On the final day of May, within the walls of Babylon, Alexander attended a dinner given by one of his trusted Companions. He pledged a toast, drank a large cup of undiluted wine, then shrieked aloud as if smitten by a violent blow. He was quickly taken to bed where a fever came, but he continued to play dice, plan with his generals, and make the proper sacrifices. On the fourth day he complained of weariness and some of his Companions noticed a lack of his normal energy. He lay quiet for several more days, sleeping in the bathhouse for coolness. Despite his weakened condition, Alexander sent word to the infantry to be ready to march in four days and for the fleet to sail in five. His plans to move west and take Arabia were about to unfold. On June 6, feeling weaker, he passed his ring to Perdiccas so the proper administration of the government could continue. This caused a panic. His troops feared he'd died and, to calm their unease, Alexander allowed them to file past his bed. He greeted each one with a smile. When the last man left he whispered, "After my death, where will you find a king who deserves such men?" He commanded that, after his death, his body should be taken to the Temple of Ammon in Egypt. But none of the Companions wanted to hear such fatalism. His condition worsened until, on June 9, his Companions asked, "To whom do you leave your kingdom?" Ptolemy said he heard, "to the brightest." Seleucus said, "to the righteous." Peithon recalls, "to the strongest." A great debate ensued as to who was right. Early during the morning of the next day, in the thirty-third year of life, twelve years and eight months into his reign, Alexander III of Macedonia died.

"People still debate those last words," she said.

"And why is it so important?" Malone asked.

"It's what he left behind," Thorvaldsen said. "His kingdom, with no rightful heir."

"And that has something to do with elephant medallions?"

"Cotton," Thorvaldsen said, "I bought that museum knowing someone would destroy it. Cassiopeia and I have been waiting for that to happen."

She said, "We had to stay a step ahead of whoever is after the medallions."

"Seems like they won. They have the thing."

Thorvaldsen cast her a look, then the older man stared at Malone and said, "Not exactly."

NINE

VIKTOR RELAXED ONLY WHEN THE DOOR TO THE HOTEL room was closed and locked. They were across Copenhagen, near Nyhavn, where boisterous waterfront cafés catered to rowdy patrons. He sat at the desk and switched on a lamp as Rafael assumed a window position, which overlooked the street four stories below.

He now possessed the fifth medallion.

The first four had been disappointments. One was a forgery, the other three in poor condition. Six months ago he knew little about elephant medallions. Now he considered himself quite proficient in their provenance.

"We should be fine," he said to Rafael. "Calm down. No one followed us."

"I'll keep watch to be sure."

He knew Rafael was trying to make amends for overreacting in the museum, so he said, "It's okay."

"He should have died."

"It's better he didn't. At least we know what we're facing."

He unzipped a leather case and removed a stereomicroscope and digital scale.

He laid the coin on the desk. They'd found it displayed in one of the museum cases, correctly noted as an "Elephant Medallion (Alexander the Great), a decadrachm, circa second century BCE."

He first measured its width. Thirty-five millimeters. About right. He flicked on the electronic scales and checked its weight. Forty point seventy-four grams. Correct, too.

With a magnifying glass he examined the image on one face—a warrior in regal splendor, complete with plumed helmet, neck guard, breastplate, and a cavalry cloak that fell to his knees.

He was pleased. An obvious flaw in the forgeries was the cloak, which in the false medallions hung to the ankles. For centuries, trade in fake Greek coins had flourished and clever forgers had become adept at fooling both the anxious and the willing.

Luckily, he was neither.

The first known elephant medallion had surfaced when it was donated to the British Museum in 1887. It came from somewhere in central Asia. A second appeared in 1926, from Iran. A third was discovered in 1959. A fourth in 1964. Then, in 1973, four more were found near the ruins of Babylon. Eight in all that had made the rounds through museums and private collectors. Not all that valuable, considering the variety of Hellenistic art and the thousands of coins available, but nonetheless collectible.

He returned to his examination.

The clean-shaven, youthful warrior grasped a sarissa in his left hand topped by a leaf-shaped point. His right hand held a bolt of lightning. Above him loomed a flying Nike, the winged goddess of victory. To the warrior's left, the die cutter had left a curious monogram.

Whether it was BA or BAB, and what the letters represented Viktor did not know. But an authentic medallion should show that odd symbol.

All seemed in order. Nothing added or missing.

He flipped the coin over.

Its edges were grossly distorted, the pewter-colored patina worn smooth as if by running water. Time was slowly dissolving the delicate engraving on both sides. Amazing, really, that any of them had managed to survive.

"All quiet?" he asked Rafael, who still stood near the window.

"Don't patronize me."

He glanced up. "I actually want to know."

"I can't seem to get it right."

He caught the defeatism. "You saw someone coming to the museum door. You reacted. That's all."

"It was foolish. Killing attracts too much attention."

"There would have been no body to find. Quit worrying about it. And besides, I approved leaving him there."

He refocused his attention on the medallion. The obverse showed the warrior, now a cavalryman, wearing the same outfit, attacking a retreating elephant. Two men sat atop the elephant, one brandishing a sarissa, the other trying to remove a cavalryman's pike from his chest. Numismatists all agreed that the regal warrior on both sides of the coin represented Alexander, and the medallions commemorated a battle with war elephants.

But the real test as to whether the thing was authentic came under the microscope.

He switched on the illuminator and slid the decadrachm onto the examining tray.

Authentic ones contained an anomaly. Tiny microletters concealed within the engraving, added by ancient die cutters using a primitive lens. Experts believed the lettering represented something akin to a watermark on a modern banknote, perhaps to ensure authenticity. Lenses were not common in ancient times, so detecting the mark then would have been nearly impossible. The lettering was noticed when the first medallion surfaced years ago. But of the four they'd stolen so far, only one had contained the peculiarity. If this medallion were genuine, within the folds of the cavalryman's clothing there should be two Greek letters—ZH.

He focused the microscope and saw tiny writing.

But not letters.

Numbers.

36 44 77 55.

He glanced up from the eyepiece.

Rafael was watching him. "What is it?"

Their dilemma had just deepened. Earlier he'd used the hotel room's phone and made several calls. His gaze shot to the telephone and the display at its base. Four sets of numbers, two each, starting with thirty-six.

Not the same ones he'd just seen through the microscope.

But he instantly knew what the digits on the supposedly ancient medallion represented.

A Danish phone number.

TEN

VINCENTI STUDIED HIMSELF IN THE MIRROR AS HIS valet creased the jacket and allowed the Gucci suit to drape his enormous frame. With a camel-haired brush, all remnants of lint from the dark wool were removed. He then adjusted his tie and made sure the dimple plunged deep. The valet handed him a burgundy handkerchief and he adjusted the silk folds into his coat pocket.

His three-hundred-pound frame looked good in the tailored suit. The Milan fashion consultant he kept on retainer had advised him that swarthy colors not only conveyed authority, they also drew attention away from his stature. Which wasn't an easy thing to do. Everything about him was big. Pouched cheeks, rolled forehead, cob-nose. But he loved rich food and dieting seemed such a sin.

He motioned and the valet buffed his Lorenzo Banfi laced shoes. He stole a last look in the mirror, then glanced at his watch.

"Sir," the valet said, "she called while you were showering."

"On the private line?"

The valet nodded.

"She leave a number?"

The valet reached into his pocket and found a slip of paper. He'd managed some sleep both before and after the Council meeting. Sleep, unlike dieting, was not a waste of time. He knew people were waiting for him, and he despised being late, but he decided to call from the privacy of his bedroom. No use broadcasting everything over a cellular.

The valet retreated from the room.

He stepped to a bedside phone and dialed international. Three buzzes shrilled in his ear before a woman's voice answered and he said, "I see, Supreme Minister, that you're still among the living."

"And it's good to know your information was accurate."

"I wouldn't have bothered you with fantasy."

"But you still haven't said how you knew someone would try to kill me today."

Three days ago he'd passed on to Irina Zovastina the Florentine's plan. "The League watches over its members, and you, Supreme Minister, are one of our most important."

She chuckled. "You're so full of it, Enrico."

"Did you win at *buzkashi*?"

"Of course. Two times into the circle. We left the assassin's body on the field and trampled it into pieces. The birds and dogs are now enjoying the rest."

He winced. That was the problem with central Asia. Wanting desperately to be a part of the twenty-first century, its culture remained entrenched in the fifteenth. The League would have to do what it could to change all that. Even if the task would be like weaning a carnivore onto a vegetarian diet.

"Do you know the *Iliad*?" she asked.

He knew she'd have to be humored. "I do."

"*Cast the souls of many stalwart heroes to Hades and their bodies to the gods and birds of prey.*"

He grinned. "You fashion yourself Achilles?"

"There's much to admire in him."

"Wasn't he a proud man? Excessive, as I recall."

"But a fighter. Always a fighter. Tell me, Enrico, what of *your* traitor? Was that problem resolved?"

"The Florentine will enjoy a lovely burial north of here, in the lake district. We'll send flowers." He decided to see if she was in the mood. "We need to talk."

"Your payment for saving my life?"

"Your end of our bargain, as we originally discussed long ago."

"I'll be ready to meet with the Council in a few days. First, there are things I need to resolve."

"I'm more interested in when you and I will meet."

She chuckled. "I'm sure you are. I am, too, actually. But there are things I must complete."

"My time on the Council ends soon. Thereafter, you'll have others to deal with. They may not be as accommodating."

She laughed. "I love that. *Accommodating.* I do enjoy dealing with you, Enrico. We so understand each other."

"We need to talk."

"Soon. First, you have that other problem we spoke about. The Americans."

Yes, he did. "Not to worry, I plan to deal with that today."

ELEVEN

"WHAT DO YOU MEAN *NOT EXACTLY*?" MALONE ASKED Thorvaldsen.

"I commissioned a fake elephant medallion. It's quite easy to do, actually. There are many counterfeits on the market."

"And why did you do that?"

"Cotton," Cassiopeia said to him, "these medallions are important."

"Gee, never would have guessed. What I haven't heard is how and why."

"What do you know of Alexander the Great, *after* he died?" Thorvaldsen asked. "With what happened to his body."

He'd read on the subject. "I know some."

"I doubt you know what we do," Cassiopeia said. She stood beside one of the bookshelves. "Last fall, I received a call from a friend who worked at the cultural museum in Samarkand. He'd found something he thought I might like to see. An old manuscript."

"How old?"

"First or second century after Christ. Ever hear of X-ray fluorescence?"

He shook his head.

"It's a relatively new procedure," Thorvaldsen said. "During the early Middle Ages, parchment was so scarce that monks developed a recycling technique where they scraped away the original ink, then reused the clean parchment for prayer books. With fluorescence, X-rays are formed from a particle accelerator, then bombarded onto the recycled parchment. Thankfully, the ink used centuries ago contained lots of iron. When the X-rays hit that ink, molecules deep in the parchment glow, and those images can be recorded. Pretty amazing, actually. Like a fax from the past. Words once thought erased, written over with new ink, reappear from their molecular signature."

"Cotton," Cassiopeia said, "what we know firsthand about Alexander is confined to the writings of four men who all lived nearly five hundred years after Alexander. *Ephemerides,* Alexander's so-called royal journal, which was supposedly contemporaneous, is useless—the victor rewriting history. The *Alexander Romance,* which many people cite as authority, is wild fiction and bears little relation to reality. The other two, though, were written by Arrian and Plutarch, both reputable chroniclers."

"I've read the *Alexander Romance.* Great story."

"But that's all it is. Alexander is like Arthur, a man whose actual life has been replaced with romantic legend. He's now regarded as some great, benign conqueror. Some sort of statesman. Actually, he slaughtered people on an unprecedented scale and totally squandered the resources of the lands he acquired. He murdered friends out of paranoia and led most of his troops to early deaths. He was a gambler who staked his life, and the lives of those around him, on chance. There's nothing magical about him."

"I disagree," he said. "He was a great military commander, the first person to unite the world. His conquests were bloody and brutal because that's war. True, he was bent on conquering, but his world seemed ready to be conquered. He was politically shrewd. A Greek, who ultimately became a Persian. From everything I've read, he seemed to have little use for petty nationalism—and I can't fault him for that. After he died his generals, the Companions, divided the empire among themselves, which ensured that Greek culture dominated for centuries. And it did. The Hellenistic Age utterly changed Western civilization. And all that started with him."

He saw that Cassiopeia did not agree with him.

"It's that legacy which was discussed in the old manuscript," she said. "What *actually* happened after Alexander died."

"We know what happened," he said. "His empire became the prey of his generals and they played finders-keepers with his body. Lots of differing accounts about how they each tried to highjack the funeral cortege. They all wanted the body as a symbol of *their* power. That's why it was mummified. Greeks burned their dead. But not Alexander. His corpse needed to live on."

"It's what happened between the time when Alexander died in Babylon and when his body was finally transported back west that concerned the manuscript," Cassiopeia said. "A year passed. A year that's critical to the elephant medallions."

A soft ring broke the room's silence.

Malone watched as Henrik removed a phone from his pocket and answered. Unusual. Thorvaldsen hated the things, and especially detested people who talked on one in front of him.

Malone glanced at Cassiopeia and asked, "That important?"

Her expression stayed sullen. "It's what we've been waiting for."

"Why you so chipper?"

"You may not believe this, Cotton, but I have feelings, too."

He wondered about the caustic comment. When she'd

visited Copenhagen during Christmas, they'd spent a few pleasant evenings together at Christiangade, Thorvaldsen's seaside home north of Copenhagen. He'd even given her a present, a rare seventeenth-century edition on medieval engineering. Her French reconstruction project, where stone by stone she was building a castle with tools and raw materials from seven hundred years ago, continued to progress. They'd even agreed that, in the spring, he'd come for a visit.

Thorvaldsen finished his call. "That was the thief from the museum."

"And how did he know to call you?" Malone asked.

"I had this phone number engraved on the medallion. I wanted to make it perfectly clear that we're waiting. I told him that if he wants the original decadrachm he's going to have to buy it."

"Knowing that, he'll probably kill you instead."

"We're hoping."

"And how do you plan to prevent that from happening?" Malone asked.

Cassiopeia stepped forward, her face rigid. "That's where you come in."

TWELVE

VIKTOR LAID THE PHONE BACK IN ITS CRADLE. RAFAEL
had stood by the window and listened to the conversation.

"He wants us to meet in three hours. At a house north
of town, on the coastal highway." He held up the elephant medallion. "They knew we were coming—and for
some time—to have this made. It's quite good. The
forger knew his craft."

"This is something we should report."

He disagreed. Minister Zovastina had sent him because he was her most trusted. Thirty men guarded her
on a daily basis. Her Sacred Band. Modeled after ancient Greece's fiercest fighting unit, which fought valiantly
until Philip of Macedonia and his son, Alexander the
Great, slaughtered them. He'd heard Zovastina speak
on the subject. The Macedonians were so impressed
with the Sacred Band's bravery that they erected a monument in their memory, which still stood in Greece.
When Zovastina assumed power, she'd enthusiastically
revived the concept. Viktor had been her first recruit,
and he'd located the other twenty-nine, including Rafael,
an Italian whom he'd found in Bulgaria, working for
that government's security forces.

"Should we not call Samarkand?" Rafael asked again.

He stared at his partner. The younger man was a
quick, energetic soul. Viktor had come to like him,
which explained why he tolerated mistakes that others

would never be allowed. Like jerking that man into the museum. But maybe that hadn't been a mistake after all?

"We can't call," he quietly said.

"If this becomes known, she'll kill us."

"Then we can't let it become known. We've done well so far."

And they had. Four thefts. All from private collectors who, luckily, kept their wares in flimsy safes or casually displayed. They'd masked each of their crimes with fires and covered their presence well.

Or, maybe not.

The man on the phone seemed to know their business.

"We're going to have to solve this ourselves," he said.

"You're afraid she'll blame me."

A knot clenched in his throat. "Actually, I'm afraid she'll blame us both."

"I'm troubled, Viktor. You carry me too much."

He threw his partner a self-deprecating expression. "We both messed this one up." He fingered the medallion. "These cursed things are nothing but trouble."

"Why does she want them?"

He shook his head. "She's not one to explain herself. But it's surely important."

"I overheard something."

He stared up into eyes alive with curiosity. "Where did you hear this *something*?"

"When I was detailed to her personal service, just before we left last week."

They all rotated as Zovastina's day-to-day guards. One rule was clear. Nothing heard or said mattered, only the Supreme Minister's safety. But this was different. He needed to know. "Tell me."

"She's planning."

He held up the medallion. "What does that have to do with these?"

"She said it did. To someone on the phone. What we're doing will prevent a problem." Rafael paused. "Her ambition is boundless."

"But she's done so much. What no one has ever been able to do. Life is good in central Asia. Finally."

"I saw it in her eyes, Viktor. None of that's enough. She wants more."

He concealed his own anxiety with a look of puzzlement.

Rafael said, "I was reading a biography of Alexander that she mentioned to me. She likes to recommend books. Especially on him. Do you know the story of Alexander's horse, Bucephalas?"

He'd heard Zovastina speak of the tale. Once, as a boy, Alexander's father acquired a handsome horse that could not be broken. Alexander chastised both his father and the royal trainers, saying he could tame the animal. Philip doubted the claim, but after Alexander promised to buy the horse from his own funds if he failed, the king allowed him the chance. Seeing that the horse seemed frightened by his shadow, Alexander turned him to the sun and, after some coaxing, managed to mount him.

He told Rafael what he knew.

"And do you know what Philip told Alexander after he broke the horse?"

He shook his head.

"He said, 'Look for a kingdom that matches your size, for Macedonia has not enough space for you.' That's her problem, Viktor. Her Federation is larger than Europe, but it's not big enough. She wants more."

"That's not for us to worry about."

"What we're doing somehow fits into her plan."

He said nothing in response, though he, too, was concerned.

Rafael seemed to sense his reluctance. "You told the

man on the phone that we'd bring fifty thousand euros. We have no money."

He appreciated the change in subject. "We won't need any. We'll get the medallion without spending anything."

"We need to eliminate whoever is doing this."

Rafael was right. Supreme Minister Zovastina would not tolerate errors.

"I agree," he said. "We'll kill them all."

THIRTEEN

THE MAN WHO ENTERED IRINA ZOVASTINA'S STUDY WAS short, squat, with a flat face and a jawline that signaled stubbornness. He was third in command of the Consolidated Federation Air Force, but he was also the covert leader of a minor political party, whose voice had, of late, acquired an alarming volume. A Kazakh who secretly resisted all Slavic influences, he liked to speak about nomadic times, hundreds of years ago, long before the Russians changed everything.

Staring at the rebel she wondered how his bald cranium and barren eyes endeared him to anyone, yet reports described him as smart, articulate, and persuasive. He'd been brought to the palace two days ago after suddenly collapsing with a raging fever, blood gushing from his nose, coughing fits that had left him exhausted, and a pounding in his hips that he'd described as hammer blows. His doctor had diagnosed a viral infection with a possible pneumonia, but no conventional treatment had worked.

Today, though, he seemed fine.

In bare feet, he wore one of the palace's chestnut bathrobes.

"You're looking good, Enver. Much better."

"Why am I here?" he asked in an expressionless tone that carried no appreciation.

Earlier, he'd been questioning the staff, who, on her orders, had dropped hints of his treachery. Interestingly, the colonel had showed no fear. He was further displaying his defiance by avoiding Russian, speaking to her in Kazakh, so she decided to humor him and kept to the old language. "You were deathly ill. I had you brought here so my doctors could care for you."

"I remember nothing of yesterday."

She motioned for him to sit and poured tea from a silver service. "You were in a bad condition. I was concerned, so I decided to help."

He eyed her with clear suspicion.

She handed him a cup and saucer. "Green tea, with a hint of apple. I'm told you like it."

He did not accept the offering. "What is it you want, Minister?"

"You're a traitor to me and this Federation. That political party of yours has been inciting people to civil disobedience."

He showed no surprise. "You say constantly that we have the right to speak out."

"And you believe me?"

She tabled the cup and decided to stop playing hostess. "Three days ago you were exposed to a viral agent, one that kills within twenty-four to forty-eight hours. Death comes from an explosive fever, fluid in the lungs, and a weakening in the arterial walls that leads to massive internal bleeding. Your infection had not, as yet, progressed to that point. But, by now, it would have."

"And how was I cured?"

"I stopped it."

"You?"

"I wanted you to experience what I'm capable of inflicting."

He said nothing for a moment, apparently digesting reality.

"You're a colonel in our air force. A man who took an oath to defend this Federation with his life."

"And I would."

"Yet you apparently have no problem inciting treason."

"I'll ask again. What do you want?" His tone had lost all civility.

"Your loyalty."

He said nothing.

She grabbed a remote control from the table. A flat-screen monitor resting on the corner of the desk sprang to life with the image of five men milling among a crowd, examining stalls beneath bright awnings burgeoning with fresh produce.

Her guest rose to his feet.

"This surveillance video came from one of the cameras in the Navoi market. They're quite useful in maintaining order and fighting crime. But they also allow us to track enemies." She saw that he recognized the faces. "That's right, Enver. Your friends. Committed to opposing this Federation. I'm aware of your plans."

She well knew his party's philosophy. Before the communists dominated, when Kazakhs lived mainly in yurts, women had been an integral part of society, occupying over a third of the political positions. But between the Soviets and Islam, women were shoved aside. Independence in the 1990s brought not only an economic depression, it also allowed women back into the forefront, where they'd steadily reacquired political influence. The Federation cemented that resurrection.

"You don't really want a return to the old ways, Enver. Back to the time when we roamed the steppes? Women ran this society then. No. You just want political power. And if you can inflame the people with thoughts of some glorious past, you'll use it to your advantage. You're as bad as I am."

He spat at her feet. "That's what I think of you."

She shrugged. "Doesn't change a thing." She pointed at the screen. "Each of those men, before the sun sets, will be infected, just like you were. They'll never realize a thing until a runny nose, or a sore throat, or a headache signals they may be coming down with a cold. You recall those symptoms, don't you, Enver?"

"You're as evil as I ever believed."

"If I were evil, I would have let you die."

"Why didn't you?"

She pointed the remote and changed channels. A map appeared.

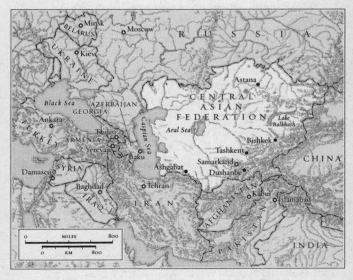

"This is what we've achieved. A unified Asian state that all of the leaders agreed to."

"You didn't ask the people."

"Really? It's been fifteen years since we achieved this

reality and the economies of all the former nations have dramatically improved. We've built schools, houses, roads. Medical care is markedly better. Our infrastructure has been modernized. Electricity, water, sewage disposal—nothing like it once was with the Soviets— now works. The Russian rape of our land and resources has stopped. International business is invested here in the multibillions. Tourism is on the rise. Our gross national product has increased a thousand percent. The people are happy, Enver."

"Not all."

"There's no way to make everyone happy. All we can do is please a majority. That's what the West preaches all the time."

"How many others have you pressured like me?"

"Not all that many. Most see the benefit of what we're doing on their own. I share the wealth, and power, with my friends. And, let me say, if any one of you has a better idea, I'm willing to listen. But so far no one has offered anything better. The little bit of opposition we've faced, you included, simply want to put themselves in power. Nothing more."

"Easy for you to be generous, while your germs can whip us all into line."

"I could have allowed you to die and solved my problem. But, Enver, killing you is foolish. Hitler, Stalin, Roman emperors, Russian tsars, and just about every European monarch all made the same mistake. They eliminated the exact people who could sustain them when they really needed help."

"Perhaps they were right? Keeping your enemies alive can be dangerous."

She sensed a slight thawing in his bitterness so she asked, "Do you know about Alexander the Great?"

"Just another Western invader."

"And in a dozen years he conquered us, taking all of

Persia and Asia Minor. More territory than the Roman Empire acquired after a thousand years of fighting. And how did he rule? Not by force. When he claimed a kingdom he always allowed the former ruler to keep power. By doing that he cultivated friends who sent men and supplies when he needed them, so more conquests could be made. Then, he shared the wealth. He was successful because he understood how to use power."

Hard to tell if she was making progress, but the Kazakh had made one valid point. Enemies did indeed surround her, and the assassination attempt from earlier still loomed fresh in her mind. She tried always to either eliminate or recruit the opposition, but new factions seemed to spring up daily. Alexander himself eventually fell victim to an unreasonable paranoia. She could not repeat that mistake.

"What do you say, Enver? Join us."

She watched as he mulled over her request. He may not have liked her, but reports noted that this warrior, an aviator trained by the Soviets who fought with them in many of their foolish struggles, hated something else far worse.

Time to see if that were true.

She pointed at the screen toward Pakistan, Afghanistan, and Iran. "These are our problem."

She saw he agreed.

"What do you plan to do?" he asked, with interest.

"End them."

FOURTEEN

MALONE STARED AT THE HOUSE. HE, THORVALDSEN, and Cassiopeia had left his bookshop a half hour ago and driven north, following a seaside route. Ten minutes south of Thorvaldsen's palatial estate, they'd veered off the main highway and parked before a modest one-story dwelling nestled among a grove of gnarly beechwoods. Spring daffodils and hyacinths wrapped its walls, the brick and wood topped by a lopsided gabled roof. Gray-brown waters of the Øresund lapped a rocky beach fifty yards behind.

"As if I have to ask who owns this place."

"It's run-down," Thorvaldsen said. "It abuts my land. I bought it for a bargain, but the waterfront location is wonderful."

Malone agreed. Prime real estate. "And who's supposed to live here?"

Cassiopeia grinned. "The owner of the museum. Who else?"

He noticed that her mood was lightening. But his two friends were clearly on edge. He'd changed clothes before leaving town and retrieved his Magellan Billet–issue Beretta from beneath his bed. He'd been ordered twice by the local police to surrender it, but Thorvaldsen had used connections with the Danish prime minister to block both attempts. Over the past year, even though retired, he'd found a lot of uses for the weapon. Which was troubling. One reason he'd quit the government was to stop carrying a gun.

They stepped inside the house. Sunlight poured through windows clouded with salt film. The interior was decorated with a mishmash of old and new—a combination of styles that seemed pleasant by merely being itself. He noticed the condition. Lots of repairs were needed.

Cassiopeia searched the house.

Thorvaldsen sat on a dusty tweed-covered couch. "Everything in that museum last night was a copy. I removed the originals after I bought the place. None of it was particularly valuable, but I couldn't allow it to be destroyed."

"You went to a lot of trouble," Malone said.

Cassiopeia returned from her reconnoiter. "There's a lot at stake."

Like he needed to hear that. "While we wait for someone to come and try to kill us—the individual you talked to on the phone three hours ago—could you at least explain why we gave them that much prep time?"

"I'm well aware of what I've done," Thorvaldsen said.

"Why are these medallions so important?"

"Do you know much about Hephaestion?" Thorvaldsen asked.

He did. "He was Alexander's closest companion. Probably his lover. Died a few months before Alexander."

"The molecular manuscript," Cassiopeia said, "that was discovered in Samarkand actually fills in the historical record with some new information. We now know that Alexander was so guilt-ridden over Hephaestion's death that he ordered the execution of his personal physician, a man named Glaucias. Had him torn apart between two trees tied to the ground."

"And what did the doctor do to deserve that?"

"He failed to save Hephaestion," Thorvaldsen said. "Seems Alexander possessed a cure. Something that had, at least once before, arrested the same fever that killed Hephaestion. It's described in the manuscript simply as the *draught*. But there are also some interesting details."

Cassiopeia removed a folded page from her pocket. "Read it for yourself."

So shameful of the king to execute poor Glaucias. The physician was not to blame. Hephaestion was told not to eat or drink, yet he did both. Had he refrained, the time needed to heal him may have been earned. True, Glaucias had none of the draught on hand, its container had been shattered days before by accident, but he was waiting for more to arrive from the east. Years earlier, during his pursuit of the Scythians, Alexander suffered a bad stomach. In return for a truce, the Scythians provided the draught, which they had long used for cures. Only Alexander, Hephaestion, and Glaucias knew, but Glaucias once administered the wondrous liquid to his assistant. The man's neck had swollen with lumps so bad he could hardly swallow, as if pebbles filled his throat, and fluid spewed forth with each exhale. Lesions had covered his body. No strength remained within any of his muscles. Each breath was a labor. Glaucias gave him the draught and, by the next day, the man recovered. Glaucias told his assistant that he'd used the cure on the king several times, once when he was near death, and always the king recovered. The assistant owed Glaucias his life, but there was nothing he could do to save him from Alexander's wrath. He watched from the Babylonian walls as the trees ripped his savior apart. When Alexander returned from the killing field he ordered the assistant to his presence and asked if he knew of the draught. Having seen Glaucias die so horribly, fear forced him to tell the truth. The king told him to speak of the liquid to no one. Ten days later Alexander lay on his deathbed, fever ravaging his body, his strength nearly gone, the same as Hephaestion. On the final day of his life, while his Companions and generals prayed for guidance, Alexander whispered that he wanted the remedy. The assistant mustered his courage and, remembering Glaucias, told Alexander no. A smile came to the king's lips. The assistant took pleasure in watching Alexander die, knowing that he could have saved him.

"The court historian," Cassiopeia said, "a man who also lost someone he loved when Alexander ordered Callisthenes executed four years previous, recorded that account. Callisthenes was Aristotle's nephew. He served as court historian until spring 327 BCE. That's when he got caught up in an assassination plot. By then, Alexander's paranoia had amplified to dangerous levels. So he ordered Callisthenes' death. Aristotle was said never to have forgiven Alexander."

Malone nodded. "Some say Aristotle sent the poison that supposedly killed Alexander."

Thorvaldsen scoffed at the comment. "The king wasn't poisoned. That manuscript proves it. Alexander died of an infection. Probably malaria. He'd been trudging through swamps a few weeks prior. But it's hard to say for sure. And this drink, the *draught,* had cured him before and it cured the assistant."

"Did you catch those symptoms?" Cassiopeia asked. "Fever, neck swelling, mucus, fatigue, lesions. That sounds viral. Yet this liquid totally cured the assistant."

He was not impressed. "You can't place much credence in a two-thousand-plus-year-old manuscript. You have no idea if it's authentic."

"It is," Cassiopeia said.

He waited for her to explain.

"My friend was an expert. The technique he used to find the writing is state of the art and doesn't lend itself to forgeries. We're talking about reading words at a molecular level."

"Cotton," Thorvaldsen said. "Alexander knew there'd be a battle for his body. He's known to have said, in the days before he died, that *his prominent friends would engage in vast funerary games* once he was gone. A curious comment, but one we're beginning to understand."

He'd caught something else and wanted to know from Cassiopeia, "You said your friend at the museum *was* an expert? Past tense?"

"He's dead."

And now he knew the source of her pain. "You were close?"

Cassiopeia did not answer.

"You could have told me," he said to her.

"No, I couldn't."

Her words stung.

"Suffice it to say," Thorvaldsen said, "that all this intrigue involves locating Alexander's body."

"Good luck. It's not been seen in fifteen hundred years."

"That's the catch," Cassiopeia coldly replied. "We might know where it is, and the man coming here to kill us doesn't."

FIFTEEN

ZOVASTINA WATCHED THE STUDENTS' EAGER FACES AND asked the class, "How many of you have read Homer?"

Only a few hands raised.

"I was at university, just like you, when I first read his epic."

She'd come to the People's Center for Higher Learning for one of her many weekly appearances. She tried to schedule at least five. Opportunities for the press, and the people, to see and hear her. Once a poorly funded Russian institute, now the center was a respectable place of academic learning. She'd seen to that because the Greeks were right. An illiterate state leads to no state at all.

She read from the copy of the *Iliad* open before her.

" 'The skin of the coward changes color all the time, he can't get a grip on himself, he can't sit still, he squats and rocks, shifting his weight from foot to foot, his heart racing, pounding inside the fellow's ribs, his teeth chattering. He dreads some grisly death. But the skin of a brave soldier never blanches. He's all control. Tense but no great fear.' "

The students seemed to enjoy her recitation.

"Homer's words from over twenty-eight hundred years ago. They still make perfect sense."

Cameras and microphones pointed her way from the back of the classroom. Being here reminded her of twenty-eight years ago. Northern Kazakhstan. Another classroom.

And her teacher.

"It's okay to cry," Sergej said to her.

The words had moved her. More so than she'd thought possible. She stared at the Ukrainian, who possessed a unique appreciation for the world.

"You're but nineteen," he said. "I remember when I first read Homer. It affected me, too."

"Achilles is such a tortured soul."

"We're all tortured souls, Irina."

She liked when he said her name. This man knew things she didn't. He understood things she'd yet to experience. She wanted to know those things. "I never knew my mother and father. I never knew any of my family."

"They're not important."

She was surprised. "How can you say that?"

He pointed to the book. "The lot of man is to suffer and die. What's gone is of no consequence."

For years she'd wondered why she seemed doomed to a life of loneliness. Friends were few, relationships nonexistent, life for her an endless challenge of wanting and lacking. Like Achilles.

"Irina, you'll come to know the joy of the challenge. Life is one challenge after another. One battle after another. Always, like Achilles, in pursuit of excellence."

"And what of failure?"

He shrugged. "The consequence of not succeeding. Remember what Homer said. Circumstances rule men, not men circumstances."

She thought of another line from the poem. "What

chilling blows we suffer—thanks to our own conflict-
ing wills—whenever we show these mortal men some
kindness."

Her teacher nodded. "Never forget that."

"Such a story," she said to the class. "The *Iliad*. A war
that raged for nine long years. Then, in its tenth, a quarrel led Achilles to stop fighting. A Greek hero, full of
pride, a fighter whose humanity stemmed from great
passion, invulnerable except for his heels."

She saw smiles on some faces.

"Everyone has a weakness," she said.

"What's yours, Minister?" one of the students asked.

She'd told them not to be bashful.

Questions were good.

"Why do you teach me these things?" she asked
Sergej.

"To know your heritage is to understand it. Do you
realize that you may well be a descendant of the
Greeks?"

She gave him a perplexed look. "How is that possi-
ble?"

"Long ago, before Islam, when Alexander and the
Greeks claimed this land, many of his men stayed
after he returned home. They settled our valleys and
took local women as wives. Some of our words, our
music, our dance, were theirs."

She'd never realized.

"My affection for the people of this Federation," she
said in answer to the question. "You're my weakness."

The students clapped their approval.

She thought again of the *Iliad*. And its lessons. The
glory of war. The triumph of military values over family

life. Personal honor. Revenge. Bravery. The impermanence of human life.

The skin of a brave soldier never blanches.

And had she blanched earlier, when she'd faced down the would-be assassin?

"You say politics interests you," Sergej said. "Then never forget Homer. Our Russian masters know nothing of honor. Our Greek forebears, they knew everything about it. Don't ever be like the Russians, Irina. Homer was right. Failing your community is the greatest failure of all."

"How many of you know of Alexander the Great?" she asked the students.

A few hands were raised.

"Do you realize that some of you may be Greek?" She told them what Sergej told her so long ago about Greeks staying in Asia. "Alexander's legacy is a part of our history. Bravery, chivalry, endurance. He joined West and East for the first time. His legend spread to every corner of the world. He's in the Bible, the Koran. The Greek Orthodox made him a saint. The Jews consider him a folk hero. There's a version of him in Germanic, Icelandic, and Ethiopian sagas. Epics and poems have been written about him for centuries. His tale is a tale of us."

She could easily understand why Alexander had been so taken with Homer. Why he lived the *Iliad*. Immortality was gained only through heroic actions. Men like Enrico Vincenti could not understand honor. Achilles was right. *Wolves and lambs can enjoy no meeting of the minds.*

Vincenti was a lamb. She was a wolf.

And there'd be no meeting.

These encounters with students were beneficial on a multitude of levels, not the least of which was a reminder to her of what came before her. Twenty-three hundred years ago Alexander the Great marched thirty-two thousand kilometers and conquered the known world. He created a common language, encouraged religious tolerance, spurred racial diversity, founded seventy cities, established new trade routes, and ushered in a renaissance that lasted two hundred and fifty years. He aspired to *arête*. The Greek ideal of excellence.

Her turn now to display the same thing.

She finished with the class and excused herself.

As she left the building, one of her guards handed her a piece of paper. She unfolded and read the message, an e-mail that had arrived thirty minutes ago, noting the cryptic return address and curt message—NEED YOU HERE BY SUNSET.

Irritating, but she had no choice.

"Have a helicopter readied," she ordered.

SIXTEEN

TO VINCENTI, VENICE SEEMED A WORK OF ART. GOBS OF Byzantine splendor, Islamic reflections, and allusions to India and China. Half Eastern, half Western—one foot in Europe, the other in Asia. A uniquely human creation born from a series of islands that once managed to weld themselves into the greatest of trading states, a supreme naval power, a twelve-hundred-year-old republic whose lofty ideals even attracted the attention of America's Founding Fathers. Envied, suspected, even feared—trading indiscriminately with all sides, friend or foe. An unscrupulous moneymaker, dedicated to profit, treating even wars as promising investments. That had been Venice through the centuries.

And himself for the past two decades.

He bought his Grand Canal villa with the first profits from his fledgling pharmaceutical company. Only fitting that both he and his corporation, now valued in the billions of euros, be headquartered here.

He especially loved Venice in the early morning, when nothing could be heard but the human voice. A morning walk from his palazzo on the canal, to his favorite *ristorante* on the square at Campo del Leon, constituted his only attempt at exercise. But it was one he couldn't avoid. Feet or boat were the only means of transportation since vehicles were banned in Venice.

Today he walked with a renewed vigor. The problem with the Florentine had worried him. With that now resolved he could turn his attention to the final few hurdles. Nothing satisfied him more than a well-executed plan. Unfortunately, few were ever so.

Especially when deceit proved necessary.

The morning air no longer carried winter's unpleasant chill. Spring had clearly returned to northern Italy. The wind seemed gentler, too, the sky a lovely salmon, brightened by a sun emerging from the eastern ocean.

He wove a path through the twisting streets, narrow enough that carrying an open umbrella would have presented a challenge, and crossed several of the bridges that tacked the city together. He passed clothing and stationery stores, a wine shop, a shoe dealer, and a couple of well-stocked groceries, all closed at this early hour.

He came to the end of the street and entered the square.

On one end rose an antique tower, once a church, now a theater. At the other end stood the campanile of a Carmine chapel. Between stretched houses and shops that shimmered with age and self-satisfaction. He didn't particularly like the campos. They tended to feel dry, old, and urban. Different from the canal fronts where palazzos pressed forward, like people in a crowd jostling for air.

He studied the empty square. Everything neat and orderly.

Just as he liked it.

He was a man possessed of wealth, power, and a future. He lived in one of the world's great cities, his lifestyle befitting a person of prestige and tradition. His father, a nondescript soul who instilled in him a love of science, told him as a child to take life as it came. Good advice. Life was about reaction and recovery. One was either in, just coming out of, or about to find trouble. The trick was knowing which state you were in and acting accordingly.

He'd just come out of trouble.

And was about to find more.

For the past two years he'd headed the Council of Ten, which governed the Venetian League. Four hundred and thirty-two men and women whose ambitions were stymied by excessive government regulation, restrictive trade laws, and politicians who chipped away at corporate bottom lines. America and the European Union were by far the worst. Every day some new impediment sapped profits. League members spent billions trying to avert more regulation. And while one set of politicos were quietly influenced to help, another set were intent on making a name for themselves by prosecuting the helpers.

A frustrating and never-ending cycle.

Which was why the League had decided to create a place where business could not only flourish, but rule. A place similar to the original Venetian republic, which, for centuries, was governed by men possessed of the mercantile ability of Greeks and the audacity of Romans—entrepreneurs who were at once businessmen, soldiers, governors, and statesmen. A city-state that ultimately became an empire. Periodically, the Venetian republic had formed leagues with other city-states—alliances that ensured survival in numbers—and the idea worked well. Their modern incarnation expounded a similar philosophy. He'd worked hard for his fortune and agreed with something Irina Zovastina had once told him. *Everybody loves a thing more if it has cost him trouble.*

He traversed the square and approached the café, which opened each day at six A.M. simply for him.

Morning was his time of day. His mind seemed most alert before noon. He entered the *ristorante* and acknowledged the owner. "Emilio, might I ask a favor? Tell my guests that I'll return shortly. There's something I must do. It won't take long."

The man smiled and nodded, assuring there'd be no problem.

He bypassed his corporate officers waiting for him in the adjacent dining room and stepped through the kitchen. An aroma of broiling fish and fried eggs teased his nostrils. He stopped a moment and admired what was simmering on the stove, then left the building through a rear exit and found himself in another of Venice's innumerable alleys, this one darkened by tall brick buildings thick with droppings.

Three Inquisitors waited a few meters away. He nodded and they walked single file. At an intersection they turned right and followed another alley. He noticed a familiar stink—half drainage, half decaying stone—the pall of Venice. They stopped at the rear entrance to a building that housed a dress shop on its ground floor and apartments on its upper three stories. He knew they were now diagonally across the square from the café.

Another Inquisitor waited for them at the door.

"She's there?" Vincenti asked.

The man nodded.

He gestured and three of the men entered the building, while the fourth waited outside. Vincenti followed them up a flight of metal stairs. On the third floor they stopped outside one of the apartment doors. He stood down the hall as guns were drawn and one of the men prepared to kick the door.

He nodded.

Shoe met wood and the door burst inward.

The men rushed inside.

A few seconds later one of his men signaled. He stepped into the apartment and closed the door.

Two Inquisitors held a woman. She was slender, fair-haired, and not unattractive. A hand was clamped over her mouth, a gun barrel pressed to her left temple. She was frightened, but calm. Expected, since she was a pro.

"Surprised to see me?" he asked. "You've been watching for nearly a month."

Her eyes offered no response.

"I'm not a fool, though your government must take me for one."

He knew she worked for the United States Justice Department, an agent with a special international unit called the Magellan Billet. The Venetian League had encountered the unit before, a few years back when the League first started investing in central Asia. To be expected, actually. America stayed suspicious. Nothing ever came from those inquiries, but now Washington again seemed fixated on his organization.

He spied the agent's equipment. Long-range camera set on a tripod, cell phone, notepad. He knew questioning her would be useless. She could tell him little, if anything, he did not already know. "You've interfered with my breakfast."

He gestured and one of the men confiscated her toys.

He stepped to the window and gazed down into the still-deserted campo. What he chose next could well determine his future. He was about to play both ends against the middle in a dangerous game that neither the Venetian League nor Irina Zovastina would appreciate. Nor, for that matter, would the Americans. He'd planned this bold move for a long time.

As his father had said many times, the meek deserve nothing.

He kept his gaze out the window, raised his right arm, and flicked his wrist. A snap signaled that the woman's neck had broken cleanly. Killing he didn't mind. Watching was another matter.

His men knew what to do.

A car waited downstairs to take the body across town where the coffin from last night waited. Plenty of room inside for one more.

SEVENTEEN

DENMARK

MALONE STUDIED THE MAN WHO'D JUST ARRIVED, alone, driving an Audi with a bright rental sticker tacked on the windshield. He was a short, burly fellow with shocks of unkempt hair, baggy clothes, and shoulders and arms that suggested he was accustomed to hard work. Probably early forties, his features suggested Slavic influences—wide nose, deep-set eyes.

The man stepped onto the front stoop and said, "I'm not armed. But you're welcome to check."

Malone kept his gun leveled. "Refreshing to deal with professionals."

"You're the one from the museum."

"And you're the one who left me inside."

"Not me. But I approved."

"Lot of honesty from a man with a gun pointed at him."

"Guns don't bother me."

And he believed that. "I don't see any money."

"I haven't seen the medallion."

He stepped aside and allowed the man to enter. "You have a name?"

His guest stopped in the doorway and faced him with hard eyes. "Viktor."

CASSIOPEIA WATCHED FROM THE TREES AS THE MAN from the car and Malone entered the house. Whether he'd come alone or not would not be a problem.

This drama was about to play itself out.

And she hoped, for Malone's benefit, that she and Thorvaldsen had calculated correctly.

MALONE STOOD OFF TO ONE SIDE AS THORVALDSEN and the man named Viktor talked. He remained alert, watching with the intensity of someone who had spent a dozen years as a government agent. He, too, had often faced an unknown adversary with only wits and wisdom, hoping to heaven nothing went wrong and he made it out in one piece.

"You've been stealing these medallions from all over the continent," Thorvaldsen said. "Why? Their value is not that great."

"I don't know about that. You want fifty thousand euros for yours. That's five times what it's worth."

"And, amazingly, you're willing to pay. Which means you're not in it for collecting. Who do you work for?"

"Myself."

Thorvaldsen gave a refined chuckle. "A sense of humor. I like that. I detect an East European accent to your English. The old Yugoslavia? Croatian?"

Viktor remained silent and Malone noticed that their visitor had not touched a thing inside the house.

"I assumed you wouldn't answer that question," Thorvaldsen said. "How do you want to conclude our business?"

"I'd like to examine the medallion. If satisfied, I'll have the money available tomorrow. Can't be done today. It's Sunday."

"Depends on where your bank is," Malone said.

"Mine's closed." And Viktor's blank stare indicated he'd offer nothing more.

"Where did you learn about Greek fire?" Thorvaldsen asked.

"You're quite knowledgeable."

"I own a Greco-Roman museum."

The hairs on the back of Malone's neck bristled. People like Viktor, who did not appear loose-lipped, only offered concessions when they knew their listeners would not be around long enough to repeat them.

"I know you're after elephant medallions," Thorvaldsen said, "and you have them all, save mine and three others. My guess is you're hired help and have no idea why these are so important, nor do you care. A faithful servant."

"And who are you? Certainly not the owner of a Greco-Roman museum."

"On the contrary. I do own it, and I want to be paid for my destroyed goods. Hence the high price."

Thorvaldsen reached into his pocket and removed a clear plastic case, which he tossed. Viktor caught it with both hands. Malone watched as their guest dropped the medallion into his open palm. About the size of a fifty-cent piece, pewter-colored, with symbols etched on both faces. Viktor removed a jeweler's loop from his pocket.

"You an expert?" Malone asked.

"I know enough."

"The microengravings are there," Thorvaldsen said. "Greek letters. ZH. Zeta. Eta. It's amazing the ancients possessed the ability to engrave them."

Viktor continued his examination.

"Satisfied?" Malone asked.

VIKTOR STUDIED THE MEDALLION, AND THOUGH HE didn't have his microscope or scales, this one seemed genuine.

Actually, the best specimen so far.

He'd come unarmed because he wanted these men to think themselves in charge. Finesse, not force, was needed here. One thing worried him, though. Where was the woman?

He glanced up and allowed the loop to drop into his right hand. "Might I examine it closer, at the window? I need better light."

"By all means," the older man said.

"What's your name?" Viktor asked.

"How about Ptolemy?"

Viktor grinned. "There were many. Which one are you?"

"The first. Alexander's most opportunistic general. Claimed Egypt for his prize after Alexander died. Smart man. His heirs held it for centuries."

He shook his head. "In the end, the Romans defeated them."

"Like my museum. Nothing lasts."

Viktor stepped close to the dusky pane. The man with the gun stood guard at the doorway. He'd only need an instant. As he positioned himself within the shafts of sunlight, his back momentarily to them, he made his move.

CASSIOPEIA SAW A MAN APPEAR FROM THE TREES ON THE far side of the house. He was young, thin, and agile. Though last night she'd not seen the faces of either of the two who'd torched the museum, she recognized the nimble gait and careful approach.

One of the thieves.

Heading straight for Thorvaldsen's car.

Thorough, she'd give them that, but not necessarily careful, especially considering that they knew someone was at least a few steps ahead of them.

She watched as the man plunged a knife into both rear tires, then withdrew.

MALONE CAUGHT THE SWITCH. VIKTOR HAD DROPPED the loop into his right hand while his left held the medallion. But as the loop was replaced to Viktor's eye and the examination restarted, he noticed that the medallion was now in the right hand, the index finger and thumb of the left hand curled inward, palming the coin.

Not bad. Combined skillfully with the act of moving toward the window and finding the right light. Perfect misdirection.

His gaze caught Thorvaldsen's, but the Dane quickly nodded that he'd seen it, too. Viktor was holding the coin in the light, studying it through the loop. Thorvaldsen shook his head, which signaled let it go.

Malone asked again, "You satisfied?"

Viktor dropped the jeweler's loop into his left hand and pocketed it, along with the real medallion. He then held up the coin he'd switched out, surely the fake from the museum, now returned. "It's genuine."

"Worth fifty thousand euros?" Thorvaldsen asked.

Viktor nodded. "I'll have the money wired. You tell me where."

"Call tomorrow to the number from the medallion, as you did earlier, and we'll arrange a trade."

"Just drop it back in its case," Malone said.

Viktor walked to the table. "This is quite a game you two are playing."

"It's no game," Thorvaldsen said.

"Fifty thousand euros?"

"Like I said, you destroyed my museum."

Malone spotted the confidence in Viktor's careful eyes. The man had entered a situation not knowing his enemy, thinking himself smarter, and that was always dangerous.

Malone, though, had committed a worse mistake.

He'd volunteered, trusting only that his two friends knew what they were doing.

EIGHTEEN

ZOVASTINA STARED OUT OF THE HELICOPTER AS THEY left Federation airspace and flew into extreme western China. Once the area had been a tightly sealed back door to the Soviet Union, guarded by masses of troops. Now the borders were open. Unrestricted transportation and trade. China had been one of the first to formally recognize the Federation, and treaties between the two nations assured that travel and commerce flowed freely.

Xinyang province constituted sixteen percent of China. Mostly mountains and desert, loaded with natural resources. Wholly different from the rest of the country. Less communism. Heavy Islam. Once called East Turkestan, its identity was traceable far more to central Asia than the Middle Kingdom.

The Venetian League had been instrumental in formalizing friendly relations with the Chinese, another reason she'd chosen to join the group. The Great Western Economic Expansion began five years ago, when Beijing started pouring billions into infrastructure and redevelopment all across Xinyang. League members had received many of the contracts for petrochemicals, mining, machine works, road improvements, and construction. Its friends in the Chinese capital were many, as money spoke as loudly in the communist world as anywhere else, and she'd used those connections to her maximum political advantage.

The flight from Samarkand was a little over an hour in the high-speed chopper. She'd made the trek many times and, as always, stared below at the rough terrain, imagining the ancient caravans that once made their way east and west along its famed Silk Road. Jade, coral, linens, glass, gold, iron, garlic, tea—even dwarfs, nubile women, and horses so fierce they were said to have sweated blood—were all traded. Alexander the Great never made it this far east, but Marco Polo had definitely walked that earth.

Ahead, she spotted Kashgar.

The city sat on the edge of the Taklimakan Desert, a hundred and twenty kilometers east from the Federation border, within the shadows of the snowy Pamirs, some of the highest and most barren mountains in the world. A bejeweled oasis, China's western-most metropolis, it had existed, like Samarkand, for over two thousand years. Once a place of bustling open markets and crowded bazaars, now it was consumed by dust, wails, and the falsetto cries of muezzins summoning men to prayer in its four thousand mosques. Three hundred and fifty thousand people lived among its hotels, warehouses, businesses, and shrines. The town walls were long gone and a superhighway, another part of the great economic expansion, now encircled and directed green taxis in all directions.

The helicopter banked north where the landscape buckled. The desert was not far to the east. Taklimakan literally meant "go in and you won't come out." An apt description for a place with winds so hot they could, and did, kill entire caravans within minutes.

She spotted their destination.

A black-glass building in the center of a rock-strewn

meadow, the beginnings of a forest a half kilometer behind. Nothing identified the two-story structure, which she knew was owned by Philogen Pharmaceutique, a Luxembourg corporation headquartered in Italy, its largest shareholder an American expatriate with the quite Italian name of Enrico Vincenti.

Early on, she'd made a point to learn Vincenti's personal history.

He was a virologist, hired by the Iraqis in the 1970s as part of a biological weapons program that the then new leader, Saddam Hussein, wanted to pursue. Hussein had viewed the Biological Toxin Weapons Convention of 1972, which banned germ warfare worldwide, as nothing more than an opportunity. Vincenti had worked with the Iraqis until just before the first Gulf War, when Hussein quickly disbanded the research. Peace brought UN inspectors, which forced a near permanent abandonment. So Vincenti moved on, starting a pharmaceutical company that expanded at a record pace during the 1990s. Now it was the largest in Europe, with an impressive array of patents. A huge multinational conglomerate. Quite an achievement for an unheralded mercenary scientist. Which had long made her wonder.

The chopper landed and she hustled inside the building.

The exterior glass walls were merely a facade. Like tables nestled together, another whole structure rose inside. A polished-slate walkway encircled the inner building and bushy indoor plants lined both sides of the walk. The inside stone walls were broken by three sets of double doors. She knew the unique arrangement was a way to quietly ensure security. No external hedgerows topped with strands of barbed wire. No outside guards. No cameras. Nothing to alert anyone that the building was anything special.

She crossed the outer perimeter and approached one

of the entrances, her path blocked by a metal gate. A security guard stood behind a marble counter. The gate was controlled by a hand scanner, but she was not required to stop.

On the other side stood an impish man in his late fifties with thinning gray hair and a mousy face. Wire-framed glasses shielded expressionless eyes. He was dressed in a black-and-gold lab coat unbuttoned in the front, a security badge labeled "Grant Lyndsey" clipped to his lapel.

"Welcome, Minister," he said in English.

She answered his greeting with a look meant to signal annoyance. His e-mail had suggested urgency, and though she'd not liked anything about the summons, she'd canceled her afternoon activities and come.

They entered the inner building.

Beyond the main entrance the path forked. Lyndsey turned left and led her through a maze of windowless corridors. Everything was hospital clean and smelled of chlorine. All of the doors were equipped with electronic locks. At the one labeled "Chief Scientist," Lyndsey unclipped the ID on his lapel and slid the card through a slot.

Modern decor dominated the windowless office. Each time she visited the same thing struck her as odd. No family pictures. No diplomas on the wall. No mementos. As if this man possessed no life. Which was probably not far from the truth.

"I need to show you something," Lyndsey said.

He spoke to her as an equal, and that she despised. His tone always clear that he lived in China and was not subject to her.

He flicked on a monitor that, from a ceiling-mounted camera, displayed a middle-aged woman perched in a chair watching television. She knew the room was on the building's second floor, in the patient ward, as she'd seen images from there before.

"Last week," Lyndsey said, "I requisitioned a dozen from the prison. Like we've done before."

She'd been unaware that another clinical trial had been performed. "Why wasn't I told?"

"I didn't know I was required to tell you."

She heard what he'd not said. *Vincenti's in charge. His lab, his people, his concoctions.* She'd lied to Enver earlier. *She'd* not cured him. Vincenti had. A technician from this lab had administered the antiagent. Though she possessed the biological pathogens, Vincenti controlled the remedies. A check and balance born of mistrust, in place from the beginning to ensure that their bargaining positions remained equal.

Lyndsey pointed a remote control and the screen changed to other patient rooms, eight in all, each occupied by a man or woman. Unlike the first, these patients lay supine, connected to intravenous drips.

Not moving.

He slipped off his glasses. "I used only twelve, since they were readily available on short notice. I needed a quick study on the antiagent for the new virus. What I told you about a month ago. A nasty little thing."

"And where did you find it?"

"In a species of rodent east of here in Heilongjiang province. We'd heard tales of how people became sick after eating the things. Sure enough, there's a complex virus floating around in the rat blood. With a little tweaking, this bugger has punch. Death in less than one day." He pointed to the screen. "Here's the proof."

She'd actually asked for a more offensive agent. Something that worked even faster than the twenty-eight she already possessed.

"They're all on life support. They've been clinically dead for days. I need autopsies to verify the infectious parameters, but I wanted to show you before we sliced them up."

"And the antiagent?"

"One dosage and all twelve were on their way to good health. Total reversal in a matter of hours. Then I substituted a placebo to all of them, except the first woman. She's the control. As expected, the others lapsed quickly and died." He brought the image on the screen back to the first woman. "But she's virus free. Perfectly normal."

"Why was this trial needed?"

"You wanted a new virus. I needed to see if the adjustments worked." Lyndsey threw her a smile. "And, like I said, I had to verify the antiagent."

"When do I get the new virus?"

"You can take it today. That's why I called."

She never liked transporting the viruses, but only she knew this lab's location. Her deal was with Vincenti. A personal arrangement between them. No way she could trust anyone with the fruits of that bargain. And her helicopter would never be stopped by the Chinese.

"Get the virus ready," she said.

"All frozen and packed."

She pointed at the screen. "What about her?"

He shrugged. "She'll be reinfected. Dead by tomorrow."

Her nerves were still on edge. Trampling the would-be assassin had vented some of her frustration, but unanswered questions remained about the murder attempt. How had Vincenti known? Perhaps because he'd ordered it? Hard to say. But she'd been caught off guard. Vincenti had been a step ahead of her. And that she did not like.

Nor did she like Lindsey.

She pointed at the screen. "Have her ready to leave, too. Immediately."

"Is that wise?"

"That's *my* concern."

He grinned. "Some amusement?"

"Would you like to come along and see?"

"No, thanks. I like it here, on the Chinese side of the border."

She rose. "And if I were you, I'd stay here."

NINETEEN

MALONE KEPT HIS GUN READY AS THORVALDSEN concluded his business with Viktor.

"We can make the exchange back here," Thorvaldsen said. "Tomorrow."

"You don't strike me as a man who requires money," Viktor said.

"Actually, I like as much as I can acquire."

Malone repressed a smile. His Danish friend actually gave away millions of euros to causes all around the world. He'd often wondered if he was one of those causes, since Thorvaldsen had made a point, two years ago, to travel to Atlanta and offer him a chance to change his life in Copenhagen. An opportunity he'd taken and never regretted.

"I'm curious," Viktor said. "The quality of the forgery was remarkable. Who's the craftsman?"

"A person of talent, who takes pride in his work."

"Pass on my compliments."

"Some of your euros will go that way." Thorvaldsen paused. "Now I have a question. Are you going after the last two medallions, here in Europe?"

"What do you think?"

"And the third one, in Samarkand?"

Viktor did not reply, but Thorvaldsen's message had surely been received. *I know your business well.*

Viktor started to leave. "I'll call tomorrow."

Thorvaldsen stayed seated as the man left the room. "Look forward to hearing from you."

The front door opened, then closed.

"Cotton," Thorvaldsen said, producing a paper bag from his pocket. "We have little time. Carefully, slide the case with the medallion into this."

He understood. "Fingerprints? That's why you gave him the coin."

"You saw how he touched nothing. But he had to hold the medallion so he could switch them."

Malone used the barrel of the gun to slide the plastic case into the bag, careful that it landed flat. He rolled the top closed, leaving an air pocket. He knew the drill. Unlike on television, paper, not plastic, was the best repository for fingerprint evidence. Far less chance of smearing.

Thorvaldsen stood. "Come, now." He watched as his friend shuffled across the room, head cocked forward. "We must hurry."

He noticed Thorvaldsen was moving toward the rear of the house. "Where are you going?"

"Out of here."

He hustled after his friend and they left through a kitchen door that opened onto a railed deck, facing the sea. Fifty yards away, a dock jutted from the rocky shoreline where a motorboat waited. The morning sky had turned overcast. Gunmetal gray clouds now hung low. A brisk northern wind cascaded across the sound, swirling the frothy brown water.

"We're leaving?" he asked, as Thorvaldsen stepped from the deck.

The Dane continued to move with surprising speed for a man with a crooked spine.

"Where's Cassiopeia?" Malone asked.

"In trouble," Thorvaldsen said. "But that's our only saving grace."

CASSIOPEIA WATCHED AS THE MAN FROM INSIDE THE house climbed into his rental car and sped back down the tree-lined lane that led to the highway. She switched on a handheld LCD monitor, linked by radio with two video cameras she'd installed the previous week—one at the highway entrance, the other mounted high in a tree fifty meters from the house.

On the tiny screen the car stopped.

Tire Slasher scampered from the woods. The driver opened his door and stepped out. Both men hustled a few meters back down the lane toward the house.

She knew exactly what they were waiting for.

So she switched off the display and rushed from her hiding place.

VIKTOR WAITED TO SEE IF HE WAS RIGHT. HE'D PARKED the car just past a bend in the hard-packed lane and watched the house from behind a tree trunk.

"They're not going anywhere," Rafael said. "Two flat tires."

Viktor knew the woman had to have been watching.

"I never let on," Rafael said. "I acted like I was on guard and sensed nothing."

Which was what Viktor had told his partner to do.

From his pocket he removed the medallion that he'd managed to steal. Minister Zovastina's orders were clear. Retrieve and return all of them intact. Five were accounted for. Only three remained.

"What were they like?" Rafael asked.

"Puzzling."

And he meant it. He'd anticipated their moves, almost too well, and that bothered him.

The same slender woman with lioness moves emerged from the woods. Surely she'd seen the tires slashed and was racing to report to her compatriots. He was pleased to know that he'd been right. But why had she not stopped the assault? Maybe her task was simply to watch? He noticed she was carrying something. Small and rectangular. He wished he'd brought binoculars.

Rafael reached into his jacket pocket and removed the radio controller.

He gently laid a hand on his partner's arm. "Not yet."

The woman stopped and examined the tires, then trotted toward the front door.

"Give her time."

Three hours ago, after arranging the meeting, they'd driven straight here. A thorough reconnaissance had confirmed that the house stood empty, so they'd stashed packs of Greek fire beneath the raised foundation and inside the attic. Instead of one of the turtles igniting this mixture, they'd rigged a radio charge.

The woman disappeared inside the house.

Viktor silently counted to ten and prepared to lift his hand from Rafael's arm.

MALONE STOOD IN THE BOAT. THORVALDSEN BESIDE him.

"What did you mean Cassiopeia is in trouble?"

"The house is loaded with Greek fire. They came before us and prepared. Now that he has the medallion, Viktor doesn't intend for us to survive the meeting."

"And they're waiting to make sure Cassiopeia is in there."

"That's my estimate. But we're about to see if it's also theirs."

CASSIOPEIA ALLOWED THE FRONT DOOR TO CLOSE, THEN raced through the house. This was chancy. She could only hope that the thieves gave her a few seconds before they detonated the mixture. Her nerves were tingling, her mind surging, her melancholy replaced with an adrenaline-driven rush.

At the museum, Malone had sensed her anxiety, seemingly knowing that something was wrong.

And there was.

But at the moment she couldn't worry about it. Enough emotion had been expended on things she could not change. Right now, finding the rear door was all that mattered.

She burst out into dull daylight.

Malone and Thorvaldsen waited in the boat.

The house blocked any view of their escape from down the lane in front. She still held the compact LCD monitor.

Sixty meters to the water.

She leaped from the wooden deck.

MALONE SPOTTED CASSIOPEIA AS SHE FLED FROM THE house and ran straight for them.

Fifty feet.

Thirty.

A massive *swoosh* and the house suddenly caught fire. One second it stood intact, the next flames poured from the windows, out from beneath, and stretched skyward through the roof. Like magician's flash paper, he thought. No explosion. Instant combustion. Total.

Complete. And, in the absence of salt water, unstoppable.

Cassiopeia found the dock and leaped into the boat.

"You cut that close," he said.

"Get down," she urged.

They crouched in the boat and he watched as she adjusted a video receiver and the image of a car appeared.

Two men climbed inside. He recognized Viktor. The car drove away, disappearing from the screen. She flicked a switch and another image showed the car turning onto the highway.

Thorvaldsen seemed pleased. "Apparently, our ruse worked."

"Don't you think you could have told me what was happening?" Malone asked.

Cassiopeia threw him a mischievous grin. "Now what fun would that have been?"

"He has the medallion."

"Which is precisely what we wanted him to have," Thorvaldsen said.

The house continued to consume itself. Smoke billowed into the sky. Cassiopeia cranked the outboard and steered the boat out into open water. Thorvaldsen's seaside estate lay only a few miles to the north.

"I had the boat delivered just after we arrived," Thorvaldsen said, as he grabbed Malone by the arm and led him to the stern. Cold salt spray misted over the bow. "I appreciate you being here. We were going to ask for your help today, after the museum was destroyed. That's why she wanted to meet with you. She needs your help, but I doubt she'll ask now."

He wanted to inquire further, but knew now was not the time. His answer, though, was never in doubt. "She's got it." He paused. "You've both got it."

Thorvaldsen squeezed his arm in appreciation. Cassiopeia kept her attention ahead, navigating the boat through the swells.

"How bad is it?" he asked.

The roar of the engine and the wind masked his question so that only Thorvaldsen heard him.

"Bad enough. But now we have hope."

TWENTY

ZOVASTINA SAT STRAPPED INTO HER SEAT IN THE HELI-copter's rear compartment. Usually she traveled by a more luxurious method, but today she'd used the faster, military-issue chopper. One of her Sacred Band piloted the craft. Half of her personal guard, including Viktor, were licensed pilots. She sat across from the female pris-oner from the laboratory, another of her guard beside the woman. She'd been brought aboard handcuffed, but Zovastina had ordered them removed.

"What's your name?" she asked the woman.

"Does it matter?"

They spoke through headsets in Khask, which she knew none of the foreigners aboard understood.

"How do you feel?"

The woman hesitated before answering, as if debating whether to lie. "The best I've felt in years."

"I'm glad. It's our goal to improve the lives of all our citizens. Perhaps when you're released from prison, you'll have a greater appreciation for our new society."

A look of contempt formed on the woman's pitted face. Nothing about her was attractive, and Zovastina wondered how many defeats had been needed to strip her of all self-respect.

"I doubt I'll be a part of your new society, Minister. My sentence is long."

"I'm told you were involved in the trafficking of cocaine. If the Soviets were still here, you would have been executed."

"The Russians?" She laughed. "They were the ones who bought the drugs."

She wasn't surprised. "The way of our new world."

"What happened to the others who came with me?"

She decided to be honest. "Dead."

Though this woman was surely accustomed to difficulties, she noticed an unease. Understandable, really. Here she was, aboard a helicopter with the Supreme Minister of the Central Asian Federation, after being whisked from prison and subjected to some unknown medical test, of which she was the only survivor. "I'll make sure your sentence is reduced. Though you may not appreciate us, the Federation appreciates your assistance."

"Am I supposed to be grateful?"

"You volunteered."

"I don't recall anyone saying I had a choice."

She glanced out the window at the silent peaks of the Pamirs, which signaled the border and friendly territory. She caught the woman's gaze. "Don't you want to be a part of what's about to happen?"

"I want to be free."

Something from her university years, what Sergej had said long ago, flashed through her mind. *Anger seemed always directed at individuals—hatred preferred classes. Time cured anger, but never hatred.* So she asked, "Why do you hate?"

The woman studied her with a blank expression. "I should have been one of those who died."

"Why?"

"Your prisons are nasty places, from which few emerge."

"As they should be, to discourage anyone from wanting to be there."

"Many have no choice." The woman paused. "Unlike you, Supreme Minister."

The bastion of mountains grew larger in the window. "Centuries ago Greeks came east and changed the world. Did you know that? They conquered Asia. Changed our culture. Now Asians are about to go west and do the same. You're helping to make it possible."

"I care nothing about your plans."

"My name, Irina—Eirene in Greek—means peace. That's what we seek."

"And killing prisoners will bring this peace?"

This woman cared not about destiny. Zovastina's entire life had seemed destined. So far, she'd forged a new political order—just as Alexander had done. Another lesson from Sergej spoke loudly. *Remember, Irina, what Arrian said of Alexander. He was always the rival of his own self.* Only in the past few years had she come to understand that malady. She stared at the woman who'd ruined her life over a few thousand rubles.

"Ever heard of Menander?"

"Why don't you tell me?"

"He was a Greek playwright from the fourth century BCE. He wrote comedies."

"I prefer tragedies."

She was tiring of this defeatism. Not everyone could be changed. Unlike Colonel Enver, who'd earlier seen the possibilities she'd offered and willingly become a convert. Men like him would be useful in the years ahead, but this pitiful soul represented nothing but failure.

"Menander wrote something I've always found to be

true. *If you want to live your whole life free from pain, you must either be a god or a corpse.*"

She reached across and unsnapped the woman's harness. The guardsman, sitting beside the prisoner, wrenched open the cabin door. The woman seemed momentarily stunned by the bitter air and the engine roar that rushed inside.

"I'm a god," Zovastina said. "You're a corpse."

The guard ripped off the woman's headset, who apparently realized what was about to happen and started to resist.

But he shoved her out the door.

Zovastina watched as the body tumbled through the crystalline air, vanishing into the peaks below.

The guard slammed the cabin door shut and the helicopter kept flying west back to Samarkand.

For the first time since this morning, she felt satisfied.

Everything was now in place.

PART
TWO

TWENTY-ONE

STEPHANIE NELLE SCRAMBLED OUT OF THE CAB AND quickly jerked up the hood of her overcoat. An April rain poured down and water puddled between the rough cobbles, furiously streaming toward the city canals. The source, a nasty storm that had blown in earlier off the North Sea, now lay hidden behind indigo clouds, but a steady drizzle remained visible within the penumbra of streetlamps.

She pushed through the rain, stuffing bare hands into coat pockets. She crossed an arched pedestrian bridge, entered the Rembrandtplein, and noticed that the torrid evening had not dampened the crowds at the peep shows, pickup clubs, gay bars, and striptease outlets.

Farther into the bowels of the red-light district, she passed brothels, their plate-glass windows littered with girls promising fulfillment with leather and lace. In one, an Asian woman, dressed in tight bondage gear, sat on a padded seat and flipped through the pages of a magazine.

Stephanie had been told that night was not the most threatening time for a visit to the renowned district. The morning desperation of passing junkies and the early-afternoon edginess of pimps waiting for the evening's business were usually more intense. But she'd been warned that the northern end, near the Nieuwmarkt, in an area just beyond the crowds, constantly exuded a quiet sense of menace. So she was on guard as she breached the invisible line and entered. Her eyes shot back and forth, like a prowling cat's, her course set straight for the café at the far end of the street.

The Jan Heuval occupied the ground floor of a three-story warehouse. A brown café, one of hundreds that dotted the Rembrandtplein. She shoved open the front door and immediately noticed the aroma of burning cannabis along with the absence of any "No Drugs Please" sign.

The café was jammed, its warm air saturated with a hallucinogenic fog scented like singed rope. The aroma of fried fish and roasted chestnuts mixed with the intoxicating waft and her eyes burned. She pushed back the hood and shook rain onto the foyer's already damp tiles.

Then she spotted Klaus Dyhr. Mid-thirties, blond-haired, pale, weathered face—exactly as he'd been described.

Not for the first time, she reminded herself why she was here. Returning a favor. Cassiopeia Vitt had asked her to contact Dyhr. And since she owed her friend at least one favor, she could hardly refuse the request. Before making contact she'd run a check and learned that Dyhr was Dutch born, German educated, and practiced chemistry for a local plastics manufacturer. His obsession was coin collecting—he supposedly possessed an impressive array—and one in particular had drawn the interest of her Muslim friend.

The Dutchman stood alone near a chest-high table, nursing a brown beer and munching fried fish. A rolled cigarette burned in an ashtray and the thick green fog curling upward was not from tobacco.

"I'm Stephanie Nelle," she said in English. "The woman who called."

"You said you were interested in buying."

She caught the curt tone that said, "Tell me what you want, pay me, and I'll be on my way." She also noticed his glassy eyes, which almost couldn't be helped. Even she was starting to feel a buzz. "Like I said on the phone, I want the elephant medallion."

He gulped a swallow of beer. "Why? It's of no consequence. I have many other coins worth much more. Good prices."

"I'm sure you do. But I want the medallion. You said it was for sale."

"I said it depends on what you want to pay."

"Can I see it?"

Klaus reached into his pocket. She accepted the offering and studied the oblong medallion through a plastic sleeve. A warrior on one side, a mounted war elephant challenging a horseman on the other. About the size of a fifty-cent piece, the images nearly eroded away.

"You know nothing of what that is, do you?" Klaus asked.

She decided to be honest. "I'm doing this for someone else."

"I want six thousand euros."

Cassiopeia had told her to pay whatever. Price was irrelevant. But staring at the sheaved piece, she wondered why something so nondescript would be so important.

"There are only eight known," he said. "Six thousand euros is a bargain."

"Only eight? Why sell it?"

He fingered the burning butt, sucked a deep drag, held it, then slowly whistled out thick smoke. "I need the money." His oily eyes returned their gaze downward, staring toward his beer.

"Things that bad?" she asked.

"You sound like you care."

Two men flanked Klaus. One was fair, the other

STEVE BERRY / 112

tanned. Their faces and features were a conflicting mixture of Arab and Asian. Rain continued to pour outside, but the men's coats were dry. Fair grabbed Klaus's arm and a knife blade was pressed flat to the man's stomach. Tan wrapped an arm around her in a seemingly friendly embrace and brought the tip of another knife close to her ribs, pressing the blade into her coat.

"The medallion," Fair said, motioning with his head. "On the table."

She decided not to argue and calmly did as he asked.

"We'll be leaving now," Tan said, pocketing the coin. His breath stank of beer. "Stay here."

She had no intention of challenging them. She knew to respect weapons pointed at her.

The men wove their way to the front door and left the café.

"They took my coin," Klaus said, his voice rising. "I'm going after them."

She couldn't decide if it was foolishness or the drugs talking. "How about you let me handle it."

He appraised her with a suspicious gaze.

"I assure you," she said. "I came prepared."

TWENTY-TWO

MALONE FINISHED HIS DINNER. HE WAS SITTING INSIDE the Café Norden, a two-story restaurant that faced into the heart of Højbro Plads. The evening had turned nasty with a brisk April shower dousing the nearly empty city square. He sat high and dry by an open window, on the upper floor, and enjoyed the rain.

"I appreciate you helping out today," Thorvaldsen said from across the table.

"Almost getting blown up? Twice? What are friends for?"

He finished the last of his tomato bisque soup. The café offered some of the best he'd ever eaten. He was full of questions, but realized answers, as always with Thorvaldsen, would be apportioned sparingly. "Back at that house, you and Cassiopeia talked about Alexander the Great's body. That you know where it is. How's that possible?"

"We've managed to learn a lot on the subject."

"Cassiopeia's friend at the museum in Samarkand?"

"More than a friend, Cotton."

He'd surmised as much. "Who was he?"

"Ely Lund. He grew up here, in Copenhagen. He and my son, Cai, were friends."

Malone caught the sadness when Thorvaldsen mentioned his dead son. His stomach also flip-flopped at the thought of that day two years ago, in Mexico City, when the young man was murdered. Malone had been there, on a Magellan Billet assignment, and brought down the shooters, but a bullet had found him, too. Losing a son. He couldn't imagine Gary, his own fifteen-year-old, dying.

"Whereas Cai wanted to serve in government, Ely loved history. He earned a doctorate and became an expert on Greek antiquity, working in several European museums before ending up in Samarkand. The cultural museum there has a superb collection, and the Central Asian Federation offered encouragements to science and art."

"How did Cassiopeia meet him?"

"I introduced them. Three years ago. Thought it would be good for them both."

He sipped his drink. "What happened?"

"He died. A little less than two months ago. She took it hard."

"She love him?"

Thorvaldsen shrugged. "Hard to say with her. Rarely do her emotions surface."

But they had earlier. Her sadness watching the museum burn. The distant stare out over the canal. Her refusal to meet his gaze. Nothing voiced. Only felt.

When they'd docked the motorboat at Christiangade, Malone had wanted answers, but Thorvaldsen had promised that over dinner all would be explained. So he'd been driven back to Copenhagen, slept a little, then worked in the bookstore the remainder of the day. A couple of times he drifted into the history section and found a few volumes on Alexander and Greece. But mainly he wondered what Thorvaldsen had meant by *Cassiopeia needs your help.*

Now he was beginning to understand.

Out the open window, across the square, he spotted Cassiopeia leaving his bookshop, dashing through the rain, something wrapped in a plastic bag tucked beneath one arm. Thirty minutes ago he'd given her the key to the store so she could use his computer and phone.

"Finding Alexander's body," Thorvaldsen said, "centers on Ely and the manuscript pages he uncovered. Ely initially asked Cassiopeia to locate the elephant medallions. But when we started to track them down, we discovered someone else was already looking."

"How did Ely connect the medallions to the manuscript?"

"He examined the one in Samarkand and found the microletters. ZH. They have a connection to the manuscript. After Ely died, Cassiopeia wanted to know what was happening."

"So she came to you for help?"

Thorvaldsen nodded. "I couldn't refuse."

He smiled. How many friends would buy an entire museum and duplicate everything inside just so it could burn to the ground?

Cassiopeia disappeared below the windowsill. He heard the café's main door below open and close, then footsteps climbing the metal stairway to the second floor.

"You've stayed wet a lot today," Malone said, as she reached the top.

Her hair was pulled into a ponytail, her jeans and pullover shirt splotched with rain. "Hard for a girl to look good."

"Not really."

She threw him a look. "A charmer tonight."

"I have my moments."

She removed his laptop from the plastic bag and said to Thorvaldsen, "I downloaded everything."

"If I'd known you were going to bring it over in the

rain," Malone said, "I'd have insisted on a security deposit."

"You need to see this."

"I told him about Ely," Thorvaldsen said.

The dining room was dim and deserted. Malone ate here three or four times a week, always at the same table, near the same hour. He enjoyed the solitude.

Cassiopeia faced him.

"I'm sorry," he said, and meant it.

"I appreciate that."

"I appreciate you saving my ass."

"You would have found a way out. I just sped things up."

He recalled his predicament and wasn't so sure about her conclusion.

He wanted to ask more about Ely Lund, curious as to how he'd managed to crack her emotional vault. Like his own, there were a multitude of locks and alarms. But he kept silent—as always when feelings were unavoidable.

Cassiopeia switched on the laptop and brought several scanned images onto the screen. Words. Ghostly gray, fuzzy in places, and all in Greek.

"About a week after Alexander the Great died, in 323 BCE," Cassiopeia said, "Egyptian embalmers arrived in Babylon. Though it was summer, hot as hell, they found his corpse uncorrupted, its complexion still lifelike. That was taken as a sign from the gods of Alexander's greatness."

He'd read about that earlier. "Some sign. He was probably still alive, in a terminal coma."

"That's the modern consensus. But that medical state was unknown then. So they went about their task and mummified the body."

He shook his head. "Amazing. The greatest conqueror of his time, killed by embalmers."

Cassiopeia smiled in agreement. "Mummification usually took seventy days, the idea being to dry the body beyond further decay. But with Alexander, they used a different method. He was immersed in white honey."

He knew about honey, a substance that did not rot. Time would crystallize, but never destroy, its basic composition, which could easily be reconstituted with heat.

"The honey," she said, "would have preserved Alexander, inside and out, better than mummification. The body was eventually wrapped in gold cartonnage, then placed into a golden sarcophagus, dressed in robes and a crown, surrounded by more honey. That's where it stayed, in Babylon, for a year, while a gem-encrusted carriage was built. Then a funeral cortege set off from Babylon."

"Which is when the funerary games began," he said.

Cassiopeia nodded. "In a manner of speaking. Perdiccas, one of Alexander's generals, called an emergency meeting of the Companions the day after Alexander died. Roxane, Alexander's Asian wife, was six months pregnant. Perdiccas wanted to wait for the birth then decide what to do. If the child was a boy, he would be the rightful heir. But others balked. They weren't going to have a part-barbarian monarch. They wanted Alexander's half brother, Philip, as their king, though the man was, by all accounts, mentally ill."

Malone recalled the details of what he'd read earlier. Fighting actually broke out around Alexander's deathbed. Perdiccas then called an assembly of Macedonians and, to keep order, placed Alexander's corpse in their midst. The assembly voted to abandon the planned Arabia campaign and approved a division of the empire. Governorships were doled out to the Companions. Rebellion quickly erupted as the generals fought among themselves. In late summer, Roxane gave birth to a boy, christened Alexander IV. To keep the peace, a joint arrangement was conceived whereby the child and Philip, the half brother, were deemed king, though the Companions governed their respective portions of the empire, unconcerned with either.

"What was it," Malone asked, "six years later when the half brother was murdered by Olympias, Alexander's mother? She'd hated that child from birth, since Philip of Macedonia had divorced her to marry the mother. Then, a few years later, Roxane and Alexander IV were both poisoned. None of them ever ruled anything."

"Eventually, Alexander's sister was murdered, too," Thorvaldsen said. "His entire bloodline eradicated. Not a single legitimate heir survived. And the greatest empire in the world crumbled away."

"So what does all that have to do with elephant medallions? And what possible relevance could that have today?"

"Ely believed a great deal," she said.

He saw there was more. "And what do *you* believe?"

She sat silent, as if unsure, but not wanting to voice her reservations.

"It's all right," he said. "You tell me when you're ready."

Then something else occurred to him and he said to Thorvaldsen, "What about the last two medallions here in Europe? I heard you ask Viktor about them. He's probably headed after those next."

"We're ahead of him there."

"Someone's already got them?"

Thorvaldsen glanced at his watch. "At least one, I hope, by now."

TWENTY-THREE

STEPHANIE STEPPED FROM THE CAFÉ BACK INTO THE rain. As she yanked the hood over her head she found her earpiece and spoke into the mike hidden beneath her jacket.

"Two men just left here. They have what I want."

"Fifty meters ahead, heading for the bridge," came a reply.

"Stop them."

She hustled into the night.

She'd brought two Secret Service agents, requisitioned from President Danny Daniels' overseas detail. A month ago the president had requested that she accompany him to the annual European economic summit. National leaders had gathered forty miles south of Amsterdam. Tonight Daniels was attending a formal dinner, secure within The Hague, so she'd managed to corral two helpers. Just insurance, she'd told them, promising dinner afterward wherever they'd like.

"They're armed," one of the agents said in her ear.

"Knives in the café," she said.

"Guns out here."

Her spine stiffened. This was turning nasty. "Where are they?"

"At the pedestrian bridge."

She heard shots and removed a Magellan Billet–issue Beretta from beneath her jacket.

More shots.

She rounded a corner.

People were scattering. Tan and Fair were huddled on a bridge behind a chest-high iron railing, shooting at the two Secret Servicemen, one on either side of the canal.

Glass shattered, as a bullet found one of the brothels.

A woman screamed.

More frightened people rushed by Stephanie. She lowered her gun, concealing it by her side. "Let's contain this," she said into the mike.

"Tell it to them," one of the agents answered.

Last week, when she'd agreed to do Cassiopeia the favor, she'd not seen the harm, but yesterday something had told her to come prepared, especially when she remembered that Cassiopeia had said she *and* Henrik Thorvaldsen appreciated the gesture. Anything Thorvaldsen was involved with signaled trouble.

More shots from the bridge.

"You're not getting out of here," she yelled out.

Fair whirled and aimed a gun her way.

She dove into a sunken alcove. A bullet pinged off the bricks a few feet away. She hugged the stairs and eased herself back up. Rain gushed down each runner and soaked her clothes.

She fired two shots.

Now the two men lay in the center of a triangle. No way out.

Tan shifted position, trying to lessen his exposure, but one of the agents shot him in the chest. He staggered until another round sent him teetering onto the bridge railing, his frame folding over the side and splashing into the canal.

Wonderful. Now there were bodies.

Fair scampered to the railing and tried to look over.

He seemed as if he wanted to jump, but more shots kept him pinned. Fair straightened, then ran forward, charging the far side of the bridge, shooting indiscriminately. The Secret Service agent ahead of him returned fire, while the one on her side rushed forward and brought the man down, from behind, with three shots.

Sirens could be heard.

She sprang from her position and trotted onto the bridge. Fair lay on the cobbles, rain ushering away the blood that poured from his body. She waved with her arms for the agents to come.

Both men raced over.

Tan floated facedown in the canal.

Red and blue lights appeared fifty yards away, speeding toward the bridge. Three police cars.

She pointed at one of the agents. "I need you in the water getting a medallion from that man's pocket. It's in a plastic sleeve and has an elephant on it. Once you get it, swim out of here and don't get caught."

The man holstered his gun and leaped over the railing. She liked that about the Secret Service. No questions, just action.

The police cars skidded to a stop.

She shook rain from her face and glanced at the other agent. "Get out of here and get me some diplomatic help."

"Where will you be?"

Her mind flashed back to last summer. Roskilde. She and Malone.

"Under arrest."

TWENTY-FOUR

CASSIOPEIA SIPPED A GLASS OF WINE AND WATCHED AS Malone digested what she and Thorvaldsen were telling him.

"Cotton," she said, "let me explain about the connection that sparked our interest. We told you some earlier, about X-ray fluorescence. A researcher at the cultural museum in Samarkand pioneered the technique, but Ely came up with the idea of examining medieval Byzantine texts. That's where he found the writing at a molecular level."

"The reused parchment is called a palimpsest," Thorvaldsen said. "Quite ingenious, actually. After monks scraped away the original ink and wrote on the cleaned pages, they would cut and turn the sheets sideways, fashioning them into what we would recognize today as books."

"Of course," she said, "much of the original parchment is lost by this mangling, because rarely were original parchments kept together. Ely, though, found several that had been kept relatively intact. In one he discovered some lost theorems of Archimedes. Remarkable, given that almost none of Archimedes' writings exist today." She stared at him. "In another he found the formula for Greek fire."

"And who did he tell?" Malone asked.

"Irina Zovastina," Thorvaldsen said. "Supreme Minister of the Central Asian Federation. Zovastina asked that the discoveries be kept secret. At least for a short while. Since she paid the bills, it was hard to refuse. She also encouraged him to analyze more of the museum's manuscripts."

"Ely," she said, "understood the need for secrecy. The techniques were new and they needed to be sure what they were finding was authentic. He didn't see the harm in waiting. He actually wanted to examine as many manuscripts as he could before going public."

"But he told you," Malone said.

"He was excited, and wanted to share. He knew I wouldn't say anything."

"Four months ago," Thorvaldsen said, "Ely stumbled onto something extraordinary in one of the palimpsests. The History of Hieronymus of Cardia. Hieronymus was a friend and countryman to Eumenes, one of Alexander the Great's generals. Eumenes also acted as Alexander's personal secretary. Only fragments of Hieronymus' works have survived, but they're known to be quite reliable. Ely discovered a full account, from Alexander's time, told by an observer with credibility." Thorvaldsen paused. "It's quite a tale, Cotton. You read some of it earlier, about Alexander's death and the draught."

Cassiopeia knew Malone was intrigued. At times, he reminded her of Ely. Both men used humor to mock reality, dodge an issue, twist an argument, or, most irritatingly, escape involvement. But where Malone exuded a physical confidence, a command of his surroundings, Ely dominated through thoughtful intelligence and gentle emotion. What a contrast she and he had been. She the dark-skinned, dark-haired, Spanish Muslim. He the pale, Protestant Scandinavian. But she'd loved being around him.

A first for her, in a long while.

"Cotton," she said, "about a year after Alexander died, in the winter of 321 BCE, his funeral cortege finally set out from Babylon. Perdiccas had, by then, decided to bury Alexander in Macedonia. This was contrary to Alexander's deathbed wish to be entombed in Egypt. Ptolemy, another of the generals, had claimed Egypt as his portion of the empire and was already there acting as governor. Perdiccas was acting as regent for the infant, Alexander IV. Under the Macedonian constitution, the new ruler was required to properly bury his predecessor—"

"And," Malone said, "if Perdiccas allowed Alexander to be buried by Ptolemy, in Egypt, that might give Ptolemy a greater claim to the throne."

She nodded. "Also, there was a prophecy common at the time that if kings stopped being buried in Macedonian earth, the royal bloodline would end. As it turned out, Alexander the Great was not buried in Macedonia and the royal bloodline did end."

"I read about what happened," Malone said. "Ptolemy highjacked the funeral cortege in what is now northern Syria and brought the body to Egypt. Perdiccas tried twice to invade across the Nile. Eventually, his officers rebelled and stabbed him to death."

"Then Ptolemy did something unexpected," Thorvaldsen said. "He refused the regency offered to him by the army. He could have been king of the entire empire, but he said no and turned his full attention to Egypt. Strange, wouldn't you say?"

"Maybe he didn't want to be king. From what I've read, there was so much treachery and cynicism going around that nobody survived long. Murder was simply part of the political process."

"But maybe Ptolemy knew something no one else did." She saw that Malone was waiting for her to explain. "That the body in Egypt was not Alexander's."

He grinned. "I read about those stories. Supposedly, after highjacking the cortege, Ptolemy fashioned a likeness of Alexander and substituted it for the real corpse, then allowed Perdiccas, and others, a chance to seize it. But those are tales. No proof exists to substantiate them."

She shook her head. "I'm talking about something entirely different. The manuscript Ely discovered tells us exactly what happened. The body sent west for burial in 321 BCE was not Alexander. A switch was made in Babylon, during the previous year. Alexander himself was laid to rest in a place only a handful knew about. And they kept their secret well. For twenty-three hundred years, no one has known."

Two days had passed since Alexander executed Glaucias. What was left of the physician's body remained outside Babylon's walls, on the ground and in the trees, the animals still picking flesh from the bones. The king's fury continued unrestrained. He was short-tempered, suspicious, and unhappy. Eumenes was called into the king's presence and Alexander told his secretary that he would soon die. The statement shocked Eumenes, as he could not imagine a world without Alexander. The king said that the gods were impatient and his time among the living was about to end. Eumenes listened, but placed little credence in the prediction. Alexander had long believed that he was not the son of Philip, but instead the mortal descendant of Zeus. A fantastic claim for sure, but after all his great conquests many had come to agree with him. Alexander spoke of Roxane and the child she carried in her womb. If it be a boy he would have a solid claim to the throne, but Alexander recognized the resentment Greeks would have toward a half-foreign ruler. He told Eumenes that his Companions would battle among themselves for his empire and he did not want to be a part of their struggle. "Let them claim their own destiny," he said. His was made. So he told Eumenes that he wanted to be buried with Hephaestion. Like Achilles, who wished that his ashes be mixed with those of his lover, Alexander wanted the same. "I shall make sure your ashes and his are joined," Eumenes said. But Alexander shook his head. "No. Bury us together." Since just days earlier Eumenes had witnessed Hephaestion's grand funeral pyre, he asked how that would be possible. Alexander told him that the body burned in Babylon was not Hephaestion's. He'd ordered Hephaestion embalmed last fall so that he could be transported to a place where he could forever lie in peace. Alexander wanted the same for himself. "Mummify me," he commanded, "then take me where I, too, can lie in clean air." He forced Eumenes to pledge that he would fulfill this wish, in secret, involving only two others, whom the king named.

Malone glanced up from the screen. Outside, the rain had quickened. "Where did they take him?"

"It becomes more confusing," Cassiopeia said. "Ely dated that manuscript to about forty years *after* Alexander died." She reached over to the laptop and scrolled through the pages on the screen. "Read this. More from Hieronymus of Cardia."

How wrong that the greatest of kings, Alexander of Macedonia, should lie forever in an unknown place. Though he sought a quiet respite, one which he arranged, such a silent fate does not seem fitting. Alexander was correct about his Companions. The generals fought among themselves, killing each other and all who posed a threat to their claims. Ptolemy may have been the most fortunate. He ruled Egypt for thirty-eight years. In the last year of his reign, he heard of my efforts in writing this account and summoned me to the palace from the library at Alexandria. He knew of my friendship with Eumenes and read with interest what I had so far written. He then confirmed that the body buried in Memphis was not that of Alexander. Ptolemy made clear that he'd known that ever since he'd attacked the funeral cortege. Years later he'd finally become curious and dispatched investigators. Eumenes was brought to Egypt and told Ptolemy that Alexander's true remains were hidden in a place only he knew. By then the grave site in Memphis, where Alexander was said to lay, had become a shrine. "We both fought by his side and would have gladly died for him," Ptolemy told Eumenes. "He should not lie forever in secret." Overcome by remorse and sensing that Ptolemy was sincere, Eumenes revealed the resting place, far away, in the mountains, where the Scythians taught Alexander about life, then Eumenes died shortly thereafter. Ptolemy recalled that when asked to whom did he leave his kingdom, Alexander had answered "to the brightest." So Ptolemy spoke these words to me:

*And you, adventurer, for my immortal voice,
    though far off, fills your ears, hear my words.
Sail onto the capital founded by Alexander's father,
    where sages stand guard.
Touch the innermost being of the golden illusion.
    Divide the phoenix.
Life provides the measure of the true grave.
But be wary, for there is but one chance of success.
    Climb the god-built walls.
When you reach the attic, gaze into the tawny eye,
    and dare to find the distant refuge.*

Ptolemy then handed me a silver medallion that showed Alexander when he fought against elephants. He told me that, in honor of those battles, he'd minted the coins. He also told me to come back when I solved his riddle. But a month later Ptolemy lay dead.

TWENTY-FIVE

SAMARKAND
CENTRAL ASIAN FEDERATION
11:50 P.M.

ZOVASTINA LIGHTLY RAPPED ON A WHITE LACQUERED door. A stately, well-groomed woman in her late fifties with dull gray-black hair answered. Like always, Zovastina did not wait to be invited inside.

"Is she awake?"

The woman nodded and Zovastina marched down the hall.

The house dominated a wooded lot on the eastern outskirts of the city, beyond the sprawl of low-slung buildings and colorful mosques, in an area where many of the newer estates had sprung, the hilly terrain once littered with Soviet-era guard towers. Federation prosperity had generated both a middle and an upper class, and those with means had begun to flaunt it. This house, built a decade ago, belonged to Zovastina, though she'd never actually lived here. Instead, she'd given it to her lover.

She surveyed the luxurious interior. An elaborately carved Louis XV console displayed an array of white porcelain figurines given to her by the French president. A coffered ceiling topped the adjacent living room, its floor covered by inlaid parquetry protected by a Ukrainian carpet. Another gift. A German mirror anchored one end of the long room and taffeta draperies adorned three towering windows.

Every time she stepped down the marbled hall, her mind wandered back six years, to one afternoon when she'd approached the same closed door. Inside the bedroom she'd found Karyn naked, a thin-chested man with curly hair and muscular arms atop her. She could still hear their moans, their ferocious exploration of each other surprisingly arousing. She'd stood for a long minute, watching, until they broke apart.

"Irina," Karyn calmly said. "This is Michele."

Karyn had climbed from the bed and brushed back her long wavy hair, exposing breasts Irina had many times enjoyed. Lean as a jackal, every inch of Karyn's unblemished skin shimmered with the color of cinnamon. Thin lips curved contemptuously, tilted nose with delicate nostrils, cheeks smooth as porcelain. Zovastina had suspected her lover's cheating, but it was an entirely different matter to witness the act firsthand.

"You're lucky I don't have you killed."

Karyn seemed unconcerned. "Look at him. He cares how I feel, gives without question. You only take. It's all you know how to do. Give orders and expect them to be obeyed."

"I don't recall any complaints from you."

"Being your whore doesn't come cheap. I've given up things more precious than money."

Zovastina's gaze involuntarily drifted to the naked Michele.

"You like him, don't you?" Karyn said.

She did not answer. Instead, she commanded, "I want you out of here, by nightfall."

Karyn stepped close, the sweet smell of an expensive perfume leading the way. "You really want me to go?" Her hand drifted to Zovastina's thigh. "Maybe you'd like to take off these clothes and join us."

She backhanded her lover across the face. Not the first time, but the first time in anger. A trickle of blood oozed from Karyn's busted lip and hatred stared back at her. "Gone. Before nightfall or, I promise, you'll not see morning."

Six years ago. A long time.

Or at least it seemed that way.

She turned the knob and entered.

The bedroom remained adorned with dainty French provincial furniture. A marble-and-gilt-bronze fireplace guarded by a pair of Egyptian porphyry lions decorated one wall. Seemingly out of place was the respirator beside the canopy bed, the oxygen bottle on the other side, and an intravenous bag suspended from a stainless-steel stand, transparent tubes snaking to one arm.

Karyn lay propped on pillows in the center of a queen-size bed, coral silk covers adjusted to her waist. Her flesh was the color of brown ash—her patina like waxed paper. Once-thick blond hair hung tangled, disheveled, thin as mist. Her eyes, which used to flash a vivid blue, now stared out of deep holes like creatures tucked away in caves. Angular cheeks were gone, replaced with a cadaverous gaunt that had transformed her pug nose into aquiline. A lace nightgown graced her emaciated frame as a flag hanging limp on a pole.

"What do you want tonight?" Karyn muttered, the voice brittle and strained. Tubing at her nostrils delivered oxygen with each breath. "Come to see if I'm dead?"

Irina crept close to the four-poster bed. The room's smell intensified. A sickening mixture of disinfectant, disease, and decay.

"Nothing to say?" Karyn managed, the voice mostly air.

She stared at the woman. Uncharacteristically for her, not a lot of planning had gone into their relationship.

Karyn had first been on her staff, then her personal secretary, and finally her concubine. Five years together. Five more apart, until last year when Karyn unexpectedly returned to Samarkand, ill.

"I actually came to see how you were."

"No, Irina. You came to see when I would die."

She wanted to say that was the last thing she wanted, but thoughts of Michele and Karyn's betrayal kept her from any emotional concessions. Instead, she asked, "Was it worth it?"

Zovastina knew that years of unprotected sex, drifting from man to man and woman to woman, taking risks, had finally caught up with Karyn. Along the way, one of them had passed along HIV. Alone, frightened, and broke, last year Karyn had swallowed her pride and returned to the only place she'd thought might provide some comfort.

"Is that why you keep coming?" Karyn asked. "To see me proven wrong?"

"You *were* wrong."

"Your bitterness will consume you."

"This from a person who has literally been consumed by hers."

"Careful, Irina, you have no idea when I was infected. Maybe I'll share this misery."

"I've been tested."

"And what doctor was foolish enough to do that?" A cough racked Karyn's words. "Is he still alive to tell what he knows?"

"You haven't answered my question. Was it worth it?"

A smile creased the withdrawn face. "You can't order me anymore."

"You came back. You wanted help. I'm helping."

"I'm a prisoner."

"You can leave whenever you want." She paused. "Why can't you share the truth?"

"And what is the truth, Irina? That you're a lesbian. Your dear husband knew. He had to. You never speak of him."

"He's dead."

"A convenient car crash. How many times have you played that sympathy card with *your* people?"

This woman knew far too much of her business, which both attracted and repelled her. Their sense of intimacy, of sharing, had been part of their bond. Here was where, at one time, she could truly be herself. "He knew what was involved when he agreed to marry me. But he was ambitious, like you. He wanted the trappings. And I come with those trappings."

"How difficult it must be to live a lie."

"You do it."

Karyn shook her head. "No, Irina. I know what I am." The words seemed to sap her strength and Karyn paused to suck a few deep breaths before saying, "Why don't you just kill me?"

Some of Karyn's old self seeped through the bitter tone. Killing this woman was not an option. Saving her . . . that was the goal. Fate denied Achilles a chance to save his Patroclus. Incompetence cost Alexander the Great his love when Hephaestion died. She would not fall victim to the same mistakes.

"Can you seriously believe that anyone deserves this?" Karyn yanked her nightgown open. Tiny pearl buttons exploded outward onto the sheets. "Look at my breasts, Irina."

It hurt to look. Since Karyn had returned, Irina had studied AIDS and knew that the disease affected people differently. Some suffered internally. Blindness, colitis, life-threatening diarrhea, brain inflammation, tubercu-

STEVE BERRY / 134

losis, and worst of all, pneumonia. Others were emasculated externally, their skin covered with the effects of Kaposi's sarcoma, or devastated by herpes simplex, or ravaged by emaciation, the epidermis inevitably drawn down to bone. Karyn seemed the much more common combination.

"Remember how beautiful I was? My lovely skin? You used to adore my body."

She did recall. "Cover yourself up."

"Can't stand to see?"

She said nothing.

"You shit until your ass aches, Irina. You can't sleep, and your stomach stays in knots. I wait every day to see what new infection will spawn inside me. This is hell."

She'd tossed the woman in the helicopter to her death. She'd ordered the elimination of countless political opponents. She'd forged a Federation through a covert campaign of biological assassination that had claimed thousands. None of those deaths meant a thing. Karyn's dying was different. That was why she'd allowed her to stay. Why she supplied the drugs needed to keep her alive. She'd lied to those students. Here was her weakness. Perhaps her only one.

Karyn smiled faintly. "Every time you come here I see it in your eyes. You care." Karyn grabbed her arm. "You can help me, can't you? Those germs you played with years ago. You had to learn something. I don't want to die, Irina."

She fought to keep an emotional distance. Achilles and Alexander both failed by not doing that. "I'll pray to the gods for you."

Karyn started to laugh. A guttural, throaty chuckle mixed with the rattle of spit. Which both surprised and hurt her.

Karyn kept laughing.

She fled the bedroom and hurried to the front door.

These visits were a mistake. No more. Not now. Too much was about to happen.

The last thing she heard before leaving was the sickening sound of Karyn choking on her own saliva.

TWENTY-SIX

VINCENTI PAID THE WATER TAXI, THEN HOISTED HIM-
self up to street level and marched into the San Silva, one
of Venice's premier hotels. No weekend specials or cut-
rate promotions applied here, just forty-two luxurious
suites overlooking the Grand Canal in what was once
the home of a Doge. Its grand lobby reflected old-world
decadence. Roman columns, veined-marble, museum-
quality accessories—the spacious surroundings busy
with people, activity, and noise.

Peter O'Conner waited patiently in a quiet alcove.
O'Conner wasn't ex-military or ex-government intelligence—just a man with a talent for gathering information coupled with a conscience that barely existed.

Philogen Pharmaceutique spent millions annually on
an extensive array of in-house security to protect trade
secrets and patents, but O'Conner reported directly to
Vincenti—a set of personal eyes and ears providing the
indispensable luxury of being able to implement whatever was needed to protect his interests.

And he was glad to have him.

Five years ago it was O'Conner who stopped a rebellion among a sizable block of Philogen stockholders
over Vincenti's decision to expand the company further
into Asia. Three years ago, when an American pharma-

ceutical giant tried a hostile takeover, O'Conner terrorized enough shareholders to prevent any wholesale stock ditching. And, just recently, when Vincenti faced a challenge from his board of directors, O'Conner discovered the dirt used to blackmail enough votes that Vincenti managed not only to keep his job as CEO, but was also reelected chairman.

Vincenti settled into a tooled-leather armchair. A quick glance at the clock etched into the marble behind the concierge's counter confirmed that he needed to be at the restaurant by nine fifteen. As soon as he was comfortable, O'Conner handed him some stapled sheets and said, "That's what we have so far."

He quickly scanned the transcripts of telephone calls and face-to-face discussions—all from listening devices monitoring Irina Zovastina. When finished, he asked, "She's after these elephant medallions?"

"Our surveillance," O'Conner said, "has been enough to know she has sent some of her personal guards after these medallions. The head guy himself, Viktor Tomas, is leading one team. Another team went to Amsterdam. They've been burning buildings all over Europe to mask those thefts."

Vincenti knew all about Zovastina's Sacred Band. More of her obsession with all things Greek. "Do they have the medallions?"

"At least four. They went after two yesterday, but I haven't heard the results."

He was puzzled. "We need to know what she's doing."

"I'm on it. I've managed to bribe a few of the palace staff. Unfortunately, electronic surveillance only works when she stays put. She's constantly on the move. She flew to the China lab earlier."

He'd already been told of the visit by his chief scientist, Grant Lyndsey.

"You should have seen her with that assassination attempt," O'Conner said. "Rode straight toward the gunman, daring him to shoot. We watched on a long-range camera. Of course, she had a sharpshooter on the palace ready to take the guy down. But still, to ride straight for him. You sure there's not a set of nuts between her legs?"

He chuckled. "I'm not going to look."

"That woman's crazy."

Which was why Vincenti had changed his mind with the Florentine. The Council of Ten had collectively ordered some preliminary investigative work on the possibility that Zovastina might have to be eliminated, and the Florentine had been contracted to perform that reconnaissance. Vincenti had initially decided to make use of the Florentine in a full-scale rush to judgment, since to accomplish what he privately planned Zovastina had to go. So he'd promised the Florentine a huge profit if he could have her killed.

Then a better idea blossomed.

If he revealed the planned assassination, that might quell any fears Zovastina harbored about the League's trustworthiness. Which would buy him time to prepare something better—something he'd actually been conceiving over the past few weeks. More subtle. Less residuals.

"She also visited the house again," O'Conner told him. "A little while ago. Slipped out of the palace, alone, in a car. Tree-mounted cameras caught the visit. She stayed a half hour."

"Do we know her former lover's current condition?"

"Holding her own. We listened to their conversation with a parabolic monitor from a nearby house. A strange pair. Love/hate thing going on."

He'd found it interesting that a woman who'd managed to govern with unfettered ruthlessness harbored such an obsession. She'd been married for a few years, the man a midlevel diplomat in the former Kazakhstan's foreign service. Surely a marriage for appearance's sake. A way to mask her questionable sexuality. Yet the reports he'd amassed noted an amicable husband/wife relationship. He died suddenly in a car crash seventeen years ago, just after she became Kazakhstan's president, and a couple of years before she managed to forge the Federation. Karyn Walde came along a few years later and remained Zovastina's only long-lasting interpersonal relationship, which ended badly. Yet a year ago, when the woman reappeared, Zovastina had immediately taken her in and arranged, through Vincenti, for needed HIV medications.

"Should we act?" he asked.

O'Conner nodded. "Wait any longer and it might be too late."

"Arrange it. I'll be in the Federation by week's end."

"Could get messy."

"Whatever. Just no fingerprints. Nothing that links anything to me."

TWENTY-SEVEN

STEPHANIE HAD EXPERIENCED THE INSIDE OF A DANISH jail last summer when she and Malone were arrested. Now she'd visited a Dutch cell. Not much different. Wisely, she'd kept her mouth shut as the police rushed onto the bridge and spotted the dead man. Both Secret Service agents had managed to escape, and she hoped the one in the water had retrieved the medallion. Her suspicions, though, were now confirmed. Cassiopeia and Thorvaldsen were into something, and it wasn't ancient coin collecting.

The door to the holding cell opened and a thin man in his early sixties, with a long, sharp face and bushy silver hair, entered. Edwin Davis. Deputy national security adviser to the president. The man who replaced the late Larry Daley. And what a change. Davis had been brought over from State, a career man, possessed of two doctorates—one in American history, the other international relations—along with superb organizational skills and an innate diplomatic ability. He employed a courte- ᴋsy way, similar to that of President Daniels him- people tended to underestimate. Three secretaries ᴋad used him to whip their ailing departments Now he worked at the White House, helping the administration finish out the last three years of its second term.

"I was having dinner with the president. In The Hague. What a place, by the way. Enjoying the evening. Food was superb, and I usually don't care for gourmet. They brought me a note that told me where you were and I said to myself, there has to be a logical explanation why Stephanie Nelle would be in Dutch custody, found with a gun beside a dead man in the rain."

She opened her mouth to speak and he held up a halting hand.

"It gets better."

She sat quietly in her wet clothes.

"As I was deciding how I could actually leave you here, since I was reasonably sure I did not want to know why you came to Amsterdam, the president himself took me aside and told me to get over here. Seems two Secret Service agents were also involved, but they weren't in custody. One of them was soaking wet from swimming in a canal to retrieve this."

She caught what he tossed her and saw again the medallion with elephants, snug in its plastic sleeve.

"The president intervened with the Dutch. You're free to go."

She stood. "Before we leave I need to know about those dead men."

"Since I already knew you'd say that, I found out that they both carried Central Asian Federation passports. We checked. Part of Supreme Minister Irina Zovastina's personal security force."

She caught something in his eye. Davis was much easier to read than Daley had been. "That doesn't shock you."

"Few things do anymore." His voice had lowered to a whisper. "We have a problem, Stephanie, and now, fortunately or unfortunately, depending on your point of view, you're part of it."

She followed Davis into the hotel suite. President Danny Daniels sat sprawled on a sofa, wrapped in a bathrobe, his bare feet propped on a gilded glass-topped table. He was a tall stretch of a man with piles of blond hair, a booming voice, and a disarming manner. Though she'd worked for him for five years, she'd only come to really know him last fall with the treachery surrounding the lost library of Alexandria. He'd then both fired and rehired her. Daniels held a drink of something in one hand and a remote control in the other.

"There's not a damn thing on this TV to watch that isn't subtitled or in a language I don't understand. And I can't bear that BBC News or CNN International any longer. They show the same stories over and over." Daniels blackened the screen and tossed the remote aside. He sipped from his drink, then said to her, "I hear you've had another career-ending night."

She caught the twinkle in his eye. "Seems to be my path to success."

He motioned and she sat. Davis stood off to the side.

"I've got some more bad news," Daniels said. "Your agent in Venice is missing. She's not been heard from in twelve hours. Neighbors in the building where she was stationed reported a disturbance early this morning. Four men. A door kicked in. Of course, no one now officially saw anything. Typical Italians." He raised one arm in a flurry. "For God's sake don't involve me." The president paused, his face darkened. "Nothing about this sounds good."

Stephanie had loaned Naomi Johns to the White House, which needed some field reconnaissance on a person-of-interest—Enrico Vincenti, an international financier with ties to an organization called the Venetian

League. She knew the group. Another of the countless cartels from around the world. Naomi worked for Stephanie for many years, and had been the agent who'd investigated Larry Daley. She'd left the Billet last year, only to return, and Stephanie had been glad. Naomi was good. The recon job should have been low risk. Just record meets and greets. Stephanie had even told her to take a couple of days off in Italy when she finished.

Now she might be dead.

"When I loaned her out, your people said this was simply information gathering."

No one answered and her gaze shifted between the two men.

Daniels pointed. "Where's the medallion?"

She handed it to him.

"You want to tell me about this?"

She felt grimy. What she wanted was a shower and sleep, but she realized that wasn't going to happen. She resented being interrogated, but he was the president of the United States and had saved her hide, so she explained about Cassiopeia, Thorvaldsen, and the favor. The president listened with an unusual attentiveness, then said, "Tell her, Edwin."

"How much do you know about Supreme Minister Zovastina?"

"Enough to know that she's no friend of ours."

Her tired mind retrieved Zovastina's pertinent history. Born to a working-class family in northern Kazakhstan, her father died fighting the Nazis for Stalin, then an earthquake, just after the war, killed her mother and the rest of her immediate relatives. She grew up in an orphanage, until one of her mother's distant cousins took her in. She eventually became an economist, trained at the Leningrad Institute, then joined the Communist Party in her twenties and worked her way to head of the local Committee of the Representatives of the Workers.

She then snagged a spot on the Central Committee of Kazakhstan and quickly rose to the Supreme Soviet. She first promoted land and other economic reforms, then became a critic of Moscow. After independence from Russia, she was one of six Party members who ran for president of Kazakhstan. When the two front-runners failed to receive a majority, under the national constitution both were disqualified from the second round of voting, which she won.

"I learned a long time ago," Daniels said, "that if you have to tell someone you're their friend, the relationship's got big problems. This woman thinks we're a bunch of idiots. Friends like her we don't need."

"But you still have to kiss her ass."

Daniels enjoyed more of his drink. "Unfortunately."

"The Central Asian Federation is not something to take lightly," Davis made clear. "Land of hardy people and long memories. Twenty-eight million men and women available for military conscription. Twenty-two million of those fit and ready for service. About one and a half million new conscripts available each year. That's quite a fighting force. Currently, the Federation spends one point two billion dollars a year on defense, but that doesn't count what we pour in there, which is twice that.

"And the real crap," Daniels continued, "is that the people love her. The standard of living has improved a thousandfold. Before her, sixty-four percent lived in poverty. Now it's less than fifteen percent. That's as good as we do. She's investing everywhere. Hydroelectric power, cotton, gold—she's loaded with surpluses. That Federation is perched in a superb geoeconomic position. Russia, China, India. Smack between them all. Smart lady, too. She's sitting on some of the world's largest oil and natural gas reserves, which the Russians once totally controlled. They're still pissed about independence, so she made a deal and sells them oil and gas at below-market prices, which keeps Moscow off her tail."

She was impressed with Daniels' command of the region.

"Then," the president said, "a few years ago she entered into a long-term lease with Russia on the Baykonur Cosmodrome. The Russian spaceport sits in the middle of the old Kazakhstan. Six thousand square miles, which Russia now has exclusive use of until 2050. In return, of course, she got some debt cancellation. After that, she stroked the Chinese by settling a centuries-old border dispute. Not bad for an economist who grew up in an orphanage."

"Do we have problems with Zovastina?" she asked. Again neither man answered her question, so she switched gears. "What does Enrico Vincenti have to do with this?"

"Zovastina and Vincenti are connected," Daniels said, "through the Venetian League. Both are members. Four hundred and some people. Lots of money, time, and ambition, but the League isn't interested in changing the world—only being left alone. They hate government, restrictive laws, tariffs, taxes, me, anything that keeps them in line. They have their hands in lots of countries—"

She saw that Daniels had read her thoughts.

The president shook his head. "Not here. Not like last time. We've checked. Nothing. The Central Asian Federation is their main concern."

Davis said, "All of the stans were heavy with foreign debt from their Soviet domination and tries at independence. Zovastina has managed to renegotiate those obligations with the various government creditors and a large chunk of that debt has been forgiven. But an influx of new capital would help. Nothing quells progress more than long-term debt." He paused. "There's three point six billion dollars on deposit in a variety of banks across the globe, traced to Venetian League members."

"An ante in a huge poker game," Daniels said.

She realized the significance, since presidents were not prone to sound an alert based on flimsy suspicion. "Which is about to play out?"

Daniels nodded. "So far, corporations organized under Central Asian Federation law have acquired, or taken over, nearly eighty companies around the world. Pharmaceuticals, information technology, automobile and truck manufacturing, and telecommunications are just a few of the areas. Get this, they even acquired the world's largest producer of tea bags. Goldman Sachs predicts that, if this continues, the Federation could well become the third or fourth largest economy in the world, behind us, China, and India."

"It's alarming," Davis noted. "Particularly since it's happening with little or no fanfare. Usually, corporations like to play up their acquisitions. Not here. Everything is being kept close."

Daniels motioned with one arm. "Zovastina needs a consistent capital flow to keep the wheels of her government turning. We have taxes, she has the League. The Federation is rich in cotton, gold, uranium, silver, copper, lead, zinc—"

"And opium," she finished.

"Zovastina," Davis said, "has even helped with that. The Federation is now third, worldwide, for opiates seizure. She's shut down that region for trafficking, which makes the Europeans love her. Can't speak ill about her at all across the Atlantic. Of course, she peddles cheap oil and gas to a lot of them, too."

"You realize," she said, "that Naomi is probably dead because of all this." The thought turned her stomach. Losing an agent was the worst thing she could imagine.

Luckily, it rarely happened. But when it did, she always had to fight a disturbing mixture of anger and patience.

"We realize that," Davis said. "And it won't go unpunished."

"She and Cotton Malone were close. They worked together at the Billet many times. A good team. He'll be upset to hear."

"Which is another reason why you're here," the president said. "A few hours ago Cotton was involved in a fire at a Greco-Roman museum in Copenhagen. Henrik Thorvaldsen owned the place and Cassiopeia Vitt helped him escape the blaze."

"You seem up on things."

"Part of my job description, though I'm coming to dislike this part more and more." Daniels gestured with the medallion. "One of these was in that museum."

She recalled what Klaus Dyhr had said. *Only eight.*

Davis pointed a long finger at the coin. "It's called an elephant medallion."

"Important?" she asked.

"Apparently so," Daniels said. "But we need your help to learn more."

TWENTY-EIGHT

MALONE GRABBED A BLANKET AND HEADED FOR THE sofa in the other room. After the fire last fall, during rebuilding he'd eliminated several of the apartment walls and rearranged others, adjusting the layout so that the fourth floor of his bookshop was now a more practical living space.

"I like the furniture," Cassiopeia said. "Fits you."

He'd opted away from Danish simplicity and ordered everything from London. A sofa, some chairs, tables, and lamps. Lots of wood and leather, warm and comfortable. He'd noticed that little ever changed in the decor unless another book found its way up from the ground floor or another picture of Gary arrived by e-mail and was added to the growing collection. He'd suggested Cassiopeia sleep here, in town, as opposed to driving back to Christiangade with Thorvaldsen, and she'd not argued. During dinner, he'd listened to their various explanations, mindful that Cassiopeia possessed a judgment-affecting personal stake in whatever was happening.

Which wasn't good.

He'd recently been there himself, when Gary had been threatened.

She sat on the edge of his bed. Lamps long on charm but short on strength illuminated mustard-colored walls. "Henrik says I may need your help."

"You don't agree?"

"I'm not sure you do."

"Did you love Ely?"

He was surprised at himself for asking and she did not immediately answer.

"Hard to say."

Not an answer. "He must have been pretty special."

"Ely was extraordinary. Smart. Alive. Funny. When he discovered those lost texts, you should have seen him. You would have thought he just found a new continent."

"How long did you see each other?"

"Off and on for three years."

Her eyes drifted again, like while the museum burned. They were so alike. Both of them masked feelings. But everyone had a limit. He was still dealing with the realization that Gary was not his natural son—the product of an affair his ex-wife had long ago. A picture of the boy rested on one of the nightstands and his gaze shot toward it. He'd determined that genes didn't matter. The boy was still *his* son, and he and his ex-wife had made their peace. Cassiopeia, though, seemed to be wrestling with her demon. Bluntness seemed in order. "What are you trying to do?"

Her neck tensed and hands stiffened. "Live my life."

"Is this about Ely or you?"

"Why does it matter?"

Partly, she was right. It shouldn't matter either way. This was her fight. Not his. But he was drawn to this woman, even though she obviously cared for someone else. So he flushed emotion from his brain and asked, "What did Viktor's fingerprints reveal? Nobody mentioned a word about that at dinner."

"He works for Supreme Minister Irina Zovastina. Head of her personal guard."

"Was anyone going to tell me?"

She shrugged. "Eventually. If you'd wanted to know."

He quelled his anger, realizing she was taunting him. "You think the Central Asian Federation is directly involved?"

"The elephant medallion in the Samarkand museum has not been touched."

Good point.

"Ely found the first tangible evidence of Alexander the Great's lost tomb in centuries. I know he passed that on to Zovastina, because he told me about her reaction. She's obsessed with Greek history and Alexander. The museum in Samarkand is well funded because of her interest in the Hellenistic Age. When Ely discovered Ptolemy's riddle about Alexander's tomb, Zovastina was fascinated." Cassiopeia hesitated. "He died less than a week after telling her."

"You think he was murdered?"

"His house burned to the ground. Not much left of it or him."

The dots connected. Greek fire. "And what of the manuscripts he uncovered?"

"We had some inquiries made by academicians. No one at the museum knew anything."

"And now more buildings are burning and medallions are being stolen."

"Something like that."

"What are we going to do?"

"I haven't decided if I need your help."

"You do."

She appraised him with suspicion. "How much do you know about the historical record regarding Alexander's grave?"

"He was first entombed by Ptolemy at Memphis, in

southern Egypt, about a year after he died. Then Ptolemy's son moved the body north to Alexandria."

"That's right. Sometime between 283 BCE, when Ptolemy I died, and 274. A mausoleum was built in a new quarter of the city, at a crossroad of two main avenues that flanked the royal palace. It eventually came to be called the Soma—Greek for body. The grandest tomb in the grandest city of the time."

"Ptolemy was smart," he said. "He waited until all of Alexander's heirs were dead then proclaimed himself pharaoh. His heirs were smart, too. They reshaped Egypt into a Greek kingdom. While the other Companions mismanaged or lost their portions of the empire, the Ptolemys kept theirs for three hundred years. That Soma was used to great political advantage."

She nodded. "An amazing story, actually. Alexander's tomb became a place of pilgrimage. Caesar, Octavian, Hadrian, Caligula, and a dozen other emperors came to pay homage. Should have been quite a site. A gold-encrusted mummy with a golden crown, encased in a golden sarcophagus, surrounded by golden honey. For a century and a half Alexander lay undisturbed until Ptolemy IX needed money. He stripped the body of all its gold and melted the coffin, replacing it with a glass one. The Soma eventually stood for six hundred years. The last record of it existing was in 391 CE."

He knew the rest of the tale. Both the building and the remains of Alexander the Great disappeared. For sixteen hundred years people had searched. But the greatest conqueror of the ancient world, a man venerated as a living god, had vanished.

"Do you know where the body is?" he asked.

"Ely thought he did." The words sounded distant, as if she were talking to his ghost.

"You think he was right?"

She shrugged. "We're going to have to go and see."

"Where?"

She finally looked at him with tired eyes. "Venice. But first we have to get that last medallion. The one Viktor is surely headed toward right now."

"And where is it?"

"Interestingly, it's in Venice, too."

TWENTY-NINE

ZOVASTINA SMILED AT THE PAPAL NUNCIO. HE WAS A handsome man with gray-streaked, auburn hair and a pair of keenly inquisitive eyes. An American. Monsignor Colin Michener. Part of the new Vatican orchestrated by the first African pope in centuries. Twice before, this emissary had come and inquired if the Federation would allow a Catholic presence, but she'd rebuked both attempts. Though Islam was the nation's dominant religion, the nomadic people who'd long populated central Asia had always placed their law ahead of even the Islamic sharia. A geographical isolation bred a social independence, even from God, so she doubted Catholics would even be welcomed. But still, she needed something from this envoy and the time had come to bargain.

"You're not a night person?" she asked, noticing the tired look Michener tried only minimally to conceal.

"Isn't this time traditionally reserved for sleeping?"

"It wouldn't be to either of our advantages to be seen meeting in the middle of the day. Your Church is not all that popular here."

"Something we'd like to change."

She shrugged. "You'd be asking the people to abandon things they've held precious for centuries. Not even the Muslims, with all their discipline and moral precepts, have been able to do that. You'll find the organizational and political uses of religion appeal far more here than spiritual benefits."

"The Holy Father doesn't want to change the Federation. He only asks that the Church be allowed the freedom to pursue those who want to practice our faith."

She grinned. "Have you visited any of our holy sites?"

He shook his head.

"I encourage you to. You'll notice quite a few interesting things. Men will kiss, rub, and circumambulate venerated objects. Women crawl under holy stones to boost their fertility. And don't overlook the wishing trees and the Mongol poles with horsehair tassels set over graves. Amulets and charms are quite popular. The people place their faith in things that have nothing to do with your Christian God."

"There's a growing number of Catholics, Baptists, Lutherans, even a few Buddhists among those people. Apparently there are some who want to worship differently. Are they not entitled to the same privilege?"

Another reason she'd finally decided to entertain this messenger was the Islamic Renaissance Party. Though outlawed years ago, it quietly thrived, especially in the Fergana Valley of the old Uzbekistan. She'd covertly infected the main troublemakers and thought she'd killed off its leaders, but the party refused to be extinguished. Allowing greater religious competition, especially from an organization such as the Roman Catholics, would force the Islamics to focus their rage on an enemy even more threatening than she. So she said, "I've decided to grant the Church access to the Federation."

"I'm glad to hear that."

"With conditions."

The priest's pleasant face lost its brightness.

"It's not that bad," she said. "Actually, I have only one simple request. Tomorrow evening, in Venice, within the basilica, the tomb of St. Mark will be opened."

A perplexed look invaded the emissary's eyes.

"Surely you're familiar with the story of St. Mark and how he came to be buried in Venice?"

Michener nodded. "I have a friend who works in the basilica. He and I have discussed it."

She knew the tale. Mark, one of Christ's twelve disciples, ordained by Peter as bishop of Alexandria, was martyred by the city's pagans in 67 CE. When they tried to burn his body, a storm doused the flames and allowed Christians time to snatch it back. Mark was mummified, then entombed secretly until the fourth century. After the Christian takeover of Alexandria, an elaborate sepulcher was built, which became so holy that Alexandria's newly appointed patriarchs were each invested upon Mark's tomb. The shrine managed to survive the arrival of Islam and the seventh-century Persian and Arab invasions.

But in 828 a group of Venetian merchants stole the body.

Venice wanted a symbolic statement of both its political and theological independence. Rome possessed Peter, Venice would have Mark. At the same time, the Alexandrian clergy were extremely concerned about the city's sacred relics. Islamic rule had become more and more antagonistic. Shrines and churches were being dismantled. So, with the aid of the tomb's guardians, the body of St. Mark was whisked away.

Zovastina loved the details.

The nearby corpse of St. Claudian was substituted to hide the theft. The aroma of the embalming fluids was so strong that, to discourage authorities from examining the departing ship's cargo, layers of cabbage leaves and pork were wrapped over the corpse. Which worked—Muslim inspectors fled in horror at the presence of pig.

The body was then sheathed in canvas and hoisted to a yardarm. Supposedly, on the sail back to Italy, a visit from the ghost of St. Mark saved the ship from foundering during a storm.

"On January 31, 828, Mark was presented to the doge in Venice," she said. "The doge housed the holy remains in the palace, but they eventually disappeared, reemerging in 1094 when the newly finished Basilica di San Marco was formally dedicated. The remains were then placed in a crypt below the church, but were moved upstairs in the nineteenth century, beneath the high altar, where they are today. Lots of missing gaps in the history of that body, wouldn't you say?"

"That's the way of relics."

"Four hundred years in Alexandria, then again for nearly three hundred years in Venice, St. Mark's body was not to be found."

The nuncio shrugged. "It's faith, Minister."

"Alexandria always resented that theft," she said. "Especially the way Venice has, for centuries, venerated the act, as if the thieves were on a holy mission. Come now, we both know the whole thing was political. The Venetians stole from around the world. Scavengers on a grand scale, taking whatever they could acquire, using it all to their advantage. St. Mark was, perhaps, their most productive theft. The whole city, to this day, revolves around him."

"So why are they opening the tomb?"

"Bishops and nobles of the Coptic and Ethiopian churches want St. Mark returned. In 1968 your Pope Paul VI gave the patriarch of Alexandria a few relics to placate them. But those came from the Vatican, not Venice, and didn't work. They want the body back, and have long discussed it with Rome."

"I served as papal secretary to Clement XV. I'm aware of those discussions."

She'd long suspected this man was more than a nuncio. The new pope apparently chose his envoys with care. "Then you're aware the Church would never surrender that body. But the patriarch in Venice, with Rome's approval, has agreed to a compromise—part of your African pope's reconciliation with the world. Some of the relic, from the tomb, will be returned. That way, both sides are satisfied. But this is a delicate matter, especially for Venetians. *Their* saint disturbed." She shook her head. "That's why the tomb will be opened tomorrow night, in secret. Part of the remains will be removed, then the sepulcher closed. No one the wiser until an announcement of the gift is made in a few days."

"You have excellent information."

"It's a subject in which I have an interest. The body in that tomb is not St. Mark's."

"Then who is it?"

"Let's just say that the body of Alexander the Great disappeared from Alexandria in the fourth century, at nearly the exact time the body of St. Mark reappeared. Mark was enshrined in his own version of Alexander's Soma, which was venerated, just as Alexander's had been for six hundred years prior. My scholars have studied a variety of ancient texts, some the world has never seen—"

"And you think the body in the Venetian basilica is actually that of Alexander the Great?"

"I'm not saying anything, only that DNA analysis can now determine race. Mark was born in Libya to Arab parents. Alexander was Greek. There would be noticeable chromosomal differences. I'm also told there are dentine isotope studies, tomography, and carbon dating that could tell us a lot. Alexander died in 323 BCE. Mark in the first century after Christ. Again, there would be scientific differences in the remains."

"Do you plan to defile the corpse?"

"No more than you plan to. Tell me, what will they cut away?"

The American considered her statement. She'd sensed, early on, that he'd returned to Samarkand with far more authority than before. Time to see if that were true. "All I want is a few minutes alone with the open sarcophagus. If I remove anything, it will not be noticed. In return, the Church may move freely through the Federation and see how many Christians take to its message. But the construction of any buildings would have to be government approved. That's as much for your protection as ours. There'd be violence if church construction wasn't handled carefully."

"Do you plan to travel to Venice yourself?"

She nodded. "I'd like a low-profile visit, arranged by your Holy Father. I'm told the Church has many connections in the Italian government."

"You realize that, at best, Minister, anything you find there would be like the Shroud of Turin or Marian visions. A matter of faith."

But she knew that there could well be something conclusive. What had Ptolemy written in his riddle? *Touch the innermost being of the golden illusion.*

"Just a few minutes alone. That's all I ask."

The papal nuncio sat silent.

She waited.

"I'll instruct the patriarch in Venice to grant you the time."

She was right. He'd not returned empty-handed. "Lots of authority for a mere nuncio."

"Thirty minutes. Beginning at one A.M., Wednesday. We'll inform the Italian authorities that you're coming to attend a private function, at the invitation of the Church."

She nodded.

"I'll arrange for you to enter the cathedral through

the Porta dei Fiori in the west atrium. At that hour, few people will be in the main square. Will you be alone?"

She was tired of this officious priest. "If it matters, maybe we should forget about this."

She saw that Michener caught her irritation.

"Minister, bring whoever you want. The Holy Father simply wants to make you happy."

THIRTY

VIKTOR SAT IN THE HOTEL BAR. RAFAEL WAS UPSTAIRS, asleep. They'd driven south from Copenhagen, through Denmark, into northern Germany. Hamburg was the prearranged rendezvous point with the two members of the Sacred Band sent to Amsterdam to retrieve the sixth medallion. They should arrive sometime during the night. He and Rafael had handled the other thefts, but a deadline was looming, so Zovastina had ordered a second team into the field.

He nursed a beer and enjoyed the quiet. Few patrons occupied the dimly lit booths.

Zovastina thrived on tension. She liked to keep people on edge. Compliments were few, criticisms common. The palace staff. The Sacred Band. Her ministers. No one wanted to disappoint her. But he'd heard the talk behind her back. Interesting that a woman so attuned to power could become so oblivious to its resentment. Shallow loyalty was a dangerous illusion. Rafael was right, something was about to happen. As head of the Sacred Band he'd many times accompanied Zovastina to the laboratory in the mountains, east of Samarkand— this one on *her* side of the Chinese border, staffed with *her* people, where she kept *her* germs. He'd seen the test subjects, requisitioned from jails, and the horrible deaths. He'd also stood outside conference rooms while she plotted with her generals. The Federation possessed an impressive army, a reasonable air force, and a limited short-range missile capability. Most provided, and funded, by the West for defensive purposes since Iran, China, and Afghanistan all bordered the Federation.

He'd not told Rafael, but he knew what she was planning. He'd heard her speak of the chaos in Afghanistan, where the Taliban still clung to fleeting power. Of Iran, whose radical president constantly rattled sabers. And Pakistan, a place that exported violence with blinded eyes.

Those nations were her initial goal.

And millions would die.

A vibration in his pocket startled him.

He located the cell phone, glanced at the display, and answered, his stomach clenching into a familiar knot.

"Viktor," Zovastina said. "I'm glad I found you. There's a problem."

He listened as she told him about an incident in Amsterdam, where two Sacred Band members had been killed while trying to obtain a medallion. "The Americans have made official inquiries. They want to know why my people were shooting at Secret Service agents. Which is a good question."

He wanted to say it was probably because they were terrified of disappointing her, so their better judgment had been overridden by recklessness. But he knew better and only noted, "I would have preferred to handle the matter there myself."

"All right, Viktor. Tonight, I'm conceding this one. You were opposed to the second team and I overruled you."

He knew better than to acknowledge that concession. Incredible enough she'd offered it. "But you, Minister, want to know why the Americans just happened to be there?"

"That did occur to me."

"It could be that we've been exposed."

"I doubt they care what we do. I'm more concerned with our Venetian League friends. Especially the fat one."

"Still, the Americans were there," he said.

"Could have been chance."

"What do they say?"

"Their representatives refused to give any details."

"Minister," he said in a hushed tone, "have we finally learned what we're actually after?"

"I've been working on that. It's been slow, but I now know that the key to deciphering Ptolemy's riddle is finding the body that once occupied the Soma in Alexandria. I'm convinced the remains of St. Mark, in the Basilica di San Marco in Venice, are what we're after."

He'd not heard this before.

"That's why I'm going to Venice. Tomorrow night."

Even more shocking. "Is that wise?"

"It's necessary. I'll want you with me, at the basilica. You'll need to acquire the other medallion and be at the church by one A.M."

He knew the proper response. "Yes, Minister."

"And you never said, Viktor. Do we have the one from Denmark?"

"We do."

"We'll have to do without the one in Holland."

He noticed she wasn't angry. Odd considering the failure.

"Viktor, I ordered that the Venetian medallion be last for a reason."

And now he knew why. The basilica. And the body of St. Mark. But he was still concerned about the Americans. Luckily, he'd contained the Denmark situation. All three of the problems who'd tried to best him were dead and Zovastina need never know.

"I've planned this for some time," she was saying. "There are supplies waiting for you in Venice, so don't drive, fly. Here's their location." She provided a warehouse address and an access code for an electronic lock. "What happened in Amsterdam is unimportant. What occurs in Venice . . . that's vital. I want that last medallion."

THIRTY-ONE

STEPHANIE LISTENED WITH GREAT INTEREST AS EDWIN Davis and President Daniels explained what was happening.

"What do you know about zoonosis?" Davis asked her.

"A disease that can be transmitted from animals to humans."

"It's even more specific," Daniels said. "A disease that *normally exists* harmlessly in animals but can infect humans with devastating results. Anthrax, bubonic plague, ebola, rabies, bird flu, even common ringworm are some of the best-known examples."

"I didn't realize biology was your strong point."

Daniels laughed. "I don't know crap about science. But I know a lot of people who do. Tell her, Edwin."

"There are about fifteen hundred known zoonotic pathogens. Half sit quietly in animals, living off the host, never infecting. But when transmitted to another animal, one for which the pathogen doesn't harbor any paternal instincts, they go wild. That's exactly how bubonic plague began. Rats carried the disease, fleas fed on the rats, then the fleas transmitted the disease to humans, where it ran rampant—"

"Until," Daniels said, "we developed an immunity to

the damn thing. Unfortunately, in the fourteenth century, that took a few decades and, in the meantime, a third of Europe died."

"The 1918 Spanish flu pandemic was a zoonosis, wasn't it?" she asked.

Davis nodded. "Jumped from birds to humans, then mutated so it could pass from human to human. And did it ever. Twenty percent of the world actually suffered from the disease. Around five percent of the entire world's population died. Twenty-five million people in the first six months. To put that in perspective, AIDS killed twenty-five million in its first twenty-five *years*."

"And those 1918 numbers are shaky," Daniels noted. "China and the rest of Asia suffered horribly with no accurate fatality count. Some historians believe that as many as a hundred million may have died worldwide."

"A zoonotic pathogen is the perfect biological weapon," Davis said. "All you have to do is find one, whether it be a virus, bacteria, a protozoa, or a parasite. Isolate it, then it can infect at will. If you're clever, two versions could be created. One that only moves from animal to human, so you'd have to directly infect the victim. Another, mutated, that moves from human to human. The first could be used for limited strikes at specific targets, a minimal danger of the thing passing beyond the person infected. The other would be a weapon of mass destruction. Infect a few and the dying never stops."

She realized what Edwin Davis said was all too real.

"Stopping these things is possible," Daniels said. "But it takes time to isolate, study, and develop countermeasures. Luckily, most of the known zoonoses have anti-agents, a few even have vaccines that prevent wholesale infection. But those take time to develop, and a lot of people would be killed in the meantime."

Stephanie wondered where this was headed. "Why is all this important?"

Davis reached for a file on the glass-topped table, beside Daniels' bare feet. "Nine years ago a pair of endangered geese was stolen from a private zoo in Belgium. At about the same time, some endangered rodents and a species of rare snails were taken from zoos in Australia and Spain. Usually, this kind of thing is not that significant. But we started checking and found that it's happened at least forty times around the world. The break came last year. In South Africa. The thieves were caught. We covered their arrest with phony deaths. The men cooperated, considering a South African prison is not a good place to spend a few years. That's when we learned Irina Zovastina was behind the thefts."

"Who ran that investigation?" she asked.

"Painter Crowe at Sigma," Daniels said. "Lots of science here. That's their specialty. But now it's passed into your realm."

She didn't like the sound of that. "Sure Painter can't keep it?"

Daniels smiled. "After tonight? No, Stephanie. This one's all yours. Payback for me saving your hide with the Dutch."

The president still held the elephant medallion, so she asked, "What does that coin have to do with anything?"

"Zovastina has been collecting these," Daniels said. "Here's the real problem. We know she's amassed a pretty hefty inventory of zoonoses. Twenty or so at last count. And by the way, she's been clever, she has multiple versions. Like Edwin said, one for limited strikes, the other for human-to-human transmission. She operates a biological lab near her capital in Samarkand. But, interestingly, Enrico Vincenti has another bio lab just across the border, in China. One Zovastina likes to visit."

"Which was why you wanted fieldwork on Vincenti?"

Davis nodded. "Pays to know the enemy."

"The CIA has been cultivating leaks inside the Federation," Daniels said, shaking his head. "Hard going. And a mess. But we've made a little progress."

Yet she detected something. "You have a source?"

"If you want to call it that," the president said. "I have my doubts. Zovastina is a problem on many levels."

She understood his dilemma. In a region of the world where America possessed few friends, Zovastina had openly proclaimed herself one. She'd been helpful several times with minor intelligence that had thwarted terrorist activity in Afghanistan and Iraq. Out of necessity, the United States had provided her with money, military support, and sophisticated equipment, which was risky.

"Ever hear the one about the man driving down the highway who saw a snake lying in the middle of the road?"

She grinned. Another of Daniels' famed stories.

"The guy stopped and saw that the snake was hurt. So he took the thing home and nursed it back to health. When the snake recovered, he opened the front door to let it go. But as the rattler crawled out, the damn thing bit him on the leg. Just before the venom drove him to unconsciousness, he called out to the snake, 'I took you in, fed you, doctored your wounds, and you repaid that by biting me?' The snake stopped and said, 'All true. But when you did that you knew I was a snake.' "

She caught the message.

"Zovastina," the president said, "is up to something and it involves Enrico Vincenti. I don't like biological warfare. The world outlawed it over thirty years ago. And this form is the worst kind. She's planning something awful, and that Venetian League, of which she and

Vincenti are members, is right there helping her. Thankfully, she's not acted. But we have reason to believe she may soon start. The damn fools surrounding her, in what they loosely call nations, are oblivious to what's happening. Too busy worrying about Israel and us. She's using that stupidity to her advantage. She thinks I'm stupid, too. It's time she knew that we're on to her."

"We would have preferred to stay in the shadows a bit longer," Davis said. "But two Secret Service agents killing her guardsmen has surely sounded an alarm."

"What do you want me to do?"

Daniels yawned and she smothered one of her own. The president waved his hand. "Go ahead. Hell, it's the middle of the night. Don't mind me. Yawn away. You can sleep on the plane."

"Where am I going?"

"Venice. If Mohammed won't come to the mountain, then by God we'll bring the mountain to him."

THIRTY-TWO

VINCENTI ENTERED THE MAIN SALON OF HIS PALAZZO and readied himself. Usually, he did not bother with these types of presentations. After all, Philogen Pharmaceutique employed an extensive marketing and sales department with hundreds of employees. This, however, was something special, something that demanded only his presence, so he'd arranged for a private presentation at his home.

He noticed that the outside advertising agency, headquartered in Milan, seemed to have taken no chances. Four representatives, three females and a male, one a senior vice president, had been dispatched to brief him.

"Damaris Corrigan," the vice president said in English, introducing herself and her three associates. She was an attractive woman, in her early fifties, dressed in a dark blue, chalk-striped suit.

Off to the side, coffee steamed from a silver urn. He walked over and poured himself a cup.

"We couldn't help but wonder," Corrigan said, "is something about to happen?"

He unbuttoned his suit jacket and settled into an upholstered chair. "What do you mean?"

"When we were retained six months ago, you wanted

suggestions on marketing a possible HIV cure. We wondered then if Philogen was on the brink of something. Now, with you wanting to see what we have, we thought maybe there'd been a breakthrough."

He silently congratulated himself. "I think you voiced the operative word. *Possible.* Certainly, it's our hope to be first with a cure—we're spending millions on research—but if a breakthrough were to happen, and you never know when that's going to occur, I don't want to be caught waiting months for an effective marketing scheme." He paused. "No. Nothing to this point, but a little preparedness is good."

His guest acknowledged the explanation with a nod, then she paraded to a waiting easel. He shot a glance at one of the women sitting next to him. A shapely brunette, not more than thirty or thirty-five, in a tight-fitting wool skirt. He wondered if she was an account executive or just decoration.

"I've done some fascinating reading over the past few weeks," Corrigan said. "HIV seems to have a split personality, depending on what part of the globe you're studying."

"There's truth to that observation," he said. "Here, and in places like North America, the disease is reasonably containable. No longer a leading cause of death. People simply live with it. Symptomatic drugs have reduced the mortality rate by more than half. But in Africa and Asia it's an entirely different story. Worldwide, last year, three million died of HIV."

"And that's what we did first," she said. "Identified our projected market."

She folded back the blank top sheet on the pad affixed to the easel, revealing a chart.

"These figures represent the latest incidents of worldwide HIV infections."

REGIONS	NUMBER
North America	1,011,000
Western Europe	988,000
Australia-Pacifica	22,000
Latin America	1,599,000
Sub-Saharan Africa	20,778,000
Caribbean	536,000
Eastern Europe	2,000
Southeast Mediterranean	893,000
Northeast Asia	6,000
Southeast Asia	<u>11,277,000</u>
Total	37,112,000

"What's the data source?" Vincenti asked.

"World Health Organization. And this represents the total current market available for any cure." Corrigan flipped to the next page. "This chart fine-tunes the available market. As you can see, the data shows roughly a quarter of worldwide HIV infections have already resulted in a manifestation of acquired immune deficiency syndrome. Nine million HIV-infected individuals now have full-blown AIDS."

REGIONS	NUMBER
North America	555,000
Western Europe	320,500
Australia-Pacifica	14,000
Latin America	573,500
Sub-Saharan Africa	6,300,000
Caribbean	160,500
Eastern Europe	10,800
Southeast Mediterranean	15,000
Northeast Asia	17,600
Southeast Asia	<u>1,340,000</u>
Total	9,306,900

Corrigan flipped to the next chart. "This shows the projections for five years from now. Again, this data came from the World Health Organization."

REGIONS	ESTIMATE
North America	8,150,000
Western Europe	2,331,000
Australia-Pacifica	45,000
Latin America	8,554,000
Sub-Saharan Africa	33,609,000
Caribbean	6,962,000
Eastern Europe	20,000
Southeast Mediterranean	3,532,000
Northeast Asia	486,000
Southeast Asia	45,059,000
Total	108,748,000

"Amazing. We could soon have one hundred ten million people infected, worldwide, with HIV. Current statistics indicate that fifty percent of these individuals will eventually develop AIDS. Forty percent of that fifty percent will be dead within two years. Of course, the vast majority of these will be in Africa and Asia." Corrigan shook her head. "Quite a market, wouldn't you say?"

Vincenti digested the figures. Using a mean of seventy million HIV cases, even at a conservative five thousand euros per year for treatment, any cure would initially generate three hundred and fifty billion euros. True, once the initial infected population was cured, the market would dwindle. So what? The money would be made. More than anyone could ever spend in a lifetime. Later, there'd surely be new infections and more sales, not the billions the initial campaign would generate, but a continuous windfall nonetheless.

"Our next analysis involved a look at the competition. From what we've been able to learn from the WHO, roughly sixteen drugs are now being used globally for the symptomatic treatment of AIDS. There are roughly a dozen players in this game. The sales from your own drugs were just over a billion euros last year."

Philogen owned patents for six medicines that, when used in conjunction with others, had proven effective in arresting the virus. Though it took, on average, about fifty pills a day, the so-called cocktail therapy was all that really worked. Not a cure, the deluge of medication simply confused the virus, and it was only a matter of time before nature outsmarted the microbiologists. Already, drug-resistant HIV strains had emerged in Asia and China.

"We took a look at the combination treatments," Corrigan said. "A three-drug regimen costs on average about twenty thousand euros a year. But that form of treatment is basically a Western luxury. It's nonexistent in Africa and Asia. Philogen donates, at reduced costs, medications to a few of the affected governments, but to treat those patients similarly would cost billions of euros a year, money no African government has to spend."

His own marketing people had already told him the same thing. Treatment was not really an option for the ravaged third world. Stopping the spread of HIV was the only cost-effective method to attack the crisis. Condoms were the initial instrument of choice, and one of Philogen's subsidiaries couldn't make the things fast enough. Sales had risen in the thousands of percent over the course of the last two decades. And so had profits. But, of late, the use of condoms had steadily dropped. People were becoming complacent.

Corrigan was saying, "According to its own propaganda, one of your competitors, Kellwood-Lafarge, spent more than a hundred million euros on AIDS-cure research last year alone. You spent about a third of that."

He threw the woman a smirk. "Competing with Kell-wood-Lafarge is akin to fishing for whales with a rod and reel. It's the largest drug conglomerate on the planet. Hard to match somebody euro for euro when the other guy has over a hundred billion in year gross revenues."

He sipped his coffee as Corrigan flipped to a clean chart.

"Getting away from all that, let's take a look at product ideas. A name of course, for any cure, is critical. Currently, of the sixteen symptomatic drugs on the market, designations vary. Things like Bactrim, Diflucan, Intron, Pentam, Videx, Crixivan, Hivid, Retrovir. Because of the worldwide use any cure will enjoy, we thought a simpler, more universal designation, like AZT utilized, might be better from a marketing standpoint. From what we were told, Philogen now has eight possible cures under development." Corrigan flipped to the next chart, which showed packaging concepts. "We have no way of knowing if any cure will be solid or liquid, taken orally or by injection, so we created variations, keeping the colors in your black-and-gold motif."

He studied the proposals.

She pointed to the easel. "We left a blank for the name, to be inserted in gold letters. We're still working on that. The important thing about this scheme is that even if the name doesn't translate in a particular language, the package will be distinctive enough to provide immediate recognition."

He was pleased, but thought it best to suppress a smile. "I have a possible name. Something I've beaten around in my head."

Corrigan seemed interested.

He stood, walked to the easel, opened a marker, and wrote ZH.

He noticed a puzzled look on everyone's face. "Zeta. Eta. Old Greek. It meant 'life.' "

Corrigan nodded. "Appropriate."

He agreed.

THIRTY-THREE

ZOVASTINA WAS THRILLED WITH THE CROWD. HER STAFF
had promised five thousand would appear. Instead, her
traveling secretary told her on the helicopter flight,
northwest from Samarkand, that over twenty thousand
were awaiting her arrival. More proof, she was told, of
her popularity. Now, seeing the bedlam of goodwill, perfect for the television cameras focused on the dais, she
could not help but be pleased.

"Look around you," she said into the microphone,
"at what we can accomplish when both our minds and
our hearts work in unison." She hesitated a moment for
effect, then motioned outward. "Kantubek reborn."

The crowd, thick as ants, cheered their approval with
an enthusiasm she'd grown accustomed to hearing.

Vozrozhdeniya Island sat in the central Aral Sea, a remote wilderness that once housed the Soviet Union's
Microbiological Warfare Group, and also provided a
tragic example of Asia's exploitation by its former masters. Here was where anthrax spores and plague bacilli
were both developed and stored. After the fall of the
communist government, in 1991, the laboratory staff
abandoned the island and the containers holding the

deadly spores, which, over the ensuing decade, developed leaks. The potential biological disaster was compounded by the receding Aral Sea. Fed by the ample Amu Darya, the wondrous lake had once been shared by Kazakhstan and Uzbekistan. But when the Soviets changed the Darya's course and diverted the river's flow into a twelve-hundred-kilometer-long canal—water used to grow cotton for Soviet mills—the inland sea, once one of the world's largest freshwater bodies, began to vanish, replaced by a desert incapable of supporting life.

But she'd changed all that. The canal was now gone, the river restored. Most of her counterparts had seemed doomed to mimic their conquerors, but her brain had never atrophied from vodka. She'd always kept her eye on the prize, and learned how to both seize and hold power.

"Two hundred tons of communist anthrax were neutralized here," she told the crowd. "Every bit of their poison is gone. And we made the Soviets pay for it."

The crowd roared their approval.

"Let me tell you something. Once we were free, away from Moscow's choke hold, they had the audacity to say we owed them money." Her arms rose into the air. "Can you imagine? They rape our land. Destroy our sea. Poison the soil with their germs. And *we* owe them money?" She saw thousands of heads shake. "That's exactly what I said, too. No."

She scanned the faces staring back at her, each bathed in bright midday sunshine.

"So we made the Soviets pay to clean up their own mess. And we closed their canal, which was sucking the life from our ancient sea."

Never did she use the singular "I." Always "we."

"Many of you I'm sure, as I do, remember the tigers,

wild boar, and waterfowl that thrived in the Amu Darya delta. The millions of fish that filled the Aral Sea. Our scientists know that one hundred and seventy-eight species once lived here. Now, only thirty-eight remain. Soviet progress." She shook her head. "The virtues of communism." She smirked. "Criminals. That's what they were. Plain, ordinary criminals."

The canal had been a failure not only environmentally but also structurally. Seepage and flooding had been common. Like the Soviets themselves, who cared little for efficiency, the canal lost more water than it ever delivered. As the Aral Sea dried to nothing, Vozrozhdeniya Island eventually became a peninsula, connected to the shore, and the fear rose that land mammals and reptiles would carry off the deadly biological toxins. Not anymore. The land was clean. Declared so by a United Nations inspection team, which labeled the effort "masterful."

She raised her fist to the air. "And we told those Soviet criminals that if we could, we'd sentence each one of them to our prisons."

The people roared more approval.

"This town of Kantubek, where we stand, here in its central plaza, has risen from the ashes. The Soviets reduced it to rubble. Now free Federation citizens will live here, in peace and harmony, on an island that is also reborn. The Aral itself is returning, its water levels rising each year, man-made desert once again becoming seabed. This is an example of what we can achieve. Our land. Our water." She hesitated. "Our heritage."

The crowd erupted.

Her gaze raked the faces, soaking in the anticipation her message seemed to generate. She loved being among the people. And they loved her. Acquiring power was one thing. Keeping it, quite another.

And she planned to keep it.

"My fellow citizens, know that we can do anything if we set our minds to it. How many across the globe declared we could not consolidate? How many said we'd split thanks to civil war? How many claimed we were incapable of governing ourselves? Twice we've conducted national elections. Free and open, with many candidates. No one can say that either contest was not fair." She paused. "We have a constitution that guarantees human rights, along with personal, political, and intellectual freedom."

She was enjoying this moment. The reopening of Vozrozhdeniya Island was certainly an event that demanded her presence. Federation television, along with three new independent broadcasting channels that she'd licensed to Venetian League members, were spreading her message nationwide. Those new station owners had privately promised control over what they produced, all part of the camaraderie League membership offered to fellow members, and she was glad for their presence. Hard to argue that she controlled the media when, from all outward appearances, she did not.

She stared out at the rebuilt town, its brick and stone buildings erected in the style of a century ago. Kantubek would once again be populated. Her Interior ministry had reported that ten thousand had applied for land grants on the island, another indication of the confidence the people placed in her since so many were willing to live where only twenty years ago nothing would have survived.

"Stability is the basis of everything," she roared.

Her catchphrase, used repeatedly over the past fifteen years.

"Today, we christen this island in the name of the people of the Central Asian Federation. May our union last forever."

She stepped from the podium as the crowd applauded.

Three of her guardsmen quickly closed ranks and escorted her off the dais. Her helicopter was waiting, as was a plane that would take her west, to Venice, where the answers to so many questions awaited.

THIRTY-FOUR

MALONE STOOD BESIDE CASSIOPEIA AS SHE PILOTED the motorboat out into the lagoon. They'd flown from Copenhagen on a direct flight, landing at Aeroporto Marco Polo an hour ago. He'd visited Venice many times in years past on assignments with the Magellan Billet. It was familiar territory, expansive and isolated, but its heart remained compact, about two miles long and a mile wide—and had wisely managed for centuries to keep the world at bay.

The boat's bow was pointed northeast, away from the center, leading them past the glass-making center of Murano, straight for Torcello, one of the many squats of land that dotted the Venetian lagoon.

They'd rented the launch near the airport, a sleek wooden craft with enclosed cabins fore and aft. Frisky outboards skimmed the low-riding hull across the choppy swells, churning the green water behind them into a lime foam.

Over breakfast, Cassiopeia had told him about the final elephant medallion. She and Thorvaldsen had charted the thefts across Europe, noticing early on that the decadrachms in Venice and Samarkand seemed to be ignored. That was why they'd been reasonably sure the Copenhagen medallion would be next. After the fourth was stolen from a private collector in France three weeks ago, she and Thorvaldsen had waited patiently.

"They held the Venice medallion last for a reason," Cassiopeia said to him over the engines. One of the city water buses chugged past, heading in the opposite direction. "I guess you'd like to know why?"

"The thought did occur to me."

"Ely believed Alexander the Great may be inside St. Mark's tomb."

Interesting idea. Different. Nuts.

"Long story," she said, "but he may be right. The body in St. Mark's basilica is supposedly of a two-thousand-year-old mummy. St. Mark was mummified in Alexandria, after he died in the first century CE. Alexander is three hundred years older and was mummified, too. But in the fourth century, when Alexander disappeared from his tomb, Mark's remains suddenly appeared in Alexandria."

"I assume you have more evidence than that?"

"Irina Zovastina is obsessed with Alexander the Great. Ely told me all about it. She has a private collection of Greek art, an expansive library, and fashions herself an expert on Homer and the *Iliad*. Now she's sending guardsmen out to collect elephant medallions and leave no trail. And the coin in Samarkand goes completely untouched." She shook her head. "They waited for this theft to be last, so they could be near St. Mark's."

"I've been inside that basilica," he said. "The saint's sarcophagus is under the main altar, which weighs tons. You'd need hydraulic lifts and lots of time to get inside it. That's impossible considering the basilica is the city's number one tourist attraction."

"I don't know how she intends to do it, but I'm convinced she's going to make a try for that tomb."

But first, he thought, they apparently needed the seventh medallion.

He retreated from the helm down three steps into the forward cabin adorned with tasseled curtains, embroidered seats, and polished mahogany. Ornate for a rental. He'd bought a Venetian guidebook at the airport and decided to learn what he could about Torcello.

Romans first inhabited the tiny island in the fifth and sixth centuries. Then, in the eighth century, frightened mainlanders fled invading Lombards and Huns and reoccupied it. By the 1500s twenty thousand people lived in a thriving colony among churches, convents, palaces, markets, and an active shipping center. The merchants who stole the body of St. Mark from Alexandria in 828 were citizens of Torcello. The guidebook noted it as a place where "Rome first met Byzantium." A watershed. To the west lay the Houses of Parliament. To the east the Taj Mahal. Then, pestilent fever, malaria, and silt clogging its canals brought a decline. Its most vigorous citizens moved to central Venice. The merchant houses folded. All of the palaces became forgotten. Builders from other islands eventually scrabbled among its rubble for the right stone or sculptured cornice, and everything gradually disappeared. Marshland reclaimed high ground and now fewer than sixty people lived there in only a handful of houses.

He stared out the forward windows and spotted a single redbrick tower—old, proud, and lonely—stretching skyward. A photograph in the guidebook matched the outline. He read and learned the bell tower stood beside Torcello's remaining claim to fame. The Basilica di Santa Maria Assunta, built in the seventh century, Venice's oldest house of worship. Beside it, according to the guidebook, sat a squat of a church in the shape of a Greek cross, erected six hundred years later. Santa Fosca.

The engines dimmed as Cassiopeia throttled down and the boat settled into the water. He climbed back to where she stood at the helm. Ahead he spotted thin streaks of ochre-colored sandbank cloaked in reeds, rushes, and gnarly cypresses. The boat slowed to a crawl and they entered a muddy canal, its bulwarks flanked on one side by overgrown fields and on the other by a paved lane. To their left, one of the city's water buses was taking on passengers at the island's only public transportation terminal.

"Torcello," she said. "Let's hope we got here first."

VIKTOR STEPPED OFF THE *VAPORETTO* WITH RAFAEL following.

The water bus had delivered them from San Marco to Torcello in a laborious chug across the Venetian lagoon. He'd chosen public transportation as the most inconspicuous way to reconnoiter tonight's target.

They followed a crowd of camera-clad tourists making their way toward the island's two famed churches, a sidewalklike street flanking a languid canal. The path ended near a low huddle of stone buildings that accommodated a couple of restaurants, a few tourist vendors, and an inn. He'd already studied the island's layout and knew that Torcello was a minuscule strip of land that supported artichoke farms and a few opulent residences. Two ancient churches and a restaurant were its claims to fame.

They'd flown from Hamburg, with a stop in Munich. After here, they would head back to the Federation and home, their European foray completed. Per the Supreme Minister's orders, Viktor needed to obtain the seventh medallion before midnight, as he was due at the basilica in San Marco by one A.M.

Zovastina's coming to Venice was highly unusual.

Whatever she'd been anticipating had apparently started.

But at least this theft should be easy.

MALONE STARED DOWN AT THE ARCHITECTURAL ELE-gance of the island's bell tower, a mass of brick and marble ingeniously held together by pilasters and arches. A hundred and fifty feet tall, like a talisman in the waste, the path to the top, on ramps that wound upward along the exterior walls, had reminded him of the Round Tower in Copenhagen. They'd paid the six euros admission and made the climb to study the island from its highest point.

He stood at a chest-high wall and stared out open arches, noting how the land and water seemed to pursue each other in a tight embrace. White herons soared skyward from a grassy marsh. Orchards and artichoke fields loomed quiet. The somber scene seemed like a ghost town from the American West.

Below, the basilica stood, nothing warm or welcoming to it, a makeshift barnlike feel to its design, as if uncompleted. Malone had read in the guidebook that it was built in a hurry by men who thought the world would end in the year 1000.

"It's a great allegory," he said to Cassiopeia. "A Byzantine cathedral right beside a Greek church. East and West, side by side. Just like Venice."

In front of the two churches stretched a grass-infested piazzetta. Once the center of city life, now no more than a village green. Dusty paths stretched outward, a couple leading to a second canal, more winding toward distant farmhouses. Two other stone buildings fronted the piazzetta, both small, maybe forty by twenty feet, two-storied, with gabled roofs. Together they comprised the Museo di Torcello. The guidebook noted they were once palazzos, occupied centuries ago by wealthy merchants, but were now owned by the state.

Cassiopeia pointed at the building on the left. "The medallion is in there, on the second floor. Not much of a museum. Mosaic fragments, capitals, a few paintings, some books, and coins. Greek, Roman, and Egyptian artifacts."

He faced her. She continued to stare out over the island. To the south loomed the outline of Venice central, its campaniles reaching for a darkening sky, the hint of a storm rising. "What are we doing here?"

She did not immediately answer. He reached over and touched her arm. She shuddered at the contact, but did not resist. Her eyes watered and he wondered if Torcello's sad atmosphere had reminded her of memories better left forgotten.

"This place is all gone," she muttered.

They were alone at the top of the tower, the lazy silence disturbed only by footfalls, voices, and laughter from others, below, making the climb.

"So is Ely," he said.

"I miss him." She bit her lip.

He wondered if her burst of sincerity implied a growing trust. "There's nothing you can do."

"I wouldn't say that."

He did not like the sound of her words. "What do you have in mind?"

She did not answer and he did not press. Instead, he stared with her across the church rooftops. A few stalls selling lace, glassware, and souvenirs flanked a short lane leading from the village to the grassy piazzetta. A group of visitors were making their way toward the churches. Among them, Malone spotted a familiar face.

Viktor.

"I see him, too," Cassiopeia said.

People arrived at the top, in the bell chamber.

"The man beside him is the one who slashed the car tires," she said.

They watched as the two men headed straight for the museum.

"We need to get down from here," he said. "They might decide to check the high ground, too. Remember they think we're dead."

"Like this whole place," she muttered.

THIRTY-FIVE

STEPHANIE HOPPED FROM THE WATER TAXI AND MADE her way through the tight warren of close-quartered streets. She'd asked directions at her hotel and was following them the best she could, but Venice was a vast labyrinth. She was deep into the Dorsoduro district, a quiet, picturesque neighborhood long associated with wealth, following busy, alleylike thoroughfares lined with bustling commerce.

Ahead, she spotted the villa. Rigidly symmetrical, casting an air of lost distinction, its beauty sprang from a pleasing contrast of redbrick walls veined with emerald vines, highlighted with marble trim.

She stepped through a wrought-iron gate and announced her presence with a knock on the front door. An older woman with an airy face, dressed in a servant's uniform, answered.

"I'm here to see Mr. Vincenti," Stephanie said. "Tell him I bring greetings from President Danny Daniels."

The woman appraised her with a curious look and she wondered if the name of the president of the United States struck a chord. So, to be sure, she handed the attendant a folded slip of paper. "Give this to him."

The woman hesitated, then closed the door.

Stephanie waited.

Two minutes later the door reopened.

Wider this time.

And she was invited in.

"Fascinating introduction," Vincenti said to her.

They sat in a rectangular room beneath a gilded ceiling, the room's elegance highlighted by the dull gleam of lacquer that had surely coated the furniture for centuries. She sniffed the dank fragrance and thought she detected the odor of cats mixed with a scent of lemon polish.

Her host held up the note. " 'The President of the United States sent me.' Quite a statement." He seemed pleased at his perceived importance.

"You're an interesting man, Mr. Vincenti. Born in upstate New York. A U.S. citizen. August Rothman." She shook her head. "Enrico Vincenti? You changed the name. I'm curious, why?"

He shrugged. "It's all about image."

"It does sound more," she hesitated, "continental."

"Actually, a lot of thought was given to that name. Enrico came from Enrico Dandolo, thirty-ninth doge of Venice, in the late twelfth century. He led the Fourth Crusade that conquered Constantinople and ended the Byzantine Empire. Quite a man. Legendary, you might say.

"Vincenti I took from another twelfth-century Venetian. A Benedictine monk and nobleman. When his entire family was wiped out in the Aegean Sea, he applied for and got permission to dispense with his monastic vows. He married and founded five new lines of his family from his children. Quite resourceful. I admired his flexibility."

"So you became Enrico Vincenti. Venetian aristocracy."

He nodded. "Sounds great, no?"

"Want me to continue on what I know?"

He motioned his assent.

"You're sixty years old. Bachelor of science from the University of North Carolina, in biology. Master's degree from Duke University. A doctorate in virology from the University of East Anglia, the John Innes Centre, in England. Recruited there by a Pakistani pharmaceutical firm with ties to the Iraqi government. You worked for the Iraqis early on, with their initial biological weapons program, just after Saddam assumed power in 1979. At Salman Pak, north of Baghdad, operated by the Technical Research Center, which oversaw their germ search. Though Iraq signed the Biological Weapons Convention in 1972, Saddam never ratified it. You stayed with them until 1990, just before the first Gulf War went to shit in a handbasket for the Iraqis. That's when they shut everything down and you hauled ass."

"All correct, Ms. Nelle, or do I get to call you Stephanie?"

"Whatever you prefer."

"Okay, Stephanie, why am I so interesting to the president of the United States?"

"I wasn't finished."

He motioned again for her to continue.

"Anthrax, botulinum, cholera, plague, ricin, salmonella, even smallpox—you and your colleagues dabbled with them all."

"Didn't your people in Washington finally figure out that was all fiction?"

"May have been in 2003 when Bush invaded, but it sure as hell wasn't in 1990. Then, it was real. I particularly liked camel pox. You assholes thought it the perfect weapon. Safer than smallpox to handle in the lab, but a great ethnic weapon since Iraqis were generally immune thanks to all of the camels they've handled through the centuries. But for Westerners and Israelis, another matter entirely. Quite a deadly zoonosis."

"More fiction," Vincenti said, and she wondered how many times he'd voiced the same lie with similar conviction.

"Too many documents, photos, and witnesses to make that cover story stick," she said. "That's why you disappeared from Iraq, after 1990."

"Get real, Stephanie, nobody in the eighties thought biological warfare was even a weapon of mass destruction. Washington could not have cared less. Saddam, at least, saw its potential."

"We know better now. It's quite a threat. In fact, many believe that the first biological war won't be a cataclysmic exchange. It'll be a low-intensity, regional conflict. A rogue state versus its neighbor. No global consensual morality will apply. Just local hatred and indiscriminate killing. Similar to the Iran/Iraq War of the nineteen-eighties where some of your bugs were actually used on people."

"Interesting theory, but isn't that your president's problem? Why do I care?"

She decided to change tack. "Your company, Philogen Pharmaceutique, is quite a success story. You personally own two point four million shares of its stock, representing about forty-two percent of the company, the single largest shareholder. An impressive conglomerate. Assets at just under ten billion euros, which includes wholly owned subsidiaries that manufacture cosmetics, toiletries, soap, frozen foods, and a chain of European department stores. You bought the company fifteen years ago for practically nothing—"

"I'm sure your research showed it was nearly bankrupt at the time."

"Which begs the question—how and why did you manage to both buy and save it?"

"Ever hear of public offerings? People invested."

"Not really. You funneled most of the start-up capital

into it. About forty million dollars, by our estimate. Quite a nest egg you amassed from working for a rogue government."

"The Iraqis were generous. They also had a superb health plan and a wonderful retirement system."

"Many of you profited. We monitored a lot of key microbiologists back then. You included."

He seemed to catch the edge in her voice. "Is there a point to this visit?"

"You're quite the businessman. From all accounts, an excellent entrepreneur. But your corporation is over-extended. Your debt service is straining every resource you possess, yet you continue onward."

Edwin Davis had briefed her well.

"Daniels looking to invest? What's left, three years on his term? Tell him I could find a place on my board of directors for him."

She reached into her pocket and tossed him the jacketed elephant medallion. He caught the offering with a surprising quickness.

"You know what that is?"

He studied the decadrachm. "Looks like a man fighting an elephant. Then a man standing, holding a spear. I'm afraid history is not my strong point."

"Germs are your specialty."

He appraised her with a look of conviction.

"When the UN weapons inspectors questioned you, after the first Gulf War, about Iraq's biological weapons program, you told them nothing had been developed. Lots of research, but the whole venture was under-funded and poorly managed."

"All those toxins you mentioned? They're bulky, difficult to store, cumbersome, and nearly impossible to control. Not practical weapons. I was right."

"Smart guys like you can conquer those problems."

"I'm not that good."

"That's what I said, too. But others disagree."

"You shouldn't listen to them."

She ignored his challenge. "Within three years after you left Iraq, Philogen Pharmaceutique was up and running and you were a member of the Venetian League." She watched to see if her words spurred a reaction. "That membership comes with a price. Quite an expensive one, I'm told."

"I don't believe it's illegal for men and women to enjoy one another's company."

"You're not the Rotary Club."

"We have a purpose, quality members, and a dedication to our mission. Sounds like any service club I know of."

"You still never answered my question," she pointed out. "Ever seen one of those coins before?"

He tossed it back to her. "Never."

She tried to read this man of commanding girth whose face was as deceptive as his voice. From everything she'd been told, he was a mediocre virologist with an ordinary education who had a knack for business. But he may also have been responsible for the death of Naomi Johns.

Time to find out.

"You're not half as smart as you think you are."

Vincenti smoothed back a rebellious lock of his thin hair. "This is becoming tiresome."

"If she's dead, so are you."

She watched again for a reaction and he seemed to be weighing the minimum truth he could voice against a lie she'd never tolerate.

"Are we finished?" he asked, still with a warm cloak of politeness.

She stood. "Actually, we're just getting started." She held up the medallion. "On the face of this coin, hidden within the folds of the warrior's cloak, are microletters.

Amazing that ancient people could engrave like that. But I checked with experts and they could. The letters were like watermarks. Security devices. This one has two. ZH. Zeta. Eta. Mean anything to you?"

"Not a thing."

But she caught a moment when his eyes flickered with interest. Or was it surprise? Perhaps even a nanosecond of shock.

"I asked some experts on Old Greek. They said ZH means 'life.' Interesting, wouldn't you say, that someone went to the trouble of engraving tiny letters with such a message, when so few at the time could have read them. Lenses were practically unknown in those days."

He shrugged. "Doesn't concern me."

VINCENTI WAITED A FULL FIVE MINUTES AFTER THE palazzo's front door closed. He sat in the salon and allowed the quiet to ease his anxiety. Only a rustle of caged wings and the clicking of his canaries' beaks disturbed the stillness. The palazzo had once been owned by a *bon viveur* of intellectual tastes who, centuries ago, made it a central location for Venetian literary society. Another owner took advantage of the Grand Canal and accommodated the many funeral processions, utilizing the room where he sat as a theater for autopsies and a holding place for corpses. Later, smugglers chose the house as a mart for contraband, deliberately surrounding its walls with ominous legends to keep the curious away.

He longed for those days.

Stephanie Nelle, employed with the U. S. Justice Department, sent supposedly by the president of the United States, had rattled him.

But not because of anything the Americans knew about his past—that would soon become irrelevant.

And not because of what may have happened to their agent sent to spy on him—she was dead and buried, never to be found. No. His stomach ached because of the letters on the coin.

ZH.

Zeta. Eta.

Life.

"You can come in now," he called out.

Peter O'Conner strolled into the room, having listened to the entire conversation from the adjacent parlor. One of Vincenti's many house cats scampered into the main parlor, too.

"What do you think?" Vincenti asked.

"She's a messenger who chose her words with care."

"That medallion she showed me is exactly what Zovastina is after. It matches the description I read yesterday in the materials you gave me at the hotel." But he still did not know why the coins were so important.

"There's something new. Zovastina is coming to Venice. Today."

"On a state visit? I've heard nothing of that."

"Not official. In and out tonight. Private plane. Special arrangement, by the Vatican, with Italian customs. A source called and told me."

Now he knew. Something was definitely happening and Zovastina was several steps ahead of him. "We need to know when she arrives and where she goes."

"I'm already on it. We'll be ready."

Time for him to move, as well. "Are we ready in Samarkand?"

"Just say the word."

He decided to take advantage of his enemy's absence. No sense waiting till the weekend. "Have the jet ready. We'll leave within the hour. But while we're gone, make sure we know exactly what the Supreme Minister is doing here."

O'Conner nodded his understanding.

Now for what really troubled him. "One more thing. I need to send a message to Washington. One that will be perfectly understood. Have Stephanie Nelle killed. And get that medallion."

THIRTY-SIX

MALONE ENJOYED HIS PLATE OF SPINACH PASTA swirled with cheese and ham. Viktor and his cohort had left the island an hour ago, after spending twenty minutes inside the museum, then surveying the area around the basilica, especially the garden that separated the church from the Canale Borgognoni, a riverlike waterway that stretched between Torcello and the next patchy island over. He and Cassiopeia had watched from varying positions. Viktor had not seemed to notice anything, surely concentrating on the task that lay ahead, comfortable in his anonymity.

After Viktor and his accomplice departed on the water bus, he and Cassiopeia retreated to the village. One of the vendors peddling souvenirs told them that the restaurant, Locanda Cipriani, which had been around for decades, was regarded as one of Venice's most famous. People boated over each evening to enjoy its ambiance. Inside, among wooden ceilings, terra-cotta brick, and impressive bas-reliefs, hung a gallery of photographs—Hemingway, Picasso, Diana and Charles, Queen Elizabeth, Churchill, countless actors and performers—each one personalized with a testament of thanks.

They were seated in the garden, beneath a pergola of sweet-smelling roses, in the shadow of the two churches and campanile, the tranquil oasis framed by blossoming pomegranate trees. He had to admit, the food was excellent. Even Cassiopeia seemed hungry. Neither one of them had eaten since breakfast in Copenhagen.

"He'll be back after dark," she quietly said.

"Another bonfire?"

"Seems their way, though it's not necessary. Nobody will miss that coin."

After Viktor left, they'd ventured inside the museum. Cassiopeia had been right. Not much there. Bits and pieces, fragments of columns, capitals, mosaics, and a few paintings. On the second floor, two rickety glass-topped cases displayed pottery shards, jewelry, and ancient household items, all supposedly found in and around Torcello. The elephant medallion lay in one of the cases, among a variety of coinage. Malone had noticed that the building possessed no alarms or security and the lone attendant, a heavyset woman in a plain white dress, seemed only concerned that no one take photographs.

"I'm going to kill the son of a bitch," Cassiopeia muttered.

The declaration did not surprise him. He'd sensed her rising anger in the bell tower. "You think Irina Zovastina ordered Ely's murder."

She'd stopped eating.

"Any proof, besides the fact that his house burned to the ground?"

"She did it. I know it."

"Actually, you don't know crap."

She sat immobile. Beyond the garden, dusk was beginning to take hold. "I know enough."

"Cassiopeia, you're leaping to conclusions. I agree, the fire is suspect, but if she did it, you need to know why."

"When Gary was threatened, what did you do?"

"I got him back. Unharmed."

He saw she knew he was right. First rule of a mission. Never lose sight of the goal.

"I don't need your advice."

"What you need to do is stop and think."

"Cotton, there's more happening here than you realize."

"That's a shocker."

"Go home. Let me be."

"Can't do that."

A vibration in his trouser pocket startled him. He removed the cell phone, noticed the number, and said to her, "It's Henrik." He answered.

"Cotton, President Daniels just called."

"I'm sure that was interesting."

"Stephanie is in Venice. She was sent there to see a man named Enrico Vincenti. The president is concerned. They've lost contact."

"Why call you?"

"He was looking for you, though I sensed he knew you were already here."

"Not a hard thing to check, what with passport scans made at the airport. Provided you know what country to check."

"Apparently he knew the right one."

"Why was Stephanie sent here?"

"He said this Vincenti is connected to Irina Zovastina. I know of Vincenti. He's a problem. Daniels also told me that another agent has been missing now for over a day and is presumed dead. He said you knew her. A woman named Naomi Johns."

He shut his eyes. They had joined the Magellan Billet together and worked as a team several times. A good agent. A better friend. That was the problem with his fomer profession—rarely was someone fired. You either quit, retired, or died. He'd attended many memorials.

"Vincenti implicated in that?" he asked.

"Daniels thought so."

"Tell me about Stephanie."

"She's staying at the Montecarlo, a block north and behind the basilica in San Marco, on the Calle degli Specchieri."

"Why not use one of their own people?"

"He said Naomi Johns was their person on the scene. No one else in position. He was hoping I could contact you and ask if you'd check on Stephanie. Is it possible?"

"I'll take care of it."

"How are things there?"

He stared across the table at Cassiopeia. "Not good."

"Tell Cassiopeia the package she ordered will be there shortly."

He clicked off and asked her, "You called Henrik?"

She nodded. "Three hours ago. After we spotted our thieves."

They'd split up and reconned the two museums separately.

"Stephanie's in Venice and may be in trouble," he said. "I have to go see about her."

"I can handle things here."

He doubted that.

"They'll wait till it's dark before returning," she said. "I asked. This island is deserted at night, except for people who come over for dinner here. Closing time is nine P.M. The last water bus leaves at ten. By then, everyone is gone."

A waiter delivered a silver box, wrapped in a red ribbon, along with a long cloth bag, maybe three feet, it, too, tied with a decorative bow. He explained that a water taxi had delivered both a few moments ago. Malone tipped him two euros.

Cassiopeia unwrapped the box, peeked, then passed

it to him. Inside lay two automatic pistols with spare magazines.

He motioned at the bag. "And that?"

"A surprise for our thieves."

He didn't like the implications.

"You check on Stephanie," she said. "Time for Viktor to see a ghost."

THIRTY-SEVEN

9:40 P.M.

MALONE FOUND THE HOTEL MONTECARLO EXACTLY where Thorvaldsen had directed, hidden along a hall-waylike street lined with shops and busy cafés a hundred feet north of the basilica. He wove his way through a dense evening crowd to the glass-fronted entrance and entered a lobby where a Middle Eastern man sporting a white shirt, tie, and black pants waited behind a counter.

"*Prego,*" Malone said. "English?"

The man smiled. "Of course."

"I'm looking for Stephanie Nelle. American. She's staying here."

Recognition instantly came to the other man's face, so he asked, "Which room?"

The man searched the key rack behind him. "Two-ten."

Malone stepped toward a marble stairway.

"But she's not there."

He turned back.

"She went out in the square a few minutes ago. For a gelato. Just dropped her key." The attendant held up a heavy chunk of brass with 210 etched on the side.

How different it was in Europe learning things. That would have cost him at least a hundred dollars at home. Still, nothing about this seemed right. Thorvaldsen said Washington had lost contact with Stephanie. But clearly she'd been in the hotel and, like all Magellan Billet agents, carried a world phone.

And yet she'd just casually left her hotel in search of an ice cream?

"Any idea where?"

"I directed her to the arcade. In front of the basilica. Good treats there."

He liked the stuff, too. So why not?

They'd both have one.

CASSIOPEIA ASSUMED A POSITION NEAR WHERE THE muddy canal drained into the lagoon, not far from Torcello's public transportation terminal. If her instincts proved correct, Viktor and his cohort would return here sometime in the next couple of hours.

Darkness cloaked the island.

Only the restaurant where she and Malone had eaten remained open, but she knew it would close in another half hour. She'd also checked the two churches and the museum. Both were locked down, all the employees departing on the water bus that left an hour ago.

Through a thickening mist shrouding the lagoon she spotted boats crisscrossing in all directions, confined, she knew, to marked channels that acted like highways on the shallow water. What she was about to do would cross a moral line—one she'd never breached before. She'd killed, but only when forced. This was different. Her blood ran cold, which frightened her.

But she owed Ely.

She thought of him every day.

Especially about their time in the mountains.

She stared out over the mass of rock sloping into steeply falling hills, ravines, gorges, and precipices. She'd learned that the Pamirs were a place of violent storms and earthquakes, of constant mists and soaring eagles. Desolate and lonely. Only a wild barking tore through the silence.

"You like this, don't you?" Ely asked.

"I like you."

He smiled. He was in his late thirties, broad-shouldered, with a bright, round face and mischievous eyes. He was one of the few men she'd encountered who made her feel mentally inadequate, and she loved that feeling. He'd taught her so much.

"Coming here is one of the great perks of my job," Ely said.

He'd told her about his retreat in the mountains, east of Samarkand, close to the Chinese border, but this was her first visit. The three-room cabin was built with stout timber, nestled in the woods off the main highway, about two thousand meters above sea level. A short walk through the trees brought them to this perch and the spectacular mountain view.

"You own the cabin?" she asked.

He shook his head. "The widow of a shopkeeper in the village owns it. She offered it to me last year, when I came here for a visit. The money I pay in rent helps her live, and I get to enjoy all this."

She loved his quiet manner. Never raised his voice or uttered a profanity. Just a simple man who loved the past. "Have you found what you wanted?"

He motioned to the rocky ground and the magenta earth. "Here?"

She shook her head. "In Asia."

He seemed to consider her question in earnest. She allowed him the luxury of his thoughts and watched as snow trickled down one of the distant flanks.

"I believe I have," he said.

She grinned at his assertion. "And what have you accomplished?"

"I met you."

Flattery never worked with her. Men tried all the time. But with Ely it was different. "Besides that," she said.

"I've learned that the past never dies."

"Can you talk about it?"

The barking stopped and the weak patter of some far-off rivulet could be heard.

"Not now," he said.

She wrapped her arm around him, brought him close, and said, "Whenever you're ready."

Her eyes moistened at the memory. Ely had been special in so many ways. His death came as a shock, similar to when she learned that her father died, or when her mother succumbed to a cancer nobody knew she'd harbored. Too much pain. Too many heartbreaks.

She spotted a pair of yellow lights heading her way, the boat plowing a course straight for Torcello. Two water taxis had already come and gone, shuttling patrons to and from the restaurant.

This could be another.

She'd meant what she'd said to Malone. Ely had been murdered. She possessed no proof. Just her gut. But that feeling had always served her well. Thorvaldsen, God bless him, had sensed she needed a resolution, which was why he'd sent, without argument, the cloth bag she cradled in a tight embrace, and the gun snuggled at her belt. She hated Irina Zovastina, and Viktor, and anyone else who'd driven her to this moment.

The boat slowed, its engine weakening.

The low-lying craft was similar to the one she and Malone had rented. Its course was straight for the canal entrance and, as the craft drew closer, in the amber light from its helm, she spotted not a nondescript taximan but Viktor.

Early.

Which was fine.

She wanted to handle this without Malone.

STEPHANIE EASED ACROSS SAN MARCO SQUARE, THE
high golden baubles of the basilica lit to the night.
Chairs and tables stretched out from the arcades across
the famous pavement in symmetrical rows. A couple of
ensembles stringed away in blithe disharmony. The
usual rabble of tourists, guides, vendors, beggars, and
touts seemed diminished by the deteriorating weather.

She passed the celebrated bronze flagpoles and the impressive campanile, closed for the night. A smell of fish,
pepper, and a hint of clove caught her attention. Somber
pools of light illuminated the square in a golden hue. Pi-
geons, which dominated by day, were gone. Any other
time the scene would be romantic.

But now she was on guard.

Ready.

MALONE SEARCHED THE CROWD FOR STEPHANIE AS THE
bells high in the campanile pealed out ten P.M. A breeze
blew in from the south and swirled the mist-muffled air.
He was glad for his jacket, beneath which he concealed
one of the guns Thorvaldsen had provided Cassiopeia.

The brightly lit basilica dominated one end of the old
square, a museum the other, everything mellowed by
years of glory and splendor. Visitors milled through the
long arcades, many searching the shop windows for
possible treasures. The trattorias, coffee shops, and
gelato stands, shielded from the weather by the arcade,
were all doing a brisk business.

He surveyed the piazza. Maybe six hundred feet long
by three hundred wide. Bordered on three sides by a

continuous row of artistic buildings that seemed to form one vast marble palace. Across the damp square, through bobbing umbrellas, he spotted Stephanie, who was walking briskly toward the south arcade.

He stood beneath the north arcade, which stretched to his right for what seemed like forever from the basilica, toward the museum at the far end.

Among the crowd, one man caught his attention.

He stood alone, dressed in an olive green overcoat, his hands stuffed into his coat pockets. Something about the way he stopped and started down the arcade, hesitating at each archway, his attention focused outward, caught Malone's attention.

Malone decided to take advantage of his anonymity and head toward the problem. He kept one eye on Stephanie and the other on the man in the olive coat. It only took a moment for him to determine that the man was definitely interested in her.

Then he spied more trouble in a beige raincoat at the far end of the arcade, the other man's attention also directed out into the piazza.

Two suitors.

Malone kept walking, taking in the voices, laughter, a fragrance of perfume, the click-clack of heels. The two men joined together, then abandoned their positions, turning left, hustling toward the south arcade, which Stephanie had now entered.

Malone veered left, out into the mist, and trotted across the square.

The two men advanced parallel to him, their images illuminated between each of the arches. The thin strain of one of the café orchestras masked all sound.

Malone slowed and wove his way through a maze of tables, empty thanks to the inclement weather. Beneath the covered arcade, Stephanie stood before a glass case studying the ice cream.

The two men rounded the corner a hundred feet away.

He stepped up beside her and said, "The chocolate chip is excellent."

Surprise invaded her face. "Cotton, what in—"

"No time. We have company, behind me, coming this way."

He saw her glance over his shoulder.

He turned.

Guns appeared.

He shoved Stephanie away from the counter and together they fled the arcade, back into the piazza.

He gripped his gun and readied himself for a fight.

But they were trapped. A football field–size open square spread out behind them. Nowhere to go.

"Cotton," Stephanie said. "I have this under control."

He stared at her, and hoped to heaven she was right.

VIKTOR INCHED THE BOAT THROUGH THE NARROW canal and passed beneath a rickety arched bridge. He wasn't planning on tying up at the waterway's end, near the restaurant, he just wanted to make sure the village had cleared out for the night. He was glad for the wet weather, a typical Italian storm had blown in from the sea, rain coming off and on, more a nuisance than a distraction, but enough to provide them with great cover.

Rafael kept an eye out on the blackened banks. High tide had arrived two hours ago, which should make their eventual landing point that much more accessible. He'd spotted the location earlier. Adjacent to the basilica, where a sluggish canal cut a broad path across the breadth of the island. A concrete dock, near the basilica, would provide the stopping point.

Ahead, he spotted the village.

Dark and quiet.

No boats.

They'd just come from the warehouse Zovastina had directed him toward. True to her word, the Supreme Minister had planned ahead. Greek fire, guns, and ammunition were stored there. He wondered, though, about torching the museum. It seemed unnecessary, but Zovastina had made clear that nothing should remain.

"Looks okay," Rafael said.

He agreed.

So he shifted the boat's throttle into neutral, then reversed the engine.

CASSIOPEIA SMILED. SHE'D BEEN RIGHT. THEY WOULDN'T be foolish enough to dock at the village. They'd intentionally reconnoitered the other canal that ran beside the basilica as their destination.

She watched the boat's outline turn one hundred eighty degrees and leave the canal. She reached back, found the gun Thorvaldsen had sent, and chambered a round. She gripped both the gun and the cloth bag and fled her hiding place, keeping her eyes locked out on the water.

Viktor and his accomplice found the lagoon.

Engines revved.

The boat veered right, beginning its circumnavigation of the island.

She trotted through the soggy night, toward the churches, one stop to make along the way.

THIRTY-EIGHT

STEPHANIE WAS PUZZLED BY MALONE'S PRESENCE. Only one way she could have been found. No time at the moment, though, to consider the implications.

"Do it now," she said into the lapel mike.

Three pops echoed across the piazza and one of the armed men crumpled to the pavement. She and Malone dove to the damp flagstones as the remaining man sought cover. Malone reacted with the skill of the agent he'd once been and rolled himself back into the arcade, firing twice, trying to flush the remaining attacker out into the open square.

People scattered in a frenzy, as a panic overtook San Marco.

Malone sprang to his feet and hugged the wet side of one of the arches. The assailant stood fifty feet away, caught in a crossfire between Malone and the rifleman Stephanie had stationed atop the building on the north side.

"Care to tell me what's happening?" Malone asked, not taking his eyes off the man.

"Ever heard of bait?"

"Yeah, and it's a bitch on that hook."

"I have men in the square."

He risked a look around, but saw nothing. "They invisible?"

She looked around, too. No one was coming their

way. Everyone was fleeing toward the basilica. A familiar anger swelled inside her.

"Police will be here any second," he said.

She realized that could be a problem. Her rules at the Magellan Billet discouraged agents from involving the locals. They were usually not helpful or were downright hostile, and she'd seen evidence of that, firsthand, in Amsterdam.

"He's on the move," Malone said, as he rushed forward.

She followed and said into the mike, "Get out of here."

Malone was running to an exit that led from the arcade, away from the square, back into the dark streets of Venice. At the exit's end a pedestrian bridge arced over one of the canals.

She saw Malone race across it.

MALONE KEPT RUNNING. CLOSED SHOPS LINED BOTH sides of the ridiculously narrow lane. Just ahead, the street right-angled. A few pedestrians turned the corner. He slowed and concealed the gun beneath his jacket, keeping his fingers tight on the trigger.

He stopped at the next corner, embracing the gleam of a wet store window. He swallowed hot, heavy gulps of air and carefully peered around the edge.

A bullet whizzed past and ricocheted off the stone.

Stephanie found him.

"Isn't this foolish?" she asked.

"Don't know. It's your party."

He risked another look.

Nothing.

He abandoned his position and rushed forward another thirty feet to where the street turned again. A glance around the corner and he saw more closed shops and deep shadows and a misty murk that could conceal almost anything.

Stephanie approached, holding a gun.

"Aren't you the little field agent?" he said. "Carrying a weapon now?"

"Seems I've had a lot of use for one lately."

So had he, but she was right. "This is foolish. We're going to get shot or arrested if we keep going. What are you doing here?"

"That was going to be my question for you. This is my job. You're a bookseller. Why did Danny Daniels send you?"

"He said they'd lost contact with you."

"No one tried to contact me."

"Seems our president apparently wants me involved, but didn't have the courtesy to ask."

Shouts and screams could be heard from behind them in the square.

But he had a greater concern. Torcello. "I have a boat docked just beyond San Marco, at the quayside." He pointed right at another alleylike street. "We should be able to get there if we head that way."

"Where are we going?" Stephanie asked.

"To help someone who needs even more help than you do."

VIKTOR KILLED THE ENGINE AND ALLOWED THE BOAT TO gently touch the stone dock. A muted scene of slate grays, muddy greens, and pale blues engulfed them. The iron silhouette of the basilica rose thirty meters away, just past a jagged patch of stubbled shadows that defined a garden and orchard. Rafael emerged from the aft cabin carrying two shoulder bags and said, "Eight packs and one turtle ought to be enough. If we torch the bottom, the rest will burn easily."

Rafael understood the ancient potion and Viktor had come to rely on that expertise. He watched as his partner gently laid the rucksacks down and stepped back into the cabin, toting up one of the robotic turtles.

"He's charged and ready."

"Why is it a 'he'?"

"I don't know. Seems appropriate."

Viktor smiled. "We need a rest."

"A few days off would be good. Maybe the minister will give us the time, as a reward."

He laughed. "The minister doesn't believe in rewards."

Rafael adjusted the straps on the two packs. "A few days in the Maldives would be great. Lying on a beach. Warm water."

"Stop dreaming. Not going to happen."

Rafael shouldered one of the heavy rucksacks. "Nothing wrong with dreaming. Especially out here, in this rain."

He grabbed the turtle as Rafael lifted the other satchel. "In and out. Quick and fast. Okay?"

His partner nodded. "Should be an easy run."

He agreed.

CASSIOPEIA STOOD ON THE BASILICA'S FRONT PORCH, using its shadows and six towering columns for cover. The mist had evolved into a drizzle, but thankfully the damp night was warm. A steady breeze kept the froth stirred and masked sounds she desperately needed to hear. Like the engine on the boat, just beyond the garden to her right, which should be there by now.

Two pebbled paths led away, one to a stone pier that

was surely Viktor's stopping point, the other to the water itself. She needed to be patient, to allow them to enter the museum and make their way to the second floor.

Then give them a dose of their own medicine.

THIRTY-NINE

S<small>TEPHANIE STOOD BESIDE</small> M<small>ALONE AS HE EASED THE</small> boat away from the concrete dock. Police cruisers were arriving, tying up at the quayside mooring posts where San Marco ended at the lagoon's edge. Emergency lights strobed the darkness.

"All hell is going to break loose out there," Malone said.

"Daniels should have thought about that before he interfered."

Malone followed the lighted channel markers northward, paralleling the shore. More police boats raced by, sirens blasting. She found her world phone, dialed a number, then stepped close to Malone and switched to "Speaker."

"Edwin," she said. "You're lucky you're not here or I'd kick your ass."

"Don't you work for me?" Davis asked.

"I had three men in that square. Why weren't they there when I needed them?"

"We sent Malone. I hear he's equal to three men."

"Whoever you are," Malone said, "flattery would normally work. But I'm with her. You called her backup off?"

"She had the roof sniper and you. That was enough."

"Now I'm really going to kick your ass," she said.

"How about we get through this, then you can have the opportunity."

"What the hell's going on?" she said, voice rising. "Why is Cotton here?"

"I need to know what happened."

She sucked in her anger and provided a brief summary. Then said, "Lots going on in that square right now. Plenty of attention."

"Not necessarily a bad thing," Davis said.

The original idea had been to see if Vincenti would act. Men had been staking out her hotel all evening and, when she'd left, they'd promptly headed upstairs, surely intent on finding the medallion. She wondered why the change in strategy—involving Malone—but held that inquiry and said into the phone, "You still haven't said why Cotton is here."

Malone steered left as they rounded the shoreline, the compass indicating northeast, and added power to the engines.

"What are you doing right now?" Davis asked.

"Heading into another problem," Malone said. "You need to answer her question."

"We want San Marco in an uproar tonight."

She waited for more.

"We've learned that Irina Zovastina is on her way to Venice. She'll be landing within the next two hours. Unusual, to say the least. A head of state making an unannounced visit to another country for no apparent reason. We need to find out what she's doing there."

"Why don't you ask her?" Malone said.

"Are you always so helpful?"

"It's one of my better traits."

"Mr. Malone," Davis said. "We know about the fire in Copenhagen and the medallions. Stephanie has one of them with her. Can you cut me some slack and help us out?"

"Is this that bad?" she asked.

"It's not good."

She saw that Malone's cooperation was never in doubt. "Where is Zovastina headed?"

"Into the basilica, around one A.M."

"You apparently have good information."

"One of those impeccable sources. So damn impeccable I have to wonder."

The line went silent a moment.

"I'm not wild about any of this," Davis finally said. "But, believe me, we have no choice."

VIKTOR STEPPED INTO THE VILLAGE GREEN, BEFORE THE basilica and its companion church, studying the Museo di Torcello. He laid his shoulder pack on a chunk of marble carved into a thronelike perch. He'd heard earlier that it was called Sedia d'Attila, Attila's Seat. Supposedly, Attila the Hun himself had sat there, but he doubted that claim.

He studied their final target. The museum was a squat two-story rectangle, maybe twenty by ten meters, with a set of double windows, top and bottom, at each end, barred with wrought iron. A bell tower jutted skyward from one side. The piazzetta around him was dotted with trees and displayed, across the trimmed grass, remnants of marble columns and carved stone.

Double wooden doors in the center of the museum's ground floor provided the only entrance. They opened outward and were barred with a thick piece of blackened lumber laid across their center, held close by iron brackets. Padlocks at each end clamped the bar in place.

He motioned at the doors and said, "Burn them off."

Rafael removed a plastic bottle from one of the shoulder bags. He followed his partner to the doors where Rafael carefully doused both padlocks with Greek fire. He stood back as Rafael removed a striker and sparked both locks into a brilliant blue blaze.

Amazing stuff. Even metal succumbed to its fury—not enough to melt, but plenty to weaken.

He watched as the flames burned for nearly two minutes before consuming themselves.

CASSIOPEIA KEPT HER VIGIL THIRTY METERS AWAY AS two points of intense blue light, like distant stars, glowed and then extinguished. Two thrusts of a crowbar and the thieves unbarred the museum's main doors.

They carried their equipment inside.

She saw that they'd brought one of the robotic gizmos, which meant the Museo di Torcello would soon be ash.

One of the men closed the double doors.

The piazzetta once again loomed dark, damp, and sinister. Only the click of rain finding puddles disturbed the silence. She stood on the basilica's porch and contemplated what she was about to do, then noticed the wooden bar that had secured the doors had been left outside.

VIKTOR CLIMBED A SPIRAL STAIRCASE TO THE MUSEUM'S second floor, his eyes adjusted to the murky night. He'd discerned enough shadows for him to navigate his way through the sparse ground-floor exhibits and up to the equally sparse top level, where three oversized glass-topped cases waited. In the middle case, right where he'd noted earlier, lay the elephant medallion.

Rafael was below, positioning Greek fire packets for maximum destruction. He carried two packs earmarked for the second floor. With a quick blow from the crowbar, he shattered the glass and, from among the shards, carefully retrieved the medallion. He then tossed one of the three-quart vacuum packs into the display case.

The other he laid on the floor.

He pocketed the medallion.

Hard to say if it was genuine but, from a casual long-distance inspection earlier, it had certainly looked authentic.

He glanced at his watch. Ten forty P.M. Ahead of schedule. More than enough time to meet the Supreme Minister. Maybe Zovastina *would* reward them with a few days' rest.

He descended the stairway to ground level.

They'd noted earlier that the flooring on both levels was wood. Once the fire below started to rage, it would only be a few minutes before the packs overhead joined the mélange.

Through the darkness he saw Rafael bent over the turtle. He heard a click and the device began to roam. The robot halted at the room's far end and started dousing the outer wall, spewing odorous Greek fire.

"Everything's ready," Rafael said.

The turtle continued its task, unconcerned that it would shortly disintegrate. Just a machine. No feelings. No remorse. Precisely, he thought, what Irina Zovastina expected from him.

Rafael pushed on the main doors.

They did not open.

His partner shoved again.

Nothing.

Viktor stepped close and pressed his palm flat against the wood. The double doors were barred. From the outside. A surge of anger swept through him and he rammed himself into the wood, but all he did was pound his shoulder. The thick slabs, held upright with iron hinges, refused to yield.

His gaze raked the darkness.

While reconnoitering the building earlier he'd noted bars on the windows. Not an obstacle since they planned to enter and leave through the front door. Now, though, the barred windows assumed a greater significance.

He stared at Rafael. Though he could not see his partner's face he knew exactly what he was thinking.

They were trapped.

PART THREE

FORTY

VINCENTI CAREFULLY DESCENDED THE STAIRWAY FROM the private jet. The trip east from Venice to the Central Asian Federation had taken nearly six hours, but he'd made the journey many times and had learned to enjoy the jet's luxury and rest during the long flight. Peter O'Conner followed him into a balmy night.

"I love Venice," Vincenti said, "but I'll enjoy when I finally live here. I won't miss all that rain."

A car waited on the tarmac and he headed straight for it, stretching his stiff legs, working his tired muscles. A driver emerged and opened the rear door. Vincenti climbed inside as O'Conner sat in the front passenger's seat. A Plexiglass partition assured the rear compartment privacy.

Already sitting in the back was a black-haired, olive-skinned man with eyes that always, even in the face of adversity, seemed to find life comic. A heavy stubble coated a square jaw and thin neck, the youthful features, even at this late hour, quick and observant.

Kamil Karimovich Revin served as the Federation's foreign minister. Barely forty, with few or no credentials, he was generally regarded as the Supreme Minister's lap-dog, doing exactly what she commanded. Several years ago, though, Vincenti had noticed something else.

"Welcome back," Kamil said to him. "It's been a few months."

"Lots to do, my friend. The League consumes much of my time."

"I've been dealing with your members. Many are beginning to select home sites."

One of the arrangements made with Zovastina had been for League members to relocate to the Federation. A good move for both sides. Their new business utopia would free them all from burdensome taxation. But the influx of their capital into the economy, in the form of goods, services, and direct investment, would more than compensate the Federation for any taxes that could be imposed. Even better, an entire upper class would be instantly established, with no trickle-down effect that Western democracies loved to impose, where—quite unfairly, Vincenti had always thought—the few paid for the many.

League members had been encouraged to purchase tracts and many had, including himself, paying the government as most Federation land, thanks to the Soviets, lay in public hands. Vincenti had actually been part of the committee that negotiated this aspect of the League's deal with Zovastina, and had been one of the first to buy, acquiring two hundred acres of valley and mountain in what was once eastern Tajikistan.

"How many have closed deals?" he asked.

"One hundred and ten so far. Lots of varied tastes in locations, but in and around Samarkand has been the most popular."

"Near the source of power. That town and Tashkent will soon become world financial centers."

The car left the air terminal and began the four-kilometer trek into town. Another improvement would be a new airport. Three League members had already drawn plans for a more modern facility.

"Why are you here?" Kamil asked. "Mr. O'Conner was not all that forthcoming when I spoke to him earlier."

"We appreciate the information on Zovastina's trip. Any idea why she's in Venice?"

"She left no word, saying only she would return shortly."

"So she's in Venice doing who knows what."

"And if she discovers you're here plotting," Kamil said, "we're all dead. Remember, her little germs cannot be defended against."

The foreign minister was one of a new breed of politicians that had risen with the Federation. And though Zovastina was the first to become Supreme Minister, she would not be the last.

"I can counter her bugs."

A smile came to the Asian's face. "Can you kill her and be done with it?"

He appreciated raw ambition. "That would be foolish."

"What do you have in mind?"

"Something better."

"Will the League stand with you?"

"The Council of Ten has authorized everything I'm doing."

Kamil grinned. "Not everything, my friend. I know better. That attempt on her life. That was you. I could tell. And you bargained that assassin away. How else would she have been ready?" He paused. "I wonder. Will I be bargained away, too?"

"Do you want to succeed her?"

"I prefer to live."

He glanced out the window at flat roofs, blue domes, and spindly minarets. Samarkand lay in a natural bowl, surrounded by mountains. Night camouflaged a hazy smog that perpetually blanketed the ancient earth. In the distance, factory lights cast a fuzzy halo. What once supplied the Soviet Union with manufactured goods now churned out Federation gross national product. The League had already invested billions for modernization. More was coming. So he needed to know, "How much do you want to be Supreme Minister?"

"It all depends. Can your League make that happen?"

"Her germs don't scare me. They shouldn't scare you, either."

"Oh, my stout friend, I've seen too many enemies die suddenly. It's amazing that no one has ever noticed. But her diseases work well. Just a cold or a flu that turns bad."

Though Federation bureaucrats, including Zovastina, detested anything Soviet, they'd learned well from their corrupt predecessors. That was why Vincenti was always careful with his words but generous with promises. "Nothing can be gained without risk."

Revin shrugged. "True. But sometimes the risks are too great."

Vincenti gazed out at Samarkand. Such an old place, dating from the fifth century before Christ. The City of Shadows, Garden of the Soul, Jewel of Islam, Capital of the World. A Christian see before Islam and the Russians conquered. Thanks to the Soviets, Tashkent, two hundred kilometers to the northeast, had grown far larger and more prosperous. But Samarkand remained the region's soul.

He stared across at Kamil Revin. "I'm personally about to take a dangerous step. My time as head of the Council of Ten ends soon. If we're going to do this, we have to do it now. Time for you, as we say where I come from, to shit or get off the pot. You in or out?"

"I doubt I would live to see tomorrow if I said out. I'm in."

"Glad we understand each other."

"And what is it you're about to do?" the foreign minister asked.

He gazed back out at the city. On one of the hundreds of mosques that dominated the landscape, in brilliantly illuminated Arabic calligraphy, letters at least a meter high proclaimed "God Is Immortal." For all its elaborate history, Samarkand still cast a bland institutional solemnity, derived from a culture that had long ago lost all imagination. Zovastina seemed intent on changing that malady. Her vision was grand and clear. He had lied when he told Stephanie Nelle that history was not his strong point. In reality, it was his goal. But he hoped he wasn't making a mistake breathing life into the past.

No matter. Too late to turn back now.

So he stared across at his coconspirator and answered the question honestly.

"Change the world."

FORTY-ONE

VIKTOR'S MIND RACED. THE TURTLE CONTINUED ITS programmed assault of the museum's ground floor, leaving a stinking trail of Greek fire. He thought about trying to force the double doors with Rafael, but he knew the wood's breadth and the bar outside would make any effort foolish.

The windows seemed the only way out.

"Get one of the vacuum packs," he said to Rafael, as his eyes raked the room and he decided on the set of windows to his left.

Rafael retrieved one of the clear plastic bags from the floor.

The Greek fire should weaken the aged wrought iron, along with the bolts that held the bars to the exterior wall, enough that they could force them. He drew one of the guns they'd obtained in the warehouse and was just about to shoot out the panes when, from the far side of the room, glass shattered.

Someone had shot out the window from outside.

He ducked for cover, as did Rafael, waiting to see what would happen next. The turtle continued its rhythmic crawl, stopping and starting as it encountered obstacles. He had no idea how many people were outside and whether or not he and Rafael were vulnerable from the three other sets of windows.

He felt the edge of danger on which they were balancing. One thing was clear. The turtle needed to be stopped. That would buy them some time.

But still.

They knew nothing.

CASSIOPEIA STUFFED THE GUN BACK AGAINST HER SPINE and gripped the fiberglass bow she'd removed from the cloth bag. Thorvaldsen had not questioned why she needed a bow and high-velocity arrows, and she'd not really known if the weapon would prove useful.

But now it certainly would.

She was standing thirty meters from the museum, dry under the basilica's porch. On her way from the other side of the island, she had stopped in the village and retrieved one of the oil lamps that illuminated the quayside near the restaurant. She'd noticed the lanterns earlier when she and Malone first arrived, which was another reason why she'd asked Thorvaldsen for the bow. She'd then found some rags in a trash bin near a vendor stall. While the thieves tended to their mission inside the museum, she'd prepared four arrows, wrapping strips of cloth around the metal tips and soaking them with lamp oil.

Matches were obtained during dinner with Malone—a few books retrieved from a tray in the restroom.

She lit the flammable rags on two of the arrows, then carefully loaded the first flaming projectile onto the bow. Her aim was for the ground-floor windows that she'd just shattered with bullets. If Viktor wanted a fire, then that was precisely what he was going to get.

She'd learned archery as a child. Never had she hunted, she detested the thought, but she regularly enjoyed target practice at her French estate. She was good, especially at distances, so thirty meters to the window

across the piazzetta was no problem. And the bars themselves should not be a deterrent. Far more air than iron.

She stretched the string.

"For Ely," she whispered.

VIKTOR SAW FLAMES STREAK THROUGH THE OPEN WIN-
dow and crash into a tall sheet of glass that backed
one of the ground-floor exhibits. Whatever propelled
the flames had pierced the glass, the sheet smashing to
the hardwood and taking the fire down with it. The turtle had already made a pass of that part of the museum,
which was confirmed by a roar, as Greek fire sprang to
life.

Orange and yellow instantly evolved into a scorching
blue and the floor consumed itself.

But the vacuum packs.

He saw that Rafael had realized the same thing. Four
lay scattered. Two atop display cases, two on the floor,
one of which announced its presence in a cascade of
mushrooming flames.

Viktor dove under one of the remaining display cases,
seeking shelter from the heat.

"Get back here," he yelled to Rafael.

His partner retreated toward him. Half the ground
floor was now ablaze. Floor, walls, ceilings, and fixtures
all burned. Where he'd taken refuge had yet to catch,
thanks to a lack of the potion, but he knew that would
only last another precious few moments. The stairway
leading up began to his right, the path toward it clear.
But the top floor would provide little refuge considering
the fire would shortly obliterate it from beneath.

Rafael came close. "The turtle. You see it?"

He realized the problem. The device was heat sensitive, programmed to explode when temperatures
reached a predetermined level. "How high is it set?"

"Low. I wanted this place to burn fast."

His eyes searched the flames. Then he spotted the turtle, still cruising across the blazing floor, each exhale from its funnel roaring like a fire-breathing dragon.

More glass shattered from the opposite side of the room.

Hard to tell if heat or bullets had been the culprit.

The turtle rolled straight for them, emerging from the fire and finding a part of the floor that had yet to catch. Rafael stood and, before Viktor could stop him, rushed toward the device. Deactivating it was the only way to shut off its program.

A flaming arrow pierced Rafael's chest.

His clothes caught fire.

Viktor came to his feet and was about to dart to his partner's aid when he saw the turtle's funnel retract and the unit halt its advance.

He knew what was about to happen.

He dove for the stairway, lunging forward through the open doorway and scampering up the metal runners.

On hands and knees he climbed in a desperate retreat.

The turtle ignited.

CASSIOPEIA HAD NOT PLANNED ON SHOOTING ONE OF the thieves, but the man had appeared just as she released the string. She watched as the flaming arrow slammed into his chest and his clothing ignited. Then a huge ball of flame consumed the museum's interior, heat surging out the open window and exploding the remaining panes.

She leaped to the wet ground.

Fire licked the night through the shattered openings.

She'd left the basilica's porch and assumed a position opposite the museum's bell tower. At least one of the men was dead. Hard to tell which one, but it didn't matter.

She came to her feet and shifted to the front of the building, watching the prison she'd fashioned burn.

One more flaming arrow ready to fire.

FORTY-TWO

ZOVASTINA STOOD BESIDE THE PAPAL NUNCIO. SHE'D landed an hour ago, Monsignor Michener waiting for her on the tarmac. She, Michener, and two of her guardsmen had traveled to central downtown from the airport via a private water taxi. They'd been unable to use the basilica's north entrance, off the Piazzetta dei Leoncini, as first arranged. A sizable portion of San Marco had been cordoned off, some sort of shooting, the nuncio had told her. So they'd detoured down a side street, behind the basilica, and entered the church from the diocese offices.

The papal nuncio looked different from yesterday, his black robes and priest's collar replaced with street clothes. The pope was apparently making good on his pledge that the visit be nondescript.

She now stood within the cavernous church, its ceiling and walls ablaze with golden mosaics. Clearly a Byzantine concoction, as if it had been erected in Constantinople instead of Italy. Five hemispherical cupolas vaulted overhead. The Domes of Pentecost, St. John, St. Leonard, the Prophets, and the one she was standing beneath, the Ascension. Thanks to a warm glow from strategically placed incandescent lights, she silently agreed that the church had earned its well-known label as the Golden Basilica.

"Quite a place," Michener said. "Isn't it?"

"It's what religion and commercial might can do when joined together. Venetian merchants were the scavengers of the world. Here's the best evidence of their pilfering."

"Are you always so cynical?"

"The Soviets taught me that the world is a tough place."

"And to *your* gods, do you ever offer any thanks?"

She grinned. This American had studied her. Never in their previous conversations had they talked of her beliefs. "My gods are as faithful to me as yours is to you."

"We're hoping you might reconsider your paganism."

She bristled at the label. The word itself implied that somehow the belief in many gods was inferior to the belief in one. She didn't view it that way. Throughout history, many of the world's cultures had agreed with her, which she made clear. "My beliefs have served me well."

"I didn't mean to imply they were wrong. It's only that we may be able to offer some new possibilities."

After tonight, she would have little use for the Catholic Church. She'd allow a limited amount of contact within the Federation, enough to keep the radical Muslims off balance, but never would an organization capable of preserving all that now surrounded her be allowed a foothold in her domain.

She motioned toward the high altar, beyond an ornate multicolored rood screen that looked suspiciously like an iconostasis. She could hear activity from its brightly lit far side.

"They're preparing to open the sarcophagus. We've decided to return a hand, arm, or some other significant relic that can be easily extracted."

She couldn't resist. "You don't see the ridiculousness in that?"

Michener shrugged. "If it'll please the Egyptians, what does it hurt?"

"What about sanctity of the dead? Your religion preaches that constantly. Yet there's apparently nothing wrong with disturbing a man's tomb, removing part of his remains, and giving them away."

"It's an unfortunate thing, but necessary."

She despised his bland innocence. "That's the thing I like about *your* church. Flexible when *necessary.*"

She stared around at the deserted nave, most of the chapels, altars, and niches cast in deep shadows. Her two guardsmen stood only a few meters away. She studied the marble floor, every bit as exquisite as the mosaic walls. Lots of colorful geometrical, animal, and flower motifs, along with unmistakable undulations—intentional, some said, to mimic the sea, but more likely the effect of a weak foundation.

She thought of Ptolemy's words. *And you, adventurer, for my immortal voice, though far off, fills your ears, hear my words. Sail onto the capital founded by Alexander's father, where sages stand guard.*

Though Ptolemy certainly believed himself clever, time had solved that part of the riddle. Nectanebo ruled Egypt, as pharaoh, during the era of Alexander the Great. While Alexander was a teenager, Nectanebo was driven into exile by invading Persians. Egyptians at the time firmly believed Nectanebo would one day return and expel the Persians. And nearly ten years after his defeat, this idea proved more or less true, when Alexander arrived and the Persians promptly surrendered and left. To elevate their liberator and make his presence more palatable, Egyptians told stories of how, early in his rule, Nectanebo had traveled to Macedonia, disguised as a magician, and coupled with Olympias, Alexander's mother, which would make Nectanebo, not Philip, Alexander's father. The story was utter nonsense but prevalent enough that five hundred years later it found its way into the *Alexander Romance*, a piece of fanciful historical fiction that many historians, she knew, erroneously cited as authority. During his reign as the last Egyptian pharaoh, history notes that Nectanebo established Memphis as his capital, which solved *sail onto the capital founded by Alexander's father.*

The next part, *where sages stand guard,* reinforced that conclusion.

At the temple of Nectanebo, in Memphis, stood a semicircle of eleven limestone statues depicting Greek sages and poets. Homer, whom Alexander worshipped, was a central figure. Plato, who taught Aristotle, and Aristotle himself, who taught Alexander, were there, too, along with other renowned Greeks to whom Alexander possessed a close connection. Only fragments of those sculptures remained, but enough to know they once existed.

Ptolemy had entombed the body he believed to be Alexander at the temple of Nectanebo. There it stayed until after Ptolemy's death, when his son moved the body north to Alexandria.

Sail onto the capital founded by Alexander's father, where sages stand guard.

Go south to Memphis and the temple of Nectanebo.

She thought of the next line of the riddle.

Touch the innermost being of the golden illusion.

And smiled.

FORTY-THREE

VIKTOR FLATTENED HIMSELF ONTO THE STAIRWAY, RAISing an arm and shielding his face from the overwhelming heat that surged upward through the ground-floor doorway. The turtle had reacted to the rising temperatures, automatically disintegrating, doing what it was created to do. No way Rafael had survived. Greek fire's initial temperatures were enormous, enough to soften metal and burn stone, but its secondary heat was even more powerful. Human flesh was no match. As with what should have happened to the man in Copenhagen, Rafael would soon be ash.

He turned back.

Fire raged ten feet away.

The heat was becoming unbearable.

He hustled to the top.

The old building was erected at a time when the first-floor ceiling doubled as the second story's flooring. The ceiling below was, by now, totally ablaze. One of the purposes of having the turtle explode was to force the destruction outward. Creaks and moans from the second-story floorboards confirmed their rapid devastation. The weight of the three display cases and the other bulky exhibits wasn't helping. Though the second story had not yet ignited, he realized that crossing the floor could be foolish. Thankfully, the stairwell where he stood was fashioned from stone.

A set of double windows broke the wall a few feet away, facing the piazzetta. He decided to risk it and stepped lightly, hugging the outer perimeter, glancing through the panes, down below.

CASSIOPEIA SAW THE FACE IN THE WINDOW. SHE INstantly dropped the bow, gripped her gun, and fired two shots.

VIKTOR LEAPED BACK INTO THE STAIRWELL AS THE WINdow shattered. He gripped his gun and prepared to return fire. He'd seen enough to know that his attacker was a woman, clear from her silhouetted shape. She'd been holding a bow, but had quickly replaced that weapon with a gun.

Before he could take advantage of his higher ground, a flaming arrow bypassed the wrought-iron bars and pierced the open window, embedding into the plaster on the opposite side of the room. Thankfully, no turtle had saturated things here. Only the two packs he'd left earlier, one on the floor, the other inside the pilfered display case, were potential problems.

He needed to do something.

So he took a cue from his attacker and shot out the double windows that opened to the rear of the building.

CASSIOPEIA HEARD VOICES TO HER LEFT, TOWARD where the restaurant and inn stood. The shots had surely attracted attention from the inn guests. She spotted darkened figures heading down the path from the village and quickly abandoned her position in the piazzetta, retreating to the basilica's porch. She'd fired the last flaming arrow hoping the second floor would ignite, too. In the fire's glow she'd clearly recognized Viktor's face in the window.

People appeared. One man held a cell phone to his ear. No police occupied the island, which should give her time, and she doubted Viktor would enlist the help of any onlookers. Too many questions about the corpse on the ground floor.

So she decided to leave.

VIKTOR STARED ACROSS THE HARDWOOD PLANKS AT THE pack of Greek fire lying on the floor. He decided a quick assault was best, so he stepped lightly, grabbed the bag, and hopped straight toward the window he'd just shot out.

The floorboards held.

He laid the pack outside across the C-shaped wrought-iron bars.

The flooring in the center of the room moaned.

He recalled crossbeams below, but they were surely weakening by the second. A few more steps toward the arrow stuck into the wall and he yanked it free. Rags wrapped around its tip still burned. He rushed across to the stairway, then, with an underhanded toss, lobbed the arrow into the open window frame. It landed on top of the pack, the flames flickering a few inches away from the plastic wrap. He knew it would only take a few moments for the bag to melt.

He sought refuge inside the stairwell.

A *woosh* and another firestorm raged.

He glanced around the doorway and saw that the wrought iron was burning. Luckily, most of the fire-power had stayed outside. The window frame had not joined the conflagration.

The second floor collapsed, swallowing the case with the other fuel pack downward. The remaining bag ignited, a cloud of heat floating upward. The Museo di Torcello would not stand much longer.

He hopped to the open windows.

He gripped the cornice that ran across the top of the frame and searched for a fingerhold, his body straining, feet powered outward, slamming into the burning bars.

Nothing moved.

Another chin-up and he kicked again, adrenaline powering each thrust as the heat began to affect his breathing.

The bars started to give.

More kicks and one corner broke free of its bolt to the exterior wall.

Two more slams and the entire assembly flew outward.

More flooring collapsed.

Another display case and pieces of a column crashed to the ground floor, churning in the fire like bits in a stew.

He stared out the window.

The drop down was three or four meters. Flames spat out the ground-floor windows.

He leaped.

MALONE KEPT THE BOAT ON A NORTHEAST HEADING, speeding as fast as the churning water would allow toward Torcello. He spotted a glow on the horizon flickering with regularity.

Fire.

Billows of smoke gushed upward, the moist air dissolving it into gray wisps. They were a good ten to fifteen minutes away.

"Looks like we're late," he said to Stephanie.

VIKTOR KEPT TO THE MUSEUM'S REAR. HE COULD HEAR shouts and voices from beyond the hedge that separated the yard from the garden and orchard that lay between here and the canal, where his boat waited.

He plowed his way through the hedge and entered the garden.

Luckily, early springtime meant not much vegetation. He was able to find a path and weave his way straight toward the concrete dock.

There, he leaped into the boat.

He untied the mooring lines and pushed off from the dock. No one had seen or followed him. The boat drifted out into the riverlike waterway and the current drove it past where the basilica and museum stood, back toward the north entrance to the lagoon. He waited until he was well beyond the dock before cranking the engine. He kept the power low and brought the bow around, slowly cruising with no lights.

The shore on either side was a good fifty meters apart, mainly mud banks, shallows, and reeds. He checked his watch—11:20 P.M.

At the mouth of the canal he revved the engines and maneuvered out into turbulent water. He finally switched on the boat's running lights and set a course around Torcello for the main channel that would lead to Venice and San Marco.

He heard a noise and turned.

Stepping from the aft cabin was a woman.

Gun in hand.

FORTY-FOUR

VINCENTI SCOOTED THE CHAIR CLOSER TO THE TABLE AS the waiter positioned his food before him. Most of the city's hotels were bleak tombs, where little or nothing worked. The Intercontinental was different, offering five-star European-quality services with what the establishment advertised as Asian hospitality. After the long flight from Italy he was hungry, so he'd ordered a meal brought to the room for both himself and a guest.

"Tell Ormand," he said to the waiter, "that I don't appreciate it taking thirty minutes to prepare these entrées, especially after I called ahead. Better yet, have Ormand come up here after we're finished and I'll tell him myself."

The waiter nodded his assent and retreated.

Arthur Benoit, sitting across from him, spread a cloth napkin onto his lap. "Do you have to be so hard on him?"

"It's your hotel. Why weren't you on his ass?"

"Because I wasn't upset. They prepared the food as fast as they could."

He could not care less. Shit was happening and he was testy. O'Conner had gone ahead to make sure things were ready. He'd decided to eat, rest a bit, and accomplish some business over a middle-of-the-night meal.

Benoit gripped a fork. "I assume the invitation to join you was not because you wanted the pleasure of my company. Why don't we cut through the garbage, Enrico. What do you want?"

He started to eat. "I need money, Arthur. Or should I say, Philogen Pharmaceutique needs money."

Benoit tabled the fork and sipped his wine. "Before my stomach becomes upset, how much do you need?"

"A billion euros. Maybe a billion and a half."

"Is that all?"

He smiled at the sarcasm. Benoit made his fortune in banks, which he still controlled across Europe and Asia. He was a billionaire several times over and a longtime Venetian League member. Hotels were a hobby and he'd recently built the Intercontinental to cater to the influx of League members and other expected luxury travelers. He'd also relocated to the Federation, one of the first League members to do so. Through the years, Benoit had several times provided money to fund Philogen's meteoric rise.

"I assume you'll want the loan below international prime."

"Nothing less." He crammed a forkful of stuffed pheasant into his mouth, savoring the tang.

"How much below?"

He heard the skepticism. "Two points."

"Why don't I just give it to you."

"Arthur, I've borrowed millions from you, every dime repaid on time, with interest. So yes, I expect preferential treatment."

"At present, as I understand it, you have several outstanding loans with my banks. Quite sizable."

"Every one of which is current."

He saw that the banker knew that to be true.

"What would be the benefit of such an arrangement?"

Now they were getting somewhere. "How much Philogen stock do you own?"

"A hundred thousand shares. Bought on your recommendation."

He speared another chunk of steaming bird. "You check yesterday's quote?"

"Never bother."

"Sixty-one and a quarter, up a half. It's really a sound investment. I bought nearly five hundred thousand new shares last week myself." He swirled pheasant into some smoked mozzarella stuffing. "In secret, of course."

Benoit's expression signaled that he got the message. "Something big?"

His fellow League member may have been a hotel dabbler, but he still liked to make money. So he shook his head and feigned, "Now, Arthur, insider trading laws forbid me from giving that kind of information. I'm ashamed you'd even ask."

Benoit smiled at the rebuke. "There are no insider trading laws here. Remember, we're writing the laws. So tell me what you're planning."

"Not going to happen." And he stood on his refusal, waiting to see if greed, as usual, would overtake better judgment.

"When would you need the billion—or billion and a half?"

He washed down a mouthful with a swallow of wine. "Sixty days, at the latest."

Benoit seemed to consider the request. "And the length of the loan? Assuming, of course, it's even possible."

"Twenty-four months."

"A billion dollars, with interest, repaid in two years?"

He said nothing. Just chewed, letting the revelation simmer.

"Like I said, your corporation is heavily in debt. This loan would not be viewed favorably by my approval committees."

He finally voiced what the man wanted to hear. "You'll succeed me on the Council of Ten."

Surprise came to Benoit's face. "How would you know that? It's a random selection from the membership."

"You'll come to learn, Arthur, that nothing is random. My time is about up. Your two years will begin shortly."

He knew Benoit desperately wanted to serve on the Council. And he needed friends there. Friends who owed him. So far, four of the five members who would not cycle off were friends. Now he'd just bought one more.

"Okay," Benoit said. "But I'll need a few days to broker out the risk among several of my banks."

He grinned and continued to eat. "You do that. But trust me, Arthur, don't forget to call your broker."

FORTY-FIVE

ZOVASTINA CHECKED HER LOUIS VUITTON WATCH, A GIFT
from the Swedish foreign minister during a state visit a
few years back. He'd been a charming man who'd actually flirted with her. She'd returned the attention even
though little about the diplomat had been stimulating.
The same was true of papal nuncio Colin Michener, who
seemed to delight in irritating her. For the past few minutes she and the monsignor had wandered the basilica's
nave—waiting, she assumed, for the altar preparations
to be completed.

"What brings you to work for the pope?" she asked.
"Once the papal secretary to the last pope, now a mere
nuncio."

"The Holy Father likes to call on me for special projects."

"Like me?"

He nodded. "You're quite special."

"And why is that?"

"You're a head of state. Why else?"

This man was good, like that Swedish diplomat and
his French watch, quick with thoughts and words, but
lacking in answers. She pointed at one of the massive
marble pillars, its base wrapped with a stone bench and
roped off to prevent anyone from sitting. "What are the
black smears?" She'd noticed them on all of the
columns.

"I asked that once myself." Michener pointed. "Centuries of the faithful sitting on the benches, leaning their heads onto the marble. Hair grease absorbed into the stone. Imagine how many millions of heads it took to leave those impressions."

She envied the West such historical nuances. Unfortunately, her homeland had been tormented by invaders who'd each made a point of eliminating all vestiges of what came before them. First Persians, then Greeks, Mongols, Turks, and finally, worst of all, Russians. Here and there a building remained, but nothing like this golden edifice.

They were standing to the left of the high altar, outside the iconostasis, her two guardsmen within shouting distance. Michener pointed down at the mosaic floor. "See the heart-shaped stone?"

She did. Small, unobtrusive, trying to blend with the exuberant designs that swirled around it.

"Nobody knew what that was. Then, about fifty years ago, during a restoration of the floor, the stone was lifted and beneath they found a small box containing a shriveled human heart. It belonged to Doge Francesco Erizzo who died in 1646. I'm told his body lies in the church of San Martino, but he willed his innermost being to be buried close to the patron saint of Venetians." Michener motioned toward the high altar. "St. Mark."

"You know of the *innermost being*?"

"The human heart? Who doesn't? The ancients saw the heart as the seat of wisdom, intelligence, the essence of the person."

Which was precisely why, she reasoned, Ptolemy had used that description. *Touch the innermost being of the golden illusion.*

"Let me show you one other thing," Michener said.

They crossed before the elaborate rood screen rich with squares, rhomboids, and quadrilobes formed in colored marble. Behind the divider, men were on their knees, working beneath the altar table, where a stone sarcophagus sat bathed in light. An iron grating that protected its front, about two meters long and a meter high, was being removed.

Michener noticed her interest and stopped. "In 1835 the altar table was hollowed out and a prominent place made for the saint. There, he's rested. Tonight will be the first time the sarcophagus has been opened since then." The nuncio checked his watch. "Nearly one A.M. They'll be ready for us shortly."

She continued to follow the irritating man to the other side of the basilica, into the dim south transept. Michener stopped before another of the towering marble columns.

"The basilica was destroyed by fire in 976," he said, "then rebuilt and dedicated in 1094. As you mentioned when I was in Samarkand, during those one hundred and eighteen years the whereabouts of St. Mark's corpse became forgotten. Then, during a mass to dedicate the new basilica, on June 26, 1094, a crumbling noise came from this pillar. A flaking of stone. A shaking. First a hand, an arm, then the entire saintly body was revealed. Priests and people crowded around, even the doge himself, and it was widely believed that, with St. Mark's reappearance, all was right with the world again."

She was more amused than impressed. "I've heard that tale. Amazing how the body suddenly reappeared just when the new church, and the doge, needed political and financial support from the Venetians. Their patron saint revealed by a miracle. Quite a show that must have been. I imagine the doge, or some clever minister, stage-managed that entire scene. A brilliant political stunt. It's still being talked about nine hundred years later."

Michener shook his head in amusement. "Such little faith."

"I focus on what's real."

He pointed. "Like Alexander the Great, lying in that tomb?"

His lack of belief bothered her. "And how do you know that it's not? The church has no idea whose body those Venetian merchants stole from Alexandria, over a thousand years ago."

"So tell me, Minister, what makes *you* so sure."

She stared at the marble pillar supporting the grand ceiling overhead and could not resist caressing its sides, wondering if the tale of the saintly body emerging from it was true.

She liked such stories.

So she told the nuncio one of her own.

Eumenes faced a formidable task. As Alexander's personal secretary, he had been entrusted to make sure that the king was entombed beside Hephaestion. Three months had elapsed since the king's death and the mummified body still lay in the palace. Most of the other Companions had long since left Babylon, venturing out to take control of their portion of the empire. Finding a suitable corpse to switch proved a challenge, but a man of Alexander's size, shape, and age was located outside the city, in a village not far away. Eumenes poisoned the man and one of the Egyptian embalmers, who had stayed on the promise of a huge payment, mummified the imposter. Afterward, the Egyptian left the city, but one of Eumenes' two accomplices killed him. The exchange of corpses happened during a summer storm that battered the city with heavy rains. Once wrapped in the golden cartonnage, dressed in golden robes, wearing a crown, no one could distinguish the two bodies.

Eumenes kept Alexander hidden for several months, until after the royal funeral cortege left Babylon, headed for Greece with the imposter. The city then slipped into a lethargy from which it never emerged. Eumenes and his two helpers managed to leave without incident, taking Alexander north, fulfilling the king's final wish.

Michener said, "So the body here may not be Alexander after all?"

"I don't recall that I promised to explain myself."

He smiled. "No, Minister. You didn't. Let me just say that I enjoyed your story."

"As entertaining as your fable of the pillar."

He nodded. "They probably both rank together in credibility."

But she disagreed. Her story had come from a molecular manuscript discovered through X-ray analysis, images that had lingered for centuries beyond the view of a human eye. Only modern technology had managed to reveal them. Hers was not a fable. Alexander the Great was never entombed in Egypt. He was taken somewhere else, a place Ptolemy, the first Greek pharaoh, ultimately discovered. A place to which the mummy in the tomb ten meters away might lead her.

A man appeared at the iconostasis and said to Michener, "We're ready."

The nuncio nodded, then motioned for her to lead the way. "Seems, Minister, it's time to see whose fable is true."

FORTY-SIX

VIKTOR WATCHED AS THE WOMAN CLIMBED THE STEPS to the boat's center deck and kept her gun trained on him.

"How'd you like the fire?" she asked.

He threw the throttle into neutral and moved toward her. "You stupid bitch, I'll show you—"

She raised the pistol. "Do it. Go ahead."

The eyes that glared back at him were full of hate. "You murder with ease."

"So do you."

"And who did I kill?"

"Maybe it was you. Maybe someone else from your Sacred Band. Two months ago. In Samarkand. Ely Lund. His house burned to the ground, thanks to your Greek fire."

He recalled the task. One he'd personally handled for Zovastina. "You're the woman from Copenhagen. I saw you at the museum, then at the house."

"When you tried to kill us."

"Seems you and your two friends invited that challenge."

"What do you know about Ely's death? You're the head of Zovastina's Sacred Band."

"How do you know that?" Then it occurred to him. "The coin I examined in that house. Fingerprints."

"Smart guy."

Her mind seemed to be struggling with some painful

conviction, so he decided to stoke her emotional furnace. "Ely was murdered."

"Your doing?"

He noticed a bow and a zippered quiver of arrows slung over her shoulder. She'd shown how cold her heart beat when she barred the museum doors and used the arrows to ignite the building. So he decided not to push her too far.

"I was there."

"Why did Zovastina want him dead?"

The boat rocked in the unseen swells and he could feel them drifting with the wind. The only illumination came from the faint glow of the instrument panel.

"You, your friends, the man Ely, all of you are involved with things that don't concern you."

"I'd say you're the one who needs to be concerned. I came to kill you both. One down. One to go."

"And what will you gain?"

"The pleasure of seeing you die."

Her gun came level.

And fired.

MALONE BROUGHT THE THROTTLE TO NEUTRAL. "YOU hear that?"

Stephanie, too, was alert. "Sounded like a gunshot. Nearby."

He stuck his head beyond the windscreen and noted that the fire on Torcello, about a mile away, burned with new vigor. The mist had lifted, weather here apparently came in quick waves, the visibility now relatively reasonable. Boat lights crisscrossed paths in all directions.

His ears searched for sound.

Nothing.

He powered up the engines.

Cassiopeia aimed at the bulkhead, sending the bullet within inches of Viktor's leg. "Ely never hurt a soul. Why did she have to kill him?" She kept the gun trained on him. "Tell me. Why?" The question came out one word at a time, through clenched teeth, more pleading than angry.

"Zovastina is a woman on a mission. Your Ely interfered."

"He was a historian. How could he have been a threat?" She hated herself for referring to him in the past tense.

Water lapped against the low-riding hull and the wind continued to batter the boat.

"You'd be surprised how easily she kills people."

His avoidance of her questions only compounded her rage. "Man the damn wheel." She watched him from the opposite side of the helm. "Move us ahead, nice and slow."

"Where to?"

"San Marco."

He turned and engaged the throttle, then suddenly spun the boat hard left, twisting the deck beneath her feet. In the moment of surprise where maintaining her balance overrode her desire to shoot, he lunged toward her.

Viktor knew he had to kill this woman. She represented failure on a multitude of levels—enough that, if she was discovered, Zovastina would lose all confidence in him.

Not to mention what happened to Rafael.

His left hand gripped the top of the rear cabin door

and he used the wooden panel to swing his body off the twisting deck, crashing his boots into the woman's arms.

She deflected his blow and fell forward.

The cockpit was a couple of meters square. Two openings on either side provided access off the boat. Engines whined as the boat, without a pilot, fought the swells. Spray crashed over the windscreen. The woman still held the gun, but was having trouble regaining her balance.

He jabbed and caught her on the jaw with the heel of his open palm. Her neck whipped back, banging her head into something. He used the moment of her confusion to spin the wheel again and decrease power. He was concerned about the shifting shoals and clinging grasses. Torcello loomed to his left, the burning museum illuminating the night. The boat twirled in the rough water and the woman grabbed for her skull.

He decided to let nature handle things.

And kicked her into the sea.

FORTY-SEVEN

ZOVASTINA STEPPED THROUGH THE ICONOSTASIS INTO the presbytery and stared at the basilica's magnificent baldachin. Four alabaster columns, each adorned with elaborate reliefs, supported a massive block of verde green marble carved into intersecting vaults. Behind, framed by the baldachin, glittered the famous Pala d'Oro, the screen rich with gold, precious stones, and enamel.

Beneath the altar, she studied the two distinct parts of the stone sarcophagus. The misshapen top was more a slab—the bottom carved smooth into a rectangle upon which was etched CORPVS DIVI MARCI EVANGELISTAE. Her Latin was enough for a rough translation. Body of the divine St. Mark. Two heavy iron rings protruded from the top, which apparently was how the massive stones had been initially lowered into place. Now, thick iron bars pierced the rings, bolted at each end to four hydraulic jacks.

"This is a real challenge," Michener said. "Not much space beneath the altar. Of course, with heavy equipment we could easily get inside, but we don't have the time or privacy for that."

She noticed the men preparing the jacks. "Priests?"

He nodded. "Assigned here. We thought it best to keep this among us."

"Do you know what's inside?" she asked.

"What you're really asking is whether the remains are

mummified." Michener shrugged. "It's been over one hundred and seventy years since this tomb was opened. No one really knows what's in there."

She resented his smugness. Ptolemy had taken advantage of Eumenes' switch, and used what the world believed to be Alexander's corpse to its fullest political potential. She had no way of knowing if what she was about to see would provide any answers, but it was imperative she find out.

Michener motioned to one of the priests and the hydraulic jacks were cranked. The iron rings atop the tomb stretched vertically, then, ever so slowly, a millimeter at a time, the jacks lifted the weighty lid.

"Powerful mechanisms," Michener said. "Small, but they can lift a house from underneath."

The lid was now two centimeters skyward, but the interior of the sarcophagus remained in shadow. She stared high above the baldachin, into the apse's brightly lit semidome, at a golden mosaic of Christ.

The four men stopped working the jacks.

The sarcophagus lid hung suspended about four centimeters above the bottom, the iron bars now flush with the underside of the altar top.

No more room to climb.

Michener gestured for them to retreat toward the iconostasis, away from the altar, where he whispered, "The Holy Father is trying to accommodate your request with the hope that you'll reciprocate his. But let's be real. You're not going to honor your promise."

"I'm not accustomed to being insulted."

"And the Holy Father is not accustomed to being lied to."

All pretense seemed to have left this diplomat. "You'll be given access to the Federation, as I assured."

"We want more."

Now she realized. He'd waited until the lid was off.

She hated herself, but because of Karyn, and Alexander the Great, and what may be out there, somewhere, to find, she had no choice.

"What do you want?"

He reached beneath his jacket and removed a folded sheaf of papers. "We've prepared a concordat between the Federation and the Church. Written assurances that we'll be given access. Per your request of yesterday, we've reserved the right to the Federation on approval of any church construction."

She unfolded the papers and saw the text had even been prepared in Kazakh.

"We thought it easier to have it in your language."

"You thought it would be easier to disseminate in my language. My signature is your insurance. No way I could deny you then."

She glanced through the concordat. The language detailed a cooperative effort between the Roman Church and the Central Asia Federation to "jointly promote and encourage the free exercise of religion through unrestricted allowance of missionary work." The paragraphs went on to assure that violence against the Church would not be tolerated and offenders would be punished. More provisions guaranteed that visas would be liberally granted to Church personnel and no reprisals would be tolerated against any converts.

She stared back at the altar. The lower half of the sarcophagus remained in shadow. Even from ten meters away she could see nothing inside.

"You'd be a good one to have on my team," she said.

"I like serving the Church."

She glanced at her watch—12:50 A.M. Viktor should already be here. He was never late. So dependable. She stared out into the nave, back toward the upper portions of the west atrium where only the golden ceilings were illuminated. Lots of dark places to hide. She wondered, when one A.M. came and she was granted her thirty minutes, if she'd really be alone.

"If signing the concordat is a problem," Michener said, "we could just forget the whole thing."

Her words from yesterday when she'd challenged him.

She called his bluff.

"You have a pen?"

FORTY-EIGHT

MALONE SPOTTED A PAIR OF RED RUNNING LIGHTS A quarter mile away, flitting erratically across the black water, as if the boat was without a pilot.

"You see that out there?" he asked Stephanie, pointing.

She stood on the other side of the helm. "It's beyond the marked channel."

He'd thought the same thing. He kept the boat churning forward. They were closer now to the drifting craft, maybe a couple hundred yards off. No question, the other boat, about the same shape and size as his, was near the shallows. Then, in the ambient glow from its helm, he saw someone plunge into the water.

Another figure appeared and three shots banged in the night.

"Cotton," Stephanie said.

"Already on it."

He whirled the wheel left and headed straight for the lights. The other boat seemed to spring to life and motored away. He cut a swath through the water and sent swells heading toward the other low-riding craft. Water slashed into the hull. Malone was still fifty feet away, the other craft passing them now. The shadowy outline of its pilot appeared at the helm, a gun at the end of an outstretched arm.

"Down," he screamed to Stephanie.

She'd apparently spotted the danger, too, and was already leaping to the wet deck. He dove with her as two bullets whizzed past, one shattering a window in the aft cabin.

He sprang to his feet and regained control of the helm. The other boat was speeding away toward Venice. He needed to pursue, but now wondered about the person in the water.

"Find a flashlight," he said, as he slowed the boat and maneuvered toward the spot where they'd initially seen the other vessel.

Stephanie scampered into the forward cabin and he heard her rummaging through the compartments. She reappeared with a light in hand.

He shifted the throttle to idle.

Stephanie raked the water with the flashlight's beam. He heard sirens in the distance and spotted three boats with flashing emergency lights rounding the shore of one of the islands, heading for Torcello.

Busy night for the Italian police.

"See anything?" he asked. "Somebody hit the water."

And he had to be careful not to plow over them, but that was going to be difficult in the pitch darkness.

"There," Stephanie hollered.

He rushed to her side and spotted a figure struggling. Only a second was needed for him to know that it was Cassiopeia. Before he could react, Stephanie tossed the flashlight aside and leaped into the water.

He bolted back to the helm and maneuvered the boat.

He returned to the other side of the deck just as Stephanie and Cassiopeia waded close. He reached down and grabbed hold of Cassiopeia, yanking her out of the water.

He laid her limp body on the deck.

She was unconscious.

A stringed bow and arrow quiver were strapped to

her shoulder. Certainly a story unto itself, he thought. He rolled Cassiopeia onto her side. "Cough it all out."

She seemed to ignore him.

He popped her on the back. "Cough."

She started to spit out water, gagging on each exhale, but at least she was breathing.

Stephanie climbed out of the lagoon.

"She's woozy. But she wasn't hit by any bullets."

"Tough shot in the dark from a wobbly deck."

He kept lightly pounding her spine and more water sprayed from her lungs. She seemed to be coming around.

"You all right?" he asked.

Her eyes seemed to reacquire their focus. He knew the look. She'd been popped on the head.

"Cotton?" she asked.

"I guess it would be pointless to ask why you have a bow and arrows?"

She rubbed her head. "That piece of—"

"Who was he?" Stephanie asked.

"Stephanie? What are you doing here?" Cassiopeia reached out and touched Stephanie's wet clothes. "You pulled me out?"

"I owed you that one."

Malone had only been told some of what had happened last fall in Washington while he was under siege in the Sinai, but apparently these two had bonded. At the moment, though, he needed to know, "How many are dead inside the Museo di Torcello?"

Cassiopeia ignored him and reached back, searching for something. Her hand reappeared with a Glock. She shook the water from it, drying the barrel. Great selling point about Glocks, which he knew from firsthand experience—the damn things were nearly waterproof.

She rose to her feet. "We need to go."

"Was that Viktor in the boat with you?" he asked, irritation now in his voice.

But Cassiopeia had recovered her wits and he saw anger again in her eyes. "I told you earlier this doesn't concern you. Not your fight."

"Yeah, right. There's all kinds of crap swirling here that you don't know a thing about."

"I know the bastards in Asia killed Ely, on orders of Irina Zovastina."

"Who's Ely?" Stephanie asked.

"Long story," he said. "One that's causing us a lot of problems at the moment."

Cassiopeia continued to shake the fog from her brain and water from her gun. "We need to go."

"You kill anybody?" he asked.

"Roasted one of them like a marshmallow."

"You'll regret that later."

"Thanks for the counseling. Let's go."

He decided to delay her and tried, "Where was Viktor headed?"

She swung the bow off her shoulder.

"Henrik sent you that thing?" he asked, recalling the cloth bag from the restaurant.

"Like I said, Cotton, this isn't your affair."

Stephanie stepped forward. "Cassiopeia. I don't know half of what's happening here, but I know enough to see that you're not thinking. Like you told me last fall, use your head. Let us help. What happened?"

"You, too, Stephanie. Back off. I've been waiting for these men for months. Finally, tonight, I had them in my sights. I got one. I want the other. And yes, it's Viktor. He was there when Ely died. They burned him to death. For what?" Her voice had steadily risen. "I want to know why he died."

"Then let's find out," Malone said.

Cassiopeia paced with an unsteady gait. At the moment she was trapped, nowhere to go, and she was apparently smart enough to know that neither of them was going to back off. She rested the palms of her hands on the deck rail and gathered her breath. Finally, she said, "Okay. Okay. You're right."

He wondered if they were being placated.

Cassiopeia stood still. "This one's personal. More than either of you realize." She hesitated. "It's more than Ely."

That was the second time she'd insinuated as much. "How about you tell us what's at stake?"

"How about I don't."

He wanted desperately to help her and arguing seemed pointless. So he glanced at Stephanie, who knew what his eyes were asking.

She nodded her approval.

He stepped toward the helm and powered up the engines. More police cruisers passed, heading for Torcello. He aimed the boat for Venice and the distant lights of Viktor's retreating craft.

"Don't worry about a corpse," Cassiopeia said. "There'll be nothing left of the body or that museum."

He wanted to know something. "Stephanie, any word on Naomi?"

"Nothing since yesterday. That's why I came."

"Who's Naomi?" Cassiopeia asked.

"That's *my* business," he said.

Cassiopeia did not challenge him. Instead she said, "Where are we going?"

He glanced at his watch. The luminous dial read 12:45 A.M. "Like I told you. Lots going on here, and we know exactly where Viktor's headed."

FORTY-NINE

VINCENTI'S SPINE TINGLED. TRUE, HE'D ORDERED PEO-
ple killed, one just yesterday, but this was different. He
was about to embark on a bold path. One that would
not only make him the wealthiest person on the planet,
but also secure him a place in history.

Dawn lay a little over an hour away. He sat in the rear
of the car while O'Conner and two other men approached a house shielded behind a thicket of blooming
chestnut trees and a tall iron fence, everything owned by
Irina Zovastina.

O'Conner drew near to the car and Vincenti lowered
the window.

"The two guards are dead. We took them out with no
trouble."

"Any other security?"

"That's it. Zovastina had this place on a loose leash."
Because she thought no one cared. "Are we ready?"

"Only the woman who watches over her is inside."

"Then let's see how agreeable they are."

Vincenti entered through the front door. The two
other men they'd hired for tonight held Karyn Walde's
nurse, an older woman with a stern face, wearing a
bathrobe and slippers. A frightened look filled her Asian
features.

"I understand," he said to her, "that you care for Ms. Walde."

The woman nodded.

"And that you resent how the Supreme Minister treats her."

"She's terrible to her."

He was pleased their intelligence had been accurate. "I understand that Karyn is suffering. Her illness is progressing."

"And the minister won't let her rest."

He signaled and the two men released their hold. He stepped close and said, "I'm here to relieve her suffering. But I need your help."

Her gaze carried suspicion. "Where are the guards?"

"Dead. Wait here while I go see her." He motioned. "Down the hall?"

She nodded again.

He switched on one of the bedside lamps and gazed at the pathetic sight lying prone beneath a pale pink comforter.

Karyn Walde breathed with the help of bottled oxygen and a respirator. An intravenous bag fed one arm. He removed a hypodermic, inserted the needle into one of its IV ports, and let it dangle.

The woman's eyes opened.

"You need to wake up," he said.

She blinked a few times, trying to register what was happening. She then pushed herself up from the pillow. "Who are you?"

"I know they've been in short supply lately, but I'm a friend."

"Do I know you?"

He shook his head. "No reason why you would. But I know you. Tell me, what was it like to love Irina Zovastina?"

Surely an odd question from a stranger in the middle of the night, but she only shrugged. "Why would you care?"

"I've dealt with her many years. Never once have I ever felt any affection either from or toward her. How did you?"

"It's a question I've asked myself many times."

He glanced around at the room's decor. Elegant and expensive, like the rest of the house. "You live well."

"Small comfort."

"Yet when you became ill, knew you were HIV positive, you returned to her. Came back after several years of estrangement."

"You know a lot about me."

"To come back you must have felt something for her."

She laid herself back on the pillow. "In some ways, she's foolish."

He listened closely.

"She fashions herself Achilles to my Patroclus. Or worse, she's Alexander and thinks of me as Hephaestion. I've listened to those stories many times. You know the *Iliad*?"

He shook his head.

"Achilles felt responsible for Patroclus' death. He allowed his lover to lead men into battle, pretending to be him. Alexander the Great felt great guilt over Hephaestion dying."

"You know your literature and history."

"I don't know a thing. I've just listened to her ramble."

"How is she foolish?"

"She wants to save me, yet can't bring herself to say it. She comes, stares at me, chastises me, even attacks me, but always she's trying to save me. When it came to me I knew she was weak, so I returned to where I knew I'd be looked after."

"Yet you obviously hate her."

"I assure you, whoever you are, that someone in my shoes has little choice."

"You speak freely to a stranger."

"I have nothing to hide or fear. My life's about over."

"You've given up?"

"Like I have a choice."

He decided to see what else he could learn. "Zovastina is in Venice. Right now. Searching for something. Are you aware of that?"

"It doesn't surprise me. She's the great hero, on the great hero's quest. I'm the weak lover. We're not to ask or challenge the hero, just accept what's offered."

"You have listened to a lot of nonsense."

She shrugged. "She imagines herself my savior, so I allow it. Why not? Besides, tormenting her is my only pleasure. Life's choices and all that bullshit."

"Sometimes life is fickle."

He could see that she was intrigued.

"Where are the guards?"

"Dead."

"And my nurse?"

"She's fine. I believe she actually cares for you."

A slight nod. "She does."

In her prime this woman would have been formidable—able to seduce both men and women—easy to see how Zovastina would have been attracted to her. But it was also easy to see how the two women would have clashed. Both alpha-females. Both accustomed to having their way.

"I've been watching you for some time," he told her.

"There's not much to see."

"Tell me, if you could have anything in this world, what would it be?"

The gravely ill soul lying before him seemed to seriously consider his inquiry. He saw the words as they formed in her mind. He'd seen the same resolution before, in others long ago, facing similar dire consequences, clinging to little or no hope since neither science nor religion could save them.

Only a miracle.

So when she drew a breath and mouthed her answer, he was not disappointed.

"To live."

FIFTY

VIKTOR HUSTLED PAST THE BASILICA'S BRIGHTLY LIT western facade. High above, St. Mark himself stood guard in the black night above a golden lion with outstretched wings. The heart of the piazza spanned to his left, cordoned off, a multitude of police swarming the broad pavement. A crowd had gathered and he'd overheard from snippets of conversation that a shooting had occurred. He skirted the spectacle and headed for the church's north entrance, the one Zovastina had told him to use.

He was unnerved by the appearance of the woman with the bow. She should have been dead in Denmark. And if *she* wasn't dead, the other two problems were surely also still breathing. Things were gyrating out of control. He should have stayed and made sure she drowned in the lagoon, but Zovastina was waiting and he could not be late.

He kept seeing Rafael die.

Zovastina would not care beyond wanting to know if the death raised any suspicion. But how could it? There'd be no body to find. Just bone fragments and ashes.

Like when Ely Lund's house burned.

"You're going to kill me?" Ely asked. *"What have I done?"* The intruder brandished a gun. *"How can I be a threat to anyone?"*

Viktor stood out of sight, in an adjacent room, and listened.

"Why don't you answer me?" Ely asked, his voice rising.

"I'm not here to talk," the man said.

"Just here to shoot me?"

"I do as I'm ordered."

"And you have no idea why?"

"I don't care."

Silence filled the room.

"I wish I could have done a few more things," Ely finally said. The tone was melancholy, full of resignation, surprisingly calm. "I always thought my illness would kill me."

Viktor listened with a renewed interest.

"You are infected?" the stranger asked, some suspicion in his voice. "You don't look sick."

"No reason I should. But it's still there."

Viktor heard the distinctive click of a gun slide.

He'd stood outside and watched the house burn. Samarkand's meager fire department had done little. Eventually, the walls collapsed onto themselves and Greek fire consumed everything.

Now he knew something else.

The woman from Copenhagen had cared enough for Ely Lund to avenge his death.

He rounded the basilica and spotted the north portal. A man waited inside the open bronze doors.

Viktor grabbed his composure.

The Supreme Minister would want him focused and controlled.

ZOVASTINA HANDED THE SIGNED CONCORDAT BACK TO Michener. "Now leave me be for my thirty minutes."

The papal nuncio motioned and all the priests withdrew from the presbytery.

"You'll regret pressuring me," she made clear.

"You might find the Holy Father tough to challenge."

"How many armies does your pope have?"

"Many have asked that question. But armies weren't needed to bring communism to its knees. John Paul II did just fine, all by himself."

"And your pope is equally astute?"

"Cross him and you'll find out."

Michener walked away, passing through the iconostasis into the nave, disappearing toward the basilica's main entrance. "I'll be back in a half hour," he called out through the darkness.

She saw Viktor advancing through the dimness. He passed Michener, who acknowledged him with a nod. Her two other guardsmen stood off to the side.

Viktor entered the presbytery. His clothes were damp and dingy, his face smoke-streaked.

All she wanted to know was, "Do you have it?"

He handed her an elephant medallion.

"What do you think?" she asked.

"Looks authentic, but I haven't had a chance to test it."

She pocketed the coin. Later.

The open sarcophagus waited ten meters away.

That's what mattered now.

MALONE WAS THE LAST TO HOP FROM THE BOAT ONTO the concrete quay. They were back downtown, in San Marco, where the famous square ended at the lagoon. Ripples slapped moving poles and jostled gondolas tied to the docks. Still lots of police around and a multitude more spectators than an hour ago.

Stephanie motioned toward Cassiopeia, who was already shouldering through a crowded row of street vendors, toward the basilica, the bow and quiver still draped across her shoulder. "Pocahontas there needs a leash."

"Mr. Malone."

Through the crowd, he spotted a man in his late forties dressed in chinos, a long-sleeve shirt, and a cotton jacket walking their way. Cassiopeia seemed to have heard the greeting, too, as she'd stopped her advance and was headed toward where Malone and Stephanie stood.

"I'm Monsignor Colin Michener," the man said as he approached.

"You don't look like a priest."

"Not tonight. But I was told to expect you, and I must say the description they gave was dead on. Tall, light-haired, with another, older woman in tow."

"Excuse me," Stephanie said.

Michener grinned. "I was told you're sensitive about your age."

"And who told you that?" Malone wanted to know.

"Edwin Davis," Stephanie said. "He mentioned he had an impeccable source. You, I assume?"

"I've known Edwin a long time."

Cassiopeia pointed at the church. "Did another man go inside that basilica? Short, stocky, dressed in jeans?"

The priest nodded. "He's there. With Minister Zovastina. His name is Viktor Tomas, the head of Zovastina's personal guard."

"You're well-informed," Malone said.

"I'd say Edwin is the one in the know. But he couldn't tell me one thing. How did you get that name? Cotton."

"Long story. Right now we need to get inside the basilica. And I'm sure you know why."

Michener motioned and they retreated behind one of the street vendors, out of the pedestrian flow. "Yesterday we came across some information on Minister Zovastina that we passed on to Washington. She wanted a peek inside St. Mark's tomb, so the Holy Father thought America might like a look at the same time."

"Can we go?" Cassiopeia asked.

"You're a nervous one, aren't you?" Michener said.

"I just want to go."

"You're carrying a bow and arrows."

"Can't fool you."

Michener ignored her quip and faced Malone. "Is this going to get out of hand?"

"No more than it already has."

Michener motioned off toward the square. "Like the man killed here earlier."

"And there's a museum burning on Torcello," Malone added, as he felt his cell phone vibrate.

He fished the unit from his pocket, checked the display—Henrik, again—and answered. "Sending her a bow and arrows was not smart."

"I had no choice," Thorvaldsen said through the phone. "I must speak with her. Is she with you?"

"Oh, yes."

He handed the phone to Cassiopeia and she walked away.

CASSIOPEIA HELD THE PHONE CLOSE, HER HAND TREMBLING.

"Listen well," Thorvaldsen said in her ear. "There are things you must know."

"THIS IS CHAOS," MALONE SAID TO STEPHANIE.

"And getting worse by the moment."

He watched Cassiopeia, her back to them, phone held close.

"She's messed up," he made clear.

"A state, I believe, we've all experienced."

He smiled at that truth.

Cassiopeia ended the call and walked back, handing him the phone.

"You have your marching orders?" he asked.

"Something like that."

He faced Michener. "You can see what I have to work with, so I hope *you're* going to tell me something productive."

"Zovastina and Viktor are in the basilica's presbytery."

"Works for me."

"But I need to speak with you privately," Michener said to Stephanie. "Information Edwin asked me to pass along."

"I'd rather go with them."

"He said it was critical."

"Do it," Malone said. "We'll handle things inside."

ZOVASTINA APPROACHED THE ALTAR TABLE AND BENT down.

One of the priests had left a light bar on the floor. She motioned for Viktor to kneel beside her. "Send the other two out into the church. Tell them to wander, especially upstairs. I want to make sure we have no watching eyes."

Viktor dispatched the guards, then returned.

She lifted the light bar and, with breath held, illuminated the interior of the stone sarcophagus. She'd imagined this moment ever since Ely Lund had first told her of the possibility. Was this the imposter? Could Ptolemy have left a clue that would lead to where Alexander the Great rested? That place far away, *in the mountains, where the Scythians taught Alexander about life.* Life in the form of the draught. She recalled what Alexander's court historian had written in one of the manuscripts Ely discovered. *The man's neck had swollen with lumps so bad he could hardly swallow, as if pebbles filled his throat, and fluid spewed forth from his mouth with each exhale. Lesions covered his body. No strength remained within any of his muscles. Each breath was a labor.* Yet in one day the draught cured him. The scientists at her biological lab believed the symptoms were viral. Was it possible that nature, which created so many assailants, had also spawned a way to stop them?

But no mummified remains lay within the stone coffin.

Instead, she saw a thin wooden box, half a meter square, richly decorated, with two brass handles. Disappointment squeezed her stomach. She instantly masked that emotion and ordered, "Remove it."

Viktor reached beneath the dangling stone lid, lifted out the ornate receptacle, and laid it on the marble pavement.

What had she expected? Any mummy would have been at least two thousand years old. True, Egyptian embalmers knew their craft and mummies that old and older had survived intact. But those had sat undisturbed in their tombs for centuries, not indiscriminately carted across the globe, disappearing for hundreds of years at a time. Ely Lund had been convinced that Ptolemy's riddle was authentic. He'd been equally convinced that the Venetians, in 828, left Alexandria not with St. Mark, but with the remains of another, perhaps even the body that had rested in the Soma for six hundred years, revered and worshipped by all as Alexander the Great.

"Open it."

Viktor released the hasps and removed the lid. The inside was lined with faded red velvet. More of the brittle cloth lay puffed within. She carefully removed it and spied teeth, a shoulder blade, a thigh bone, part of a skull, and ash.

She closed her eyes.

"What did you expect?" a new voice asked.

FIFTY-ONE

VINCENTI CONSIDERED KARYN WALDE'S ANSWER TO HIS question and asked, "What would you be willing to do to have your life?"

"There's little I can do. Look at me. And I don't even know your name."

This woman had spent a lifetime manipulating and, even now, she was still capable.

"Enrico Vincenti."

"Italian? You don't look it."

"I liked the name."

She grinned. "I have a feeling, Enrico Vincenti, that you and I are a lot alike."

He agreed. He was a man of two names, many interests, but one ambition. "What do you know about HIV?"

"Only that it's killing me."

"Did you know it has existed for millions of years? Which is incredible, considering it's not even alive. Just ribonucleic acid—RNA—surrounded by a protective protein coat."

"You're some kind of scientist?"

"As a matter of fact, I am. Did you know HIV has no cell structure? It can't produce a single speck of energy. The only characteristic of a living organism it ever displays is the ability to reproduce. But even that requires genetic material from a host."

"Like me?"

"I'm afraid so. There are roughly a thousand viruses we know of. New ones, though, are found every day. Roughly half dwell in plants, the rest in animals. HIV is an animal dweller, but superbly unique."

He saw the puzzled look on her wizened face. "Don't you want to know what's killing you?"

"Does it matter?"

"Actually, it could matter a great deal."

"Then, my new friend, who's here for who knows what, please continue."

He appreciated her attitude. "HIV is special because it can replace another cell's genetic makeup with its own. That's why it's called a retrovirus. It latches onto the cell and changes it into a duplicate of itself. It's a burglar that robs another cell of its identity." He paused and let the metaphor take hold. "Two hundred thousand HIV cells clumped together would scarcely be visible to the naked eye. It's super resilient, almost indestructible, but it needs a precise mixture of protein, salts, sugars, and, most critical, the exact pH to live. Too much of one, too little of another and"—he snapped his fingers—"it dies."

"I assume that's where I come in?"

"Oh, yes. Warm-blooded mammals. Their bodies are perfect for HIV. Brain tissue, cerebrospinal fluid, bone marrow, breast milk, cervical cells, seminal fluid, mucous membranes, vaginal secretions—they can all harbor it. Blood and lymph, though, are its favorite haunts. Like you, Ms. Walde"—he pointed—"the virus simply wants to survive."

He glanced at the clock on the bedside table. O'Conner and the other two men were standing guard outside. He'd chosen to have his talk here since no one would bother them. Kamil Revin had told him that the guards on the house changed by the week. None of the Sacred Band enjoyed the duty, so, unless it was their turn, no one paid the location much attention. Just another of Zovastina's many obsessions.

"Here's the interesting thing," he said. "HIV shouldn't even be able to live inside you. Too many infection-fighting cells roaming in your blood. But it adopted a refined form of microscopic guerrilla warfare, playing hide-and-seek with your white blood cells. It learned to secrete itself away in a place where they would never even consider looking."

He let the moment dangle, then said, "Lymph nodes. Pea-size nodules scattered throughout the body. They act as filters, trapping unsuspecting intruders so the white cells can destroy them. The nodes are the lion's den of your immune system, the last place a retrovirus should use as a hiding place, but they proved the perfect location. Quite amazing, really. HIV learned to duplicate the protein coating the immune system naturally produces within the lymph nodes. So, undetected, right under the nose of the immune system, it patiently lives, converting lymph nodes' cells from infection-fighting enemies to duplicates of itself. For years it does this, until the nodes swell, then deteriorate, and the blood-stream is flooded with HIV. Which explains why it takes such a long time from actual infection to know the virus is in your blood."

His mind flashed with the analytical thinking of the scientist he was for many years. Now, though, he was a global entrepreneur, a manipulator, much like Karyn Walde, about to perform the greatest manipulation of all.

"And do you know what's even more amazing?" he asked. "Each replication of a cell by HIV is individual. So when the lymph nodes collapse, instead of one invader, there are billions of different invaders, an army of variant retrovirus strains, running unchecked through your blood. Your immune system reacts, like it's supposed to, but it's forced to generate new and different white cells to battle each strain. Which is impossible. And to make matters worse, all of the variant strains of the retrovirus can destroy any of the white cells. The odds are billions against one, the results all but inevitable—of which you are living proof."

"Surely, you came for more than a science lesson."

"I came to see if you wanted to live."

"Unless you're an angel or God himself, that's impossible."

"Now, you see, that's the thing. HIV can't kill anybody. But it does render you defenseless when another virus, bacteria, fungus, or parasite enters your bloodstream in search of a home. Not enough white blood cells to cleanse the stream. So the only question is which infection will be the cause of your death?"

"How about you screw off and leave me to die."

Karyn Walde was indeed a bitter woman, but talking to her had stirred his dreams. He imagined himself addressing the press, reporters hanging on his every word, becoming, overnight, a worldwide recognized authority. He envisioned book deals, movie rights, television specials, speaking engagements, awards. Certainly the Albert Lasker Prize. The National Medal for Science. Perhaps even a Nobel Prize. Why not?

But all that hinged on the decision he was about to make.

He stared down at the shell of a human being. Only her eyes seemed alive.

He reached for the hypodermic protruding from the IV port.

"What is that?" she asked, noting the clear liquid the syringe contained.

He did not answer her.

"What are you doing?"

He gripped the plunger and emptied the contents into the IV stream.

She tried to lift herself, but the effort proved futile. She collapsed back to the bed, her pupils wild. He watched as her eyelids acquired weight, then her breathing slowed. She went limp. Her eyes closed.

And did not open.

FIFTY-TWO

ZOVASTINA ROSE AND FACED THE INTRUDER. HE WAS short, with a crooked spine, bushy hair and eyebrows, and spoke in a brittle voice of maturity. His crinkly features, gaunt cheeks, coarsened hair, and veined hands all belonged to age.

"Who are you?" she asked.

"Henrik Thorvaldsen."

She knew the name. One of the wealthiest men in Europe. A Dane. But what was he doing here?

Viktor instantly reacted to the visitor, pointing his weapon. She reached over and restrained him, her eyes saying, *Let's see what he wants.*

"I know of you."

"And I of you. Risen from Soviet bureaucrat to a forger of nations. Quite an achievement."

She wasn't in the mood for compliments. "What are you doing here?"

The older man shuffled close to the wooden box. "Did you really think Alexander the Great was in there?"

This man knew her business.

"*And you, adventurer, for my immortal voice, though far off, fills your ears, hear my words. Sail onto the capital founded by Alexander's father, where sages stand guard. Touch the innermost being of the golden illusion.*

Divide the phoenix. Life provides the measure of the grave. Be wary, for there is but one chance of success."

She fought to conceal her shock at Thorvaldsen's recitation.

This man truly did know her business.

"Do you think you're the only one who knows?" he asked. "How pompous are you?"

She grabbed Viktor's gun and leveled the barrel at Thorvaldsen. "Enough to shoot you."

MALONE WAS CONCERNED. HE AND CASSIOPEIA WERE fifty feet up and three quarters of a football field away from where Thorvaldsen was challenging Irina Zovastina while Viktor watched. Michener had brought them into the basilica via the west atrium and led them to a steep stairway. At its top, the walls, arches, and domes reflected the architecture below, but instead of a stunning marble facade and glinting mosaics, the basilica's upper-story museum and gift shop were encased only by brick walls.

"What the hell is he doing here?" Malone muttered. "He just called you outside."

They were huddled behind a stone balustrade, beyond which was a panoramic view of the towering vaulted domes, each resting on massive marble pillars. Golden ceiling mosaics shimmered from incandescent lamps— the marble floor and unlit side chapels cast in varying shades of black and gray. The presbytery, at the far end, where Thorvaldsen stood, loomed like a bright stage in a dark theater.

"You're not going to answer me?"

Cassiopeia stayed silent.

"You two are about to piss me off."

"I told you to go home."

"Henrik may have bit off more than he can chew."

"She's not going to shoot him. At least not until she knows why he's here."

"And why is he here?"

More silence.

They needed to shift position. "How about we move over there." He pointed left to the north transept and another gallery that overlooked the presbytery. "This museum winds around that way. We'll be closer and can hear."

She motioned right. "I'll go that way. There's surely an opening to the upper south transept from here. That way we'll be on either side."

VIKTOR'S HEART RACED. FIRST THE WOMAN, NOW THE supposed museum owner. Surely the second man was also alive. And probably nearby. Yet he noticed Thorvaldsen paid him no mind.

Not a hint of recognition.

ZOVASTINA STARED DOWN THE GUN'S SIGHTS AT THORvaldsen.

"I realize you're a pagan," the Dane calmly said. "But would you shoot me, here, on the altar of a Christian church?"

"How do you know Ptolemy's riddle?"

"Ely told me."

She lowered the weapon and appraised her intruder. "How did you know him?"

"He and my son were close. Ever since they were children."

"Why are you here?"

"Why is it important to find the tomb of Alexander the Great?"

"Is there any reason I would discuss that with you?"

"Let's see if I can provide you with some. At present you possess nearly thirty zoonoses that you've harvested from a variety of exotic animals, many of which you stole from zoos and other private collections. You have at least two biological weapons laboratories at your disposal, one operated by your government, the other by Philogen Pharmaceutique, a corporation controlled by a man named Enrico Vincenti. Both of you are also members of the Venetian League. Am I making any progress?"

"You're still breathing, aren't you?"

Thorvaldsen smiled in seeming satisfaction. "For which I'm grateful. You also have a formidable military. Nearly a million troops. One hundred and thirty fighter jets. Various transports and support aircraft, adequate bases, an excellent communications network—everything an ambitious despot would need."

She didn't like that Viktor was listening, but she desperately needed to hear more, so she turned to him and said, "Find out what the other two guards are doing, and make sure we're alone."

THE OTHER TWO?

Malone heard the words as he assumed a position behind another stone railing, this one high above the presbytery, less than a hundred fifty feet above Thorvaldsen and Zovastina. Cassiopeia was fifty yards across the nave, in the south transept, with an equally high perch.

He couldn't see her, but he hoped she'd heard.

ZOVASTINA WAITED UNTIL VIKTOR LEFT, THEN GLARED at Thorvaldsen. "Is there a problem with wanting to defend my nation?"

"Beware the toils of war. Soon they'll raze your sturdy citadel to the roots."

"What Sarpedon said to Hector in the *Iliad*. You have studied me. Let me offer a quotation. *Nor do I think you'll find us short on courage, long as our strength will last.*"

"You're not planning on defending anything. You're preparing an attack. Those zoonoses are offensive. Iran, Afghanistan, Pakistan, India. Only one man ever conquered them. Alexander the Great. And he could only hold the land for just a handful of years. Ever since, conquerors have tried and failed. Even the Americans attempted with Iraq. But you, Supreme Minister, you intend to best them all."

She possessed a leak—a massive one. She needed to return home and resolve that problem.

"You want to do what Alexander did, only in reverse. Not the West conquering the East. This time the East will dominate. You intend to acquire all of your neighbors. And you actually believe the West will allow you the luxury, thinking you'll be their friend. But you don't plan to stop there, do you? The Middle East and Arabia, you want those, too. You have oil. The old Kazakhstan is rich with it. But you sell most of that to Russia and Europe cheap. So you want a new source, one that would give you even greater world power. Your zoonoses might just make all that possible. You could devastate a nation in a matter of days. Bring it to its knees. None of your potential victim-states are particularly adept at war in the first place, and when your germs finish, they'll be defenseless."

She still held the gun. "The West should welcome that change."

"We prefer the devils we know. And contrary to all those Arab states' varied beliefs, the West isn't their enemy."

He pointed straight at her.

"You are."

MALONE LISTENED CAREFULLY. THORVALDSEN WAS NO fool, so he was challenging Zovastina for a reason. The Dane even being here was highly unusual. The last trip the man took was to Austria last fall. Yet here he was, inside an Italian basilica in the middle of the night, poking sticks into the spokes of an armed despot.

He'd watched as Viktor left the presbytery and turned into the south transept, below Cassiopeia's position. Malone's immediate concern was an open stairway twenty feet away that led down to the nave. If there was a portal on this side, in the north transept, surely another opened in the south since medieval builders, if nothing else, loved symmetry.

He was surrounded by more undressed masonry walls along with art, tapestries, lace, and paintings, most displayed in glass cases or on tables.

A shadow appeared in the lighted stairway and danced across the marble walls, growing in size.

One of Zovastina's guards.

Climbing to the second floor.

Straight for him.

FIFTY-THREE

STEPHANIE FOLLOWED MONSIGNOR MICHENER DOWN the halls of the diocese offices, into a nondescript cubicle, where Edwin Davis sat beneath a framed portrait of the pope.

"Still want to kick my ass?" Davis asked.

She was too tired to fight. "What are you doing here?"

"Trying to stop a war."

She didn't want to hear it. "You realize there could be trouble inside that church."

"Which is why you're not in there."

Realization dawned. "Malone and Cassiopeia can be denied."

"Something like that. We have no idea what Zovastina may do, but I didn't want the head of the Magellan Billet involved."

She turned to leave.

"I'd stay here if I were you," Davis said.

"Screw off, Edwin."

Michener blocked her way in the doorway.

"Are you part of this insanity?" she asked.

"As I said outside, we came across something and passed it on to a place we thought might be interested. Irina Zovastina is a threat to the world."

"She's planning a war," Davis said. "Millions will die, and she's just about ready to start."

She turned back. "So she took the time to risk a trip

to Venice and look at a two-thousand-year-old body? What is she doing here?"

"Probably getting angry," Michener said.

She saw a twinkle in his eye. "You set her up?"

The priest shook his head. "She did that all by herself."

"Somebody's going to get shot in there. Cassiopeia is way beyond the end of her rope. You don't think gunfire is going to attract the attention of all those police out in the square?"

"The basilica's walls are several feet thick," Michener said. "Totally soundproof. No one will disturb them."

"Stephanie," Davis said, "we're not sure why Zovastina took the chance coming here. But it's obviously important. We thought since she was so intent on coming, we'd accommodate her."

"I get the point. Out of her sandbox and into ours. But you have no right to place Malone and Cassiopeia in jeopardy."

"Come now. I didn't do that. Cassiopeia was already involved, with Henrik Thorvaldsen—who, by the way, involved you. And Malone? He's a big boy and can do what he wants. He's here because he wants to be here."

"You're fishing for information. Hoping to learn something."

"And using the only bait we have. She's the one who wanted a look inside that tomb."

Stephanie was puzzled. "You seem to know her overall plan. What are you waiting for? Move on her. Bomb her installations. Shut her down. Bring political pressures on her."

"It's not that simple. Our information is sketchy. And we have no concrete proof. Certainly not anything she can't simply deny. You can't bomb biologicals. And, unfortunately, we don't know it all. That's what we need Malone and the others to zero in on for us."

"Edwin, you don't know Cotton. He doesn't like to be played."

"We know Naomi Johns is dead."

He'd held that one for the right moment, and the words pounded her gut.

"She was stuffed into a coffin with another man, a small-time hood from Florence. Her neck was broken and he had a bullet to the head."

"Vincenti?" she asked.

Davis nodded. "Who's also on the move. He left earlier for the Central Asian Federation. An unscheduled visit."

She could see he knew even more.

"He just kidnapped a woman that Irina Zovastina has been caring for since last year, a woman that she was once romantically involved with."

"Zovastina's a lesbian?"

"Wouldn't that be a shocker to her People's Assembly? She and this woman were involved for a long time. But her former lover is dying of AIDS, and Vincenti apparently has a use for her."

"And there's a reason you're allowing Vincenti to do whatever it is he's doing?"

"He's up to something, too. And it's more than just supplying Zovastina with germs and antiagents. It's more than providing the Venetian League with a safe haven for all their business activities. We want to know what that is."

She needed to leave.

Another priest appeared in the office doorway and said, "We just heard a shot, from inside the basilica."

MALONE DOVE BEHIND ONE OF THE DISPLAY CASES AS the guardsman fired. He'd tried to hide before the man topped the stairs, but apparently a fleeting glance of his retreat was enough to generate an attack.

The bullet thudded into one of the tables that displayed medieval textiles. The laminated wood deflected the round and allowed Malone the instant he needed to scurry farther into the shadows. The gunshot echoed through the basilica and had surely attracted everyone's attention.

He scrambled across slick hardwood, taking refuge behind a long exhibit of panel paintings and illuminated manuscript pages.

His gun was ready.

He needed to draw the man farther in.

Which didn't seem a problem.

Footsteps were coming his way.

ZOVASTINA HEARD THE SHOT FROM THE UPPER NORTH transept. She spotted movement to her right, beyond the stone railing, and saw the head of one of her guards.

"I didn't come alone," Thorvaldsen said.

She kept her gun aimed at the Dane.

"San Marco is littered with police. Going to be tough for you to leave. You're a head of state, in a foreign country. Are you really going to shoot me?" He paused. "What would Alexander do?"

She couldn't decide if he was being serious or patronizing, but she knew the answer. "He'd kill you."

Thorvaldsen shifted his position, easing to her left. "I disagree. He was a great tactician. And clever. The Gordian knot, for example."

She called out, "What's happening up there?"

Her guardsman did not answer.

"In the village of Gordium," Thorvaldsen was saying, "that complicated knot attached to a wagon. Nobody could untie the thing. A challenge Alexander solved by simply cutting the rope with his sword, then untying it. A simple solution to a complex problem."

"You talk too much."

"Alexander did not allow confusion to affect his thinking."

"Viktor," she called out.

"Of course," Thorvaldsen said, "there are many tales to that knot's story. One says Alexander withdrew a pole connected to the wagon yoke, found the rope ends, and untied it. So who knows?"

She was tiring of this man's rambles.

Head of state or not.

She pulled the trigger.

FIFTY-FOUR

SAMARKAND

Vincenti remembered the first indication of a problem. Initially, the malady possessed all the characteristics of a cold, then he thought it the flu, but soon the full effects of a viral invasion became apparent.

Contamination.

"Am I going to die?" Charlie Easton screamed from the cot. "I want to know, dammit. Tell me."

He dabbed Easton's sopping brow with a damp rag, like he'd done for the past hour, and quietly said, "You need to calm down."

"Don't bullshit me. It's over, isn't it?"

Three years they'd worked side by side. No sense hedging. "There's nothing I can do."

"Shit. I knew it. You've got to get some help."

"You know I can't."

The station's remote location had been selected by the Iraqis, and the Soviets, with great care. Secrecy was paramount. And the price of that secrecy was fatal when a mistake occurred, and a mistake was exactly what happened.

Easton jerked the cot with his restrained arms and legs. "Cut these damn ropes. Let me out of here."

He'd tied the idiot down knowing their options were limited. "We can't leave."

"Screw policy. Screw you. Cut these damn ropes."

Easton stiffened, his breath grew labored, then he succumbed to the fever and relaxed into unconsciousness.

Finally.

Vincenti turned from the cot and grabbed a notebook that he'd started three weeks back, the first page labeled with his partner's name. Inside, he'd noted a progressive shift in skin color. Normal, to jaundiced, to such ashiness that the man now appeared dead. There'd been an incredible weight loss, forty pounds all told, ten over one two-day period alone, the intestinal intake dwindling to an occasional gulp of warm water and a few sips of liquor.

And the fever.

A raging torrent of a constant one hundred and three, sometimes peaking higher, moisture escaping faster than it was being replaced, the body literally evaporating before his eyes. For years they'd used animals in their research, Baghdad providing an endless supply of gibbons, baboons, green monkeys, rodents, and reptiles. But here, for the first time, the effects on a human being could be accurately gauged.

He stared down at his partner. Easton's chest heaved with more labored breaths, mucus rattling deep in the throat, sweat beading off the skin like rain. He noted every observation in the journal, then pocketed the pen.

He stood from the cot and tried to work some feeling into his rubbery legs. He lumbered outside into a crisp night. He wondered how much more Easton's ravaged tissues could take.

Which raised the problem of what to do with the body.

No protocol existed for handling this type of emergency, so he'd have to improvise. Luckily, the station's builders had thoughtfully provided an incinerator for disposing of the animal carcasses used in experimentation. But making the oven work on something as large as a human body was going to take ingenuity.

"I see angels. They're here. All around," Easton cried from the cot.

Vincenti walked back inside.

Easton was now blind. He wasn't sure if the fever or a secondary infection had destroyed the retina.

"God's here. I see him."

"Of course, Charlie. I'm sure you do."

He took a pulse. Blood snapped through the carotid artery. He listened to the heart, which pounded like a drum. He checked blood pressure. On the verge of bottoming. The body temperature was a steady one hundred and three.

"What do I tell God?" Easton asked.

He stared down at his partner. "Say hello."

He pulled a chair close and watched death take hold. The end came twenty minutes later and seemed neither violent nor painful. Just a final breath. Deep. Long. No exhale.

He noted the date and time in the journal, then extracted a blood and tissue sample. He then rolled the thin mattress and filthy sheets around the body and carried the stinking bundle out of the building into an adjacent shed. A scalpel was already there, sharpened to the degree of broken glass, along with a surgeon's saw. He slipped on a pair of thick rubber gloves and sawed the legs from the torso. The emaciated flesh cut soft and loose, the bone brittle, the intervening muscle offering the resistance of a boiled chicken. He amputated both arms and stuffed all four limbs into the incinerator, watching with no emotion as the flames consumed them. Without extremities, the torso and head fit easily through the iron door. He then cut the *bloodied mattress into quarters and quickly stuffed it, the sheets, and gloves into the fire.*

He slammed the portal shut and staggered outside. Over. Finally.

He fell to the rocky ground and stared up at the night. Against the indigo backdrop of a mountain sky, silhouetted as an even darker shadow, the incinerator's brick flue reached skyward. Smoke escaped, carrying with it the stench of human flesh.

He lay back and welcomed sleep.

Vincenti recalled that sleep from over twenty-five years ago. And Iraq. What hell. Hot and miserable. A lonely, desolate spot. What had the UN Commission concluded after the first Gulf War? *Given their mission, the facilities were wholly archaic, but within the frantic atmosphere of the time they were thought state of the art.* Right. Those inspectors weren't there. He was. Young and skinny with a head full of hair and brains. A hotshot virologist. He and Easton had eventually been detailed to a remote lab in Tajikistan, working in conjunction with the Soviets who controlled the region, at a station hidden away in the Pamir foothills.

How many viruses and bacteria had they searched for? Natural organisms that could be used as biological weapons. Something that eliminated an enemy yet preserved a culture's infrastructure. No need to bomb the population, waste bullets, risk nuclear contamination, or put troops in jeopardy. A microscopic organism could do all of the heavy lifting—simple biology the catalyst for certain defeat.

The working criteria for whatever they found had been simple. Fast-acting. Biologically identifiable. Containable. And, most important, curable. Hundreds of strains were discarded simply because no practical way could be found to stop them. What good would infecting an enemy be if you couldn't protect your own population? All four criteria had to be satisfied before a specimen was cataloged. Nearly twenty had made the grade.

He'd never accepted what the press reported after the Biological Toxin Weapons Convention of 1972—that the United States quit the germ-warfare business and destroyed all of its arsenals. The military wouldn't discard decades of research simply because a few politicians unilaterally decided it was the thing to do. At least a few of those organisms, he believed, were hidden in cold storage at some nondescript military institution.

He personally found six pathogens that met all of the criteria.

But sample 65-G failed on every count.

He first discovered it in 1979, within the bloodstream of the green monkeys that had been shipped for experimentation. Conventional science then would never have noticed, but thanks to his unique virology training, and special equipment the Iraqis provided, he found it. A strange-looking thing—spherical—filled with RNA and enzymes. Expose it to air and it evaporated. In water, the cell wall collapsed. Instead, it craved warm plasma and seemed prevalent throughout all of the green monkeys that came his way.

Yet none of the animals seemed affected.

Charlie Easton, though, had been another matter. Damn fool. He'd been bitten two years prior by one of the monkeys, but told no one until three weeks before he died, when the first symptoms appeared. A blood sample confirmed 65-G roamed through him. He'd eventually used Easton's infection to study the viral effects on humans, concluding the organism was not an efficient biological weapon. Too unpredictable, sporadic, and far too slow to be an effective offensive agent.

He shook his head.

Amazing how ignorant he'd been.

A miracle he'd survived.

He was back in his hotel room at the Intercontinental, dawn coming slowly to Samarkand. He needed to rest, but was still energized from his encounter with Karyn Walde.

He thought again about the old healer.

Was it 1980? Or '81?

In the Pamirs, about two weeks before Easton died. He'd visited the village several times before, trying to learn what he could. The old man was surely dead by now. Even then he was well up in age.

But still.

The old man scampered barefoot up the liver-colored slope with the agility of a cat, on feet with soles like leather. Vincenti followed and, even through heavy boots, his ankles and toes ached. Nothing was flat. Rocks arched everywhere like speed breakers, sharp, unforgiving. The village lay a mile back, nearly a thousand feet above sea level, their current journey taking them even higher.

The man was a traditional healer, a combination family practitioner, priest, fortune teller, and sorcerer. He knew little English but could speak passable Chinese and Turkish. He was a near-dwarf with European features and a forked Mongol beard. He wore a gold-threaded quilt and a bright skullcap. Back in the village, Vincenti had watched while the man treated the villagers with a concoction of roots and plants, meticulously administered with an intelligence born from decades of trial and error.

"Where are we going?" he finally asked.

"To answer your question and find what will stop the fever in your friend."

Around him, a stadium of white peaks formed a gallery of untouched heights. Thunder clouds steamed from the highest summits. Streaks of silvers and autumnal reds and dense groves of walnut trees added color to the otherwise mummified scene. A rush of water could be heard somewhere far off.

They came to a ledge and he followed the old man through a purple vein in the rock. He knew from his studies that the mountains around him were still alive, slowly pushing upward about two and a half inches a year.

They exited into an oval-shaped arena, walled in by more stone. Not much light inside, so he found the flashlight the old man had encouraged him to bring.

Two pools dotted the rock floor, each about ten feet in diameter, one bubbling with the froth of thermal energy. He brought the light close and noticed their contrasting color. The active one was a russet brown, its calm companion a sea foam green.

"The fever you describe is not new," the old man said. "Many generations have known that animals deliver it."

To learn more about the yaks, the sheep, and the huge bears that populated the region was one of the reasons he'd been sent. "How do you know that?"

"We watch. But only sometimes do they pass the fever. If your friend has the fever, this will help." He pointed to the green pool, its still surface marred only by an array of floating plants. They looked like water lilies, only bushier, the center flower straining through the shade for precious drops of sunlight. "The leaves will save him. He must chew them."

He dabbed the water and brought two moist fingers to his mouth. No taste. He half expected the hint of carbonate found in other springs of the region.

The man knelt and gulped a cupped handful. "It is good," he said, smiling.

He drank, too. Warm, like a cup of tea, and fresh. So he slurped more.

"The leaves will cure him."

He needed to know. "Is this plant common?"

The old man nodded. "Only ones from this pool work."

"Why is that?"

"I do not know. Perhaps divine will."

He doubted that. "Is this known to other villages? Other healers?"

"I am the only one who uses it."

He reached down and pulled one of the floating pods closer, assessing its biology. It was a tracheophyta, the leaves peltate with the stalk and filled with an elaborate vascular system. Eight thick, pulpous stipules surrounded the base and formed a floating platform. The epidermal tissue was a dark green, the leaf walls full of glucose. A short stem projected from the center and probably acted as a photosynthetic surface because of the limited leaf space. The flower's soft white petals were arranged in a whorl and emitted no fragrance.

He glanced underneath. A raccoon tail of stringy, brown roots extended out in the water, searching for nutrients. From all appearances, it seemed a well-adapted species.

"How did you learn that it worked?"

"My father taught me."

He lifted the plant from the water and cradled the pod. Warm water seeped through his fingers.

"The leaves must be chewed completely, the juice swallowed."

He broke off a clump and brought it to his mouth.

He looked at the old man—rapier eyes staring back quiet and confident. He stuffed the leaf in his mouth and chewed. The taste was bitter, sharp, like alum—and terrible, like tobacco.

He extracted the juice and swallowed, almost gagging.

FIFTY-FIVE

Cassiopeia's attention was drawn first across the nave to the north transept where somebody was shooting at Malone. Beyond the waist-high railing she'd seen the head and chest of one of the guards, but not Malone. Then she'd watched as Zovastina fired her weapon, the bullet careening off the marble floor inches from Thorvaldsen. The Dane had stood his ground, never moving.

Movement to her right drew her attention. A man appeared in the stairway arch, gun in hand. He spotted her and raised his weapon, but never gained the chance to fire.

She shot him in the chest.

He was thrown back, arms flailing. She finished the kill with one more well-placed shot. Across the nave, forty meters away, she saw the other guardsman advancing deeper into the museum's exhibits. She unshouldered the bow and found an arrow, but kept a position back from the railing so as not to give Zovastina a chance at her.

She was concerned. Just before the attacker appeared, Viktor had disappeared below into the lower transept. Where had he gone?

She mated the arrow's nock to the bowstring and gripped the bow's handle.

She retracted the string.

The guard winked in and out through the dim light of the opposite transept.

MALONE WAITED. HIS GUN WAS DRAWN, ALL HE NEEDED was for the guardsman to advance a few feet closer. He'd managed to retreat to the end cap of one of the exhibits, using the shadows for protection, his steps light on the wood flooring, three gunshots from out in the nave masking his movements. Impossible to say where they'd originated since the resounding echoes camouflaged any sense of direction. He really didn't want to shoot the guard.

Booksellers, generally, did not kill people.

But he doubted there was going to be much choice.

He drew a breath and made his move.

ZOVASTINA STARED AT HENRIK THORVALDSEN AS MORE gunshots erupted above. Her thirty minutes alone in the basilica had turned into a crowded mélange.

Thorvaldsen motioned to the wooden box on the floor. "Not what you expected, was it?"

She decided to be honest. "Worth a try."

"Ptolemy's riddle could be a hoax. People have searched for Alexander the Great's remains for fifteen hundred years with no success."

"And does anyone actually believe St. Mark was in that box?"

He shrugged. "An awful lot of Venetians certainly do."

She needed to leave, so she called out, "Viktor."

"Is there a problem, Minister?" a new voice asked.

Michener.

The priest stepped into the lighted presbytery.

She pointed her gun at him. "You lied to me."

MALONE CREPT LEFT AS THE GUARDSMAN KEPT TO THE railing and moved right. He sidestepped a wooden lion attached to a carved ducal throne and crouched behind a waist-high exhibit of tapestries that separated him from his pursuer.

He scampered ahead, intent on doubling around before the man had a chance to react.

He found the end of the exhibit, turned, and prepared to move.

An arrow pierced the guardsman's chest, sucking the breath away. He saw a shocked look sweep over the man's face as he groped for the implanted shaft. Life left him as his body collapsed to the floor.

Malone's head whirled left.

Across the nave Cassiopeia stood, bow in hand, her face frozen, bearing no emotion. Behind her, high in the outer wall loomed a darkened rose window. Below the window, Viktor emerged from the shadows and moved toward Cassiopeia, a gun coming shoulder high.

ZOVASTINA WAS ANGRY. "YOU KNEW THERE WAS NOTHing in that tomb," she said to Michener.

"How could I know that? It hasn't been opened in over a hundred and seventy years."

"You can tell your pope the Church will not be allowed within the Federation, concordat or no."

"I'll pass the message along."

She faced Thorvaldsen. "You never said. What's your interest in all this?"

"To stop you."

"You'll find that difficult."

"I don't know. You have to leave this basilica and the airport is a long boat ride away."

She'd come to realize that they'd chosen their trap with care. Or, more accurately, they'd allowed her to choose it. Venice. Surrounded by water. No cars. Buses. Trains. Lots of slow-moving boats. Leaving could well pose a problem. What was it? An hour's ride to the airport?

And the confident glare of the two staring at her from five meters away was no comfort.

VIKTOR APPROACHED THE WOMAN WITH THE BOW. Rafael's killer. The woman who'd just speared another of his guardsmen in the opposite transept. She needed to die, but he realized that was foolish. He'd listened to Zovastina and knew that things were not going well. To leave, they'd need insurance. So he pressed the barrel of his gun into the nape of her neck.

The woman did not move.

"I should shoot you," he spit out.

"What sport would that be?"

"Enough to even the score."

"I'd say we're even. Ely, for your partner."

He fought a rising anger and forced his mind to think. Then an idea dawned. A way to bring the situation back under control. "Move to the railing. Slowly."

She strode three steps forward.

"Minister," he called out over the balustrade.

He glanced past his captive and saw Zovastina looking up, her gun still pointed at the two men.

"This one," he said to her, "will be our pass out of here. A hostage."

"Excellent idea, Viktor."

"She doesn't know what a mess you've made, does she?" the woman whispered to him.

"You'll die before uttering the first word."

"Not to worry. I won't tell her."

MALONE SAW CASSIOPEIA'S PREDICAMENT. HE SPRANG to the railing and aimed his gun across the nave.

"Toss it down," Viktor called out.

He ignored the command.

"I'd do as he says," Zovastina said from below. Her gun was still trained on Michener and Thorvaldsen. "Or I will shoot these two."

"Supreme Minister of the Central Asian Federation committing murder in Italy? I doubt it."

"True," Zovastina said. "But Viktor can easily kill the woman, which should not be a problem for me."

"Toss it," Cassiopeia said to him.

He realized that to comply was foolish. Just retreat into the shadows and remain a threat.

"Cotton," Thorvaldsen said from below, "do as Cassiopeia says."

He had to trust that both his friends knew what they were doing. Wrong? Probably. But he'd done stupid things before.

He allowed the pistol to drop over the railing.

"BRING HER DOWN," ZOVASTINA CALLED OUT TO VIKtor. "You," she said to the other man who'd just tossed away his gun. "Come here."

He did not move from his perch.

"Please, Cotton," Thorvaldsen said. "Do as she says."

A hesitation and the man disappeared from the railing.

"You control him?" she asked.

"No one does."

Viktor and his female captive entered the presbytery.

The other man, the one Thorvaldsen commanded, followed them a moment later.

"Who are you?" she asked him. "Thorvaldsen called you Cotton."

"Name's Malone."

"And you?" she said, staring at the woman with the archer's bow.

"A friend of Ely Lund."

What was happening? She desperately needed to know, so she thought fast and motioned at Viktor's female captive. "That one is coming with me. To ensure safe passage."

"Minister," Viktor said. "I think it would be better if she stays here, with me. I can hold her until you're away."

She shook her head and pointed at Thorvaldsen. "Take him with you. Somewhere safe. Once I'm in the air, I'll call and you can let him go. Any problems, kill him and make sure the body is never found."

"Minister," Michener said, "since I'm the cause of all this chaos, how about me as a hostage and let's leave this gentleman out of it."

"And how about taking me with you instead of her?" Malone asked. "Never been to the Central Asian Federation."

She appraised the American. Tall and confident. Probably an agent. But she wanted to know more of the woman's connection to Ely Lund. Anyone who knew Lund closely enough to risk her life to avenge him bore further investigation. But Michener. She could only hope Viktor was allowed the opportunity to kill the lying scum. "All right, priest, you go with Viktor. As for you, Mr. Malone, perhaps another time."

FIFTY-SIX

VINCENTI AWOKE.

He was reclined in the helicopter's comfortable leather seat. Flying east, away from the city.

The phone lying in his lap was vibrating.

He read the LCD screen. Grant Lyndsey. Chief scientist at the China lab. He stuffed a fob into his ear and pushed "Phone."

"We're done," his employee said to him. "Zovastina has all of the organisms and the lab is converted. Clean and complete."

With what Zovastina had planned, he had no intention of the West, or the Chinese government, raiding his facility and linking him to anything. Only eight scientists had worked on the project, Lyndsey their head. All vestiges of their work were now gone.

"Pay everyone and send them on their way. O'Conner will visit them and provide for their retirement." He heard the silence from the other end of the phone. "Not to worry, Grant. Gather the computer data and head to my house over the border. We'll have to wait and see what the Supreme Minister actually does with her arsenal before we act."

"I'll leave immediately."

That's what he wanted to hear. "I'll be seeing you before the day is out. We have work to do. Get moving."

He clicked off the phone and lay back in the seat.

He thought again about the old dwarf in the Pamir mountains. Back then Tajikistan had been primitive and hostile. Little medical research had ever been done there. Few strangers visited. That was why the Iraqis thought the region a promising place to investigate for unknown zoonoses.

Two pools high in the mountains.

One green, the other brown.

And the plant whose leaves he'd chewed.

He recalled the water. Warm and clear. But when he'd pointed his flashlight into their shallow depths, he recalled an even stranger sight.

Two carved letters. One in each pool.

Z and H.

Chiseled from blocks of stone, lying on the bottom.

He thought of the medallion Stephanie Nelle had made a point to show him. One of the several Irina Zovastina seemed intent on acquiring.

And the microletters supposedly on its face.

ZH.

Coincidence? He doubted it. He knew what the letters meant since he'd sought out scholars who told him that in Old Greek they represented the concept of life. He'd thought his idea of labeling any future cure for HIV with that ancient designation clever. Now he wasn't so sure. He felt like his world was collapsing and the anonymity that he'd once enjoyed was quickly evaporating. The Americans were after him. Zovastina was after him. The Venetian League itself might well be after him.

But he'd cast his die.

No going back.

MALONE'S GAZE ALTERNATED BETWEEN THORVALDSEN and Cassiopeia. Neither of his friends showed the slightest concern with their predicament. Between him and Cassiopeia, they could take Zovastina and Viktor. He tried to voice that intent with his eyes, but no one seemed to be listening.

"Your pope doesn't scare me," Zovastina said to Michener.

"It's not our intent to scare anyone."

"You're a sanctimonious hypocrite."

Michener said nothing.

"Not much to say?" she asked.

"I'll pray for you, Minister."

She spit at his feet. "I don't need your prayers, priest." She motioned toward Cassiopeia. "Time to go. Leave the bow and arrows. You won't be needing them."

Cassiopeia dropped both to the floor.

"Here's her gun," Viktor said, and he handed over the weapon.

"Once we're away, I'll call. If you don't hear from me in three hours, kill the priest. And Viktor," she paused, "make sure he suffers."

Viktor and Michener left the presbytery and walked through the darkened nave.

"Shall we?" Zovastina said to Cassiopeia. "I assume you'll behave yourself?"

"Like I have a choice."

"The priest will appreciate it."

They left the presbytery.

Malone turned to Thorvaldsen. "And they're just going to leave, with no response from us?"

"It had to be done," Stephanie said, as she and another man stepped from the shadows of the south transept. She introduced the lean man as Edwin Davis, deputy national security adviser, the voice from the phone earlier. Everything about him was neat and restrained, from the pressed slacks and stiff cotton shirt, to his shiny, narrow calf-leather shoes. Malone ignored

Davis and asked Stephanie, "Why did it have to be done?"

Thorvaldsen answered. "We weren't sure what was going to happen. We were just trying to make something happen."

"You wanted Cassiopeia to be taken?"

Thorvaldsen shook his head. "I didn't. But Cassiopeia apparently did. I could see it in her eyes, so I seized the moment and accommodated her. That's why I asked you to drop your weapon."

"Are you nuts?"

Thorvaldsen stepped closer. "Cotton, three years ago I introduced Ely and Cassiopeia."

"What does that have to do with anything?"

"When Ely was young, he foolishly experimented with drugs. He wasn't careful with needles and, sadly, contracted HIV. He managed the disease well, taking various cocktail combinations, but the odds were not in his favor. Most of those infected eventually contract AIDS and die. He was lucky."

He waited for more.

"Cassiopeia shares his illness."

Had he heard right?

"A blood transfusion, ten years ago. She takes the symptomatic drugs and manages her disease, as well."

He was shocked, but a lot of her comments now made sense. "How's that possible? She's so active. Strong."

"Take the drugs every day and you can be, provided the virus cooperates."

He stared at Stephanie. "You knew?"

"Edwin told me before we came out here. Henrik told him. He and Henrik have been waiting for us to arrive. That's why Michener took me aside."

"So what were me and Cassiopeia? Expendables? With deniability?" he asked Davis.

"Something like that. We had no idea what Zovastina would do."

"You sorry son of a bitch." He moved toward Davis.

"Cotton," Thorvaldsen said, "I approved it. Be mad at me."

He stopped and stared at his friend. "What gave you that right?"

"When you and Cassiopeia left Copenhagen, President Daniels called. He told me what happened to Stephanie in Amsterdam and asked what we knew. I told him. He suggested I could be useful here."

"Along with me? That why you lied to me about Stephanie being in trouble?"

Thorvaldsen cast a glance toward Davis. "Actually, I'm a bit perturbed about that, too. I only told you what they told me. It seems the president wanted all of us involved."

He looked at Davis. "I don't like the way you do business."

"Fair enough. But I have to do what I have to do."

"Cotton," Thorvaldsen said, "there was little time to think this through. I was improvising as it happened."

"You think?"

"But I didn't believe Zovastina would do anything foolish here in the basilica. She couldn't. And she'd be caught totally off guard. That's why I agreed to challenge her. Of course, Cassiopeia was another matter. She killed two people."

"And one more on Torcello." He cautioned himself to stay focused. "What is all this about?"

"One part," Stephanie said, "is to stop Zovastina. She's planning a dirty war and has the resources to make it a costly one."

"She contacted the Church and they tipped us off," Davis said. "That's why we're here."

"You could have told us all that," he said to Davis.

"No, Mr. Malone, we couldn't. I've read your service record. You were a superb agent. A long list of successful missions and commendations. You don't strike me as naive. You, of all people, should understand how the game is played."

"That's just it," he said. "I don't play anymore."

He paced about and allowed himself a moment to calm down. Then he approached the wooden box lying open on the floor. "Zovastina risked everything just to look at these bones?"

"That's the other part to all of this," Thorvaldsen said. "The more complicated portion. You read some of the manuscript pages Ely found about Alexander the Great and his draught. Ely came to believe, perhaps foolishly, that from the symptoms described, the draught might have some effect on viral pathogens."

"Like HIV?" he asked.

Thorvaldsen nodded. "We know there are substances found in nature—tree bark, leafy plants, roots—that can combat bacteria and viruses, maybe even some cancers. He was hoping this might be one of those."

His mind recalled the manuscript. *Overcome by remorse and sensing that Ptolemy was sincere, Eumenes revealed the resting place, far away, in the mountains, where the Scythians taught Alexander about life.* "The Scythians are the ones who showed Alexander the draught. Eumenes said Alexander was buried where the Scythians taught him about life."

Something occurred to him. He said to Stephanie, "You have one of the medallions, don't you?"

Stephanie handed him the coin. "From Amsterdam. We recovered it after Zovastina's men tried to take it. We're told it's authentic."

He held the decadrachm high in the light.

"Concealed within the warrior are tiny letters. ZH," Stephanie said. "Old Greek for life."

More of the History of Hieronymus of Cardia. *Ptolemy then handed me a silver medallion that showed Alexander when he fought against elephants. He told me that, in honor of those battles, he'd minted the coins. He also told me to come back when I solved his riddle. But a month later Ptolemy lay dead.*

Now he knew. "The coins and the riddle go together."

"No question," Thorvaldsen answered. "But how?"

He wasn't ready to explain. "None of you ever answered me. Why did you just let them leave here?"

"Cassiopeia clearly wanted to go," Thorvaldsen said. "Between her and me, we dangled enough information about Ely to intrigue Zovastina."

"Is that why you called her outside on the phone?"

Thorvaldsen nodded. "She needed information. I had no idea what she would do. You have to understand, Cotton, Cassiopeia wants to know what happened to Ely and the answers are in Asia."

That obsession bothered Malone. Why? He wasn't sure. But it clearly did. As did her pain. And her illness. Too much to keep track of. Too many emotions for a man who worked hard at ignoring them. "What is she going to do when she gets to the Federation?"

Thorvaldsen shrugged. "I have no idea. Zovastina knows that I'm wise to her overall plan. I made that clear. She knows Cassiopeia is associated with me. She'll use the opportunity we gave her to try and learn from Cassiopeia what she can—"

"Before she kills her."

"Cotton," Stephanie said, "that's a chance Cassiopeia freely accepted. No one told her to go."

More of his melancholy arose. "No. We just let her go. Is that priest involved?"

"He has a job to do," Davis said. "That's why he volunteered."

"But there's more," Thorvaldsen said. "What Ely

found, Ptolemy's riddle, it's real. And we now have all the pieces to discover its solution."

He pointed to the box. "There's nothing there. It's a dead end."

Thorvaldsen shook his head. "Not true. Those bones lay beneath us, in the crypt, for centuries, before they were moved up here." Thorvaldsen motioned toward the open sarcophagus. "When they were first removed, in 1835, something else was found with them. Only a few know." Thorvaldsen pointed toward the darkened south transept. "It's in the treasury and has been for a long time."

"And you needed Zovastina gone before taking a look?"

"Something like that." The Dane held up a key. "Our ticket to see."

"You realize Cassiopeia may have bitten off more than she can ever chew."

Thorvaldsen nodded heavily. "Fully."

He had to think, so he gazed toward the south transept and asked, "Do you know what to do with whatever is in there?"

Thorvaldsen shook his head. "Not me. But we have someone who might."

He was puzzled.

"Henrik believes," Stephanie said, "and Edwin seems to agree—"

"It's Ely," Thorvaldsen said. "We think he's still alive."

PART
FOUR

PART
FOUR

FIFTY-SEVEN

VINCENTI STEPPED FROM THE HELICOPTER. THE TRIP from Samarkand had taken about an hour. Though there were new highways leading east all the way to the Fergana Valley, his estate lay farther south, in the old Tajikistan—and air travel remained the fastest and safest route.

He'd chosen his land with care, high in cloud-girdled mountains. No one had questioned the purchase, not even Zovastina. He'd explained only that he was tired of the flat, muddy, Venetian terrain, so he bought two hundred acres of forested valley and rocky Pamir highlands. This would be his world. Where he could not be seen nor heard, surrounded by servants, at a commanding height, amid scenery once wild but now shorn and shaven with touches of Italy, Byzantium, and China.

He'd christened the estate Attico, and noticed on the flight in that the main entrance now was crowned by an elaborate stone arch containing the label. He also noticed more scaffolding had been erected around the house, the exterior rapidly moving toward completion. Construction had been slow but constant, and he'd be glad when the walls stood totally finished.

He escaped the whirling blades and passed through a garden he'd taught to bloom upon a mountain slope so the estate would bristle with hints of the English countryside.

Peter O'Conner waited on the uneven stones of the rear terrace.

"Everything okay?" he asked his employee.

O'Conner nodded. "No problems here."

He lingered outside, catching his breath. Storm clouds wreathed the distant eastern peaks into China. Crows patrolled the valley. He'd carefully orientated his castle in the air to maximize the spectacular view. So different from Venice. No uncomfortable miasma. Only crystalline air. He'd been told that the Asian spring had been unusually warm and dry and he was grateful for the respite.

"What about Zovastina?" he asked.

"She's leaving Italy, as we speak, with another woman. Dark-skinned, attractive, provided the name Cassiopeia Vitt to Customs."

He waited, knowing O'Conner had been thorough.

"Vitt lives in southern France. Is presently financing the reconstruction of a medieval castle. A big project. Expensive. Her father owned several Spanish manufacturing concerns. Huge conglomerates. She inherited it all."

"What about her? The person."

"Muslim, but not devout. Highly educated. Engineering and history degrees. Unmarried. Thirty-eight years old. That's about all I could get on short notice. You want more?"

He shook his head. "Not now. Any clue what's she doing with Zovastina?"

"My people didn't know. Zovastina left the basilica with her and went straight to the airport."

"She on her way back here?"

O'Conner nodded. "Should arrive in another four to five hours."

He saw there was more.

"Our men who went after Nelle. One was taken down by a rooftop sniper. The other escaped. Seems Nelle was prepared for us."

He did not like the sound of that. But that problem would have to wait. He'd already leaped from the cliff. Too late to climb back now.

He entered the house.

A year ago he'd finished decorating, having spent millions on paintings, wall coverings, lacquered furniture, and objets d'art. But he'd insisted that comfort not be sacrificed for magnificence, so he'd included a theater, cozy parlors, private bedrooms, baths, and the garden. Unfortunately, he'd only been able to enjoy a precious few weeks here, staffing it with locals O'Conner personally vetted. Soon, though, Attico would become his personal refuge, a place of high living and plain thinking, and he'd provided for that eventuality by installing sophisticated alarms, state-of-the-art communications equipment, and an intricate network of concealed passages.

He passed through the ground-floor rooms, which flowed into one another in the French style, every corner of which seemed as cool and shadowy as the spring twilight. A fine atrium in the classical vein accommodated a winding marble staircase to the second floor.

He climbed.

Frescoes representing the march of the liberal sciences loomed overhead. This part of the house reminded him of Venice's best, though the towering mullion windows framed mountain landscapes instead of the Grand Canal. His destination was the closed door to his left, just beyond the top of the staircase, one of several spacious guest rooms.

He quietly entered.

Karyn Walde lay still on the bed.

O'Conner had brought her and the nurse from

Samarkand in another helicopter. Her right arm was once again connected to an intravenous drip. He stepped close and gripped one of the syringes resting on a stainless-steel table. He injected the contents into one of the ports. A few seconds later the stimulant forced Walde's eyes open. In Samarkand, he'd sent her into unconsciousness. Now he needed her alert.

"Come around," he said. "Wake up."

She blinked and he saw her pupils focus.

Then she closed them again.

He grabbed a pitcher of ice water from the night stand and doused her face.

She sprang awake, spewing mist, shaking the water from her eyes.

"You son of a bitch," she blurted out, pushing herself up.

"I told you to wake up."

She was not restrained. No need. Her gaze raked her surroundings. "Where am I?"

"You like it? It's just as elegant as you're accustomed to."

She noticed the sunlight streaming in through the windows and the open terrace doors. "How long have I been out?"

"Quite a while. It's morning."

Disorientation reappeared as she comprehended reality. "What's going on?"

"I want to read you something. Will you indulge me?"

"Do I have a choice?"

Her wits had returned.

"Not really. But I think the time will be worth it."

I was suspicious of Clinical Trial W12-23 from the start. Initially, Vincenti assigned only himself and me to its supervision. That was strange since rarely does

Vincenti personally involve himself with such things, especially on a trial with only twelve participants, which was another reason why I became suspicious. Most of the trials we conduct have upwards of a hundred to (on at least one occasion) a thousand or more participants. A sample of only twelve patients would not ordinarily reveal anything about the effectiveness of any substance, particularly given the all-important criterion of toxicity, the danger being that the conclusions could be simply random.

When I expressed these concerns to Vincenti, he explained that toxicity was not the goal of this trial. Which again seemed strange. I asked about the agent being tested and Vincenti said it was something he personally developed, curious to see if his laboratory results could be duplicated in humans. I was aware Vincenti worked on projects regarded as internally classified (meaning only certain people were allowed data access) but, in the past, I was always one of those granted access. On this trial, Vincenti made it clear that only he was to handle the testing substance, known as Zeta Eta.

Using specific parameters Vincenti provided, I secured a dozen volunteers from various health clinics throughout the country. Not an easy task since HIV is a subject Iraqis do not openly discuss and the disease is rare. Eventually, after money was offered, subjects were found. Three in the early stages of HIV infection came with white cell counts approaching one thousand and only a tiny percentage of virus. None of these people displayed any outward symptoms of AIDS. Five others had progressed from HIV to AIDS, their bloodstreams full of virus, white cell counts low, each already encountering a wide range of specific symptoms. Four more were well on their way to death, white cell counts below two hundred, a variety *of secondary infections already clear, the end only a matter of time.*

Once a day I traveled to the clinic in Baghdad and administered intravenous doses at levels specified by Vincenti. At the same time, I obtained blood and tissue samples. From the first injection all twelve showed marked improvement. White cell counts dramatically rose and, with a reemergence of their immune system, secondary infections dissipated as their bodies started to ward off the various diseases. Some, like the cancerous Kaposi outbreaks five of the twelve developed, were beyond a cure, but infections the immune system could effectively handle started to diminish by the beginning of the second day.

By the third day the immune systems in all twelve had reemerged. White cells regenerated. Counts rose. Appetites returned. Weight was gained. HIV viral load dropped to nearly zero. If the injections had continued there was little doubt they would have all been cured, at least of HIV and AIDS. But the injections were stopped. On the fourth day, after Vincenti became convinced the substance worked, he changed the injection solution to saline. All twelve patients quickly relapsed. Their T-cell counts bottomed and HIV regained control. What exactly the testing substance was remains a mystery. The few chemical tests I ran revealed only a slightly alkaline, water-based compound. More out of curiosity than anything else, I microscopically examined a sample and was shocked to discover living organisms in the solution.

He noted that Karyn Walde was listening closely. "This is a report from a man who once worked under me. He wanted to file it with my superiors. Of course, he never did. I paid to have him killed. In Iraq, during the nineteen-eighties, when Saddam ruled supreme, that was fairly easy to do."

"And why did you kill him?"

"He was nosy. Paying way too much attention to something that did not concern him."

"That isn't an answer. Why did he need to die?"

He held up a syringe filled with a clear liquid.

"More of your sleep drug?" she asked.

"No. It's actually your greatest desire. What you told me in Samarkand you wanted more than anything."

He paused.

"Life."

FIFTY-EIGHT

MALONE SHOOK HIS HEAD. "ELY LUND IS ALIVE?"

"We don't know," Edwin Davis said. "But we've suspected Zovastina was being schooled by somebody. Yesterday we learned that Lund was her initial source of information—Henrik told us about him—and the circumstances of his death are certainly suspect."

"Why does Cassiopeia believe he's dead?"

"Because she had to believe that," Thorvaldsen said. "There was no way to prove otherwise. But I suspect a part of her has doubted whether his death was real."

"Henrik thinks, and I have to agree with him," Stephanie said, "that Zovastina will try and use the link between Ely and Cassiopeia to her advantage. All of what happened here has to be a shock for her, and paranoia is one of her occupational hazards. Cassiopeia can play off that."

"This woman is planning a war. She's not going to worry about Cassiopeia. She needed her to get to the airport. After that, Cassiopeia is nothing but baggage. This is crazy."

"Cotton," Stephanie said. "There's more."

He waited.

"Naomi's dead."

He ran a hand through his hair. "I'm sick and tired of friends dying."

"I want Enrico Vincenti," she said.

So did he.

He started thinking like a field agent again, fighting hard the desire for quick revenge. "You said there's something in the treasury. Okay. Show me."

ZOVASTINA WATCHED THE WOMAN SITTING ACROSS FROM her in the jet's luxury cabin. A personality of courage, no doubt. And like the prisoner from the laboratory in China, this beauty knew fear, yet unlike that weak soul, she also knew how to control it.

They'd not spoken since leaving the basilica, and she'd used the time to gauge her hostage. She was still unsure if the woman's presence was planned or happenstance. Too much happened too fast.

And the bones.

She'd been certain there'd be something to find, sure enough to risk the journey. Everything had pointed to success. But over two thousand years had passed. Thorvaldsen may have been right. What realistically could remain?

"Why were you in the basilica?" she asked.

"Did you bring me along to chitchat?"

"I brought you to find out what you know."

This woman reminded her too much of Karyn. That damnable self-confidence, worn like a badge. And a peculiar expression of wariness, which strangely kept Zovastina both interested and off balance.

"Your clothes. Your hair. You look like you've been swimming."

"Your guardsman shoved me into the lagoon."

That was news. "My guardsman?"

"Viktor. He didn't tell you? I killed his partner in the museum on Torcello. I wanted to kill him, too."

"That could prove a challenge."

"I don't think so." The voice was cold, acid, and superior.

"You knew Ely Lund?"

Vitt said nothing.

"You think I killed him?"

"I know you did. He told you about Ptolemy's riddle. He taught you about Alexander and how the body in the Soma was never Alexander's. He connected that body to the theft of St. Mark by the Venetians and that's how you knew to go to Venice. You killed him to make sure he told no one else. Yet he did tell someone. Me."

"And you told Henrik Thorvaldsen."

"Among others."

That was a problem, and Zovastina wondered if there was any connection between this woman and the failed assassination attempt. And Vincenti? Henrik Thorvaldsen was certainly the kind of man who could be a member of the Venetian League. But since the membership roster was highly confidential she had no way of confirming his status. "Ely never mentioned you."

"He mentioned you."

This woman was indeed like Karyn. Same haunting allure and frank manner. Defiance attracted Zovastina. Something that took patience and determination to tame.

But it could be done.

"What if Ely isn't dead?"

FIFTY-NINE

MALONE FOLLOWED THE OTHERS INTO THE BASILICA'S south transept, stopping at a dimly lit doorway surmounted by an elaborate Moorish-style arch. Thorvaldsen produced a key and opened the bronze doors.

Inside, a vaulted vestibule led into a sanctuary. To the left, wall niches held icons and reliquaries. To the right was the treasury, where more fragile and precious symbols of a vanished republic rested against the walls or lay gathered in showcases.

"Most of this came from Constantinople," Thorvaldsen said, "when Venice sacked the city in 1204. But restorations, fires, and robberies have taken their toll. When the Venetian republic fell, much of the collection was melted down for its gold, silver, and precious stones. Only two hundred and eighty-three items managed to survive."

Malone admired the shiny chalices, reliquaries, caskets, crosses, bowls, and icons, fashioned of rock, wood, crystal, glass, silver, or gold. He also noticed amphorae, ampullae, manuscript covers, and elaborate incense burners, each an ancient trophy from Egypt, Rome, or Byzantium.

"Quite a collection," he said.

"One of the finest on the planet," Thorvaldsen declared.

"What are we looking for?"

Stephanie pointed. "Michener said it was over here."

They approached a glass case that exhibited a sword, a bishop's crozier, a few hexagonal bowls, and several gilt relic boxes. Thorvaldsen used another of the keys and unlocked the case. He then hinged open one of the relic boxes. "They keep it in here. Out of sight."

Malone recognized the object lying inside. "A scarab."

During the mummification process, Egyptian embalmers routinely adorned the purified body with hundreds of amulets. Many were simply for decoration, others were positioned to strengthen dead limbs. The one he was staring at was named for the insect that adorned the top—*Scarabæidæ*—a dung beetle. He'd always thought the association odd, but ancient Egyptians had noticed how the bugs seemed to spring from the dung, so they identified the insect with Chepera, the creator of all things, father of the gods, who made himself out of the matter he produced.

"This one's a heart amulet," he said.

Stephanie nodded. "That's what Michener said."

He knew that all bodily organs were removed during mummification, save for the heart. A scarab was always laid atop the heart to symbolize everlasting life. This one was typical. Made of stone. Green. Probably carnelian. But one thing he noticed. "No gold. Usually they were either made of or decorated with it."

"Which is probably how it survived," Thorvaldsen said. "History notes that the Soma, in Alexandria, was raided by the later Ptolemies. All of the gold was stripped away, the golden sarcophagus melted down, everything of value taken. That chunk of rock would have meant nothing to them."

Malone reached down and lifted the amulet. Maybe

four inches long by two inches wide. "It's larger than normal. These things are usually about half this size."

"You know a lot about them," Davis said.

Stephanie grinned. "The man reads. After all, he is a bookseller."

Malone smiled but continued to admire the amulet and noticed, in the beetle's wings, three carved hieroglyphs.

"What are they?" he asked.

"Michener said they mean life, stability, and protection," Thorvaldsen answered.

He turned the amulet over. The bottom was dominated by the image of a bird.

Thorvaldsen said, "This was found with the bones of St. Mark when they were removed from the crypt, in 1835, and brought up to the altar. St. Mark was martyred in Alexandria and mummified, so it was thought this amulet was simply part of that process. But since it has pagan overtones, the Church fathers decided not to include it with the remains. They recognized its historical value, though, and placed it here, in the treasury. When the Church learned of Zovastina's interest in St. Mark, the amulet took on a greater importance. But when Daniels told me about it, I recalled what Ptolemy said."

So did he.

Touch the innermost being of the golden illusion.

Pieces clicked into place. "The golden illusion was the body itself in Memphis, since it was wrapped in gold. The innermost being? The heart." He held up the amulet. "This."

"Which means," Davis said, "that the remains out there in the basilica are not St. Mark."

Malone nodded. "They're something else entirely. Something that has nothing to do with Christianity."

Thorvaldsen pointed to the bottom side. "That's the Egyptian hieroglyph for the phoenix, the symbol of re-birth."

More of the riddle flashed through his brain.

Divide the phoenix.

And he knew exactly what to do.

CASSIOPEIA REALIZED SHE WAS BEING PLAYED BY ZO-vastina's question. *What if Ely isn't dead?* So she controlled her emotions and calmly said, "But he is dead, and has been for months."

"You're sure?"

Cassiopeia had many times wondered—how could she not?—but she fought the pain of wishing and declared, "Ely's dead."

Zovastina reached for a phone and pushed one of the keys. A few seconds passed, then she said into the unit, "Viktor, I need you to tell someone about what happened the night Ely Lund died."

Zovastina offered her the phone.

Cassiopeia did not move. She recalled what he'd said on the boat. Which was nothing.

"Can you afford not to listen to what he has to say?" Zovastina asked, a nauseating look of satisfaction in her dark eyes.

This woman knew her weakness, and somehow that realization frightened Cassiopeia more than what Viktor might say. She wanted to know. The past few months had been torment. Yet . . .

"Shove that phone up your ass."

Zovastina hesitated, then smiled. Finally, she said into the unit, "Maybe later, Viktor. You can let the priest go now."

She clicked off.

The plane continued to climb into the clouds, heading east for Asia.

"Viktor was watching Ely's house. On my orders."

Cassiopeia didn't want to listen.

"He entered from the rear. Ely was bound to a chair and the assassin was preparing to shoot him. Viktor shot the assassin first, then brought Ely to me and burned the house with the killer inside."

"You can't expect me to believe that."

"There are people within my government who would like to see me gone. Unfortunately, treachery is part of our political way. They fear me and knew Ely was assisting me. So they ordered him killed, just as they'd ordered others, who were my allies, eliminated."

Cassiopeia remained skeptical.

"Ely is HIV positive."

That truth arrested Cassiopeia's attention. "How do you know?"

"He told me. I've been supplying him with his medications these past two months. Unlike you, he trusts me."

Cassiopeia knew that Ely would have never told anyone that he was infected. Only Henrik and Ely knew about her malady.

Now she was confused.

But she wondered.

Had that been the whole idea?

MALONE CARESSED THE SMOOTH PATINA OF THE HEART amulet, his fingers tracing the outline of the bird that represented the Egyptian phoenix. "Ptolemy said to divide the phoenix."

He shook the artifact, listening.

Nothing moved inside.

Thorvaldsen seemed to understand what he was about to do. "That thing is over two thousand years old."

Malone could not care less. Cassiopeia was in trouble and the world may soon be experiencing a biological war. Ptolemy had penned a riddle that obviously led to where Alexander the Great had wanted to be entombed. The Greek warrior-turned-pharaoh apparently had been privy to good information. And if he said *divide the phoenix,* then Malone was damn well going to do it.

He pounded the amulet, bottom-side first, into the marble floor.

It recoiled and about a third of the scarab broke away, like a nut cracking. He settled the pieces on the floor and examined them.

Something spilled out from the sides.

The others knelt with him.

He pointed and said, "The inside was cleaved, ready to split, and packed with sand."

He lifted the larger chunk and emptied the granules.

Edwin Davis pointed. "Look."

Malone saw it, too. He gently brushed the sand aside and spotted a cylindrical object, maybe a half inch in diameter. Then he noticed that it wasn't a cylinder at all.

A strip of gold.

Coiled.

He carefully tipped the tiny bundle onto its side and spotted random letters etched into one side.

"Greek," he said.

Stephanie bent down closer. "And look how thin that foil is. Like leaf."

"What is it?" Davis asked.

Malone's mind starting clicking the final pieces into place. The next part of Ptolemy's riddle now became important. *Life provides the measure of the grave. Be wary, for there is but one chance of success.* He reached into his pocket and found the medallion Stephanie had shown him. "Concealed on this are microletters. ZH. And we know Ptolemy minted these medallions, when he created the riddle."

He noticed a tiny symbol— ♋ —on one side and instantly knew the connection. "That same symbol was on the manuscript you showed me. At the bottom, below the riddle." He saw the wording clearly in his mind. *Life provides the measure of the true grave.*

"How do the elephant medallions and that strip of gold connect to each other?" Davis asked.

"To know that," Malone said, "you have to know what that strip is."

He saw that Stephanie was reading him.

"And you do?" she asked.

He nodded. "I know exactly what this is."

VIKTOR CUT THE THROTTLE AND ALLOWED THE BOAT TO drift back toward the quay at San Marco. He'd taken Michener from the basilica, straight to where he'd docked, thinking the safest place to wait for Zovastina's departure was on water. There he'd stayed, staring at the floodlit domes and pinnacles, the pink-and-white doge's palace, the campanile, and rows of antique buildings, solid and high, dotted with balconies and windows, all matted by the black yawn of night. He'd be glad when he was gone from Italy.

Nothing here had gone right.

"It's time you and I had a talk," Michener said.

He'd kept the priest in the boat's forward cabin, alone, while he waited for Zovastina's call, and Michener had sat casually and stayed silent.

"What could we have to talk about?"

"Perhaps the fact that you're an American spy."

SIXTY

VINCENTI ALLOWED KARYN WALDE TIME TO DIGEST what he'd said. He remembered the moment when *he* first realized that he'd discovered the cure for HIV.

"I told you about the old man in the mountains—"

"Is that where you found it?" she asked, anticipation in her voice.

"I think *re*found would be more accurate."

He'd never spoken of this to anyone. How could he have? So he found himself eager to explain. "It's ironic how the simplest things can solve the most complex problems. In the early 1900s, beriberi flourished all over China, killing hundreds of thousands. You know why? To make the rice more marketable, merchants started polishing the kernels, which removed thiamine—vitamin B1—from the hull. Without thiamine in their diet, beriberi passed unchecked through the population. When the polishing stopped, the thiamine took care of the disease.

"The bark from the Pacific yew tree is an effective cancer treatment. It's no cure, but it can slow down the disease. Simple bread mold led to highly effective antibiotics that kill bacterial infections. And something as basic as a high-fat, ketogenic diet can actually arrest epilepsy in some children. Simple stuff. I found that same principle true for AIDS."

"What was it in that plant you chewed that worked?" she asked.

"Not *it. They.*"

He saw her fear subside, as what might have been a threat was rapidly changing into salvation.

"Thirty years ago, we spotted a virus in the bloodstream of green monkeys. Our knowledge of viruses at the time was rudimentary, considering what we know now. We actually thought it a form of rabies, but the shape, size, and biology of the organism was different.

"It eventually was labeled simian immunodeficiency virus—SIV. We now know SIV can live in monkeys indefinitely without harming the animal. We first thought the monkeys had some kind of resistance, but we later learned the resistance came from the virus, which chemically realized that it couldn't ravage every biological organism it contacted. The virus learned to exist within the monkeys, without the monkeys knowing they even carried it."

"I've heard this," she said. "And the AIDS epidemic started with a monkey bite."

He shrugged. "Who knows? Could have been a bite or a scratch, could have been ingested. Monkeys are a regular part of many diets. No matter how it happened, the virus left monkeys and found humans. I saw this firsthand with a man named Charlie Easton, where the virus changed inside him from SIV to HIV."

He told her more about what happened decades ago, not all that far from where he stood, when Easton died.

"HIV harbored no parental instinct for humans, the way SIV did for monkeys. It went to work, quickly cloning cells in lymph nodes into duplicates of itself. Charlie was dead in a matter of weeks.

"But he wasn't the first. The first case that can be definitively diagnosed was a man from England. In 1959. A frozen serum sample tested in the early nineteen-nineties showed HIV in his blood, and medical records confirmed the symptoms of AIDS. Most likely SIV and HIV have both been around for centuries. People dying in isolated villages, nobody noticing. Secondary infections like pneumonia actually killed the people, so doctors routinely mistook AIDS for other things. Originally, in the United States, it was labeled 'the gay pneumonia.' The best guess now is that in the nineteen-fifties and -sixties, when Africa started to modernize and people began congregating in cities, the disease spread. Eventually, an outsider carried the virus off the continent. By the nineteen-eighties, HIV had made it across the globe."

"One of your natural biological weapons made good."

"We actually thought it lousy for that purpose. Too hard to contract, too long to kill. Which isn't bad. Any easier and we'd have a modern-day black death."

"We do," she said. "It's just not killing the right people yet."

He knew what she meant. Presently, there were two main strains. HIV-1, prevalent in Africa, while HIV-2 remained strong within intravenous drug users and homosexuals. Lately, new variant strains had started appearing, like a nasty one in Southeast Asia, recently acquiring the label of number three.

"Easton," she said. "Did you think you'd been infected by him?"

"We knew so little about how the virus passed back then. Remember, any offensive biological weapon is useless without a cure. So when that old healer offered to take me up into the mountains, I went. He showed me the plant and told me the juice from its leaves could stop what he called the fever-disease. So I ate some."

"And didn't give Easton any? You let him die?"

"I gave him the juice from the plant. But it did nothing for him."

She looked puzzled and he allowed her question to hang.

"Once Charlie died, I cataloged the virus as an unacceptable specimen. The Iraqis only wanted to know about successes. We were told to leave the failures in the field. In the mid-nineteen-eighties, when HIV was finally isolated in France and the United States, I recognized the biology. Initially, I didn't give it much thought. Hell, nobody outside the gay community was all that concerned. But by 1985 I heard the talk among the pharmaceutical community. Whoever found the cure was going to make a lot of money. So I decided to start looking. By then I knew a lot more. So I went back to central Asia, hired a guide to take me up to the high ground, and found the plant again. I brought back samples and tested it and, sure enough, the damn thing wiped HIV out almost on contact."

"You said it didn't work on Easton."

"The plant's useless. By the time I gave it to Charlie, the leaves were dry. It's not the leaves. It's the water. That's where I found them."

He held up the syringe.

"Bacteria."

SIXTY-ONE

"EVER HEARD OF A SCYTALE?" MALONE ASKED.

None of them had.

"You get a stick, wrap a strip of leather around it, write your message on the leather, then unwrap the strip and add a bunch of other letters. The person who you intend to get the message has a similar stick, same diameter, so that when he wraps the strip around it the message is readable. Use a different size stick and all you get is jumbled letters. The ancient Greeks used the scytale all the time to communicate secretly."

"How in the world do you know these things?" Davis asked.

Malone shrugged. "The scytale was fast, effective, and not prone to mistakes—which was important on the battlefield. A great way to send a concealed message. And, to answer your question, I read."

"We don't have the right stick," Davis said. "How are we going to decipher the thing?"

"Remember the riddle. *Life provides the measure of the grave.*" He held up the medallion. "ZH. Life. This coin is the measure."

"*Be wary, for there is but one chance of success,*" Stephanie said. "That gold foil is thin. No way to unravel and wrap it again. Apparently, you get one shot."

Malone nodded. "That's my guess, too."

He led the search as they left the basilica and headed back to the diocese offices with the foil and the elephant medallion. He estimated the decadrachm to be about an inch in diameter, so they started looking for something that would work. A couple of broom handles found in a storage closet proved too large, a few other items too small.

"All the lights are on," Malone said. "But nobody's around."

"Michener cleared the building when Zovastina was left alone in the basilica," Davis said. "We needed as few witnesses as possible."

Near a copier, on a shelf, he spotted candles. Malone grabbed the box and noticed that their diameter was only slightly larger than the medallion. "We'll make our own scytale."

Stephanie instantly understood. "There's a kitchen down the hall. I'll get a knife."

He cradled the strip of gold in his palm, protected within a crumpled sheet of paper they'd found in the treasury ticket booth.

"Anybody here speak Old Greek?" he asked.

Davis and Thorvaldsen shook their heads.

"We're going to need a computer. Any word that comes off this strip will be in Old Greek."

"There's one in the office we were in before," Davis said. "Down the hall."

Stephanie returned with a peeling knife.

"You know, I'm concerned about Michener," Malone said. "What's to stop Viktor from killing him, regardless of Zovastina leaving safely?"

"Not going to be a problem," Davis said. "I wanted Michener to go with Viktor."

Malone was puzzled. "For what?"

Edwin Davis's eyes fixed on him, as if deciding if he was someone to be trusted.

Which irritated Malone. "What is it?"

Stephanie nodded and Davis said, "Viktor works for us."

VIKTOR WAS STUNNED. "WHO ARE YOU?"

"A priest with the Catholic Church, just like I said. But you're much more than you seem to be. The president of the United States wants me to talk to you."

The boat was still drifting toward the dock. In a few moments Michener would be gone. This priest had timed his revelation well.

"I was told Zovastina hired you from the Croatian security force, where you were first recruited by the Americans. You were helpful to them in Bosnia, and once they realized you were working for Zovastina, the Americans rekindled their relationship."

Viktor realized the proffered information, all true, was being offered to convince him that this envoy was real.

"Why do you do it?" Michener asked him. "Living a lie?"

He decided to be honest. "Let's say that I prefer not to be tried in a war-crimes court. I fought for the other side in Bosnia. We all did things we regret. I eased my conscience by changing sides and helping the Americans capture the worst offenders."

"Which means the other side would hate you, too, if they knew."

"Something like that."

"The Americans still hold that stick over you?"

"There's no statute of limitations on murder. I have family in Bosnia. Retaliation in that part of the world includes everyone close to you. I left there to get away from things. But when the Americans learned I was working for Zovastina, they gave me a choice. They'd sell me out either to the Bosnians or to her. I decided it was easier to join them."

"A dangerous game you're playing."

He shrugged. "Zovastina didn't know a thing about me. That's one of her weaknesses. She believes everyone around her is either too scared or too awed to challenge her." He needed to know. "The woman tonight, in the basilica, Cassiopeia Vitt, who left with Zovastina—"

"She's part of this."

Viktor now realized the gravity of the mistake he'd made. He truly could be compromised. So he needed to say, "She and I dealt with each other in Denmark. I tried to kill her, and the other two from the basilica. I had no idea. But once she tells Zovastina about what happened, I'll be dead."

"Cassiopeia won't do that. She was told about you before she came to the basilica tonight. She's counting on your help in Samarkand."

Now he understood her strange whispers in the transept gallery, and why no one who'd been in Denmark had said anything about that in front of Zovastina.

The boat eased to the dock. Michener hopped out. "Help her. I'm told she's resourceful."

And she killed with no emotion.

"May God be with you, Viktor. You seem like you're going to need him."

"He's useless."

A smile came to the priest's face. "That's what I used to think." Michener shook his head. "But I was wrong."

Viktor was like Zovastina. A pagan. Though not for religious or moral reasons. Just simply because he could not care less about what happened after he died.

"One more thing," Michener said. "In the basilica, Cassiopeia mentioned a man named Ely Lund. The Americans want to know if he's alive."

The name again. First from the woman, now from Washington.

"He was. But I'm not sure anymore."

MALONE SHOOK HIS HEAD. "YOU'VE GOT SOMEBODY ON the inside? Then what do you need us for?"

"We can't compromise him," Davis said.

"Did you know this?" he asked Stephanie.

She shook her head. "Not until a short while ago."

"Michener became the perfect conduit," Davis said. "We weren't sure how things were going to drop here, but with Zovastina ordering Viktor to take him, it worked out perfectly. We need Viktor to help Cassiopeia."

"Who is Viktor?"

"Not one of ours, born and bred," Davis said. "The CIA adopted him years ago. A random asset."

"Friendly or unfriendly adoption?" He knew a lot of assets were forced into service.

Davis hesitated. "Unfriendly."

"That's a problem."

"Last year, we renewed contact. He's been quite helpful."

"He's so deep, there's no way he can be trusted. I can't tell you how many times I've been double-crossed by random assets. They're whores."

"Like I said, so far he's proven helpful."

He was not impressed. "You apparently haven't been at this game long."

"Long enough to know that you have to take risks."

"The distance between risk and foolishness isn't much."

"Cotton," Stephanie said, "I'm told that Viktor is the one who pointed us to Vincenti."

"Which is why Naomi is dead. All the more reason not to trust him."

He laid the ball of crumpled paper on top of the copier and grabbed the knife from Stephanie. He mated the elephant medallion to the end of one candle. The coin was misshapen, worn from the centuries, but the diameter was nearly right. Only a few strokes were needed to whittle off the excess wax.

He handed the candle to Stephanie and carefully unwrapped the paper. His palms were moist, which surprised him. He grasped the gold leaf by the edge, lightly gripping it between his index finger and thumb. He plucked the end of the coil free and wrapped the strip onto the candle, which Stephanie held steady.

Slowly, he unwound the crinkly foil.

The otherwise unconnected letters rearranged as the original spiral course was restored. He recalled something he read once about a scytale. *That which follows is joined to that which precedes.*

The message became clear.

Six Greek letters.

ΚΛΙΜΑΞ.

"A good way to send a cipher, then, and now. This one has been delivered twenty-three hundred years after the fact."

The gold conformed to the candle and he realized Ptolemy's warning to *be wary, for there is but one chance of success* had been good advice. No way to unwrap the foil, since the strip would break into pieces.

"Let's find that computer," he said.

SIXTY-TWO

VINCENTI LIKED THAT HE WAS IN CONTROL. "YOU'RE A smart woman. And you clearly want to live. But how much do you know about life?"

He did not wait for Karyn Walde to answer.

"Science had always taught us that there are basically two kinds—bacteria and everything else. The difference? Bacteria have free-floating DNA, everything else has their DNA packed into a nucleus. Then in the nineteen-seventies, a microbiologist named Carl Woese found a third type of life. He called them archaea. A cross between bacteria and everything else. When first discovered, they seemed to live only in the harshest of environments—the Dead Sea, in the middle of hot springs, miles below the ocean, Antarctica, oxygen-starved swamps—and we thought that was the extent of their existence. But over the last twenty years archaea have been found everywhere."

"These bacteria you found destroy the virus?" she asked.

"With a vengeance. And I'm talking about HIV-1, HIV-2, SIV, and every hybrid strain I could find to test, including the newest from Southeast Asia. The bacteria have a protein lining that obliterate the proteins holding HIV together. They ravage the virus, just like the virus ravages host cells. And fast. The only trick is to keep the body's immune system from destroying the archaea before the bacteria can consume the virus." He pointed toward her. "In people like you, whose immune system is virtually gone, that isn't a problem, there just aren't enough white cells left to kill the invading bacteria. But where HIV has only recently taken a stand, where the immune system is still relatively strong, the white cells kill the bacteria before it gets to the virus."

"You found a way to prevent that?"

He nodded. "The bacteria actually survive digestion. That's how the old healer managed to get them into people, only he thought it was the plant. I not only chewed the plant, I drank the water, so if any of that virus was in me that day, they took care of it. I've since found it's better to administer a dose through injection. You can control the percentage. In early HIV infections, when the immune system is still strong, more bacteria are needed. In later stages, like you, when the white cell count is near zero, not as many are needed."

"That's why you wanted a varied infection rate in that clinical trial? You needed to know how strong a dose."

"Smart girl."

"So whoever wrote that report you read to me, and thought it strange you weren't concerned with toxicity, was wrong."

"I was obsessed with toxicity. I needed to know how much of the archaea would be needed to kill off various stages of an HIV infection. The great thing is that the bacteria, by themselves, are harmless. You could ingest billions and nothing would happen."

"So you used those Iraqis like research animals."

He shrugged. "Had to in order to know if the archaea worked. They didn't know. I eventually adapted a shell to preserve the bacteria's effectiveness, which gives them more time to devour the virus. The amazing thing is that the shell eventually sheds and the immune system absorbs the archaea, like any other circulatory invader. Cleans it right out. The virus is gone, and so are the archaea. You just don't want too many of the bacteria—overworks the immune system. But, overall, it's a simple, totally effective cure to one of the deadliest viruses in the world. And not one side effect that I've discovered."

He knew she'd experienced, firsthand, the havoc of the symptomatic HIV drugs. Rashes, ulcers, fever, fatigue, nausea, low blood pressure, headaches, vomiting, nerve damage, insomnia—all were common.

He again held up the syringe. "This will cure you."

"Give it to me." Desperation laced her plea.

"You know Zovastina could have done this." He saw the lie had the desired effect. "She knows."

"I knew she did. Her and those germs. She's been obsessed with them for years."

"She and I worked together. Yet she never offered a thing to you."

She shook her head. "Never. She'd just come and watch me die."

"She had total control. There was nothing you could do. I understand your breakup, years ago, was difficult. She felt cheated. When you returned, asking for help, you realize you gave her an opportunity to exact a measure of revenge. She would have let you die. Would you like to return the favor?"

He watched as the moment of truth weighed on her mind but, just as he'd suspected, her conscience had long since dissolved.

"I just want to breathe. If that's the price, I'll pay it."

"You're going to be the first person cured of AIDS—"

"Who gets to tell the tale."

He nodded. "That's right. We're going to make history."

She didn't seem impressed. "If your cure is so simple, why couldn't somebody just steal or copy it?"

"Only I know where this particular archaea can be

found naturally. Believe me, there are many kinds, but only this one works."

Her oily eyes narrowed. "We know why I want to do this. What about you?"

"Lots of questions from a dying woman."

"You seem like a man who wants to provide answers."

"Zovastina is an impediment to my plans."

"Cure me, and I'll help you eliminate that problem."

He doubted her unconditional assurance, but keeping this woman alive made sense. Her anger could be channeled. He'd first thought assassinating Zovastina the answer, which was why he'd allowed the Florentine a free reign. But he'd changed his mind and ratted out his co-conspirator. An assassination would only make her a martyr. Disgracing her—that was the better way. She had enemies. But they were all afraid. Maybe he could provide them with courage through the bitter soul staring up at him.

Neither the League nor he were interested in world conquest. Wars were expensive in a great many ways, the most critical of which was the depletion of wealth and national resources. The League wanted its new utopia just as it is, not as Zovastina envisioned it should be. For himself, he wanted billions in profits and to savor his status as the man who conquered HIV. Louis Pasteur, Linus Pauling, Jonas Salk, and, now, Enrico Vincenti.

So he emptied the contents of the hypodermic into the IV port.

"How long does it take?" she asked, her voice expectant, her tired face alive.

"In a few hours you'll feel much better."

MALONE SAT BEFORE THE COMPUTER AND FOUND Google. There, he located websites that dealt with Old Greek and eventually opened one that offered translations. He typed in the six letters—ΚΛΙΜΑΞ—and was surprised at both the pronunciation and the meaning.

"Klimax in Greek. Ladder in English," he said.

He found another site that also offered a conversion. He typed in the same letters from the alphabet supplied and received the same response.

Stephanie still held the candle wrapped with gold leaf.

"Ptolemy," Thorvaldsen said, "went to a lot of trouble to leave this. That word must have great relevance."

"And what happens when we figure it out?" Malone asked. "What's the big deal?"

"The big deal," a new voice said, "is that Zovastina is planning to kill millions of people."

They all turned and saw Michener standing in the doorway.

"I just left Viktor out in the lagoon. He was shocked that I knew about him."

"I imagine he was," Thorvaldsen said.

"Is Zovastina gone?" Malone asked.

Michener nodded. "I checked. Left the ground a little while ago."

Malone wanted to know, "How does Cassiopeia know about Viktor?" Then it hit him. He faced Thorvaldsen. "The call. Out at the dock when we first got here. You told her then."

The Dane nodded. "Information she needed. We're lucky she didn't kill him on Torcello. But, of course, I didn't know any of this then."

"More of that 'plan as you go,' " Malone said, directing his comment to Davis.

"I'll take the blame for that one. But it worked out."

"And three men are dead."

Davis said nothing.

He wanted to know, "And if Zovastina had not insisted on a hostage for safe passage to the airport?"

"Luckily, that didn't happen."

"You're too damn reckless for me." He was becoming irritated. "If you have Viktor on the inside, why don't you know if Ely Lund's alive?"

"That fact wasn't important, until yesterday, when you three became involved. Zovastina had a teacher, we just didn't know who. It makes sense it's Lund. Once we learned that, we needed Viktor contacted."

"Viktor said Ely Lund was alive. But probably not now," Michener told them.

"Cassiopeia has no idea what she's facing," Malone said. "She's in there blind."

"She set all that up herself," Stephanie said, "perhaps hoping that Ely might still be alive."

He didn't want to hear that. For a variety of reasons. None of which he needed to face at the moment.

"Cotton," Thorvaldsen said, "you asked why all this matters. Beyond the obvious disaster of a biological war, what if this draught is some sort of natural cure? The ancients thought it so. Alexander thought it so. The chroniclers who wrote those manuscripts thought it so. What if something *is* there? I don't know why, but Zovastina wants it. Ely wanted it. And Cassiopeia wants it."

He remained skeptical. "We don't know a damn thing."

Stephanie motioned with the candle. "We know this riddle is real."

She was right about that and, he had to admit, he was curious. That godforsaken curiosity which always seemed to keep him in trouble.

"And we know Naomi is dead," she said.

He'd not forgotten.

He stared again at the scytale. Ladder. A location? If

so, it was a designation that would have made more sense in Ptolemy's time. He knew Alexander the Great had insisted that his empire be accurately mapped. Cartography was then an infant art, but he'd seen reproductions of those ancient charts. So he decided to see what was on the web. Twenty minutes of searching found nothing that indicated what ΚΛΙΜΑΞ—klimax, ladder— might be.

"There might be another source," Thorvaldsen said. "Ely had a place in the Pamirs. A cabin. He'd go there to work and think. Cassiopeia told me about it. He kept his books and papers there. Quite an array on Alexander. She said there were lots of maps from his time."

"That's in the Federation," Malone pointed out. "I doubt Zovastina is going to grant us a visa."

"How near is the border?" Davis asked.

"Thirty miles."

"We can enter through China. They're cooperating with us on this."

"And what is *this*?" Malone asked. "Why are *we* even involved? Don't you have a CIA and a multitude of other intelligence agencies?"

"Actually, Mr. Malone, you involved yourself, as did Thorvaldsen and Stephanie. Zovastina, publicly, is the only ally we possess in that region, so politically we can't be seen challenging her. Using official assets comes with the risk of exposure. Since we had Viktor on the inside, keeping us informed, we knew most of her moves. But this is escalating. I understand the dilemma with Cassiopeia—"

"Actually, you don't. But that's why I'm staying in. I'm going after her."

"I'd prefer you go to the cabin and see what's there."

"That's the great thing about being retired. I can do what I please." He turned to Thorvaldsen. "You and Stephanie go to the cabin."

"I agree," his friend said. "See about her."

Malone stared at Thorvaldsen. The Dane had aided Cassiopeia and cooperated with the president, involving them all. But his friend didn't like the idea of Cassiopeia being there alone.

"You have a plan," Thorvaldsen said. "Don't you?"

"I think I do."

SIXTY-THREE

ZOVASTINA DRANK FROM A BOTTLED WATER AND AL-
lowed her passenger the continued luxury of her troubled thoughts. They'd flown in silence for the past hour,
ever since she'd tantalized Cassiopeia Vitt with the possibility that Ely Lund might still be alive. Clearly, her
captive was on a mission. Personal? Or professional?
That remained to be seen.

"How do you and the Dane know my business?"

"A lot of people know your business."

"If they know it so well, why hasn't anyone stopped
me?"

"Maybe we're about to?"

She grinned. "An army of three? You, the old man,
and Mr. Malone? By the way, is Malone a friend of
yours?"

"United States Justice Department."

She assumed what happened in Amsterdam had generated official interest, but the situation made little
sense. How would the Americans have mobilized so
quickly—and known she'd be in Venice? Michener?
Maybe. United States Justice Department. The Americans. Another problem flashed through her mind. Vincenti.

"You have no idea," Vitt said to her, "how much we
do know."

"I don't need an idea. I have you."

"I'm expendable."

She doubted that declaration. "Ely taught me a great deal. More than I ever knew existed. He opened my eyes to the past. I suspect he opened yours, too."

"It's not going to work. You can't use him to get to me."

She needed to break this woman. Her whole plan had been based on moving in secret. Exposure would open her not only to failure but also to retaliation. Cassiopeia Vitt represented, for the moment, the quickest and easiest way to ascertain the full extent of her problem.

"I went to Venice to find answers," she said. "Ely pointed me there. He believed the body in the basilica might lead to Alexander the Great's true grave. He thought that location may hold the secret of an ancient cure. Something that might help even him."

"That's dreaming."

"But it's a dream he shared with you, wasn't it?"

"Is he alive?"

Finally, a direct question. "You won't believe me no matter how I answer."

"Try me."

"He didn't die in that house fire."

"That's not an answer."

"It's all you're going to get."

The plane dipped as turbulence buffeted the wings and the engines continued their constant whine, driving them farther east. The cabin was empty save for them. Both of her guardsmen, who'd made the flight to Venice, were dead, their bodies now Michener's and the Church's problem. Only Viktor had kept faith and performed, as usual.

She and her captive were a lot alike. Both of them cared for people afflicted with HIV. Cassiopeia Vitt to the point that she'd risked her life, Zovastina to the point that she gambled on a questionable journey to Venice and placed herself in physical and political jeopardy. Foolishness? Perhaps.

But heroes, at times, had to be fools.

SIXTY-FOUR

VINCENTI WAS HOLED UP IN THE LAB HE'D BUILT BE-neath his estate, only he and Grant Lyndsey inside. Lynd-sey had come straight from China, his duties there done. Two years ago he'd taken Lyndsey into his confidence. He'd needed somebody out front to supervise all the testing on the viruses and antiagents. Also, somebody had to placate Zovastina.

"How's the temperature?" he asked.

Lyndsey checked the digital readouts. "Stable."

The lab was Vincenti's domain. A passive, sterile space encased within cream-colored walls atop a black tile floor. Stainless-steel tables ran in two rows down the center. Flasks, beakers, and burettes towered on metal stands above an autoclave, distilling equipment, a cen-trifuge, analytical balances, and two computer termi-nals. Digital simulation played a key role in their experimentation, so different from his days with the Iraqis, when trial and error cost time, money, and mis-takes. Today's sophisticated programs were able to du-plicate most any chemical or biological effect, so long as there were parameters. And, over the past year, Lyndsey had done an admirable job establishing parameters for the cyber-testing of ZH.

"The solution is at room temperature," Lyndsey said. "And they're swimming like crazy. Amazing."

The pool where he'd found the archaea was thermal fed, its temperature pushing one hundred degrees Fahrenheit. Producing the bacteria in the trillions that would be needed, then safely transporting them around the world at such high temperatures, could prove impossible. So they'd changed them. Slowly adapting the archaea to lower and lower thermal environments. Interestingly, at room temperature their activity only slowed, almost going dormant, but once inside a warm bloodstream at ninety-eight point six degrees, they quickly reactivated.

"The clinical trial I finished a few days ago," Lyndsey said, "confirmed that they can be stored at room temperature for a prolonged time. I'd held those for over four months. It's incredible, their adaptability."

"Which is how they've survived billions of years, waiting for us to find them."

He huddled close to one of the tables, fleshy hands inserted through rubber gloves into a hermetically sealed container. Air purred overhead, forced through laminar microfilters, cleansed of impurities, the constant rumble nearly hypnotic. He stared through a plexiglass portal and deftly manipulated the evaporating dish. He dabbed a sample of active HIV culture onto a slide, swirling the drop with another already there. He then clipped the slide onto the built-in microscope's stage. He freed his hands of the sweaty rubber and focused the objective.

Two adjustments and he found the right power.

One look was all he required.

"The virus is gone. Almost on contact. It's like they've been waiting to devour it."

He knew their biological modifications were the key to success. A few years ago a New York law firm he'd engaged advised him that a new mineral discovered in the earth, or a new plant found in the wild, was not something that could be patented. Einstein could not patent his celebrated $E=mc^2$, nor could Newton have patented the law of gravity. Those were manifestations of nature, free to all. But genetically engineered plants, man-made multicellular animals, and archaea-bacteria altered from their natural state, these were patentable.

He'd make a call to the same law firm later and start the patent process. FDA approval would also be needed. Twelve years was the average time for an experimental solution to travel from lab to medicine chest—the American system of drug approvals the most rigorous in the world. And he knew the odds. Only five in four thousand compounds screened in FDA preclinical testing made it to human testing. Only one of those five ultimately gained approval. Seven years ago a new fast-track testing procedure for compounds that targeted life-threatening diseases had been okayed—AIDS treatments specifically in that category. Still, quick by FDA standards was six to nine months. European approval processes were stringent, but nothing like the FDA. African and Asian nations, where the major problem existed, didn't require government approvals.

So that's where he'd start selling.

Let the world see them being cured while American and European AIDS patients died. Approval would come then, without him even asking.

"I've never asked," Lyndsey said, "and you've never said. But where did you find these bacteria?"

The time for silence was over. He needed Lyndsey on board—completely. But answering his question about *where* also meant discussing *when*.

"Have you ever considered the value of a company that manufactured condoms prior to HIV? Sure, there was a market. What? Several million a year? But *after* the resurgence of AIDS, billions were manufactured and sold worldwide. And what about the symptomatic drugs? Treating AIDS is the perfect money machine. A triple drug cocktail treatment is twelve to eighteen thousand U.S. dollars a year. Multiply that by the millions infected and you're talking billions spent on drugs that cure nothing.

"Think about the supply benefits—things like latex gloves, gowns, sterile needles. You have any idea how many millions of sterile needles are bought and distributed in trying to stop the HIV spread among drug users? And, like condoms, the price has gone through the roof. The range here is endless. For a medical supply and manufacturing house, like Philogen, HIV has been a huge cash bonanza.

"Over the past eighteen years, our business has soared, our condom manufacturing plant has tripled in size. Sales went through the roof for all of our products. We even developed a couple of symptomatic drugs that sold well. Ten years ago I took the company public, raised capital, and used the expanding medical supply and drug divisions to fund more expansion. I bought a cosmetics firm, a soap company, a department store chain, and a frozen food business, knowing one day Philogen could easily pay all the debt back."

"How did you know?"

"I found the bacteria almost thirty years ago. I realized their potential twenty years ago. Then I held the cure for HIV, knowing I could release it at any time."

He watched the realization take hold.

"And you told no one?"

"Not a soul." He needed to know if Lyndsey was as amoral as he believed him to be. "Is that a problem? I simply let the market build."

"Knowing that you didn't have a partial fix, something the virus would eventually work around. Knowing you had *the* cure. The one way to totally destroy HIV.

Even if somebody eventually found a drug to quell the virus, yours worked better, faster, safer, and costs pennies to produce."

"That was the idea."

"It didn't matter to you that people were dying by the millions?"

"And you think the world cares about AIDS? Get real, Grant. Lots of talk, little action. It's a unique disease. The perception is that it mainly kills blacks, gays, and drug users. The whole epidemic has rolled back a big rotting log and revealed all the squirming life underneath—the main themes of our existence—sex, death, power, money, love, hate, panic. In nearly every way that AIDS has been conceptualized, imagined, researched, and financed, it's become the most political of diseases."

And what Karyn Walde said earlier came to mind. *It's just not killing the right people yet.*

"What about the other pharmaceutical companies?" Lyndsey said. "Weren't you afraid they'd find a cure?"

"A risk, but I've kept a close eye on our competition. Let's just say that their research bought little more than mistakes." He was feeling good. After all this time, he liked talking about it. "Would you like to see where the bacteria live?"

The man's eyes lit up. "Here?"

He nodded. "Close by."

SIXTY-FIVE

CASSIOPEIA WAS TAKEN FROM THE PLANE BY TWO OF Zovastina's guardsmen. She'd been told that they would escort her to the palace, where she'd be held.

"You realize," she said to Zovastina, from beside the open car door, "that you've bargained for trouble."

Zovastina surely would not want to have this conversation here, on an open tarmac, with an airport crew and her guardsmen nearby. On the plane, alone, would have been the time. But Cassiopeia had purposefully stayed silent the last two hours of the flight.

"Trouble is a way of life here," Zovastina said.

As she was guided into the rear seat, her hands cuffed behind her back, Cassiopeia decided to insert the knife. "You were wrong about the bones."

Zovastina seemed to consider the challenge. Venice had, for all intents and purposes, been a failure, so it was no surprise when Zovastina approached and asked, "How so?"

The whine of jet engines and a stiff spring breeze stirred the fume-filled air. Cassiopeia sat calmly in the rear seat and stared out through the front windshield. "There was something to find." She faced the Supreme Minister. "And you missed it."

"Taunting me will not help."

She ignored the threat. "If you want to solve the riddle, you're going to have to bargain."

This demon was easy to read. Certainly, Zovastina had suspected she knew things. Why else bring her? And Cassiopeia had been careful so far, knowing that she could not reveal too much. After all, her life literally depended on how much information she could effectively withhold.

One of the guardsmen stepped forward and whispered in Zovastina's ear. The Minister listened, and she saw a momentary shock sweep across her face. Then Zovastina nodded and the guardsman withdrew.

"Trouble?" Cassiopeia asked.

"The perils of being Supreme Minister. You and I will talk later."

And she marched off.

THE FRONT DOOR OF THE HOUSE STOOD OPEN. NOTHing damaged. No evidence of forced entry. Inside, two of her Sacred Band waited. Zovastina glared at one and asked, "What happened?"

"Both of our men were shot through the head. Sometime last night. The nurse and Karyn Walde are gone. Their clothes are still here. The nurse's alarm clock was set and on for six A.M. Nothing shows they intended to voluntarily leave."

She walked back to the master bedroom. The respirator stood silent, the intravenous drip connected to no one. Had Karyn escaped? And where would she go? She stepped back to the foyer and asked her two men, "Any witnesses?"

"We asked at the other residences, but no one saw or heard anything."

It had all happened while she was gone. That could not be a coincidence. She decided to play a hunch. She stepped to one of the house phones and dialed her personal secretary. She told her what she wanted and waited three minutes until the woman returned on the line and said, "Vincenti entered the Federation last night at 1:40 A.M. Private plane using his open visa."

She still believed Vincenti had been behind the assassination attempt. He must have known she'd left the Federation. Her government clearly possessed a multitude of leaks—Henrik Thorvaldsen and Cassiopeia Vitt were proof of that—but what to do about those things?

"Minister," her secretary said through the phone, "I was about to try and locate you. You have a visitor."

"Vincenti?" she asked, a bit too quickly.

"Another American."

"The ambassador?" Samarkand was dotted with foreign embassies, and many of her days were filled with visits from their various representatives.

"Edwin Davis, the deputy national security adviser to the American president. He entered the country a few hours ago on a diplomatic passport."

"Unannounced?"

"He simply appeared at the palace, asking to see you. He will not discuss with anyone why he's here."

That was not a coincidence, either.

"I'll be there shortly."

SIXTY-SIX

MALONE DRANK A COCA-COLA LIGHT AND WATCHED AS
the Lear Jet 36A approached the terminal. Samarkand's
airport lay north of the city, a single runway facility that
accommodated not only commercial traffic, but also private and military. He'd beaten both Viktor and Zovastina back from Italy thanks to an F-15-E Strike Eagle
that President Daniels had ordered placed at his disposal. Aviano Air Base, fifty miles north of Venice, had
been a quick chopper ride and the flight east, thanks to
supersonic speeds at over thirteen hundred miles an
hour, had taken just over two hours. Zovastina and the
Lear Jet he was now watching taxi closer had needed almost five hours.

Two F-15-Es had arrived in Samarkand without incident, as the United States possessed unrestricted landing
rights at all Federation airports and bases. Ostensibly,
the U.S. was an ally, but that distinction, he knew, was
fleeting at best in this part of the world. The other
fighter had carried Edwin Davis, who was, by now, at
the palace. President Daniels had not liked involving
Davis, he had preferred to keep him at a distance, but
wisely recognized that Malone was not going to take no
for an answer. Besides, as the president had said with a

chuckle, the whole plan had at least a ten percent chance of working, so what the hell.

He gulped the last of the soft drink, weak by American standards but tasty enough. He'd slept an hour on the flight, the first time he'd been inside a strike fighter in twenty years. He'd been trained to fly them early in his navy career, before he became a lawyer and switched to the Judge Advocate General's corps. Naval friends of his father had urged him to make the choice.

His father.

A full commander. Until one August day when the submarine he captained sank. Malone had been ten, but the memory always brought a pang of sadness. By the time he'd enlisted in the navy, his father's contemporaries had risen to high rank and they had plans for Forrest Malone's son. So out of respect, he'd done as they'd asked and ended up as an agent with the Magellan Billet.

He never regretted his choices, and his Justice Department career had been memorable. Even in retirement the world had not ignored him. Templars. The Library of Alexandria. Now Alexander the Great's grave. He shook his head. Choices. Everybody made them.

Like the man now deplaning from the Lear Jet. Viktor. Government informant. Random asset.

Problem.

He tossed the bottle into the trash and waited for Viktor to step into the concourse. An AWACS E3 Sentry, always in orbit over the Middle East, had tracked the Lear Jet from Venice, Malone knowing precisely when it would arrive.

Viktor appeared as in the basilica, his face chapped, his clothes dirty. He walked with the stiffness of a man who'd just endured a long night.

Malone retreated behind a short wall and waited until

Viktor was inside, turning toward the terminal, then he stepped out and followed. "Took you long enough."

Viktor stopped and turned. Not a hint of surprise clouded the other man's face. "I thought I was to help Vitt."

"I'm here to help you."

"You and your friends set me up in Copenhagen. I don't like being played."

"Who does?"

"Go back where you came from, Malone. Let me handle this."

Malone withdrew a pistol. One of the advantages of arriving by military jet had been no Customs checks for U.S. military personnel or their passengers. "I've been told to help you. That's what I'm going to do, whether you like it or not."

"You going to shoot me?" Viktor shook his head. "Cassiopeia Vitt killed my partner in Venice and tried to kill me."

"At the time, she didn't know you wore the white hat."

"You sound like you think that's a problem."

"I haven't decided whether you're a problem or not."

"That woman is the problem," Viktor said. "I doubt she's going to let either one of us help her."

"Probably right, but she's going to get it." He decided to try a pat on the back. "I'm told you've been a good asset. So let's help her."

"I planned to. I just didn't count on an assistant."

He stuffed the gun back beneath his jacket. "Get me into the palace."

Viktor seemed puzzled by the request. "Is that all?"

"Shouldn't be a problem for the head of the Sacred Band. No one would question you."

Viktor shook his head. "You people are insane. Do you all have a death wish? Bad enough she's in there.

Now you? I can't be responsible for all this. And, by the way, it's foolish for us to even be talking. Zovastina knows your face."

Malone had already checked. The concourse was not equipped with cameras. Those were farther on, in the terminal. No one else was around, which was why he'd decided here was a good place for a chat. "Just get me into the palace. If you point me in the right direction, I can do the heavy lifting. That'll give you cover. You don't have to do anything, except watch my back. Washington wants to protect your identity at all costs. That's why I'm here."

Viktor shook his head in disbelief. "And who came up with this ridiculous plan?"

He grinned. "I did."

SIXTY-SEVEN

VINCENTI LED LYNDSEY BEYOND THE HOUSE GROUNDS, onto a rocky trail that inclined up into the highlands. He'd ordered the ancient path smoothed, steps carved into the rock at places, and electricity wired, knowing that he'd be making the trek more than a few times. Both the path and the mountain were within the estate's boundaries. Every time he returned to this place he thought of the old healer who'd clambered up the rock face, catlike, clinging to the path with bare toes and fingers. Vincenti had followed, climbing with anticipation, like a child after his parent up the stairs wondering what awaited in the attic.

And he'd not been disappointed.

Gray rock streaked with mottled veins of gleaming crystals surrounded them in what seemed like a natural cathedral. His legs ached from the exertion and the breath tore at his lungs. He dragged himself up another stretch of cliff and beads of sweat gathered on his brow.

Lyndsey, a thin and wiry man, seemed unaffected.

Vincenti gave a deep exhale of thankfulness as he stopped on the final ledge. "To the west, the Federation. The east, China. We're standing at the crossroad."

Lyndsey stared out at the vista. An afternoon sun spotlighted a distant stretch of towering scarps and pyramids. A herd of horses rushed in silence through the valley beyond the house.

Vincenti was enjoying sharing this. Telling Karyn

Walde had ignited within him a need for recognition. He'd discovered something remarkable and managed to gain exclusive control of it, no small feat considering this whole region was once Soviet-dominated. But the Federation had changed all that, and through the Venetian League, he'd helped navigate those changes to his personal advantage.

"This way," he said, motioning toward a crease in the rock. "Through there."

Three decades ago the narrow slit had been easy to traverse, but he'd been a hundred and fifty pounds lighter. Now it was a tight squeeze.

The crevice opened a short way into a gray chamber beneath an irregular vault of sharp rock, walled in on all sides. Dim light leaked in from the entrance. He stepped to a switch box and powered on incandescent lighting that hung from the ceiling. Two pools dotted the rock floor, each about ten feet in diameter—one, a russet brown; the other, a sea foam green—both illuminated by cabled lights suspended in the water.

"Hot springs dot these mountains," he said. "From ancient times until today, the locals believed they contained valuable medicinal properties. Here, they were right."

"Why light them?"

He shrugged. "I needed to study the water and, as you can see, they're stunning with the contrasting color."

"This is where the archaea live?"

He pointed at the green-tinted pool. "That's their home."

Lyndsey bent down and stroked the surface. A host of ripples shivered across its transparent surface. None of the plants that had been there the first time Vincenti had been there dotted the pool. They'd apparently died out long ago. But they weren't important.

"Just over a hundred degrees," he said of the water.

"But our modifications now allow them to live at room temperature."

One of Lyndsey's tasks had been to prepare an action plan—what the company would do once Zovastina acted—when massive amounts of antiagent would supposedly be needed, so Vincenti asked, "Are we ready to go?"

"Growing the small quantities we've been using on the zoonoses was easy. Full-scale production will be different."

He'd thought as much, which was why he'd secured the loan from Arthur Benoit. Infrastructure would have to be built, people hired, distribution networks created, more research completed. All of which required massive amounts of capital.

"Our production facilities in France and Spain can be converted into acceptable manufacturing sites," Lyndsey said. "Eventually, though, I'd recommend a separate facility, since we'll need millions of liters. Luckily, the bacteria reproduce easily."

Time to see if the man was truly interested. "Have you ever dreamed of going down in history?"

Lyndsey laughed. "Who doesn't?"

"I mean seriously go down in history, as someone who made a tremendous scientific contribution. What if I could bestow that honor? You interested?"

"Like I said, who wouldn't be?"

"Imagine schoolchildren, decades from now, looking up HIV and AIDS in an encyclopedia, and there's your name as the man who helped conquer the scourge of the late twentieth century." He recalled the first pleasure of that vision. Not all that dissimilar from Lyndsey's current look of curiosity and amazement. "Would you like to be a part of that?"

No hesitation. "Of course."

"I can give you that. But there'd be conditions. Needless to say, I can't do this by myself. I need someone to personally oversee production, someone who understands the biology. Security is, of course, a great concern. Once our patents are filed, I'll feel better, but somebody still has to manage this on a daily basis. You're the logical choice, Grant. In return, you'll receive some discovery credit and generous compensation. And by generous, I'm talking millions."

Lyndsey opened his mouth to speak, but Vincenti silenced him with an upright finger.

"That's the good part. Here's the bad. If you become a problem, or you become greedy, I'll have O'Conner plant a bullet in your head. Back at the house I told you about how we controlled our competition. Let me explain further."

He told Lyndsey about a Danish microbiologist found in 1997, comatose in the street near his laboratory. Another, in California, who vanished, his abandoned rental car parked near a bridge, his body never located. A third in 2001 found on the side of an English country road, the apparent victim of a hit and run. A fourth murdered in a French farmhouse. Another died uniquely, his body discovered ten years ago trapped in the airlock to the walk-in refrigerator at his lab. Five died simultaneously in 1999 when their private plane crashed into the Black Sea.

"All worked for our competitors," he said. "They were making progress. Too much. So, Grant, do as I say. Be grateful for the opportunity I've given you, and we'll both live to be rich, old men."

"You won't have any trouble from me."

He thought he'd guessed right choosing this soul. Lyndsey had handled Zovastina masterfully, never once compromising the antigents. He'd also maintained security at the lab. Everything had played out perfectly, in no small part thanks to this man.

"I am curious about one thing," Lyndsey said.

He decided to indulge him.

"Why now? You've held the cure. Why not wait longer?"

"Zovastina's war plan makes the time right. We had a vehicle, through her, where the research could be completed without anyone knowing any better. I see no reason to wait any longer. I just have to stop Zovastina before she goes too far. And what of you, Grant? Now that you know, does all this bother you?"

"You held that secret twenty years. I only found out an hour ago. Not my problem."

He smiled. Good attitude. "There'll be a spate of publicity. You'll be a part of that. But I control everything you say, so watch your words. You should be seen far more than heard. Soon your name will be ranked with the greats." He swept his hands across an invisible marquee. "Grant Lyndsey, one of the slayers of HIV."

"Has a nice ring to it."

"We're going public within the next thirty days. In the meantime I'm going to want you to work with my patent lawyers. I plan to tell them tomorrow of our breakthrough. When the actual announcement is made, I want you at the podium. I also want samples—they'll make great photo ops. And slides of the bacteria. We'll have the PR people make pictures. It'll be quite a show."

"Do others know about this?"

He shook his head. "Not a soul, save for a woman back at the house who is, at this moment, experiencing the benefits. We need someone to show off and she's as good as any."

Lyndsey stepped to the other pool. Interesting that he'd not noticed what lay in the bottom of each, which was another reason he'd chosen this man. "I told you that this is an ancient place. See the letters at the bottom of the pools?"

Lyndsey found both.

"They mean life in old Greek. How they got there, I have no idea. I managed to learn from that old healer that Greeks once worshipped this area, so that might explain it. They called this mountain Klimax. Ladder, in English. Why? Probably had a lot to do with what the Asians named this place. Arima. I decided to use their name for the estate."

"I saw the sign at the gate when I drove in. Attico. What does it mean?"

"It's Italian for Arima. Means the same. Place at the top, like an attic."

SIXTY-EIGHT

SAMARKAND

ZOVASTINA MARCHED INTO THE PALACE'S AUDIENCE chamber and faced a thin man with bushy gray hair. Her foreign minister, Kamil Revin, was also there, sitting to one side. Protocol demanded his presence. The American introduced himself as Edwin Davis and produced a letter from the president of the United States that attested to his credentials.

"If I may, Minister," Davis said in a light tone, "could we speak in private?"

She was puzzled. "Anything you would tell me, I would pass on to Kamil anyway."

"I doubt you would pass on what we'll be discussing."

The words came out as a challenge, but the envoy's facial expression never broke, so she decided to be cautious. "Leave us," she said to Kamil.

The younger man hesitated. But after Venice and Karyn, she was not in the mood.

"Now," she said.

Her foreign minister rose and left.

"Do you always treat your people like that?"

"This is not a democracy. Men like Kamil do as told, or—"

"One of your germs will visit their bodies."

She should have known that even more people knew her business. But this time it ran straight to Washington.

"I don't recall your president ever complaining of the peace the Federation has brought to this region. Once this whole area was a problem, now America enjoys the benefits of a friend. And governing here is not a matter of persuasion. It's about strength."

"Don't misunderstand, Minister. Your methods are not our concern. We agree. Having a friend is worth the occasional"—Davis hesitated—"personnel replacement." His cold eyes communicated a look of begrudging respect. "Minister, I've come here to personally tell you something. The president did not think the usual diplomatic channels appropriate. This conversation needs to remain between us, as friends."

What choice did she have? "All right."

"Do you know a woman named Karyn Walde?"

Her legs tightened as emotions ricocheted through her. But she held her composure and decided to be honest. "I do. What of it?"

"She was kidnapped last night. From a house here in Samarkand. She was once your lover, and is currently afflicted with AIDS."

She fought to maintain a dull look. "You seem to know a lot about my life."

"We like to know all we can about our friends. Unlike you, we live in an open society where all of our secrets are either on television or the Internet."

"And what brought you to delve into mine?"

"Does that matter? It's fortuitous that we did."

"And what do you know about Karyn's disappearance?"

"A man named Enrico Vincenti took her. She's being held at his estate, here in the Federation. Land he purchased as part of your deal with the Venetian League."

The message was clear. This man knew many things.

"I'm also here to say that Cassiopeia Vitt is not your problem."

She concealed her surprise.

"Vincenti. *He's* your problem."

"And why is that?"

"I'll admit that this is just speculation on our part. In most places of the world, nobody would care about your sexual orientation. True, you were once married but, from what we've been able to learn, it was for appearances. He died tragically—"

"He and I never had a cross word. He understood why he was there. I actually liked him."

"That's not our concern, and I didn't mean to insult. But you have remained unmarried since. Karyn Walde worked for you for a time. One of your secretaries. So, I imagine, having a private relationship with her proved easy. No one paid much attention, so long as you were careful. But central Asia is not western Europe." Davis reached into his jacket and removed a small recorder. "Let me play something for you." He activated the unit and stood it upright on the table between them.

"*And it's good to know your information was accurate.*"

"*I wouldn't have bothered you with fantasy.*"

"*But you still haven't said how you knew someone would try to kill me today.*"

"*The League watches over its members, and you, Supreme Minister, are one of our most important.*"

"*You're so full of it, Enrico.*"

Davis switched off the recorder. "You and Vincenti, talking on the phone two days ago. An international call. Easily monitored."

He pushed "Play" again.

"*We need to talk.*"

"*Your payment for saving my life?*"

"*Your end of our bargain, as we originally discussed long ago.*"

"*I'll be ready to meet with the Council in a few days. First, there are things I need to resolve.*"

"*I'm more interested in when you and I will meet.*"

"*I'm sure you are. I am, too, actually. But there are things I must complete.*"

"*My time on the Council ends soon. Thereafter, you'll have others to deal with. They may not be as accommodating.*"

"*I do enjoy dealing with you, Enrico. We so understand each other.*"

"*We need to talk.*"

"*Soon. First, you have that other problem we spoke about. The Americans.*"

"*Not to worry, I plan to deal with that today.*"

Davis switched off the machine. "Vincenti dealt with the problem. He killed one of our agents. We found her body, along with another man, the one who arranged for your assassination."

"You allowed her to die? Knowing of the conversation?"

"Unfortunately, we did not have this recording until after she disappeared."

She didn't like the way Davis' eyes flickered between her and the recorder—along with the strange uneasiness that accompanied her growing anger.

"Apparently, you and Vincenti are engaged in some sort of joint venture. I'm here—again, as your friend—to tell you that he intends to change that deal. Here's what we think. Vincenti needs you out of power. With Karyn Walde, he can shame you from office or, at a minimum, cause you enormous political problems. Homosexuality is not accepted here. Religious fundamentalists, whom you keep on a tight leash, would finally have the ammunition to fire back. You'd have problems so massive, not even your germs could ease them."

She'd never considered the possibility before, but

what the American said made sense. Why else would Vincenti take Karyn? Yet there was something that needed to be mentioned. "Like you said, she's dying of AIDS and may already be dead."

"Vincenti's no fool. Maybe he believes a dying declaration could actually carry more weight. You'd have a lot of questions to answer—about that house, why Walde was there, the nurse. I'm told that she knows things, along with many of your Sacred Band, who guarded the house. Vincenti has the nurse, too. That's a lot of people to contain."

"This isn't America. Television can be controlled."

"But can fundamentalism? Along with the fact that you have plenty of enemies who'd like to take your place. I think the man who just left here falls into that category. By the way, he met with Vincenti last night, too. Picked him up at the airport and drove him into the city."

This man was superbly informed.

"Minister, we don't want Vincenti to succeed with whatever he's planning. That's why I'm here. To offer our assistance. We're aware of your trip to Venice and of Cassiopeia Vitt returning here with you. Again she's not a problem. In fact, she knows quite a bit about what you were seeking in Venice. There's information you missed."

"Tell me what it is."

"If I knew, I would. You'll have to ask Vitt. She and her two associates, Henrik Thorvaldsen and Cotton Malone, are aware of something called Ptolemy's riddle and objects known as elephant medallions." Davis held up his hands in a mock surrender. "Don't know. Don't care. That's your business. All I know is that there was something to find in Venice, which you apparently missed. If you already are aware, I apologize for wasting your time. But President Daniels wanted you to know that, like the Venetian League, he, too, looks after his friends."

Enough. This man needed to be put in his place. "You must take me for an idiot."

They exchanged glances, but no words.

"Tell your president I don't need his help."

Davis appeared offended.

"If I were you," she said, "I'd leave this Federation as quickly as you came."

"A threat, Minister?"

She shook her head. "Just a comment."

"Strange way to talk to a friend."

She stood. "You're not my friend."

The door closed as Edwin Davis left the chamber. Her mind churned with an ability she'd always managed when seizing an opportune moment.

Kamil Revin reentered and walked to her desk. She studied her foreign minister. Vincenti thought himself clever, cultivating him to be a spy. But this Russian-educated Asian, who professed to be a Muslim but never entered a mosque, had acted as the perfect conduit for disinformation. She'd dismissed him earlier from her meeting with Davis because he could not repeat what he did not know.

"You failed to mention that Vincenti was in the Federation," she said.

Revin shrugged. "He came in last night on business. He's at the Intercontinental, as always."

"He's at his estate in the mountains."

She noticed the surprise in the younger man's eyes. Real? Or an act? Hard to say with this one. But he seemed to sense her suspicion.

"Minister, I've been your ally. I've lied for you. I've delivered enemies to you. I've watched Vincenti for years and have faithfully acted as you instructed."

She had not the time to argue. "Then show your loyalty. I have a special task that only you can perform."

SIXTY-NINE

STEPHANIE LIKED SEEING HENRIK THORVALDSEN FRAZ-
zled. They'd flown from Aviano Air Base in two F-15-Es,
she in one, Thorvaldsen the other. They'd followed Malone and Edwin Davis, who'd landed in Samarkand, then
she and Thorvaldsen continued eastward, landing at
Kashgar, just across the Federation border into China.
Thorvaldsen did not like to fly. A necessary evil, he
called it before they'd suited up. But a ride on a supersonic fighter jet was no ordinary flight. She'd ridden behind the pilot, where the weapons system officer usually
sat. Exhilarating and terrifying, the bumps and grinds at
over thirteen hundred miles per hour had kept her on
edge the entire two hours.

"I cannot believe I did that," Thorvaldsen was saying.

She noticed that he was still shaking. A car had been
waiting for them at the Kashgar airport. The Chinese
government had cooperated fully with all of Daniels' re-
quests. They were apparently quite concerned about
their neighbor and willing even to partner with Washington in order to discover if their fears were real or
imagined.

"It wasn't that bad," she said.

"Here's a memo to file. Never, ever, no matter what
anyone says, fly in one of those things."

She grinned. They were driving through the Pamirs, in
Federation territory, the border crossing nothing more
than a welcome sign. They'd climbed in elevation, pass-

ing through a succession of barren rounded spurs and equally barren valleys. She knew that *pamir* was the name for this particular type of valley, places where winter loomed long and rainfall was sparse. Lots of coarse wormwood scrub, dwarf pine, with occasional patches of rich pasture. Mostly uninhabited country, villages here and there and the occasional yurts, which clearly distinguished the scenery from the Alps or the Pyrenees, where she and Thorvaldsen had last been together.

"I've read about this area," she said. "But I've never been to this part of the world before. Pretty incredible."

"Ely loved the Pamirs. He spoke of them religiously. And I can see why."

"Did you know him well?"

"Oh, yes. I knew his parents. He and my son were close. He practically lived at Christiangade when he and Cai were boys."

Thorvaldsen appeared weary in the passenger seat, and not because of the flight. She knew better. "Cotton will look after Cassiopeia."

"I doubt if Zovastina has Ely." Thorvaldsen seemed suddenly resigned. "Viktor's right. He's probably dead."

The road flattened as they motored through one of the mountain passes and into another valley. The air outside was surprisingly warm, the lower elevations devoid of snow. Without question, the Central Asian Federation was blessed with natural wonder, but she'd read the CIA fact sheets. The Federation had targeted the entire area for economic development. Electricity, telephone, water, and sewer services were being extended, along with an upgrade of roads. This highway seemed a prime example—the asphalt appeared new.

The candle with the gold leaf still wrapped around it lay within a stainless-steel container on the rear seat. A modern-day scytale displaying a single Old Greek word. ΚΛΙΜΑΞ. Where did it lead? They had no idea, but maybe something in Ely Lund's mountain retreat would help explain its significance. They'd also come armed. Two 9mms and spare magazines. Courtesy of the U.S. military and allowed by the Chinese.

"Malone's plan," she said, "might work."

But she agreed with Cotton. Random assets, like Viktor, were not reliable. She much preferred a seasoned agent, someone who cared about retirement.

"Malone cares for Cassiopeia," Thorvaldsen said. "He won't say it, but he does. I see it in his eyes."

"I saw the pain on his face when you told him she's sick."

"That's one reason why I thought she and Ely could relate to each other. Their mutual afflictions somehow became part of their attraction."

They passed through two more sparse villages and kept driving west. Finally, just as Cassiopeia had told Thorvaldsen, the road forked, and they veered north. Ten kilometers later the landscape became more wooded. Ahead, beside a hard-packed drive that disappeared into the blackened woods, she spotted a sarissa plunged into the earth. Hanging from it was a small sign upon which was painted "Soma."

"Ely named the place appropriately," she said. "Like Alexander's tomb in Egypt."

She turned and the car bumped and swayed up the rough path. The lane climbed a quarter mile into the trees where it ended at a single-storied cabin, fashioned of rough-hewn timber planks. A covered porch shielded the front door.

"Looks like something from northern Denmark," Thorvaldsen said. "Doesn't surprise me. I'm sure it was a bit of home for him."

She parked and they stepped out into the warm afternoon. The woods all around them loomed quiet. Through the trees, northward she believed, more mountains could be seen. An eagle soared overhead.

The cabin's front door opened.

They both turned.

A man stepped out.

He was tall and handsome, with wavy blond hair. He wore jeans and a long-sleeved shirt with boots. Thorvaldsen stood rigid but his eyes instantly softened, the Dane's thoughts easily read as to the man's identity.

Ely Lund.

SEVENTY

CASSIOPEIA SMELLED WET HAY AND HORSES AND KNEW she was being held near a stable. The room was some sort of guesthouse, the furnishings adequate but not elegant, probably for staff. Boarded shutters closed the windows from the world, the door was locked and, she assumed, guarded. On the walk from the palace she'd noticed armed men on rooftop perches. Fleeing from this prison could prove dicey.

The room was equipped with a phone that did not work, and a television fed by no signal. She sat on the bed and wondered what was next. She'd managed to get herself to Asia. Now what? She'd tried to bait Zovastina, playing off the woman's obsessions. How successful she'd been was hard to tell. Something had bothered the Supreme Minister at the airport. Enough that Cassiopeia suddenly was not a priority. But at least she was still alive.

A key scraped the lock and the door swung open.

Viktor entered, followed by two armed men.

"Get up," he said.

She sat still.

"You shouldn't ignore me."

He lunged forward and backhanded her across the face, propelling her off the bed and to the carpet. She recovered and sprang to her feet, ready for a fight. Both of the men standing behind Viktor leveled their guns.

"That was for Rafael," her captor said.

Rage filled her eyes. But she knew this man was doing exactly what was expected of him. Thorvaldsen had said he was an ally, albeit a secret one. So she played along. "You're tough when backed up by men with guns."

Viktor chuckled. "I'm afraid of you? Is that what you're saying?"

She dabbed her busted lower lip.

Viktor leaped onto her and twisted an arm behind her back. He wrenched her wrist toward her shoulders. He was strong, but she had trust that he knew what he was doing, so she surrendered. Cuffs clamped one wrist, then the other. Her ankles were likewise shackled while Viktor held her down, then rolled her onto her back.

"Bring her," he ordered.

The two men grabbed her by the feet and shoulders, carrying her outside, down a graveled path to the stables. There, she was tossed, stomach first, across the back of a horse. Blood rushed to her head as she dangled, facing the ground. Viktor tied her secure with a coarse rope, then led the horse outside.

He and three other men walked with the animal in silence, across a grassy stretch about the size of two soccer fields. Goats dotted the field, feeding, and tall trees lined its perimeter. Leaving the open expanse, they entered a forest and threaded a path to a clearing encircled by more trees.

She was untied, slid from the horse's back, and stood upright. It took a few moments for the blood to drain from her head. The scene flashed in and out, then clarity came and she saw two tall poplars had been bent to the ground and tied to a third tree. Ropes led from the top of each tree and lay on the ground. She was dragged toward them, her hands freed from the cuffs, her wrists tied to each rope.

Then the shackles were removed.

She stood, arms extended, and realized what would happen if the two trees were freed from their restraint.

Out of the woods, another horse approached. A tall, gangly steed atop which rode Irina Zovastina. The Supreme Minister was dressed in leather boots and a quilted leather jacket. She surveyed the scene, dismissed Viktor and the other men, then dismounted.

"Just you and me," Zovastina said.

VIKTOR SPURRED THE HORSE AND RACED BACK TO THE stables. As soon as he'd arrived at the palace, Zovastina had ordered him to prepare the trees. It was not the first time. Three years ago she'd similarly executed a man who'd plotted revolution. No way to convert him, so she'd tied him between the trunks, brought his coconspirators to watch, then slashed the bindings herself. His body had been ravaged as the trees righted themselves, part of him dangling from one, the rest from the other. Afterward, his compatriots had been easily converted.

The horse galloped into the corral.

MALONE WAITED IN THE TACK ROOM. VIKTOR HAD smuggled him into the palace inside the trunk of a car. No one had questioned or searched the chief of the guard. Once the car was parked in the palace garage, he'd slipped out and Viktor had provided him with palace credentials. Only Zovastina would recognize him and, with Viktor as his escort, they'd easily walked to the stables, where Viktor said he could wait in safety.

He did not like anything about this situation. Both he and Cassiopeia were at the mercy of a man they knew nothing about, besides Edwin Davis' assurance that Viktor had, so far, proven reliable. He could only hope that Davis would confuse Zovastina enough to buy them time. He still carried his gun and he'd sat patient for the past hour. No sounds came from outside the door.

The stables themselves were magnificent, befitting the supreme leader of a massive Federation. He'd counted forty bays when Viktor had first brought him inside. The tack room was equipped with a variety of quality saddles and expensive equipment. He was no expert rider, but knew how to handle a horse. The room's one window opened to the stable's rear, and offered no view.

Enough. Time to act.

He drew his gun and opened the door.

No one in sight.

He turned right and headed for the open barn doorway at the far end, passing stalls accommodating some impressive-looking steeds.

He spotted a rider, beyond the doors, racing straight for the stables. He shifted and hugged the wall, approaching the exit, gun ready. Hooves ground to a halt and he heard the coarse exhales of the horse, exhausted from the gallop.

The rider slid from the saddle.

Feet pounded the earth.

He readied himself. A man rushed inside, then stopped abruptly and turned. Viktor.

"You don't follow instructions well. I told you to stay in the tack room."

He lowered the gun. "Needed some air."

"I ordered this place cleared, but somebody might still have come out."

He wasn't in the mood for a lecture. "What's happening?"

"It's Vitt. She's in trouble."

SEVENTY-ONE

STEPHANIE WATCHED THORVALDSEN CLAMP ELY LUND in a fervent embrace, like the affection of a father who'd found a lost son.

"It's so wonderful to see you," Thorvaldsen said. "I thought you were gone."

"What in the world are you doing here?" Ely asked, amazement in his voice.

Thorvaldsen seemed to recover his composure and introduced Stephanie.

"Ely," she said, "we're kind of like an Egyptian mummy. Pressed for time. Lots happening. Can we talk?"

He led them both inside. The cabin was a dull place, sparsely furnished with lots of books, magazines, and papers. She noticed nothing electrical.

"No power here," he said. "I cook with gas and heat with wood. But there's clean water and lots of privacy."

"How did you get here?" Thorvaldsen asked. "Is Zovastina holding you?"

A puzzled look came to the man's face. "Not at all. She saved my life. She's been protecting me."

They listened as Ely explained how a man had barged into his Samarkand house and held him at gunpoint. But before anything had happened, another man saved him, killing the first. Then, his house was burned with the attacker inside. Ely had been taken to Zovastina, where she explained that her political enemies had targeted him. He was secretly brought to the cabin, where he'd remained the past few months. Only a solitary guard, who lived in the village, came to check on him twice a day and brought supplies.

"The guard has a mobile phone," Ely said. "That's how Zovastina and I communicate."

Stephanie needed to know, "You told her about Ptolemy's riddle? About elephant medallions and Alexander's lost tomb?"

Ely grinned. "She loves to talk about it. The *Iliad* is a passion of hers. Anything Greek, for that matter. She's asked me lots of questions. Still does, almost every day. And, yes, I told her all about the medallions and the lost tomb."

She could see that Ely had no conception of what was happening, of the danger all of them, including him, were in. "Cassiopeia is Zovastina's prisoner. Her life could be at stake."

She saw all of the confidence leave him. "Cassiopeia's here? In the Federation? Why would the Supreme Minister want to harm her?"

"Ely," Thorvaldsen said, "let's just say that Zovastina is not your savior. She's your jailer, though she's constructed a clever jail—one that kept you contained without much effort."

"You don't know how many times I wanted to call Cassiopeia. But the Supreme Minister said we needed secrecy right now. I might place others in jeopardy, including Cassiopeia, if I involved them. She assured me all this would be over soon, and I could call who I wanted and go back to work."

Stephanie decided to get to the point. "We solved Ptolemy's riddle. We found a scytale that contained a word." She handed him a square of paper upon which was written ΚΛΙΜΑΞ. "Can you translate it?"

"Klimax. Old Greek for ladder."

ALEXANDER'S
BACTRIAN
CONQUESTS

0   MILES   200

0   KM   200

"What possible significance could that have?" she
asked.

He seemed to shake himself free of any speculation.
"Is this in the context of the riddle?"

"It's supposedly the place where the grave is located.
*Touch the innermost being of the golden illusion. Divide
the phoenix. Life provides the measure of the true grave.*

We did all that and"—she pointed to the paper—"that's what we found."

Ely seemed to grasp the enormity with no prompting. He stepped across to one of the tables and plucked a book from one of the stacks. He thumbed through, found what he was after, then flattened the volume on the table. She and Thorvaldsen stepped close and saw a map labeled "Alexander's Bactrian Conquests."

"Alexander swept eastward and took what is today Afghanistan and the Federation—what was once Turkmenistan, Tajikistan, and Kyrgyzstan. He never crossed the Pamirs into China. Instead, he veered south to India, where his conquests ended when his army revolted." Ely pointed to the map. "The area here, between the Jaxartes and Oxus Rivers, Alexander conquered in 330 BCE. To the south was the land of Bactria. To the north Scythia."

She instantly connected the dots. "That's where Alexander learned about the draught from the Scythians."

Ely seemed impressed. "That's right. Samarkand existed then, in a region called Sogdiana, though the city itself was named Maracanda. Alexander established one of his many Alexandrias, here, calling it Alexandria Eschate, the Furthest. It was the city most east in his empire, and one of the last he founded."

Ely traced his finger on the map and noted, with a pen, an X. "Klimax was a mountain, here, in what was once Tajikistan, now in the Federation. A place revered by the Scythians and, later, by Alexander, after he negotiated a peace with them. It was said that their kings were buried in these mountains, though no evidence of that has ever been found. The museum in Samarkand sent a couple of expeditions to look around, but found nothing. Pretty barren place, in fact."

"It's exactly where the scytale points," Thorvaldsen said. "Have you been to the area?"

Ely nodded. "Two years ago. Part of an expedition. I'm told that a good bit of this is now privately owned. One of my colleagues at the museum said there's a huge estate at the base of the mountain. A monstrous thing. Under construction."

Stephanie recalled what Edwin Davis had told her about the Venetian League. Members were buying property, so she played a hunch. "Do you know who owns it?"

He shook his head. "No idea."

"We need to go," Thorvaldsen said. "Ely, can you lead us there?"

The younger man nodded. "It's about three hours south."

"How are you feeling?"

Stephanie realized what the Dane meant.

"She knows," Thorvaldsen said. "Ordinarily, I would have never said a thing, but these are far from ordinary times."

"Zovastina has been supplying my daily medications. I told you she's been good to me. How's Cassiopeia?"

Thorvaldsen shook head. "Unfortunately, I'm afraid her health may well be the least of her worries."

A car engine grew louder outside.

Stephanie stiffened and raced to the window. A man slid out of an Audi with an automatic rifle.

"My guard," Ely said over her shoulder. "From the village."

The man shot out the tires on their car.

SEVENTY-TWO

CASSIOPEIA WAS HAVING TROUBLE GAUGING ZOVASTINA.

"I was just visited by the deputy national security adviser to the American president. He told me the same thing you said at the airport. That I missed something in Venice and that you know what that is."

"And you think this is going to get me to tell you?"

Zovastina admired the two stout trees, their trunks held close to the ground by a coiled rope. "I had this clearing prepared years ago. Several have felt the agony of being torn apart alive. A couple of them actually survived their arms being ripped from their bodies. It took a few minutes for them to bleed to death." She shook her head. "Horrible way to leave this world."

Cassiopeia was helpless. Little she could do but try and bluff her way out. Viktor, who was supposedly here to help, had done nothing but make her situation worse.

"After Hephaestion died, Alexander killed his personal physician this same way. I thought it ingenious, so I resurrected the practice."

"I'm all you have," she said in a flat tone.

Zovastina seemed curious. "Really? And what is it you have?"

"Apparently, Ely didn't share with you what he did with me."

Zovastina stepped close. She was a muscular woman,

sallow-faced. Worrisome was the transient look of madness that occasionally revealed itself in anxious dark eyes. Especially now, when her guts were being stoked with both curiosity and anger. "Do you know the *Iliad*? When Achilles finally vents his anger and kills Hector, he says something interesting. *I only wish my fury would compel me to cut away your flesh and eat it raw for what you've done. No one can keep the dogs off of your head, not if they brought me ransom of ten or twenty times as much, or more.* Tell me, why are you here?"

"You brought me."

"You never resisted."

"You risked a lot coming to Venice. Why? It couldn't be all political."

She noticed that Zovastina's eyes seemed a bit less belligerent.

"Sometimes we're called upon to act for others. To risk things. No quest worth the effort is without risk. I've been searching for Alexander's grave, hoping there might be answers there to some perplexing problems. Ely surely told you about Alexander's draught. Who knows if there's anything there? But to find the place. How glorious that would be."

Zovastina spoke more in wonder than anger. She seemed genuinely moved by the thought. On the one hand she cast herself a foolish romantic, consumed with notions of greatness gained from dangerous quests. On the other, according to Thorvaldsen, she was plotting the death of millions.

Zovastina clamped Cassiopeia's chin in a strong hold. "You need to tell me now what you know."

"The priest lied to you. In the basilica's treasury is an amulet that was found in the remains of St. Mark. A heart scarab with a phoenix carved into it. Remember the riddle. *Touch the innermost being. Divide the phoenix.*"

Zovastina seemed not to hear her. "You are beauti-ful." Her breath stank of onion. "But you're a liar and a cheat. Here to deceive me."

Zovastina released her grip and stepped away.

Cassiopeia heard the bleating of goats.

MALONE MOUNTED THE HORSE.

"None of the roof guards will pay us any attention," Viktor said. "You're with me."

Viktor hopped back onto his ride. "They're beyond the playing field, in the woods. She's planning on killing Vitt."

"What are we waiting for?"

Viktor kicked his horse. Malone followed.

They galloped from the corral toward an open field. He noticed striped poles at each end and an earthen pan in its center and knew what was played here. *Buzkashi.* He'd read about the game, its violence, how deaths were routine, the barbarity and beauty it simultaneously dis-played. Zovastina was apparently a connoisseur and the stabled horses were surely bred to participate, like the steed beneath him, loping forward with uncanny speed and ability. Littered across the grassy field were goats that seemed to provide an excellent manicure service. Maybe a hundred or more, and large, scattering as the horses thundered past.

He glanced back and noticed gun posts atop the palace. As Viktor had predicted, no one seemed alarmed, surely accustomed to their Supreme Minister's exploits. Ahead, at the far end of the field, stood a thick stand of trees. Two paths cut a route into them. Viktor brought his horse to a stop. Malone reined his in, too. His legs dangled against dark streaks of sweat on the animal's flanks.

"They're maybe a hundred meters down that trail, in another clearing. It's up to you now."

He slid from the saddle, gun in hand.

"WE HAVE A PROBLEM," STEPHANIE SAID. "IS THERE AN-other way out of here?"

Ely motioned toward the kitchen.

She and Thorvaldsen rushed forward just as the cabin's front door burst inward. The man barked orders in a language she did not understand. She found the kitchen door and opened it, cautioning Thorvaldsen for quiet. Ely was speaking to the man in the same language.

She slipped outside. Thorvaldsen followed.

Automatic gunfire exploded from inside the cabin and bullets ripped into the heavy timbers behind them.

They fell to the ground as a window exploded. Glass showered outward. Bullets found trees. She heard Ely yell something to their attacker and used that instant to spring to her feet and race around the cabin toward the car. Thorvaldsen remained on the ground, struggling to stand, and she could only hope Ely delayed the guard long enough.

She reached the car, opened the rear door, and gripped one of the automatics.

Thorvaldsen rounded the cabin.

She assumed a defensive position with the car as a buffer, aiming across the hood, and motioned with the gun for Henrik to go right onto the front porch. He veered out of her line of fire, just as the guard appeared, his rifle leveled waist high. He seemed to spot Thorvaldsen first and pivoted to adjust his aim.

She fired twice.

Both bullets found the man's chest.

She fired twice more.

The guard collapsed to the ground.

Silence gripped her. She did not move until Ely appeared from behind the dead guardsman. Thorvaldsen stepped off the porch. Her gun was still aimed, both hands locked on the stock. Shaking. She'd killed a man.

Her first.

Thorvaldsen walked toward her. "You okay?"

"I've heard others talk about it. I told them it was their job. But now I understand. Killing someone is a big deal."

"You had no choice."

Ely walked over. "He wouldn't listen. I told him you weren't a threat."

"But we are," Thorvaldsen said. "I'm sure his orders were for no one to make contact with you. That would be the last thing Zovastina would want."

Stephanie's mind began to clear. "We need to leave."

SEVENTY-THREE

MALONE ADVANCED INTO THE WOODS, BLACK AND silent and seemingly filled with threats. He spied a clearing ahead where sunshine spread unaffected by the leafy canopy. He glanced back and did not see Viktor, but understood why the man had disappeared. He heard voices, so he increased his pace, stopping behind a thick trunk near the path's end.

He saw Cassiopeia. Tied between two trees. Her arms stretched outward. Irina Zovastina standing beside her.

Viktor was right.

Big trouble.

ZOVASTINA WAS BOTH INTRIGUED AND IRRITATED WITH Cassiopeia Vitt. "You don't seem to care that you're about to die."

"If I cared, I wouldn't have come with you."

She decided it was time to give the woman a reason to live. "You asked on the plane about Ely. Whether he was alive. I didn't answer you. Don't you want to know?"

"I wouldn't believe a word you said."

She shrugged. "That's a fair statement. I wouldn't, either."

She found a phone in her pocket and pushed one of the buttons.

STEPHANIE HEARD A RINGING. HER GAZE SHOT TO THE dead man lying on the rocky ground.

Thorvaldsen heard it, too.

"It's Zovastina," Ely said. "She calls me on the phone he brings."

She darted to the body, found the unit, and said to Ely, "Answer it."

CASSIOPEIA LISTENED AS ZOVASTINA SAID, "THERE'S someone here who wants to talk to you."

Zovastina placed the phone close to her ear. She had no intention of saying anything, but the voice that came from the other side of the call sent an electric shock down her spine.

"What is it, Minister?" A pause. "Minister?"

She could not help herself. The voice confirmed all her doubts.

"Ely. It's Cassiopeia."

Silence greeted her.

"Ely? Are you there?" Her eyes burned.

"I'm here. Just shocked. It's good to hear your voice."

"Yours, too." Emotion surged through her. Everything had changed.

"What are you doing here?" Ely asked.

"Looking for you. I knew . . . I *hoped* you weren't dead." She tried to maintain a tight grip on her emotions. "Are *you* okay?"

"I'm fine, but I'm worried about you. Henrik's here with a woman named Stephanie Nelle."

That was news. Cassiopeia tried to shove her apprehension aside and focus. Apparently, Zovastina was unaware of what was happening wherever Ely was being held. "Tell the minister what you just told me."

Zovastina listened into the phone.

STEPHANIE HEARD ELY REPEAT HIMSELF. SHE UNDER-stood the shock Cassiopeia must be experiencing, but why did Cassiopeia want Ely to tell the Supreme Minister they were here?

ZOVASTINA SAID INTO THE PHONE, "WHEN DID YOUR friend Thorvaldsen and this woman arrive?"

"A short while ago. Your guard tried to kill them, but he's dead."

"Minister," a new voice said in her ear, one she instantly recognized.

Thorvaldsen.

"We have Ely."

"And I have Cassiopeia Vitt. I'd say she has another ten minutes or so to live."

"We solved the riddle."

"Lots of talk. From you and Vitt. Anything to back it up?"

"Oh, yes. We'll be at the grave before nightfall. But you'll never know."

"You're in my Federation," she made clear.

"Except that we were able to enter, take your prisoner, and leave with him without you ever knowing."

"But you made a point to tell me."

"The only thing you have that I want is Cassiopeia. Call back if you want to bargain."

And the call ended.

"YOU THINK THAT WAS SMART?" STEPHANIE ASKED Thorvaldsen.

"We have to keep her off balance."

"But we don't know what's happening there."

"Tell me what I don't know."

She could see Thorvaldsen was worried.

"We have to trust that Cotton is handling things," he said.

———✳———

ZOVASTINA FOUGHT THE FEELING OF UNEASINESS THAT swept through her. These people fought hard, she'd give them that.

She freed a knife from its leather sleeve. "Your friends are here. And they have Ely. Unfortunately, contrary to what Thorvaldsen may think, he has nothing I want."

She stepped close to the bundle of rope. "I'd much prefer to watch you die."

———✳———

MALONE SAW AND HEARD EVERYTHING. ELY LUND WAS apparently on the phone. He saw how Cassiopeia had been affected, but he also realized that someone else had come onto the call. Henrik? Stephanie? They were surely with Lund by now.

He could wait no longer. He rushed from his hiding place. "That's enough."

Zovastina stood with her back to him. He saw that she'd stopped her assault on the ropes.

"The knife," he said. "Let it go."

Cassiopeia watched him with a look of anticipation. He felt it, too. A bad feeling. Almost as if he'd been expected.

Two men stepped from the trees, weapons trained on him.

"Mr. Malone," Zovastina said, as she turned toward him with a grim look of satisfaction on her face. "You can't kill us all."

PART
FIVE

SEVENTY-FOUR

VINCENTI STEPPED INTO HIS LIBRARY, CLOSED THE door, and poured himself a drink. Kumis. A local specialty he'd come to enjoy. Fermented mare's milk. Not much alcohol but quite a buzz. He downed the shot in one swallow and savored its almond aftertaste.

He poured another.

His stomach growled. He was hungry. He should tell the chef what he wanted for dinner. A thick slab of teriyaki horse steak would be good. He'd come to like that local specialty, too.

He sipped more Kumis.

Everything was about to unfold. His intuition from all those years ago had proven correct. All that stood in the way was Irina Zovastina.

He stepped to his desk. The house was equipped with a sophisticated satellite communications system, with direct links to Samarkand and his corporate headquarters in Venice. Drink in hand, he saw an e-mail had arrived from Kamil Revin about a half hour ago. Unusual. Revin, for all his joviality, distrusted any form of communication save face-to-face, with him controlling the time and location.

He opened the file and read the message.

THE AMERICANS WERE HERE.

His tired mind snapped alert. Americans? He was about to hit "Reply" when the study door burst open and Peter O'Conner rushed in.

"Four helicopter gunships bearing down on us. Federation."

He darted to the windows and gazed west. At the far end of the valley four dots pricked the bright sky, growing larger.

"They just appeared," O'Conner said. "I'm assuming this is not a social call. You expecting anyone?"

He wasn't.

He returned to the computer and deleted the e-mail.

"They'll be on the ground in less than ten minutes," O'Conner said.

Something was wrong.

"Is Zovastina coming for the woman?" O'Conner asked.

"It's possible. But how would she know this fast?"

Zovastina would never have imagined what he was planning. True, she distrusted him as he distrusted her, but there was no reason for any show of force. Not now, anyway. Then there was Venice, and what happened when he'd moved on Stephanie Nelle. And the Americans?

What didn't he know?

"They're swinging around to land," O'Conner said from the windows.

"Go get her."

O'Conner dashed from the room.

Vincenti slid open one of the desk drawers and removed a pistol. They'd yet to hire the full security contingent the estate would ultimately require. That would all be done in the coming weeks, while Zovastina occupied herself preparing for war. He'd planned to use that diversion to its fullest.

Karyn Walde entered the library, wearing a bathrobe and slippers. Standing, on her own. O'Conner followed.

"How do you feel?" he asked.

"Better than I have in months. I can walk."

Already, a doctor was en route from Venice who would treat her secondary infections. Lucky for her, they were remediable. "It'll take a few days for your body to start a full recovery. But the virus is right now being assaulted by a predator against which it has no defense. As, by the way, are we."

O'Conner assumed a position at the window. "They're on the ground. Troops. Asians. Looks like they're hers."

He faced Walde. "Seems Irina may want you back. We're not sure what's happening."

He stepped across the room to a built-in bookcase with ornate glass-fronted doors. The wood had come from China, along with the craftsman who'd made the piece. But O'Conner had added something extra. He pressed a button on a pocket controller and a spring-loaded mechanism above and below the cabinet released, allowing the heavy case to rotate one hundred and eighty degrees. Beyond was a lighted passageway.

Walde was impressed. "Like in a damn horror movie."

"Which is what this may become," he said. "Peter, see what they want and express my regrets that I wasn't here to greet them." He motioned to Walde. "Follow me."

STEPHANIE'S HANDS STILL SHOOK AS SHE WATCHED ELY drag the body around to the rear of the cabin. She still did not like the fact that Zovastina knew they were in the Federation. Not particularly smart to alert a person with the kind of resources at her disposal. She had to trust that Thorvaldsen knew what he was doing, particularly since his butt was on the line, too.

Ely emerged from the cabin's front door, followed by Thorvaldsen. He held an arm full of books and paper. "I'll need these."

She was watching the lane leading back to the highway. All seemed quiet. Thorvaldsen came up beside her. He noticed her shaking hand and calmly grasped it. Neither of them said a word. She still held the gun, her palm sweaty. Her mind needed to focus, so she asked, "What exactly are we going to do?"

"We know the location," Ely said. "Klimax. So let's go see what's there. It's worth a look."

She fought to recall Ptolemy's words and repeated them, "*Climb the god-built walls. When you reach the attic, gaze into the tawny eye, and dare to find the distant refuge.*"

"I remember the riddle," Ely said. "I need to check some information, spur my memory, but I can do that along the way."

She wanted to know, "Why did Zovastina go after the elephant medallions?"

"I pointed out a connection between a mark on the medallions and the riddle. A symbol, like two Bs joined to an A. It's on one side of the medallion and in the riddle. They had to be significant. Since there were only eight known, she said she'd acquire them all for comparison. But she told me she was going to buy them."

"Not hardly," Stephanie said. "I'm still baffled. All of this is over two thousand years old. Wouldn't anything that existed have been found by now?"

Ely shrugged. "Hard to say. Let's face it, the clues have not been out in the open. It took X-ray fluorescence to find the important stuff."

"But Zovastina wants it. Whatever it is."

Ely nodded. "In her mind, which I always thought

was a little weird, she's Alexander, or Achilles, or some other epic hero. It's a romantic vision she seems to enjoy. A quest. She believes there might be some sort of cure out there. She talked about that a lot. That was most important to her, but I don't know why." Ely paused. "I won't say that it wasn't important to me, too. Her enthusiasm became infectious. I actually started to believe there might be something to find."

She could see he was troubled by all that had happened, so she offered, "You might be right."

"That would be amazing, wouldn't it?"

"But how could there be any connection between St. Mark and Alexander the Great?" Thorvaldsen asked.

"We know that Alexander's body was in Alexandria up to 391 CE, when paganism was finally outlawed. But there's no mention of it ever again, anywhere, after that. St. Mark's body reappears in Alexandria around 400 CE. Remember, pagan relics were routinely adopted for Christian purposes.

"There are lots of examples I've read about from Alexandria. A bronze idol of Saturn in the Caesareum was melted down to cast a cross for the patriarch of Alexandria. The Caesareum itself became a Christian cathedral. My theory, from reading everything I could on St. Mark and Alexander, was that some fourth-century patriarch conceived a way to not only preserve the corpse of the city's founder, but to furnish Christianity with a potent relic. A win/win. So Alexander simply became St. Mark. Who'd know the difference?"

"Sounds like a long shot," she said.

"I don't know. You tell me Ptolemy left something in that mummy in the basilica that led you straight here. I'd say theory is now firmly entrenched in reality."

"He's right," Thorvaldsen said. "It's worth going south to take a look."

She didn't necessarily agree, but any place was preferable to here. At least they'd be on the move. But something occurred to her. "You said the area where Klimax is located is now privately owned. We could have trouble gaining access."

Ely smiled. "Maybe the new owner will let us have a look around."

SEVENTY-FIVE

MALONE WAS TRAPPED. HE SHOULD HAVE KNOWN. VIK-tor had led him straight to Zovastina.

"Come to save Ms. Vitt?"

He still held the gun.

Zovastina motioned. "Who do you plan to kill? Choose between the three of us." She pointed at her guardsmen. "One of them will shoot you before you can shoot the other." She displayed her knife. "And then I'll cut these ropes."

All true. His options were limited.

"Take him," she ordered the guards.

One of the men rushed forward, but a new sound captured Malone's attention. Baying. Growing louder. The guard was ten feet away when goats rushed from the other path that led back to the *buzkashi* field. First a few, then the entire herd exploded into the clearing.

Hooves thumped the earth.

Malone spotted Viktor atop a horse, keeping the oversized animals bunched, trying not to break their advance. A lumbering pace increased into a rush, the rear shoving the front, forcing the confused goats forward. Their unexpected appearance seemed to generate the desired effect. The guards were momentarily confused and Malone used that instant to shoot the one in front of him.

Another pop and the second guard dropped to the ground.

Malone saw that Viktor had fired the shot.

The goats crowded the clearing, milling into one another, still baffled, slowly realizing the only way out was through the trees.

Dust stirred the air.

Malone spotted Zovastina and pushed his way through the stinking animals toward her and Cassiopeia.

The herd retreated into the woods.

He arrived just as Viktor slid from the saddle, gun in hand. Zovastina stood with her knife, but Viktor was holding her at bay, a few feet from the ropes that anchored the two bent trees.

"Drop the knife," Viktor said.

Zovastina seemed shocked. "What are you doing?"

"Stopping you." Viktor motioned with his head. "Free her, Malone."

"Tell you what," Malone said. "You free Cassiopeia and I'll keep an eye on the minister."

"Still don't trust me?"

"Let's just say I prefer to do this my way." He raised his gun. "Like he said, drop the knife."

"Or what?" Zovastina said. "You'll shoot me?"

He fired into the ground, between her legs, and she recoiled. "The next one's in your head."

She released the knife.

"Kick it this way."

She did.

"What are you doing here?" Cassiopeia asked him.

"I owed you. Goats?" he said to Viktor, as the other man untied Cassiopeia.

"You use what you have. Seemed like a good diversion."

He couldn't argue.

"You work for the Americans?" Zovastina asked Viktor.

"That's right."

Fire boiled in her eyes.

Cassiopeia shook the ropes free and lunged toward Zovastina, swinging her fist and catching the other woman square in the face. A kick to the knees and Zovastina stumbled back. Cassiopeia continued her attack, planting her foot into Zovastina's stomach and slamming the woman's head into the trunk of one of the trees.

Zovastina shrunk to the ground and lay still.

Malone had calmly watched the assault. "You get all that out of your system?"

Cassiopeia breathed hard. "I could have given her more." She paused, rubbing her wrists from the ropes. "Ely's alive. I talked to him on the phone. Stephanie and Henrik are with him. We need to go."

Malone faced Viktor. "I thought Washington wanted your cover protected?"

"I had no choice."

"You sent me into this trap."

"Did I tell you to confront her? You didn't give me a chance to do anything. When I saw your problem, I did what I had to."

He didn't agree, but there was no time to argue. "What do we do now?"

"We're going to leave. We'll have a little time. No one will disturb her back here."

"What about the gunfire?" Malone asked.

"It won't be noticed." Viktor motioned around him. "This is her killing field. Many enemies have been eliminated back here."

Cassiopeia was lifting Zovastina's limp body from the ground.

"What are you doing?" Malone asked.

"Tying this bitch to those ropes, so she can see what it feels like."

STEPHANIE DROVE WITH HENRIK IN THE FRONT SEAT and Ely in the rear. They'd had no choice but to commandeer the guard's car since theirs had four flat tires. They quickly left the cabin, found the highway, and began the trek south, paralleling the Pamir foothills, heading toward what over two thousand years ago had been known as Mt. Klimax.

"This is amazing," Ely said.

She saw in the rearview mirror that he was admiring the scytale.

"When I read Ptolemy's riddle, I wondered how he would convey any message. It's really clever." Ely held up the scytale. "How did you figure it out?"

"A friend of ours did. Cotton Malone. He's the one with Cassiopeia."

"Shouldn't we go see about her?"

She heard the anticipation in his question. "We have to trust that Malone will handle his end. Our problem's here." She was talking again like the dispassionate head of an intelligence agency, cool and indifferent, but she was still rattled from what happened at the cabin. "Cotton's good. He'll deal with it."

Thorvaldsen seemed to sense Ely's quandary. "And Cassiopeia is not helpless. She can take care of herself. Why don't you tell us what we need to know to understand all this? We read in the manuscript about the draught, from the Scythians. What do you know about them?"

She watched as Ely carefully laid the scytale aside.

"A nomadic people who migrated from central Asia to southern Russia in the eighth and seventh centuries before Christ. Herodotus wrote about them. They were bloody and tribal. Feared. They'd cut off the heads of their enemies and make leather-bound drinking cups from the skulls."

"I'd say that would build you a reputation," Thorvaldsen said.

"What's their connection to Alexander?" she asked.

"In the fourth and third centuries BCE, they settled in what became Kazakhstan. They successfully resisted Alexander, blocking his way east across the Syr Darya river. He fought them fiercely, was wounded several times, but eventually made a truce. I wouldn't say Alexander feared the Scythians, but he respected them."

"And the draught?" Thorvaldsen said. "It was theirs?"

Ely nodded. "They showed it to Alexander. Part of their peace with him. And he apparently used it to cure himself. From what I read, it appeared as some kind of natural potion. Alexander, Hephaestion, and that physician's assistant mentioned in one of the manuscripts were all cured by it. Assuming the accounts are accurate.

"The Scythians were a strange people," Ely said. "For example, in the midst of one fight with the Persians, they all abandoned the battlefield to chase a rabbit. Nobody knows why, but it's noted in an official account.

"They were gold connoisseurs, using and wearing enormous amounts. Ornaments, belts, plates, even their weapons were gold adorned. Scythian burial mounds are full of gold artifacts. But their main problem was language. They were illiterate. No written record of them survives. Just pictures, fables, and accounts from others. Only a few of their words are even known, and that's thanks to Herodotus."

She could see his face in the rearview mirror and realized there was more. "What is it?"

"Like I said, only a few of their words survived. *Pata* meant kill. *Spou,* eye. *Oior,* man. Then there's *arima.*" He shuffled through some of the papers he'd brought.

"It didn't mean much, until now. Remember the riddle. *When you reach the attic.* Ptolemy fought the Scythians with Alexander. He knew them. *Arima* means, roughly, place at the top."

"Like an attic," she said.

"Even more important. The place the Greeks once called Klimax, where we're headed, the locals have always called Arima. I remember that from the last time I was there."

"Too many coincidences?" Thorvaldsen asked.

"It seems all roads point here."

"And what do we hope to find?" Stephanie asked.

"The Scythians used mounds to cover their kings' tombs, but I've read that mountain locations were chosen for some of their most important leaders. This was the farthest reach of Alexander's empire. Its eastern border. A long way from home. He would not have been disturbed here."

"Maybe that's why he chose it?" she asked.

"I don't know. The whole thing seems odd."

And she agreed.

ZOVASTINA OPENED HER EYES. SHE WAS LYING ON THE ground and immediately recalled Cassiopeia Vitt's attack. She shook confusion from her brain and realized something was tightly gripping both wrists.

Then she realized. She was tied to the trees, just as Vitt had been. She shook her head. Humiliating.

She stood and stared out into the clearing.

The goats, Malone, Vitt, and Viktor were gone. One of the guardsmen lay dead. But the other was still alive, propped against a tree, bleeding from a shoulder wound.

"Can you move?" she asked.

The man nodded, but was clearly in pain. All of her Sacred Band were tough, disciplined souls. She'd made sure of that. Her modern incarnation was every bit as fearless as the original from Alexander's time.

The guard struggled to his feet, his right hand clamped onto his left arm.

"The knife," she said. "There, on the ground."

Not a hint of pain seeped from the man's mouth. She tried to remember his name, but could not. Viktor had hired each one of the Sacred Band, and she'd made a point not to become attached to any of them. They were objects. Tools to be used. That's all.

The man staggered to the knife and managed to lift it from the ground.

He came close to the ropes, lost his balance, and fell to his knees.

"You can do it," she said. "Fight the agony. Focus on your duty."

The guard seemed to steel himself. Sweat poured down his brow and she noticed fresh blood oozing from the wound. Amazing he wasn't in shock. But this burly soul seemed in superb physical shape.

He raised the knife, sucked a few breaths, then cut the bindings that held her right wrist. She steadied his shaking arm as he passed her the knife, and she freed herself from the other rope.

"You did well," she said.

He smiled at her compliment, his breath labored, still on his knees.

"Lie down. Rest," she said.

She heard him settle on the ground as she searched the forest floor. Near the other body she found a gun.

She returned to the injured guardsman.

He'd seen her vulnerable and, for the first time in a long while, she'd felt vulnerable.

The man lay on his back, still gripping his shoulder.

She stood over him. His dark eyes focused on her and, in them, she saw that he knew.

She smiled at his courage.

Then aimed the gun at his head and fired.

SEVENTY-SIX

MALONE GLANCED DOWN AT THE ROUGH TERRAIN, A mixture of parched earth, greenlands, rolling hills, and trees. Viktor piloted the chopper, a Hind, which had been parked on a concrete pad a few miles from the palace. He knew the craft. Russian made, twin top-mounted turboshaft engines driving a main and tail rotors. The Soviets called it a flying tank. NATO dubbed the mean-looking thing the Crocodile, due to its camouflage color and distinct fuselage. All in all a formidable gunship, this one modified with a large rear compartment for low-capacity troop transport. Thankfully, they'd managed to leave both the palace and Samarkand with no problems.

"Where'd you learn to fly?" he asked Viktor.

"Bosnia. Croatia. That's what I did in the military. Search and destroy."

"Good place to build your nerves."

"And get killed."

He couldn't argue with that.

"How far?" Cassiopeia asked through the headset.

They were flying east, at nearly three hundred kilometers an hour, toward Ely's cabin in the Pamirs. Zovastina would soon be free, if not already, so he asked, "What about anyone coming after us?"

Viktor motioned ahead. "Those mountains will give us cover. Tough to track anything in there. We'll be into

them shortly, and we're only minutes from the Chinese border. We can always escape there."

"Don't act like you didn't hear me," Cassiopeia said. "How far?"

Malone had intentionally avoided answering. She was anxious. He wanted to tell her he knew she was sick. Let her know somebody cared. That he understood her frustration. But he knew better. Instead, he said, "We're moving as fast as we can." He paused. "But this is probably better than being tied to trees."

"I assume I'll never live that one down."

"Something like that."

"Okay, Cotton, I'm a little upset. But you have to understand, I thought Ely was dead. I wanted him to be alive, but I knew—I thought—" She caught herself. "And now—"

He turned and saw excitement in her eyes, which both energized and saddened him. Then he caught himself and finished her thought, "And now he's with Stephanie and Henrik. So calm down."

She was seated alone in the rear compartment. He saw her tap Viktor on the shoulder. "Did you know about Ely being alive?"

Viktor shook his head. "I was taunting you on the boat in Venice when I told you he was dead. I had to say something. Truth is, I'm the one who saved Ely. Zovastina thought someone might move on him. He was her adviser and political murder is commonplace in the Federation. She wanted Ely protected. After that attempt on his life, she hid him. I haven't had anything to do with him since. Though I was head of the guard, she was in charge. So I really don't know what happened to him. I learned not to ask questions, just do what she said."

Malone caught the past tense observation concerning Viktor's job status. "She'll kill you if she finds you."

"I knew the rules before all this started."

They continued flying smooth and straight. He'd never flown in a Hind. Its instrumentation was impressive, as was its firepower. Guided missiles. Multibarrel machine guns. Twin cannon pods.

"Cotton," Cassiopeia said, "do you have a way of communicating with Stephanie?"

Not a question he wanted to answer at the moment, but he had no choice. "I do."

"Give it to me."

He found the world phone—Magellan Billet–issue, provided by Stephanie in Venice—and dialed the number, slipping off his headset. A few seconds were needed before a pulsating buzz confirmed a connection and Stephanie's voice greeted him.

"We're headed your way," he said.

"We left the cabin," she said. "We're driving south on a highway marked M45 to what was once Mt. Klimax. Ely knows where it is. He says the locals call the place Arima."

"Tell me more."

He listened, then repeated the information to Viktor, who nodded. "I know where that is."

Viktor banked the copter southeast and increased speed.

"We're on our way," he told Stephanie. "Everyone here is fine."

He saw that Cassiopeia wanted the phone, but that wasn't going to happen. He motioned no with his head, hoping she'd understand that now was not the time. But to comfort her, he asked Stephanie, "Ely okay?"

"Yeah, but anxious."

"I know what you mean. We'll be there before you. I'll call. We can do some aerial recon until you get there."

"Viktor any help?"

"Wouldn't be here now if it wasn't for him."

He clicked off the phone and told Cassiopeia where Ely was headed.

An alarm sounded in the cabin.

His gaze found the radar display that indicated two targets approaching from the west.

"Black Sharks," Viktor said, "coming straight for us."

Malone knew those choppers, too. NATO called them Hokums. KA-50s. Fast, efficient, loaded with guided missiles and 30mm cannons. He saw that Viktor also realized the threat.

"They found us quick," Malone said.

"There's a base near here."

"What do you plan to do?"

They started to climb, gaining altitude, changing course. Six thousand feet. Seven. Nine. Leveling at ten.

"You know how to use the guns?" Viktor asked.

He was sitting in the weapons officer's seat, so he scanned the instrument panel. Luckily, he could read Russian. "I can manage."

"Then get ready for a fight."

SEVENTY-SEVEN

ZOVASTINA WATCHED AS HER GENERALS CONSIDERED the war plan. The men sitting around the conference table were her most trusted subordinates, though she tempered that trust with a realization that one or more of them could be a traitor. After the past twenty-four hours she could not be sure of anything. These men had all been with her from the beginning, rising as she rose, steadily building the Federation's offensive strength, readying themselves for what was about to come.

"We'll take Iran first," she declared.

She knew the calculations. The current population of Pakistan was a hundred and seventy million. Afghanistan, thirty-two million. Iran, sixty-eight million. All three were targets. Originally, she'd planned a simultaneous assault, now she believed a strategic strike better. If infection points were chosen with care, places of maximum density, and the viruses planted with skill, the computer models predicted a population reduction of seventy percent or more would occur within fourteen days. She told the men what they already knew, then added, "We need a total panic. A crisis. The Iranians have to want our assistance. What do you have planned?"

"We'll start with their military forces and government," one of the generals said. "Most of the viral agents work in less than forty-eight hours. But we'll vary which ones we use. They'll identify a virus fairly quickly, but then they'll have another to deal with. That should keep them off guard and prevent any productive medical response."

She'd been concerned on that point, but not anymore. "The scientists tell me the viruses have all been modified, making their detection and prevention even more difficult."

Eight men surrounded the table, all from her army and air force. Central Asia had long languished between China, the USSR, India, and the Middle East, not part of any of them, but desired by all. The Great Game had played itself out here two centuries ago when Russia and Britain battled each other for dominance, neither caring what the native populations wanted.

Not anymore.

Central Asia now spoke with unity through a democratically elected parliament, ministers, elections, courts, and a rule of law.

One voice.

Hers.

"What of the Europeans and the Americans?" a general asked. "How will they react to our aggression?"

"That's what it cannot be," she made clear. "No aggression. We'll simply occupy and extend aid and relief to the embattled populations. They'll be far too busy burying the dead to worry about us."

She'd learned from history. The world's most successful conquerors—the Greeks, Mongols, Huns, Romans, and Ottomans—all practiced tolerance over the lands they claimed. Hitler could have changed the course of World War II if he'd simply enlisted the aid of millions of Ukrainians, who hated the Soviets, instead of annihilating them. Her forces would enter Iran as savior, not oppressor, knowing that by the time her viruses finished there'd be no opposition left to challenge her. Then she'd annex the land. Repopulate. Move people from the Soviet-ruined regions of her nation into new locales. Blend the races. Do precisely what Alexander the Great had done with his Hellenistic revolution, only in reverse, migrating east to west.

"Can we be sure the Americans will not intervene?" one of the generals asked.

She understood the apprehension. "The Americans will not say or do a thing. Why will they care? After the Iraqi debacle, they won't interfere, especially if we're handling the load. They'll actually be thrilled at the prospect of eliminating Iran."

"Once we move on Afghanistan, there'll be American deaths," one of the men noted. "Their military is still present."

"When that time comes, let's try to minimize those," she said. "We want the end result to be that the Americans withdraw from the country as we take control. I'm assuming that will be a popular decision in the United States. Use a virus there that's containable. Strategic infections, targeted at specific groups and regions. The majority of the dead must be natives, especially Taliban, make sure U.S. personnel are only a consequence."

She met the gaze of each of the men at the table. Not one of them said a word about the bruise on her face— leftover from her bout with Cassiopeia Vitt. Was her leak here? How had the Americans learned so much about her intentions?

"Millions are about to die," one of the men said in a whisper.

"Millions of problems," she made clear. "Iran is a harbinger of terrorists. A place governed by fools. That's what the West says over and over. Time to end that problem, and we have the way. The people who survive will be better off. We will, too. We'll have their oil and their gratitude. What we do with those will determine our success."

She listened as troop strengths, contingency plans, and strategies were discussed. Squads of men had been trained in deploying the viruses and were ready to move south. She was pleased. Years of anticipation were finally over. She imagined how Alexander the Great must have felt when he crossed from Greece into Asia and began his global conquest. Like him, she, too, envisioned total success. Once she controlled Iran, Pakistan, and Afghanistan, she'd move on to the rest of the Middle East. That dominance, though, would be more subtle, the viral rampages made to appear as simply a spread of the initial infections. If she'd read the West correctly, Europe, China, Russia, and America would withdraw into themselves. Restrict their borders. Minimize travel. Hope the public health disaster was contained in countries that, by and large, none of them cared about. Their inaction would give her time to claim more links in the chain of nations that stood between the Federation and Africa. Played right, she could conquer the entire Middle East in a matter of months and never fire a shot.

"Do we have control of the antiagents?" her chief of staff finally asked.

She'd been waiting for the question. "We will." The uneasy peace that connected her and Vincenti was about to end.

"Philogen has not provided stockpiles to treat our population," one of the men noted. "Nor do we have the quantities needed to stop the viral spread in the target nations, once victory is assured."

"I'm aware of the problem," she said.

A chopper was waiting.

She stood. "Gentlemen, we're about to start the greatest conquest since ancient times. The Greeks came and defeated us, ushering in the Hellenistic Age, which eventually molded Western civilization. We will now begin a new dawn in human development. The Asiatic Age."

SEVENTY-EIGHT

CASSIOPEIA STRAPPED HERSELF ONTO THE STEEL BENCH in the rear compartment. The chopper lurched as Viktor began evasive maneuvers to elude their pursuers. She knew Malone was aware that she'd wanted to talk to Ely, but she also saw that now was not the time. She appreciated Malone risking his neck. How would she have escaped from Zovastina without him? Doubtful that she would have, even with Viktor there. Thorvaldsen had told her that Viktor was an ally, but he'd also warned about his limitations. His mission was to remain undetected, but apparently that directive had changed.

"They're firing," Viktor said through the headset.

The chopper banked left, knifing through the air. Her harness held her secure against the bulkhead. Her hands gripped the bench. She was fighting a rising nausea since, truth be told, she was prone to motion sickness. Boats she generally avoided and planes, as long as they flew straight, weren't a problem. This, though, was a problem. Her stomach seemed to roll up into her throat as they constantly changed altitude, like an elevator out of control. Nothing she could do but hold on and hope to heaven Viktor knew what he was doing.

She saw Malone work the firing controls and heard cannon shots from both sides of the fuselage. She gazed ahead into the cockpit, through the windshield, and spotted mountain haunches lurching from the clouds on both sides.

"They still back there?" Malone asked.

"Coming fast," Viktor said. "And trying to fire."

"Missiles we don't need."

"I agree. But firing those in here would be tricky for us and them."

They emerged into clearer skies. The helicopter angled right and plummeted in altitude.

"Do we have to do that?" she asked, trying to keep her stomach under control.

"Afraid so," Malone answered. "We need to use these valleys to avoid them. In and out, like a maze."

She knew Malone had once flown fighter jets and still held a pilot's license. "Some of us don't like this kind of thing."

"You're welcome to toss your cookies anytime."

"I wouldn't give you the pleasure." Thank goodness she hadn't eaten since lunch yesterday on Torcello.

More sharp banks as they roared through the afternoon sky. The engine noise seemed deafening. She'd only flown on a few helicopters, never in a combat situation, the ride like a three dimensional roller coaster.

"Two more choppers within radar range," Viktor said. "But they're off to our north."

"Where are we headed?" Malone asked.

The copter veered into another steep turn.

"South," Viktor said.

MALONE STARED AT THE RADAR MONITOR. THE MOUNtains were both a shield and a problem that compounded tracking their pursuers. The targets steadily winked in and out. The American military relied more on satellites and AWACᶜ planes to provide a clear picture. Luckily, the Central Asian Federation did not enjoy those high-tech amenities.

The radar screen cleared.

STEVE BERRY / 432

"Nothing behind us," Malone said.

He had to admit, Viktor could fly. They were winding a path through the Pamirs, rotors dangerously close to steep gray precipices. He'd never learned to fly a helicopter, though he'd always wanted to, and he'd not been behind the controls of a supersonic fighter in ten years. He'd maintained his jet fighter proficiency for a few years after transferring to the Billet, but he'd let the certification slide. At the time he hadn't minded. Now he wished he'd kept those skills current.

Viktor leveled the chopper off at six thousand feet and asked, "You hit anything?"

"Hard to say. I think we just forced them to keep their distance."

"Where we're headed is about a hundred and fifty kilometers south. I know Arima. I've been there before, but it's been a while."

"Mountains all the way?"

Viktor nodded. "And more valleys. I think I can stay beneath any radar. This area is not a security zone. The border with China has been open for years. Most of Zovastina's resources are directed to the south, on the Afghan and Pakistani lines."

Cassiopeia came up behind them. "That over?"

"Looks like it."

"I'm going to take a roundabout way," Viktor said, "to avoid any more encounters. It'll take a little longer, but the farther east I go the safer we'll be."

"How long will that slow us up?" Cassiopeia asked.

"Maybe a half hour."

Malone nodded and Cassiopeia did not offer any objections. Dodging bullets was one thing, but air-to-air missiles were another matter. Soviet offensive equipment, like their missiles, were top-notch. Viktor's suggestion was a good one.

Malone settled into his seat and watched the naked

rush of rounded spurs. In the distance, haze claimed a stadium of white-tipped peaks. A river cleaved purple veins through the foothills in a silty torrent. Both Alexander the Great and Marco Polo had walked that sooty earth—the whole place once a battleground. British dependencies to the south, Russian to the north, and the Chinese and Afghans to the east and west. For most of the twentieth century, Moscow and Peking fought for control, each testing the other, ultimately settling into an uneasy peace, only the Pamirs themselves emerging a victor.

Alexander the Great chose his last resting place wisely.

But he wondered.

Was he really down there?

Waiting?

SEVENTY-NINE

Zovastina flew from Samarkand to Vincenti's estate in a direct path aboard the fastest helicopter her air force owned.

Vincenti's house loomed below. Excessive, expensive, and, like its owner, expendable. Allowing capitalism to flourish within the Federation may not be a smart idea. Changes would be needed. The Venetian League would have to be reined in.

But first things first.

The chopper touched down.

After Edwin Davis left the palace, she'd ordered Kamil Revin to contact Vincenti and alert him of the visit. But the warning had been delayed long enough to allow her troops time to arrive. She'd been told that the house was now secure, so she'd ordered her men to leave in the choppers that had brought them, save for nine soldiers. The house staff had also been evacuated. She possessed no quarrel with locals who were only trying to earn a living—her dispute was with Vincenti.

She stepped from the helicopter and marched across manicured grounds to a stone terrace where she entered the mansion. Though Vincenti thought she was disinterested in the estate, she'd closely followed its construction. Fifty-three rooms. Eleven bedrooms. Sixteen baths. Its architect had willingly provided her a set of plans.

She knew of the regal dining hall, elaborate parlors, gourmet kitchen, and wine cellar. Staring firsthand at the decor it was easy to see why it carried an eight-figure price tag.

In the main foyer two of her troops guarded the front entrance. Two more men flanked a marble stairway. Everything here reminded her of Venice. And she'd never liked to recall failure.

She caught the attention of one of the sentinels, who motioned right with his rifle. She paraded down a short hall and entered what appeared to be a library. Three more armed men occupied the room along with another man. Though they'd never met, she knew his name and background.

"Mr. O'Conner, you have a decision to make."

The man stood from a leather settee and faced her.

"You've worked for Vincenti a long time. He depends on you. And, frankly, without you he may not have made it so far."

She allowed her compliment to be absorbed as she inspected the opulent room. "Vincenti lives well. I'm curious, does he share the wealth with you?"

O'Conner said nothing.

"Let me tell you some things you may or may not know. Last year, Vincenti netted over forty million euros from his company. He owns stock worth over a billion euros. What does he pay you?"

No answer.

"One hundred fifty thousand euros." She saw the look on his face as the truth sank in. "You see, Mr. O'Conner, I know quite a lot. One hundred fifty thousand euros for all that you do for him. You've intimidated, coerced, even killed. He makes tens of millions and you received one hundred and fifty thousand euros. He lives like this and you," she hesitated, "simply live."

"I've never complained," O'Conner said.

She stopped behind Vincenti's desk. "No. You haven't. Which is admirable."

"What do you want?"

"Where's Vincenti?"

"Gone. Left before your men arrived."

She grinned. "There it is. Another thing you do so well. Lie."

He shrugged. "Believe what you will. Surely your men have searched the house."

"They have and, you're right, Vincenti is not to be found. But you and I both know why that's so."

She noticed the lovely alabaster carvings that dotted the desk. Chinese figurines. She never really cared for Oriental art. She lifted one of the figurines. A contorted fat man, half-dressed. "During the construction of this obscene monstrosity, Vincenti incorporated back passages, ostensibly for servants' use, but you and I know what they're really used for. He also had a large underground room hewn from the rock beneath us. That's probably where he is right now."

O'Conner's face never flinched.

"So, as I said, Mr. O'Conner, you have a choice. I'll find Vincenti, with or without your assistance. But your aid will speed the process and, I must admit, time is of the essence. That's why I'm willing to bargain. I could use a man like you. Resourceful." She paused. "Without greed. So here's your choice. Do you switch sides or stay with Vincenti?"

She'd offered the same alternative to others. Most were members of the national assembly, part of her government, or a rising opposition. Some weren't worth recruiting, far easier to kill them and be done with it, but the majority had proven worthy converts. They'd all been either Asian or Russian or some combination. Here, she was dangling bait to an American and was curious how the lure would be received.

"I choose you," O'Conner said. "What can I do for you?"

"Answer my question."

O'Conner reached into his pocket and one of the troops instantly leveled a rifle. O'Conner quickly displayed empty hands. "I need something to answer your question."

"Go ahead," she said.

He retrieved a silver controller with three buttons. "Those rooms are accessed from doors throughout the house. But the underground room can only be entered from here." He displayed the device. "One button opens every portal in case of a fire. The other activates the alarm. The third button," he pointed across the room and pressed, "opens that."

An eloquent Chinese cabinet rotated, revealing a dimly lit passage.

The warmth of victory filled her.

She approached one of her infantrymen and unholstered his Makarov 9mm.

She then turned and shot O'Conner in the head.

"Loyalty that shallow I don't need."

EIGHTY

THINGS WERE WRONG AND VINCENTI KNEW IT. BUT IF HE sat tight, kept calm, and was careful, this could play itself out. O'Conner would handle things, like always. But Karyn Walde and Grant Lyndsey were another matter.

Karyn was pacing the lab like a caged animal, her strength apparently returning, fueled by anticipation.

"You need to relax," he said. "Zovastina needs me. She won't be doing anything stupid."

He knew the antiagents would keep her in line, which was precisely why he'd never allowed her to learn much about them.

"Grant, secure your computer. Password protect everything, like we discussed."

He could see Lyndsey was even more anxious than Karyn, but where she seemed fueled by anger, Lyndsey was gripped with fear. He needed the man to think clearly, so he said, "We're fine down here. Don't sweat it."

"She resented me from the start. Hated having to deal with me."

"She may have hated you, but she needed you, and still does. Use that to your advantage."

Lyndsey was not listening. He was pounding on a keyboard, muttering to himself in a panicked frenzy.

"Both of you," he said, voice rising. "Calm down. We don't even know if she's here."

Lyndsey stared up from the computer. "It's been a long time. What are those troops doing here? What the hell's going on?"

Good questions, but he had to rely on O'Conner.

"That woman she took from the lab the other day," Lyndsey said. "I'm sure she never made it back to the Federation. I saw it in her eyes. Zovastina was going to kill her. For amusement. She's ready to slaughter millions. What are we to her?"

"Her salvation."

Or at least he hoped.

STEPHANIE TURNED OFF THE HIGHWAY ONTO A PAVED lane guarded by tall poplars lined like sentries. They'd made good time, driving the hundred and fifty kilometers in less than two hours. Ely had commented on how travel had changed over the past few years, road quality being a top priority for the Federation, along with tunneling. A new system had been blasted through the mountains, greatly shortening the distances from north to south.

"This place is different," Ely said from the rear seat. "It's been two years since I was here. This road was rock and gravel."

"This asphalt is recent," she said.

A fertile valley floor, checkered with pastures, spread beyond the trees, ending at stark rolling foothills that steadily rose into highlands, then mountains. She spotted shepherds tending flocks of sheep and goats. Horses roamed freely. The road stretched straight between the trees, taking them due east toward a distant gallery of silver flanks.

"We came here on an exploratory mission," Ely said. "Lots of *chids*. The local Pamiri house, built of stone and plaster with flat roofs. We stayed in one. There was a small village out there, in that valley. But it's gone."

She'd not heard any more from Malone, and she dare not try and reach him. She had no idea of his situation, other than that he'd apparently managed to free Cassiopeia and compromise Viktor. Edwin Davis and President Daniels would not be happy, but rarely did things go according to plan.

"Why is everything so green?" Henrik asked. "I always thought of the Pamirs as dry and barren."

"Most of the valleys are, but where there's water the valleys can be quite beautiful. Like a piece of Switzerland. We've been dry lately with warm temperatures. Way above normal for here."

Up ahead, through the thin line of trees, she spotted a massive stone structure perched on a grassy promontory, backdropped by mountain spurs devoid of snow. The house rose in sharp verticals, broken by steep gables topped with black slate, the exterior a mosaic of flat stone in varying shades of brown, silver, and gold. Mullioned windows symmetrically broke the elegant facade, each outlined with thick cornices, reflecting ribbons of light from the afternoon sun. Three stories. Four stone chimneys. Scaffolding wrapped one side. The whole thing reminded her of one of the many mansions that dotted north Atlanta, or something from *Architectural Digest*.

"That's a house," she said.

"Which was not here two years ago," Ely noted.

Thorvaldsen stared out the windshield. "Apparently the new owner of all this is a person of means."

The dwelling loomed about a half mile away, across a green valley that steadily rose toward the promontory. Ahead, an iron gate blocked the drive. Two stone pillars, like compact minarets, support a wrought-iron arch that displayed the word "Attico."

"Italian for attic," Thorvaldsen said. "Seems the new owner is attuned to the local designation."

"Place names are sacred in this part of the world," Ely said. "That's one reason why the Asians hated the Soviets. They changed all of them. Of course, they were changed back when the Federation was created. Another reason Zovastina is so popular."

Stephanie searched for a way to contact the house from the gate, a call box or a switch, but saw nothing. Instead, two men appeared from behind the minarets. Young, thin, dressed in camouflage fatigues, bearing AK-74s. One pointed his weapon while the other opened the gate.

"Interesting welcome," Thorvaldsen said.

One of the men approached the car and motioned, yelling something in a language she did not understand.

But she didn't need to.

She knew exactly what he wanted.

ZOVASTINA ENTERED THE PASSAGEWAY. SHE'D RETRIEVED the controller from O'Conner's dead grasp and used it to close the portal. A series of bulbs, linked by wire, hung inside iron brackets at periodic intervals. The narrow corridor ended ten meters ahead at a metal door.

She approached and listened.

No sound from the other side.

She tried the latch.

It opened.

The top of a stone staircase, chiseled from the bedrock, began on the other side and dropped steeply.

Impressive.

Her opponent had certainly thought ahead.

VINCENTI CHECKED HIS WATCH. HE SHOULD HAVE heard from O'Conner by now. The phone affixed to the wall provided a direct line upstairs. He'd resisted calling, not wanting to reveal himself. They'd been ensconced here now pushing three hours and he was starving, though his gut churned more from anxiety than hunger.

He'd occupied the time securing data on the lab's two computers. He'd also brought to a conclusion a couple of experiments that he and Lyndsey had been running to verify that the archaea could be safely stored at room temperature, at least for the few months needed between production and sale. Concentrating on the experiments had helped with Lyndsey's apprehension, but Walde remained agitated.

"Flush everything," he said to Lyndsey. "All the liquids. The keeping solutions. Samples. Leave nothing."

"What are you doing?" Karyn asked.

He didn't feel like arguing with her. "We don't need them."

She rose from the chair where she'd been seated. "What about my treatment? Did you give me enough? Am I cured?"

"We'll know tomorrow or the next day."

"And if I'm not? What then?"

He appraised her with a calculating look. "You're awful demanding for a woman who was dying."

"Answer me. Am I cured?"

He ignored her question and concentrated on the computer screen. A few flicks of the mouse and he copied all of its data onto a flash drive. He then enabled the hard drive's encryption.

Karyn grabbed his shirt. "You're the one who came to me. You wanted my help. You wanted Irina. You gave me hope. Don't let me hang."

This woman may prove more trouble than she was

worth. But he decided to be conciliatory. "We can make more," he calmly said. "It's easy. And if we need to, we can take you where the bacteria live and let you drink them. They work that way, too."

But his assurance did not seem to satisfy her.

"You lying son of a bitch." She released her hold. "I can't believe I'm in this mess."

Neither could he. But it was too late now.

"Everything done?" he asked Lyndsey.

The man nodded.

Glass shattering caught Vincenti's attention. He turned to see Karyn holding the jagged remains of a flask and lunging toward him. She brought the improvised dagger close to his belly and stopped, her eyes alive with fire. "I need to know. Am I cured?"

"Answer her," a new voice said.

He turned toward the lab's exit.

Irina Zovastina stood in the doorway, with a gun. "Is she cured, Enrico?"

EIGHTY-ONE

MALONE SPOTTED A HOUSE ABOUT TWO MILES AWAY. Viktor had flown them in from the north, after veering east and skirting the Chinese border. He assessed the structure and estimated forty or so thousand square feet spread over three levels. They faced its rear, the front overlooking a valley that scooped a cul-de-sac out of the mountains on three sides. The house seemed to have been situated intentionally on a flat, rocky hillock overlooking the broad plain. Scaffolding wrapped one side where, it appeared, masons had been working. He noticed a sand pile and a mortar mixer. Beyond the promontory, iron fencing was being erected, some already standing, more stacked nearby. No workers. No security. Nobody in sight.

A six-bay garage stood off to one side, the doors closed. A garden that showed evidence of careful tending sprouted between a terrace and the beginnings of a grove that ended at the base of one of the rising peaks. The trees sprouted brassy new spring leaves.

"Who owns that house?" Malone asked.

"I have no idea. The last time I was here, maybe two or three years ago, it wasn't there."

"Is this the place?" Cassiopeia asked, looking out over his shoulder.

"This is Arima."

"Damn quiet down there," Malone said.

"The mountains shielded our approach," Viktor pointed out. "Radar's clean. We're alone."

Malone noticed a defined trail that routed through a bushy grove, then worked a path up the rocky incline, disappearing into a shadowy cleft. He also saw what looked like a power conduit marching up the rock waste, parallel to the trail, fastened close to the ground. "Looks like somebody is interested in that mountain."

"I saw that, too," Cassiopeia said.

He said, "We need to find out who owns this place. But we also need to be prepared." He still carried the gun that he'd brought with him into the country. But he'd used a few rounds. "You have weapons on board?"

Viktor nodded. "The cabinet in back."

He looked at Cassiopeia. "Get us each one."

ZOVASTINA ENJOYED THE SHOCK ON BOTH LYNDSEY and Vincenti's faces. "Did you think me that stupid?"

"Damn you, Irina," Karyn said.

"That's enough." Zovastina leveled her gun.

Karyn hesitated at the challenge, then retreated to the far side of one of the tables. Zovastina turned her attention back to Vincenti. "I warned you about the Americans. Told you they were watching. And this is how you show your gratitude?"

"You expect me to believe that? If it wasn't for the antiagents, you'd have killed me long ago."

"You and your League wanted a haven. I gave you one. You wanted financial freedom. You have it. You wanted land, markets, ways to clean your dirty money. I gave you all those. But that wasn't enough, was it?"

Vincenti stared back at her, seemingly keeping a tight grip on his own expression.

"You apparently have a different agenda. Something, I assume, not even your League knows about. Something that involves Karyn." She fully realized Vincenti would never admit any allegations. But Lyndsey. He was another matter. So she focused on him. "And you're a part of this, too."

The scientist watched her with undisguised terror.

"Get out of here, Irina," Karyn said. "Leave him be. Leave them both be. They're doing great things."

Bewilderment attacked her. "Great things?"

"He's cured me, Irina. Not you. Him. *He* cured me."

Her curiosity rose as she sensed that Karyn may provide the information she lacked. "HIV is not curable."

Karyn laughed. "That's your problem, Irina. You think nothing is possible without you. The great Achilles on a hero's journey to save his beloved. That's you. A fantasy world that exists only in your mind."

Her neck tensed and the hand that held the gun stiffened.

"I'm not some epic poem," Karyn said. "This is real. It's not about Homer or the Greeks or Alexander. It's about life and death. My life. My death. And this man," she clutched Vincenti by the arm, "this man has cured me."

"What nonsense have you told her?" she asked Vincenti.

"Nonsense?" Karyn shot back. "He found it. The cure. One dose and I haven't felt this good in years."

What had Vincenti discovered?

"Don't you see, Irina?" Karyn said. "You did nothing. *He* did it all. He has the cure."

She stared at Karyn. A bundle of raw energy. A tangle of emotions. "Do you have any idea what I did to try and save you? The chances I took. You came back to me in need, and I helped you."

"You did nothing for me. Only for yourself. You watched me suffer, you wanted me to die—"

"Modern medicine had nothing to offer. I was trying

to find something that might help. You ungrateful *whore*." Her voice rose with indignation.

Sadness clouded Karyn's face. "You don't get it, do you? You never got it. A possession. That's all I was to you, Irina. Something you could control. That's why I cheated on you. Why I sought other women, and men. To show you that I couldn't be dominated. You never got it and still don't."

Her heart rebelled as her mind agreed with what Karyn said. She faced Vincenti. "You found the cure for AIDS?"

He glared at her, unresponsive.

"Tell me," she shouted. She had to know. "Did you find Alexander's draught. The place of the Scythians?"

"I have no idea what that is," he said. "I know nothing about Alexander, the Scythians, or any draught. But she's right. Long ago I found a cure in the mountain behind the house. A local healer told me about the place. He called it, in his language, Arima, the attic. It's a natural substance that can make us all rich."

"That's what this is about? A way to make more money?"

"*Your* ambition will be the ruin of us all."

"So you tried to have me killed? To stop me? Yet you warned me. Lost your nerve?"

He shook his head. "I decided on a better way."

She heard again what Edwin Davis had told her and realized its truth. She motioned at Karyn. "You were going to use her to discredit me. Turn the people against me. First, cure her. Then, use her. Then, what, Enrico? Kill her?"

"Didn't you hear me?" Karyn said. "He saved me."

Zovastina was beyond caring. Taking Karyn back had been a mistake. Lots of foolish chances had been taken for her expense.

And all for nothing.

"Irina," Karyn yelled, "if the people of this damned Federation knew what you really were no one would follow you. You're a fraud. A murderous fraud. All you know is pain. That's your pleasure. Pain. Yes, I wanted to destroy you. I wanted you to feel as small as I do."

Karyn was the only one to whom she'd bared her soul, a closeness she'd never felt with another human being. Homer was right. *Once harm has been done, even a fool understands it.*

So she shot Karyn in the chest.

Then again, in the head.

VINCENTI HAD BEEN WAITING FOR ZOVASTINA TO ACT. He still held the flash drive in his closed left hand. He kept that hand resting on the waist-high table, while his right hand slowly opened the top drawer.

The weapon he'd brought from upstairs lay inside.

Zovastina shot Karyn Walde a third time.

He gripped the gun.

ZOVASTINA'S ANGER SURGED WITH EACH PULL OF THE trigger. Bullets ripped through Karyn's emaciated frame, pinging off the block wall behind her. Her former lover never realized what happened, dying quickly, her body contorted on the floor, bleeding.

Grant Lyndsey had sat silent throughout their exchange. He was nothing. A weak soul. Useless. Vincenti, though, was different. He would not go down without a fight, and surely he realized he was about to die.

So she swung the gun in his direction.

His right hand came into view, holding a pistol.

She shot him four times, emptying the magazine of its remaining rounds.

Blood roses blossomed on Vincenti's shirt.

Eyes rolled skyward and his grip on the gun released, clattering away as his bulky frame fell to the floor.

Two problems solved.

She stepped close to Lyndsey and pointed the empty weapon at his face. Horror stared back. It mattered not that the magazine was empty. The gun itself was more than sufficient to make her point.

"I warned you," she said, "to stay in China."

EIGHTY-TWO

STEPHANIE, HENRIK, AND ELY WERE BEING HELD INSIDE the house. They'd been driven from the gate to the mansion, their car stashed inside a separate garage. Nine infantrymen guarded the interior. Stephanie had seen no staff. They were standing in what appeared to be a library, the room spacious and elegant with towering windows that framed panoramic views of the lush valley beyond the house. Three men with AK-74s, their hair cropped into a utilitarian black brush, stood at the ready, one by the window, another by the door, and a third near an Oriental cabinet. A corpse lay on the floor. Caucasian, middle age, perhaps American, with a bullet to the head.

"None of this is good," she whispered to Henrik.

"I can't see an upside."

Ely appeared calm. But he'd lived under a threat for the past couple months, probably still confused as to what was happening, but willing to trust Henrik. Or, more realistically, Cassiopeia, who he knew was nearby. It was obvious the younger man cared for her. But any reunion was not going to happen soon. Stephanie hoped Malone would be more careful than she'd been. Her cell phone remained in her pocket. Curiously, though she'd been searched, they'd allowed her to keep it.

A click attracted her attention.

She turned to see the Oriental cabinet rotate inward, stopping halfway and revealing a passageway. A small, impish man with balding hair and a worried face emerged from the darkness followed by Irina Zovastina, who held a gun. The guard gave his Supreme Minister a wide berth, retreating to the windows. Zovastina pressed a button on a controller and the cabinet closed. She then tossed the device onto the corpse.

Zovastina handed her gun to one of the guards and gripped the man's AK-74. She walked straight to Thorvaldsen and rammed the butt into his stomach. The breath left the Dane as he doubled over and grabbed his gut.

Both Stephanie and Ely moved to help, but the other guards quickly aimed their weapons.

"I decided," Zovastina said, "instead of calling you back, as you suggested earlier, to come in person."

Thorvaldsen battled for breath and stood upright, fighting the pain. "Good to know . . . I made such . . . a strong impression . . ."

"Who are you?" Zovastina asked Stephanie.

She introduced herself and added, "U.S. Justice Department."

"Malone works for you?"

She nodded and lied, "He does."

Zovastina faced Ely. "What have these spies told you?"

"That you're a liar. That you've been holding me against my will, without me even knowing." He paused, perhaps to summon courage. "That you're planning a war."

ZOVASTINA WAS ANGRY WITH HERSELF. SHE'D ALLOWED emotion to rule. Killing Vincenti had been necessary. Karyn? She regretted killing her, though there was no choice. Had to be done. The cure for AIDS? How was that possible? Were they deceiving her? Or simply mis-

leading? Vincenti had been up to something for sometime. She'd known that. That was why she'd recruited
spies of her own, like Kamil Revin, who'd kept her informed.

She stared at her three prisoners and made clear to
Thorvaldsen, "You may have been ahead of me in
Venice, but you're not anymore."

She motioned with the rifle at Lyndsey. "Come here."

The man stood rooted, his gaze locked on the gun.
Zovastina gestured and one of the soldiers shoved Lyndsey toward her. He stumbled to the floor and tried to
stand, but she cut him off as he came to one knee,
nestling the barrel of the AK-74 into the bridge of his
nose. "Tell me exactly what's happening here. You have
to the count of three. One."

Silence.

"Two."

More silence.

"Three."

MALONE'S BAD FEELING WAS GROWING WORSE. THEY
were still hovering a couple of miles from the house,
using the mountains for cover. Still, no signs of activity
either inside or out. Without question, the estate below
cost tens of millions of dollars. It sat in a region of the
world where there simply weren't that many people who
could afford such luxury, except perhaps Zovastina herself.

"That place needs checking," he said.

He again noticed the trail leading up the stark mountain and the ground conduit. Afternoon heat danced in
waves along the rock face. He thought again of
Ptolemy's riddle. *Climb the god-built walls. When you
reach the attic, gaze into the tawny eye, and dare to find
the distant refuge.*

God-built walls.

Mountains.

He decided they could not keep hovering.

So he slid off the headset and grabbed his phone.

━━━━✳━━━━

STEPHANIE WATCHED THE MAN KNEELING ON THE FLOOR sob uncontrollably, as Zovastina counted to three.

"Please, God," he said. "Don't kill me."

The rifle was still pointed at him and Zovastina said, "Tell me what I want to know."

"Vincenti was right. What he said in the lab. They live in the mountain behind here, up the trail. In a green pool. He has power and lights there. He found them a long time ago." He was speaking fast, the words blurring together in a frenzy of confession. "He told me everything. I helped him change them. I know how they work."

"What are *they*?" she calmly asked.

"Bacteria. Archaea. A unique form of life."

Stephanie heard a change in tone, as if the man sensed a new ally.

"They eat viruses. Destroy them, but they don't hurt us. That's why we did all those clinical trials. To see how they work on your viruses."

Zovastina seemed to consider what she was hearing. Stephanie heard the reference to Vincenti and wondered if this house belonged to him.

"Lyndsey," Zovastina said, "you're talking nonsense. I don't have time—"

"Vincenti lied to you about the antiagents."

That interested her.

"You thought there was one for each zoonosis." Lyndsey shook his head. "Not true. Only one." He pointed in the opposite direction of the room's windows, toward the back of the house. "Back there. The bacteria in the green pool. They were the antiagents to every virus we found. He lied to you. Made you think there were many countermeasures. There weren't. Only one."

Zovastina pressed the gun barrel harder into Lyndsey's face. "If Vincenti lied to me. Then so did you."

Stephanie's cell phone jingled in her pocket.

Zovastina looked up. "Mr. Malone. Finally." The gun swung her way. "Answer it."

Stephanie hesitated.

Zovastina aimed her rifle at Thorvaldsen. "He's of no use to me, except to get you to answer."

Stephanie flipped open the phone. Zovastina came close and listened.

"Where are you?" Malone asked.

Zovastina shook her head.

"Not there yet," Stephanie answered.

"How long?"

"Another half hour. Farther than I thought."

Zovastina nodded her approval of the lie.

"We're here," Malone said. "Looking at one of the biggest damn houses I've ever seen, especially out in the middle of nowhere. Place looks deserted. There's a paved lane, maybe a mile or so, that leads in from the highway. We're hovering a couple miles behind the place. Can Ely offer any more information? There's a trail leading up the mountain into a cleft. Should we check that out?"

"Let me ask."

Zovastina nodded again.

"He says that's a good idea."

"We'll have a look. Call me when you arrive."

Stephanie clicked off the phone and Zovastina relieved her of it. "Now we'll see how much Cotton Malone and Cassiopeia Vitt really know."

EIGHTY-THREE

CASSIOPEIA FOUND THREE GUNS IN THE WEAPONS CABI-
net. She knew the make. Makarovs. A little stubbier
than a standard-issue military Beretta, but all in all a
fairly good weapon.

The helicopter descended and she noticed the ground
rising fast out the windows. Malone had been talking to
Stephanie on the phone. They were apparently not here
yet. She wanted to see Ely. Badly. To know he was all
right. She'd grieved for him, but not fully, always doubt-
ing, always hoping. Not anymore. She'd been right to
continue the quest for the elephant medallions. Right to
zero in on Irina Zovastina. Right to kill the men in
Venice. Even though she'd been wrong about Viktor, she
felt no remorse about his partner. Zovastina, not she,
had started this battle.

The copter touched ground and the turbine wound
down. The motor's roar was replaced with an eerie silence. She slid open the compartment door. Malone and
Viktor started their exit. The afternoon was dry, the sun
welcome, the air warm. She checked her watch—3:25
P.M. This had been a long day, and there was no end in
sight. Her only sleep had been a couple of hours on the
plane from Venice with Zovastina, but that had been an
uneasy slumber.

She handed each man a gun.

Malone tossed his other pistol into the copter and
stuffed the gun into his belt. Viktor did the same.

They were maybe one hundred fifty meters behind the house, just beyond the grove of trees. The trail leading up the mountain stretched to their right. Malone bent down and felt the thick electrical conduit that paralleled its course. "Humming. Somebody definitely wants power up there."

"What's there?" Viktor asked.

"Maybe what your former boss has been searching for."

STEPHANIE CHECKED ON HENRIK AS ZOVASTINA ordered two of the soldiers down into the lab.

"You all right?" she asked him.

He nodded. "I've taken worse."

But she wondered. He was on the other side of sixty, with a crooked spine, and not in what she thought was the best physical condition.

"You should not listen to these people," Zovastina said to Ely.

"Why not? You're the one pointing guns at everyone. Striking old men. Want to try me?"

Zovastina chuckled. "An academician who likes a fight? No, my smart friend. You and I don't need to battle. I need you helping me."

"Then stop all this, let them go, and you got it."

"I wish it were that simple."

"She's right. It can't be that simple," Thorvaldsen said. "Not when she's planning a biological war. A modern-day Alexander the Great, who will kill millions to reconquer all that he did and more."

"Don't mock me," Zovastina warned.

Thorvaldsen seemed unfazed. "I'll talk to you however I please."

Zovastina raised the AK-74.

Ely jumped in front of Thorvaldsen. "If you want that tomb," he made clear, "lower the gun."

Stephanie wondered if this despot coveted that ancient treasure enough to be openly challenged in front of one of her men.

"Your usefulness is rapidly declining," Zovastina made clear.

"That tomb could well be within walking distance of here," Ely said.

Stephanie admired Ely's determination. He was dangling a piece of meat to an uncaged lion, hoping an intense hunger overrode the instinctive desire to attack. But he seemed to have read Zovastina perfectly.

She lowered the gun.

The two soldiers returned with a computer mainframe cradled in each of their arms.

"It's all on there," Lyndsey said. "The experiments. Data. Methodology of dealing with the archaea. All encrypted. But I can undo that. Only me and Vincenti knew the passwords. He trusted me. Told me everything."

"There are experts who can unencrypt anything. I don't need you."

"But it'll take others time to duplicate the chemistry that's needed to deal with the bacteria. Vincenti and I worked on that for the past three years. You don't have that time. You won't have the antiagent."

Stephanie realized that the spineless fool was offering the only collateral he possessed.

Zovastina barked out something in a language Stephanie did not understand and the two men cradling the computers left the room. She then motioned with her gun and told them to follow the men out.

They walked down the hall into the main foyer and headed toward the ground floor rear. Another soldier appeared and Zovastina asked something in what sounded like Russian. The man nodded and pointed at a closed door.

They were halted before it, and after it was opened, she, Thorvaldsen, Ely, and Lyndsey were herded inside and the door closed behind them.

She surveyed their prison.

An empty storage closet, maybe eight feet by ten, paneled in unfinished wood. The air smelled of antiseptic.

Lyndsey lunged at the door and banged on the thick wood. "I can help you," he screamed. "Let me out of here."

"Shut up," Stephanie spat out.

Lyndsey went quiet.

She studied their predicament, her mind racing. Zovastina seemed in a hurry. Preoccupied.

The door reopened.

"Thank God," Lyndsey said.

Zovastina stood with the AK-74 still gripped tightly.

"Why are you doing—" Lyndsey started.

"I agree with her," Zovastina said. "Shut up." Zovastina set her gaze on Ely. "I need to know. Is this the place from the riddle?"

Ely did not immediately answer and Stephanie wondered if it was courage or foolishness that fueled his obstinance. Finally, he said, "How would I know? I've been locked away in that cabin."

"You came straight here from that cabin," Zovastina said.

"How do you know that?" Ely asked.

But Stephanie knew the answer. The pieces clicked into place and she realized the worst. They'd been played. "You ordered that guard to shoot out the tires on our car. You wanted us to take his car. It's trackable."

"Easiest way I could think of to see what you knew. I was alerted to your presence at the cabin by electronic surveillance I had installed around it."

But Stephanie had killed the guard. "That man had no idea."

Zovastina shrugged. "He did his job. If you got the better of him, that was his mistake."

"But I killed him," she said, her voice rising.

Zovastina seemed puzzled. "You worry far too much about something that means nothing."

"He didn't need to die."

"That's your problem. That's the West's problem. You can't do what needs to be done."

Stephanie now knew that their situation was worse than she imagined, and she suddenly realized something else. So was Malone's and Cassiopeia's. And she saw that Henrik read her bleak thoughts.

Behind Zovastina, several of the troops walked by, each carrying a strange-looking contraption. One was deposited on the floor beside Zovastina. A funnel extended from its top and she'd spotted wheels beneath.

"This is a big house. It will take a little while to prepare it."

"For what?" she asked.

"To burn," Thorvaldsen answered.

"Quite right," Zovastina said. "In the meantime I'm going to visit Mr. Malone and Ms. Vitt. Don't go away."

And Zovastina slammed the door.

EIGHTY-FOUR

MALONE LED THE WAY UP THE INCLINE AND NOTICED, at places, that steps had been chipped from the rock recently. Cassiopeia and Viktor followed, both keeping a lookout behind. The distant house remained quiet and Ptolemy's riddle kept playing through his mind. *Climb the god-built walls.* This certainly qualified, though he imagined the climb in Ptolemy's time would have been much different.

The trail leveled off on a ledge.

The power conduit continued to snake a path into a dark cleft in the rock wall. Narrow, but passable.

When you reach the attic.

He led the way into the passage.

His eyes were not accustomed to the diminishing light and needed a few seconds to adjust. The path was short, maybe twenty feet, and he used the conduit as a guide. The corridor ended inside a larger chamber. Weak ambient light revealed that the power line hooked left and ended at a junction box. He stepped close and saw four flashlights piled on the floor. He flicked one on and used the bright beam to survey the room.

The chamber was maybe thirty feet long and that much or more wide, the ceiling a good twenty feet away. Then he noticed two pools about ten feet apart.

He heard a click and the room sprang to life with incandescent light.

He turned to see Viktor at the electrical box.

He switched off the flashlight. "I like to check things out before acting."

"Since when?" Cassiopeia said.

"Take a look," Viktor said, motioning at the pools.

Both were illuminated by underwater lights fed through ground cables. The one on the right was oblong shaped and carried a brown tint. The other was luminous with greenish phosphorescence.

"Gaze into the tawny eye," Malone said.

He stepped close to the brown pool and noticed that the water was swimming-pool clear, its color coming from the tint of the rocks below the surface. He crouched down. Cassiopeia bent down beside him. He tested the water. "Warm, but not too bad. Like a hot tub. Must be thermal vented. These mountains are still active."

Cassiopeia brought wet fingers to her lips. "No taste."

"Look at the bottom."

He watched as Cassiopeia registered what he'd just spotted. Maybe ten feet down in the crystalline water, carved from a slab of rock, lying flat, was the letter Z.

He walked to the green pool. Cassiopeia followed. More water clear as air, colored by tinted stone. At its bottom lay the letter H.

"From the medallion," he said. "ZH. Life."

"Seems this is the place."

He noticed Viktor had stayed close to the electrical box, not all that concerned with their discovery. But there was something else. Now he knew what the last line of the riddle meant.

And dare to find the distant refuge.

He returned to the brown pool. "Remember on the medallion, and at the bottom of that manuscript Ely found. That odd symbol." With his finger he traced its outline in the sandy topsoil.

"I couldn't determine what it was. Letters? Like two B's joined to an A? Now I know exactly what it is. There." He pointed at the rock wall six feet beneath the brown pool's surface. "See that opening. Look familiar?"

Cassiopeia focused on what he'd already noticed. The opening appeared like two B's joined to an A. "It does look like it."

"*When you reach the attic, gaze into the tawny eye, and dare to find the distant refuge.* You know what that means?"

"No, Malone. Tell us what that means."

He turned.

Irina Zovastina stood just outside the exit.

STEPHANIE NESTLED CLOSE TO THE DOOR AND LISTENED for any sound on the other side. She heard the whine of an electrical motor, starting, stopping, then a bump to the door. A hesitation, then the mechanical hum began again.

"It's canvassing," Thorvaldsen said. "The robots spread the potion before exploding and setting everything off."

She noticed an odor. Sickeningly sweet. Strongest at the bottom of the door. "Greek fire?" she asked.

Thorvaldsen nodded, then said to Ely, "Your discovery."

"That crazy bitch is going to fry us all," Lyndsey said. "We're trapped in here."

"Tell us something we don't know," Stephanie muttered.

"Did she kill anyone with it?" Ely asked.

"Not that I know of," Thorvaldsen said. "We may have the honor of being first. Though Cassiopeia certainly used it to her advantage in Venice." The older man hesitated. "She killed three men."

Ely seemed shocked. "Why?"

"To avenge you."

The younger man's amiable face hardened into a puzzled frown.

"She was hurt. Angry. Once she found out Zovastina was behind things, there was no stopping her."

Stephanie examined the door. Steel hinges top and bottom. Bolts held their pins in place and no screwdriver in sight. She pounded her hand against the wood. "Does Vincenti own this monstrosity?" she asked Lyndsey.

"He did. She shot him."

"She's apparently consolidating her power," Thorvaldsen said.

"She's a fool," Lyndsey said. "There's so much more happening here. I could have had it all. The frickin' golden rainbow. He offered it to me."

"Vincenti?" she asked.

Lyndsey nodded.

"Don't you get it?" Stephanie said. "Zovastina has those computers with the data. She has her viruses. And you even told her there's only one antiagent and where they can be found. You're useless to her."

"But she does need me," he spit out. "She knows."

Her patience was wearing thin. "Knows what?"

"Those bacteria. They're the cure for AIDS."

EIGHTY-FIVE

VIKTOR HEARD ZOVASTINA'S DISTINCTIVE VOICE. How many times had she commanded him with the same brittle tone? He'd stayed near the exit, off to the side, out of Malone and Vitt's way, listening. He was also out of Zovastina's sight, as she'd yet to enter the lit chamber, staying in the shadowy passageway.

He watched as Malone and Vitt faced Zovastina. Neither of them betrayed his presence. Slowly, he inched closer to where the rock opened. He gripped the gun firmly in his right hand and waited for the moment Zovastina stepped inside to bring the weapon level with her head.

She stopped.

"My traitor. I wondered where you were."

He noticed she'd come unarmed.

"Going to shoot me?" she asked.

"If you give me reason."

"I have no weapon."

That worried him. And a quick glance toward Malone saw he was concerned, too.

"I'll have a look," Cassiopeia said, moving toward the exit.

"You'll regret attacking me," Zovastina said to Cassiopeia.

"I'd be glad to give you the opportunity to get even."

Zovastina smiled. "I doubt Mr. Malone, or my traitor here, would allow me the pleasure."

Cassiopeia disappeared into the cleft. A few seconds later she reappeared. "Nobody out there. The house and grounds are still quiet."

"Then where'd she come from?" Malone asked. "And how did she know to come here?"

"When you avoided my emissaries in the mountains," Zovastina said, "we decided to back off and see where you were headed."

"Who owns this place?" Malone asked.

"Enrico Vincenti. Or at least he did. I just killed him."

"Good riddance," Malone said. "If you hadn't, I would have."

"And the reason for your hatred?"

"He killed a friend of mine."

"And you also came to save Ms. Vitt?"

"Actually, I came to stop you."

"That may prove problematic."

Her cavalier attitude worried him.

"May I examine the pools?" Zovastina asked.

He needed time to think. "Go ahead."

Viktor lowered his gun, but kept the weapon ready. Malone wasn't sure what was happening. But their situation posed problems. Only one way in and out. And that was never good.

Zovastina stepped to the brown pool and gazed down. She then walked to the green pool. "ZH. From the medallions. I wondered why Ptolemy had the letters added to the coins. He's probably the one who laid those carvings at the bottom of the pools. Who else would have done that? Ingenious. It took a long time to decipher his riddle. Who do we have to thank? You, Mr. Malone?"

"Let's say it was a team effort."

"A modest man. A shame we didn't meet sooner and under different circumstances. I'd love to have you working for me."

"I have a job."

"American agent."

"Actually, I'm a bookseller."

She laughed. "And a sense of humor."

Viktor stood ready, on guard, behind Zovastina. Cassiopeia watched the exit.

"Tell me, Malone. Did you solve all of the riddle? Is Alexander the Great here? You were just about to explain something to Ms. Vitt when I interrupted."

Malone still held the flashlight. Heavy duty. Seemed waterproof. "Vincenti wired this place with lights. Even lit the pools. Aren't you curious why these were so important to him?"

"It looks like there's nothing here."

"That's where you're wrong."

Malone laid the flashlight on the ground and removed his jacket and shirt.

"What are you doing?" Cassiopeia asked.

He slipped off his shoes and socks and emptied his trouser pockets of the phone and his wallet. "That symbol carved into the side of the pool. It leads to the *distant refuge*."

"Cotton," Cassiopeia said.

He eased himself into the water. Hot at first, but then its warmth soothed his tired limbs. "Keep an eye on her."

He grabbed a breath and dove under.

"THE CURE FOR AIDS?" STEPHANIE ASKED LYNDSEY.

"A local healer showed Vincenti pools in the mountain years ago, when he worked for the Iraqis. He found out then that the bacteria destroy HIV."

She saw that Ely was listening with a clear intensity.

"But he didn't tell anybody," Lyndsey said. "He held it."

"For what?" Ely asked.

"The right time. He let the market build. Allowed the disease to spread. Waited."

"You can't be serious," Ely said.

"He was about to spring it."

Now Stephanie understood. "And you were going to share in the spoils?"

Lyndsey seemed to catch the reservation in her tone. "Don't give me that sanctimonious crap. I'm not Vincenti. I didn't know about any cure until today. He just told me."

"And what were you going to do?" she asked.

"Help produce it. What's wrong with that?"

"While Zovastina killed millions? You and Vincenti helped make that possible."

Lyndsey shook his head. "Vincenti said he was going to stop her before she did anything. He held the anti-agent. She couldn't move without that."

"But now she controls it. You're both idiots."

"You realize, Stephanie," Thorvaldsen said, "that Vincenti had no idea there was anything else up there. He bought this place to preserve the bacteria source. He named it after the Asian designation. He apparently knew nothing about Alexander's grave."

She'd already connected those dots. "The draught and the tomb are together. Unfortunately, we're trapped inside this closet."

At least Zovastina had left the light on. She'd examined every inch of the unfinished walls and stone floor. No way out. And more of that nauseating odor seeped in from under the door.

"Do those two computers have all the data about the cure on them?" Ely asked Lyndsey.

"Doesn't matter," she said. "Getting out of here is what matters. Before the bonfire begins."

"It does matter," Ely said. "We can't let her have those."

"Ely, look around you. What can we do about it?"

"Cassiopeia and Malone are out there."

"True," Thorvaldsen said. "But I'm afraid Zovastina may be a step ahead of them."

Stephanie agreed, but that was Malone's problem.

"There's something she doesn't know," Lyndsey said.

She heard it in his tone and was not in the mood. "Don't try and bargain with me."

"Vincenti copied everything onto a flash drive just before Zovastina showed up. He was holding the drive when she shot him. It's still down in the lab. With that drive and me, you'd have the antiagent for her bugs and the cure."

"Believe me," she said. "Even though you're a slimy SOB, if I could get you out of here, I would."

She banged again on the door.

"But it's not to be."

Cassiopeia kept one eye on Zovastina, whom Viktor was holding at bay with his gun, and one eye on the pool. Malone had been gone nearly three minutes. No way he'd held his breath that long.

But then a shadow appeared underwater as Malone emerged from the odd-shaped opening and broke the surface, resting his arms on the rocky edge, one hand gripping the flashlight.

"You need to see this," he said to her.

"And leave them? No way."

"Viktor's got the gun. He can handle her."

She still hesitated. Something wasn't right. Her mind may have been on Ely, but she wasn't oblivious to reality. Viktor was still an unknown, albeit for the past few hours a helpful one. Parts of her would be hanging from two trees right now if not for him. But still.

"You need to see this," Malone said again.

"Is it there?" Zovastina asked.

"Wouldn't you like to know?"

Cassiopeia still wore the tight-fitting leather suit from Venice. She removed the top and left the bottoms. She laid the gun down, out of reach of Zovastina, beside Malone's. A black sports bra covered her chest and she noticed Viktor's gaze. "Keep your eye on her," she made clear.

"She's not going anywhere."

She slipped into the pool.

"Grab a good breath and follow me," Malone said.

She saw him submerge and wedge himself into the opening. She followed a few feet behind, swimming through one of the B-shaped portals. Her eyes were open and she saw that they were navigating a rock tunnel, maybe a meter and a half wide. The pool sat about two meters from the chamber wall, so they were now swimming into the mountain. Malone's flashlight beam danced across the tunnel and she wondered how much farther.

Then she saw Malone rise.

She emerged from the water right beside him.

His light revealed another enclosed chamber, this one dome-shaped, the naked limestone streaked with deep blue shadows. Niches cut into the walls held what looked like alabaster jars with finely sculpted lids. Overhead, the gaunt limestone was dotted with openings, rough-hewn and irregularly shaped. Cold silvery light seeped into the lofty hall from each portal, their dusty shafts dissolving into the rock.

"Those openings have to point downward," Malone said. "It's dry as hell in here. They're to allow light, but not moisture. They also naturally ventilate."

"Were they cut?" she asked.

"I doubt it. My guess is this place was chosen because they're here." He levered himself out of the pool. Water poured from his soaked pants. "We have to hurry."

She climbed out.

"That tunnel is the only thing that connects this chamber to the other," he said. "I took a quick look around to be sure."

"Certainly explains why it's never been found."

Malone used the flashlight to trace the walls and she noticed faint paintings. Bits and pieces. A warrior in his chariot, holding a scepter and reins in one hand, clutching a woman around her waist in another. A stag hit by a javelin. A leafless tree. A man on foot with a spear. Another man moving toward what looked like a boar. What color remained seemed striking. The violet of the hunter's mantle. Maroon of the chariot. Yellow for the animals. She noticed more scenes on the opposite wall. A young rider with a spear and a wreath in his hair, clearly in his prime, about to attack a lion already beset by dogs. A white background nearly faded with intermediate shades of orange-yellow, pale red, and brown mixed with cooler shades of green and blue.

"I'd say Asian and Greek influences," Malone said. "But I'm no expert."

He motioned with the light across stones squared like a parquet floor. A doorway bursting with Greek influence— fluted shafts and ornamented bases—emerged from the darkness. Cassiopeia, a student of ancient engineering, clearly recognized the Hellenistic flair.

Above spread a shallow-carved inscription in Greek letters.

"Through there," he said.

EIGHTY-SIX

VINCENTI FORCED HIS EYES OPEN. PAIN IN HIS CHEST racked his brain. Each breath seemed a labor. How many bullets had hit him? Three? Four? He didn't remember. But somehow his heart still beat. Maybe it wasn't all that bad to be fat. He recalled falling, then a deep blackness sweeping over him. He never fired a shot. Zovastina seemed to have anticipated his move. Almost like she'd wanted him to challenge her.

He forced himself to roll over and he clutched a table leg. Blood oozed from his chest and a new wave of pain drove electric nails through his spine. He struggled harder to breathe. The pistol was gone, but he realized he was holding something else. He brought his hand close and saw the flash drive.

Everything he'd worked for over the past ten years lay in his bloodied palm. How had Zovastina found him? Who had betrayed him? O'Conner? Was he still alive? Where was he? O'Conner had been the only other person with the ability to open the cabinet in the study.

Two controllers.

Where was his?

He struggled to focus and finally spotted the device lying on the tile floor.

Everything seemed lost.

But maybe not.

He was still alive and perhaps Zovastina was gone.

He gathered his strength and scooped the controller into his hand. He should have provided the house with full security before he abducted Karyn Walde. But he'd never thought Zovastina would link him to her disappearance—certainly not so quickly—and he'd never believed that she'd turn on him. Not with what she had planned.

She needed him.

Or did she?

Blood pooled in his throat and he spit out the sour taste. A lung must have been hit. More blood caused him to cough, which sent new bolts of agony through his body.

Maybe O'Conner could get to him?

He fumbled with the controller and could not decide which of the three buttons to push. One opened the door in the study. The other released all of the concealed doors throughout the house. The last activated the alarm.

No time to be right.

So he pushed all three.

ZOVASTINA STARED AT THE BROWN POOL. MALONE AND Vitt had been submerged for several minutes.

"There must be another chamber," she said.

Viktor stayed silent.

"Lower that gun."

He did as ordered.

She faced him. "Did you enjoy tying me to those trees? Threatening me?"

"You wanted it to appear that I was one of them."

Viktor had succeeded beyond her expectations, leading them straight to her goal. "Is there anything else I need to know?"

"They seemed to know what they're looking for."

Viktor had been her double-agent ever since the Americans first reenlisted his aid. He'd come straight to her and told her of his predicament. For the past year she'd used him to funnel what she wanted the West to know. A dangerous balancing act, but one she'd been forced to maintain because of Washington's renewed interest in her.

And everything had worked.

Until Amsterdam.

And until Vincenti decided to kill his American watchdog. She'd encouraged him to eliminate the spy, hoping Washington might focus its attention on him. But the subterfuge had not worked. Luckily, today's deceptions had been more successful.

Viktor had promptly reported Malone's presence within the palace and she'd quickly conceived how to take maximum advantage of the opportunity with an orchestrated palace escape. Edwin Davis had been the other side's attempt to divert her attention but, knowing Malone was there, she'd seen through that ruse.

"There has to be another chamber," she repeated, slipping off her shoes and removing her jacket. "Grab two of those flashlights and let's go see."

STEPHANIE HEARD A CLAXON REVERBERATE THROUGH the house, the sound dulled by the thick walls that encased them. Movement caught her eye and she saw a panel swing open at the opposite end of the closet.

Ely quickly shifted out of its way.

"A frickin' doorway," Lyndsey exclaimed.

She moved toward the exit, suspicious, and examined

its top. Electric bolts—connected to the alarm. Had to be. Beyond was a passageway lit by bulbs.

The alarm stopped.

They all stood in contemplative silence.

"What are we waiting for?" Thorvaldsen asked.

She stepped through the portal.

EIGHTY-SEVEN

MALONE LED CASSIOPEIA THROUGH THE DOORWAY AND watched as she gazed in wonder. His light revealed carvings that sprang with life from the rock walls. Most of the images were of a warrior in his prime—young, vigorous, a spear in hand, a wreath in his hair. One frieze showed what appeared to be kings paying homage. Another a lion hunt. Still another a fierce battle. In each, the human element—muscles, hands, face, legs, feet, toes—were all depicted with painstaking care. Not a hint of color. Only a silvery monochrome.

He focused the beam on the center of the wigwam-shaped chamber and two stone plinths that each supported a stone sarcophagus. The exterior of both were adorned with lotus and palmetto patterns, rosettes, tendrils, flowers, and leaves. He pointed to the coffin lids. "That's a Macedonian star on each."

Cassiopeia bent down before the tombs and examined the lettering. Her fingers traced the words on each with a gentle touch. ΑΛΕΞΑΝΔΡΟΣ. ΗΦΑΙΣΤΙΩΝ. "I can't read this, but it has to be Alexander and Hephaestion."

He understood her awe. But there was a more pressing matter. "That'll have to wait. We have a bigger problem."

She stood upright.

"What is it?" she asked.

"Take off those wet clothes and I'll explain."

Zovastina leaped into the pool, followed by Viktor, and swam through the opening that looked so similar to the symbol on the elephant medallion. She'd noticed the resemblance immediately.

Easy strokes propelled her forward. The water was soothing, like a dip in one of the saunas at her palace.

Ahead, the overhead rock wall gave way.

She surfaced.

She'd been correct. Another chamber. Smaller than the one on the other side. She shook the water from her eyes and saw that the high ceiling seemed backlit by ambient light that leaked in from openings high in the rock. Viktor emerged beside her and they both climbed out. She surveyed the room. Faded murals decorated the walls. Two portals opened into more darkness.

No one in sight.

No other beams of light.

Apparently, Cotton Malone was not as naive as she'd thought.

"All right, Malone," she called out. "You have the advantage. But could I have a look first?"

Silence.

"I'll take that as a yes."

Her light studied the sandy floor, spangled with mica, and she spotted a moisture trail through the doorway to her right.

She entered the next chamber and spotted two funerary plinths. Both exteriors were adorned with carvings and letters, but she wasn't fluent in Old Greek. That was why she'd recruited Ely Lund. One image caught her eye and she stepped close and gently blew away debris that clogged its outline. Bit by bit a horse was revealed. Maybe five centimeters long, with an upstanding mane and a lifted tail.

"Bucephalas," she whispered.

She needed to see more so she said to the darkness, "Malone. I came here unarmed because I didn't need a gun. Viktor was mine, as you apparently know. But I have your three friends. I was there when you called on the phone. They're in the house, sealed away, about to be consumed by Greek fire. Just thought you'd like to know."

Still silence.

"Keep an eye out," she whispered to Viktor.

She'd come this far, wished too long, fought too hard, not to see. She laid her light atop one of the sarcophagi's lid, the one with the horse, and pushed. After a moment of valiant tugging, the thick slab moved. A few more shoves and she cleared a pie-shaped opening.

She grabbed the light and, unlike in Venice, hoped she would not be disappointed.

A mummy lay inside.

Sheathed and masked in gold.

She wanted to touch it, to lift the mask away, but thought better. She did not want to do anything that might damage the remains.

But she wondered.

Was she the first in over twenty-three hundred years to gaze upon the remains of Alexander the Great? Had she found the conqueror, along with his draught? Seems she had. Best of all, she knew precisely what to do with both. The draught would be used to fulfill her conquests and, as she now knew, make her an unexpected windfall of profit. The mummy, from whom she could not remove her eyes, would symbolize all that she did. The possibilities seemed endless, but the danger that surrounded her brought her thoughts back to the reality.

Malone was playing his hand quite carefully.

She needed to do the same.

Malone saw the anticipation on Cassiopeia's face. Ely, Stephanie, and Henrik were in trouble. They'd watched from the other doorway, the one Zovastina had avoided, as she and Viktor followed the water trail and entered the funerary chamber.

"How did you know Viktor was lying to us?" she whispered.

"Twelve years of dealing with random assets. That whole thing with you at the palace? Too easy. And something Stephanie told me. Viktor's the one who fed them Vincenti. Why? Makes no sense. Except if Viktor was playing both sides."

"I should have seen that."

"How? You didn't hear what Stephanie told me in Venice."

They stood with bare shoulders scraping against oblique walls. They'd removed their pants and wrung the water from them so as not to leave any further trail. Once through the tomb's other two rooms, filled with artifacts, they had quickly re-dressed and waited. The tomb consisted of only four interconnected rooms, none of which were large, two of which opened to the pool. Zovastina was most likely enjoying a moment of triumph. But the information about Stephanie, Ely, and Henrik had changed things. True or not, the possibility had grabbed his attention. Which was surely the idea.

He glanced out toward the pool. Light danced in the funerary room. He hoped the sight of Alexander the Great's grave might buy them a few moments.

"You ready?" he asked Cassiopeia.

She nodded.

He led the way.

Viktor stepped from the other doorway.

EIGHTY-EIGHT

STEPHANIE NOTICED THAT THE SICKENINGLY SWEET aroma was not as strong in the back passages, but nonetheless lingered. At least they weren't trapped any longer. Several turns had led them deeper into the house and she'd yet to see another open exit.

"I've seen how this concoction works," Thorvaldsen said. "Once Greek fire ignites, these walls will burn quickly. We need to be out of here before that happens."

She was aware of their dilemma, but their choices were limited. Lyndsey was still anxious, Ely amazingly calm. He had the countenance of an agent, not an academician, a coolness she admired considering their predicament. She wished she possessed more of his nerve.

"What do you mean by *quickly*?" Lyndsey asked Thorvaldsen. "How fast will this place burn?"

"Fast enough that we'll be trapped."

"So what are we doing in here?"

"You want to go back to that storage closet?" she asked.

They turned another corner, the dark hall reminding her of a corridor in a train. The path ended just ahead at the base of a steep stairway, leading up.

No choice.

They climbed.

MALONE STEADIED HIMSELF.

"Going somewhere?" Viktor asked.

Cassiopeia stood behind him. He wondered about Zovastina's location. Was the dancing light merely a ploy to draw them out?

"Thought we'd leave."

"Can't let you do that."

"If you think you can stop me, you're welcome to—" Viktor lunged forward. Malone sidestepped the move, then locked his attacker in a bear hug.

They dropped to the floor and rolled.

Malone found himself on top. Viktor struggled beneath him. He clamped a hand onto the other man's throat and sank his knee deep into Viktor's chest. Quickly, with both hands, he yanked Viktor upward and slammed the back of his skull into the rocky floor.

CASSIOPEIA READIED HERSELF TO LEAP INTO THE POOL as soon as Malone broke free. At the same instant Viktor's body went limp beneath Malone, movement out of the corner of her eye drew her attention to the doorway where they'd been hiding.

"Malone," she called out.

Zovastina rushed toward her.

Malone sprang off Viktor and found the water.

Cassiopeia dove in after him and swam hard for the tunnel.

STEPHANIE TOPPED THE STAIRS AND SAW THERE WAS A choice of routes. Left or right? She turned left. Ely headed right.

"Over here," Ely called out.

They all rushed his way and saw an open doorway.

"Careful," Thorvaldsen said. "Don't let those things out there spray you. Avoid them."

Ely nodded, then pointed at Lyndsey. "You and I are going after that flash drive."

The scientist shook his head. "Not me."

Stephanie agreed. "That's not a good idea."

"You're not sick."

"Those robots," Thorvaldsen said, "are programmed to explode, and we don't know when."

"I don't give a damn," Ely said, his voice rising. "This man knows how to cure AIDS. His dead boss has known that for years, but let millions die. Zovastina has that cure now. I'm not going to let her manipulate it, too." Ely grabbed Lyndsey by the shirt. "You and I are going to get that drive."

"You're nuts," Lyndsey said. "Frickin' nuts. Just go up to the green pool and drink the water. Vincenti said it worked that way. You don't need me."

Thorvaldsen watched the younger man closely. Stephanie realized that the Dane was perhaps seeing his own son standing before him, youth in all its glory, simultaneously defiant, brave, and foolish. Her own son, Mark, was the same way.

"Your butt," Ely said, "is going with me into that lab."

She realized something else. "Zovastina went after Cotton and Cassiopeia. She left us in this house for a reason. You heard her. She purposefully told us those machines would take a little time."

"We're insurance," Thorvaldsen said.

"Bait. Probably for Cotton and Cassiopeia. But this guy," she pointed at Lyndsey, "him, she wants. His babbling made sense. She doesn't have time to be sure an antiagent works, or that he's being truthful. Though she may not admit it, she needs him. She'll be back for him before this place burns. You can count on it."

ZOVASTINA LEAPED INTO THE POOL. MALONE HAD bested Viktor and Cassiopeia Vitt had managed to elude her.

If she swam fast she could catch Vitt in the tunnel.

MALONE PLANTED HIS PALMS AND PUSHED HIMSELF UP from the pool. He felt a rush beneath him and saw Cassiopeia surface. She deftly sprang from the warm water and, dripping wet, grabbed one of the guns that lay a few feet away.

"Let's go," he said, retrieving his shoes and shirt.

Cassiopeia backed toward the exit, gun leveled at the pool.

A shadow clouded the water.

Zovastina's head found air.

Cassiopeia fired.

THE FIRST EXPLOSION STARTLED ZOVASTINA MORE than frightened her. Water cleared from her eyes and she saw Vitt aiming one of the guns straight at her.

Another bang. Unbearably loud.

She plunged beneath the surface.

CASSIOPEIA FIRED TWO TIMES AT THE ILLUMINATED pool. The gun seemed to jam so she worked the slide, ejecting a cartridge, loading a new round. Then she noticed something and faced Malone.

"Feel better?" he asked.

"Blanks?" she asked.

"Of course. Rounds stuffed with wadding, I imagine,

so there'd be enough kick to at least partially work the slide. But not enough, obviously. You don't think Viktor would have given us bullets?"

"I never thought about it."

"That's the problem. You're not thinking. Can we go now?"

She tossed the gun away. "You're such a joy to work with."

And they both fled the chamber.

VIKTOR RUBBED THE BACK OF HIS HEAD AND WAITED. Another few seconds and he'd roll into the pool, but Zovastina returned, breathing hard as she emerged from the water, and rested her arms on the rocky edge.

"I forgot about the guns. They have us trapped. The only way out is guarded."

Viktor's head hurt from the pounding and he fought an irritating dizziness. "Minister, the guns are loaded with blanks. I changed all the magazines before we escaped from the palace. I didn't think it wise to give them loaded guns."

"Nobody noticed?"

"Who checks rounds? They simply assumed the guns aboard a military chopper were loaded."

"Good thinking, but you could have mentioned that to me."

"Everything happened so fast. There wasn't time and, unfortunately, Malone gave my skull a good pop on these rocks."

"What about Malone's gun from the palace? That *was* loaded. Where is it?"

"In the chopper. He changed it out for one of ours."

He watched as her mind rolled through the possibilities.

"We need Lyndsey from the house. He's all that's left here now."

"What about Malone and Vitt?"

"I have men waiting. And their guns *are* loaded."

EIGHTY-NINE

STEPHANIE STARED OUT THROUGH THE OPEN PANEL into one of the mansion's bedchambers. The room was elaborately furnished in an Italian style and quiet save for a mechanical whir from outside an open door, which led to the second-floor hall.

They stepped from the back passage.

One of the Greek fire machines whizzed passed in the hall, spewing mist. A pall hung heavy in the room, evidence that the robots had already visited.

"They're quickly basting this house," Thorvaldsen said as he moved to the hall door.

She was just about to caution him to stop when the Dane stepped out and a new voice—male, foreign—shouted.

Thorvaldsen froze, then slowly raised his arms.

Ely crept close to her ear. "One of the troops. He told Henrik to halt and raise his hands."

Thorvaldsen kept his head toward the guard, who apparently was positioned to their right, without a way to see inside the room. She'd wondered about the troops, hoping that they'd been evacuated when the machines started their patrol.

More loud words.

"What now?" she whispered.

"He wants to know if he's alone."

MALONE AND CASSIOPEIA CLAMBERED DOWN THE IN-
cline in their wet clothes. Malone buttoned his shirt as
they descended.

"You could have mentioned that the guns were
duds," Cassiopeia said to him.

"And when would I have done that?" He hopped
over rocks and hastened down the steep slope.

Breaths came fast. He certainly wasn't thirty years old
anymore, but his forty-eight-year-old bones weren't totally out of shape. "I didn't want Viktor to even sense
we knew anything."

"*We* didn't. Why'd you give up your gun?"

"Had to play his game."

"You're an odd bird," she said to him, as they found
level ground.

"I'll take that as a compliment, coming from someone
who traipsed around Venice with a bow and arrow."

The house lay a football field away. He still saw no
one roaming the exterior and no movement inside, past
the windows.

"We need to check something."

He raced toward the chopper and leaped into the rear
compartment. He found the weapons locker. Four AK-74s
stood upright, ammunition clips stacked beneath.

He examined them. "All blanks." Barrel plugs had
been carefully inserted to accommodate the phony
rounds and allow the cartridges to be ejected. "Thorough little cuss. I'll give him that."

He found the gun he'd brought from Italy and
checked the magazine. Five live rounds.

Cassiopeia grabbed an assault rifle and popped in a
clip. "Nobody else knows these are useless. They'll do
for now."

He reached for one of the AK-74s. "I agree. Perception is everything."

ZOVASTINA AND VIKTOR EMERGED FROM THE POOL. Malone and Vitt were gone.

All the guns lay on the sandy floor.

"Malone's a problem," she made clear.

"Not to worry," Viktor said. "I owe him."

STEPHANIE LISTENED AS THE TROOPER IN THE HALL CON-tinued to bark orders at Thorvaldsen, the voice coming closer to the doorway. Lyndsey's face froze in panic and Ely quickly clamped a hand over the man's mouth and dragged him to the other side of a poster bed, where they crouched out of sight.

With a coolness that surprised her, she locked her gaze on a Chinese porcelain statuette resting on the dresser. She grabbed it and slipped behind the door.

Through the hinge crack she saw the guard enter the bedchamber. As he stepped clear, she planted the statue into the nape of his neck. He staggered and she finished him off with another head blow, then snatched the rifle.

Thorvaldsen darted close and retrieved the side arm. "I was hoping you'd improvise."

"I was hoping these men were gone."

Ely brought Lyndsey.

"Good job with him," she told Ely.

"He has the backbone of a banana."

She studied the AK-74. She'd learned about hand-guns, but assault rifles were another matter. She'd never fired one. Thorvaldsen seemed to sense her hesitation and offered her his gun. "Want to switch?"

She did not refuse. "You can handle one of those?"

"I've had a little experience."

She made a mental note to inquire more about that later. She approached the doorway and carefully spied into the hall. No one in either direction. She led the way as they crept down the hall toward the second-floor foyer, where a staircase led down to the main entrance. Another of the Greek fire machines appeared behind them, darting from one room into another. Its sudden appearance drew her attention momentarily away from what lay ahead.

The wall to her left ended, replaced by a thick stone balustrade.

Movement below caught her gaze.

Two soldiers.

Who instantly reacted by leveling their rifles and firing.

CASSIOPEIA HEARD THE RAT-TAT-TAT OF AUTOMATIC weapon fire from inside the house.

Her first thought was Ely.

"Just remember," he said. "We've only got five good rounds."

They leaped from the chopper.

ZOVASTINA AND VIKTOR EMERGED FROM THE FISSURE and studied the scene a hundred meters below. Malone and Vitt were rushing from the helicopter carrying two assault rifles.

"Are those loaded?" she asked.

"No, Minister. Blanks."

"Which Malone clearly knows, so they're carrying them for show."

Gunfire from inside the house caused her alarm.

"Those turtles will explode if damaged," Viktor said.

She needed Lyndsey before that happened.

"I hid loaded magazines for the pistols and clips for

the rifles on board," Viktor said. "Just in case we needed them."

She admired his preparedness. "You've done well. I might have to reward you."

"First we need to finish this."

She clasped his shoulder. "That we do."

NINETY

BULLETS RICOCHETED OFF THE THICK MARBLE RAILING. A wall mirror shattered, then crashed to the floor. Stephanie sought cover past where the balustrade began, the others huddled behind her.

More bullets obliterated plaster to her right.

Luckily the angle gave them an element of protection. To obtain a clearer shot, the soldiers would have to climb the stairway, which would also give her an opportunity.

Thorvaldsen came close. "Let me."

She stepped back and the Dane sent a salvo from the AK-74 down to the ground floor. The rounds produced the intended result. All shooting from below stopped.

A robot reappeared behind them from another of the bedchambers. She paid it no mind until the whine from its electric motor steadily increased in volume. She turned her head and spotted the mechanism approaching the spot where Ely and Lyndsey stood.

"Stop that thing," she mouthed to Ely.

He stuck out his foot and halted the machine's advance. It sensed an impediment, hesitated, then sprayed Ely's pants with mist. She saw him wince from the odor, strong even from her vantage, six feet away.

The thing turned and headed in the opposite direction.

More shots rang out from below as the second floor was peppered with bullets. They needed to retreat and use the concealed passages, but before she could give the order, ahead, on the other side of the railing, one of the soldiers rounded a corner.

Thorvaldsen saw him, too, and before she could raise her gun, he chopped the man down with a burst from the AK-74.

MALONE APPROACHED THE HOUSE WITH CAUTION. He gripped the pistol in one hand, the assault rifle slung over the other shoulder. They entered through a rear terrace into an opulent salon.

A familiar smell greeted him.

Greek fire.

He saw Cassiopeia register the scent, too.

More gunfire.

From somewhere on the ground floor.

He headed toward the ruckus.

VIKTOR FOLLOWED ZOVASTINA AS THEY DREW CLOSER to the house. They'd stayed concealed and watched as Malone and Vitt entered. Lots of rounds being discharged from inside.

"There are nine militia inside," Zovastina said. "I told them not to use their weapons. Six robots are trolling, set to go when I push this."

She produced one of the remote controllers he'd many times used to detonate the turtles. He thought another warning in order. "A bullet into any one of those machines that disables it will trigger an explosion, regardless of that controller."

He saw that she did not require a reminder, but also she did not react with her usual arrogance. "Then we'll just have to be careful."

"It's not us I'm worried about."

CASSIOPEIA WAS ANXIOUS. ELY WAS SOMEWHERE IN THIS house, probably trapped, with Greek fire everywhere. She'd seen its destructive force.

The layout was a problem. The ground floor wound around itself like a labyrinth. She heard voices. Straight ahead, beyond another parlor dotted with gilt-framed art.

Malone led the way.

She admired his courage. For someone who complained all the time about not wanting to play the game, he was a damn good player.

Into another room oozing baroque charm, Malone crouched behind a high-backed chair and motioned for her to head left. Beyond a wide archway, ten meters away, she saw shadows dance across the walls.

More voices, in a language she did not know.

"I need a diversion," Malone whispered.

She understood. He had bullets. She didn't.

"Just don't shoot me," she mouthed back as she assumed a position adjacent to the doorway.

Malone shifted quickly behind another chair that offered a clear view. She drew a breath, counted to three, and told her pounding heart to stay calm. This was foolish, but she should have a second or two of advantage. She leveled the rifle, swung around and planted her feet in the archway. Finger on the trigger, she let loose a volley of blank rounds. Two soldiers stood on the other side of the foyer, their guns pointed toward the second-floor railing, but her shots produced the desired effect.

Startled faces stared back at her.

She stopped firing and dropped to the ground.

Then came two new bangs, as Malone shot both men.

STEPHANIE HEARD THE PISTOL ROUNDS. SOMETHING new. Henrik was crouched beside her, his finger ready on the rifle trigger.

Two more of the soldiers appeared on the second floor, beyond where their comrade lay dead.

Thorvaldsen instantly shot them both.

She was beginning to form a new opinion of this Dane. She'd known him to be conniving, with a disappearing conscience, but he was also cold-nerved, clearly prepared to do whatever needed to be done.

The soldiers' bodies flew back as high-powered rounds ripped through flesh.

She saw the robot and heard the pings at the same time.

One of the machines had turned the corner, behind the two dying soldiers.

Bullets had pierced its casing. The motor stuttered and jerked, like a wounded animal. Its funnel retracted.

Then the whole thing erupted in flames.

NINETY-ONE

MALONE HEARD SHOTS FROM ABOVE, THEN A SWOOSH, followed by an intense rush of unnatural heat.

He realized what had happened and fled from behind the chair, darting to the archway as Cassiopeia sprang to her feet.

He glanced around.

Flames poured from the second floor, engulfing the marble railing and consuming the walls. Glass in the tall outer windows shattered from the fiery assault.

The floor ignited.

STEPHANIE SHIELDED HERSELF FROM THE WAVES OF heat that rushed past. The robot did not actually explode, more vaporized in an atomiclike flash. She lowered her arm to see fire stretching in all directions, like a tsunami—walls, ceiling, even the floor succumbing.

Fifty feet away and closing.

"Come on," she said.

They fled the approaching maelstrom, running fast, but the flames were gaining ground. She realized the danger. Ely had been sprayed.

She glanced over her shoulder.

Ten feet away and closing.

The door to the bedchamber where they'd first exited the hidden passage was open just ahead. Lyndsey found it first. Ely next.

She and Thorvaldsen made it inside just as danger arrived.

"HE'S UP THERE," CASSIOPEIA SAID TO THE SCENE OF the second floor burning, then she yelled, "Ely."

Malone wrapped his arm around her neck and clamped her mouth shut.

"We're not alone," he whispered in her ear. "Think. More soldiers. And Zovastina and Viktor. They're here. You can count on it."

He released his hand.

"I'm going after him," she made clear. "Those guards had to be shooting at them. Who else?"

"We have no way of knowing anything."

"So where are they?" she asked the fire.

He motioned and they retreated into the parlor. He heard furniture crashing and more glass shattering from above. Luckily, none of the flames had descended the stairway, as in the Greco-Roman museum. But one of the priming mechanisms, as if sensing the heat, appeared across the foyer, which raised a concern.

If one exploded, more could, too.

ZOVASTINA HEARD SOMEONE CALL OUT ELY'S NAME, but she'd also felt the heat from the robot's disintegration and smelled burning Greek fire.

"Fools," she whispered to her troops, somewhere in the house.

"That was Vitt who shouted," Viktor said.

"Find our men. I'll find her and Malone."

STEPHANIE SPOTTED THE CONCEALED DOOR, STILL OPEN, and led the way inside, quickly closing it behind them.

"Thank God," Lyndsey said.

No smoke had yet accumulated in the hidden passage, but she heard fire trying to find its way through the walls.

They retreated to the stairway and scampered down to ground level.

She kept an eye out for the first available exit and saw an open door just ahead. Thorvaldsen saw it, too, and they exited into the mansion's dining hall.

MALONE COULD NOT ANSWER CASSIOPEIA'S QUESTION about the whereabouts of Stephanie, Henrik, and Ely, and he, too, was concerned.

"It's time you back off," Cassiopeia said to him.

That surliness from Copenhagen had returned. He thought a dose of reality might help. "We only have three bullets."

"No, we don't."

She brushed past him, retrieved the assault rifles from the two dead guards, and checked the clips. "Plenty of rounds." She handed him one. "Thanks, Cotton, for getting me here. But I have to do this." She paused. "On my own."

He saw that arguing with her was fruitless.

"There's certainly another way up there," she said. "I'll find it."

He was about to resign himself to follow her when movement to his left set off an alarm and he whirled, gun ready.

Viktor appeared in the doorway.

Malone fired a burst from the AK-74 and instantly sought cover in the foyer. He could not see if he hit the man but, looking around, one thing he knew for certain.

Cassiopeia was gone.

STEPHANIE HEARD SHOTS FROM SOMEWHERE ON THE ground floor. The dining hall spread out before her in an elaborate rectangle with towering walls, a vaulted ceiling, and leaded glass windows. A long table with a dozen chairs down each side dominated.

"We need to leave," Thorvaldsen said.

Lyndsey bolted away, but Ely cut him off and slammed the scientist to the tabletop, jostling some of the chairs. "I told you we were going to the lab."

"You can go to hell."

Forty feet away, Cassiopeia appeared in the doorway. She was wet, looked tired, and carried a rifle. Stephanie watched as her friend spotted Ely. She'd taken a huge chance going with Zovastina from Venice, but the gamble had now paid off.

Ely spotted her, too, and released his grip on Lyndsey.

Behind Cassiopeia, Irina Zovastina materialized and nestled the barrel of a rifle against Cassiopeia's spine.

Ely froze.

The Supreme Minister's clothes and hair were also wet. Stephanie debated challenging her, but the odds shifted when Viktor and three soldiers appeared and leveled their weapons.

"Lower the guns," Zovastina said. "Slowly."

Stephanie locked her gaze on Cassiopeia and shook her head, signaling this was a battle they could not win. Thorvaldsen took the lead and laid his weapon on the table. She decided to do the same.

"Lyndsey," Zovastina said. "Time for you to come with me."

"No way." He started to back away, toward Stephanie. "I'm not going anywhere with you."

"We don't have time for this," Zovastina said, and she motioned to one of the soldiers, who rushed toward Lyndsey, who was retreating back to where the concealed panel remained open.

Ely moved like he was going to grab the scientist, but when the soldier arrived, he shoved Lyndsey into him and slipped into the back passage, closing the door behind him.

Stephanie heard guns raised.

"No," Zovastina yelled. "Let him go. I don't need him and this place is about to burn to the ground."

MALONE NAVIGATED THE MAZE OF ROOMS. ONE AFTER the other. Corridor to room to another corridor. He'd seen no one, but continued to smell fire burning on the upper stories. Most of the smoke seemed to have risen to the third floor, but it wouldn't be long before the air here became tainted.

He needed to find Cassiopeia.

Where had she gone?

He passed a door that opened to what looked like an oversized storage closet. He glanced inside and noticed something unusual. Part of the unfinished paneled wall stood open, revealing a concealed passage. Beyond, bulbs tossed down stagnant pools of weak light.

He heard footsteps from inside the opening.

Approaching.

He gripped the rifle and flattened himself against the stinking wall, just outside the closet.

Fast steps kept coming.

He readied himself.

Someone emerged from the doorway.

With one hand he slammed the body into the wall,

jamming the gun, his finger on the trigger, into the man's jaw. Fierce blue eyes stared back at him, the face younger, handsome, without fear.

"Who are you?" he asked.

"Ely Lund."

NINETY-TWO

ZOVASTINA WAS PLEASED. SHE CONTROLLED LYNDSEY, all of Vincenti's data, Alexander's tomb, the draught, and now Thorvaldsen, Cassiopeia Vitt, and Stephanie Nelle. She lacked only Cotton Malone and Ely Lund, neither one of which were of any real importance to her.

They were outside, heading for the chopper, two of her remaining soldiers parading the prisoners at gunpoint. Viktor had taken the other two militia and retrieved Vincenti's computers and two of the robots they'd not used inside the house.

She needed to return to Samarkand and personally supervise the covert military offensive that would soon begin. Her tasks here had ended with total success. She'd long hoped that if Alexander's tomb were ever found it would lie within her jurisdiction, and thanks be to the gods that it did.

Viktor approached, carrying the computer mainframes.

"Load them onto the chopper," she said.

She watched as he deposited them into the rear compartment along with the two robots, both marvels of Asian engineering, developed by her engineers. The programmable bombs worked with near perfection, delivering Greek fire with an expert precision, then detonating on command. Expensive, too, so she was careful with her inventory and glad these two could be salvaged for reuse elsewhere.

She handed Viktor the controller for the machines still inside. "Take care of the house as soon as I'm away." The upper floors were all ablaze, only a matter of a few minutes before the whole house became an inferno. "And kill them all."

He nodded his consent.

"But before I go, I have a debt to repay."

She gave Viktor her gun, stepped toward Cassiopeia Vitt, and said, "You made me an offer up at the pools. About giving me a chance to be even with you."

"I'd love it."

She smiled. "I thought you might."

"WHERE ARE THE OTHERS?" MALONE ASKED ELY, AS HE lowered the rifle.

"Zovastina has them."

"What are you doing?"

"I slipped away." Ely hesitated. "There's something I have to do."

He waited for an explanation, which had better be good.

"The cure for AIDS is in this house. I have to get it."

Not bad. He understood the urgency of that quest. For both Ely and Cassiopeia. To his left, one of the spewing dragons passed by at the intersection of two corridors. He was pushing it, hanging around inside the house. But he needed to know, "Where did the others go?"

"I don't know. They were in the dining hall. Zovastina and her men had them. I managed to get inside the wall before they could follow."

"Where's the cure?"

"In a lab below the house. There's an entrance in the library, where we were first held."

The excitement in his voice could not be disguised.

Foolishness, surely. But what the hell? That seemed to be the story of his life.

"Lead the way."

CASSIOPEIA CIRCLED ZOVASTINA. STEPHANIE, HENRIK, and Lyndsey stood, at gunpoint, to one side. The Supreme Minister apparently wanted a show, a display of prowess before her men. Fine. She'd give her a fight.

Zovastina struck first, wrapping her arms around Cassiopeia's neck and hinging her spine forward. The woman was strong. More than she'd anticipated. Zovastina deftly dropped and tossed Cassiopeia over her, through the air.

She hit hard.

Brushing off the pain, she sprang to her feet and planted her right foot into Zovastina's chest, which staggered the other woman. She used the moment to shake the pain from her limbs, then lunged.

Her shoulder connected with rock-hard thighs and together the two women found the ground.

MALONE ENTERED THE LIBRARY. THEY'D SEEN NO SOLDIERS on their careful trek across the ground floor. Smoke and heat were rising. Ely darted straight for a corpse that lay on the floor.

"Zovastina shot him. Vincenti's man," Ely said, as he found a silver controller. "She used this to open the panel."

Ely pointed and pushed one of the buttons.

A Chinese wall cabinet rotated one hundred eighty degrees.

"Place is like an amusement park," Malone said, and he followed Ely into the darkened passage.

———✳———

ZOVASTINA'S ANGER BOILED. SHE WAS ACCUSTOMED TO winning. In *buzkashi*. In politics. In life. She'd challenged Vitt because she wanted this woman to know who was better. She also wanted her men to see that their leader was not afraid of anyone. True, there were only a few present, but tales of a few had long been the foundations of legends.

This entire site was now hers. Vincenti's house would be razed and a proper memorial erected in honor of the conqueror who chose this spot as his final resting place. He may have been Greek by birth, but he was Asian at heart, and that was what mattered.

She pivoted her legs and again threw Vitt off her, but maintained a savage grip on one arm, which she used to yank the woman upward.

Her knee met Vitt's chin. A blow she knew would send shock waves through the brain. She'd felt that agony herself. She slammed a fist hard into Vitt's face. How many times had she attacked another *chopenoz* on the playing field? How long had she held a weighty *boz*? Her strong arms and hands were accustomed to pain.

Vitt teetered on her knees, dazed.

How dare this nothing think her an equal? Vitt was through. That much seemed clear. No fight left in her. So Zovastina gently nestled the butt of her heel against Vitt's forehead and, with one thrust, rudely shoved her opponent to the ground.

Vitt did not move.

Zovastina, as much out of breath as anger, steadied herself, and swiped the dirt from her face. She turned, satisfied with the fight. No wit, humor, or sympathy seeped from her eyes. Viktor nodded his approval. Looks of admiration filled her soldiers' faces.

It was good to be a fighter.

MALONE ENTERED THE SUBTERRANEAN LABORATORY. They were at least thirty feet underground, surrounded by bedrock with a burning house above them. The air reeked of Greek fire and he'd felt a familiar stickiness on the steps leading down.

Apparently, biological research was being conducted here, as several gloved containers and a refrigerator labeled with a bright biohazard warning filled the lab. He and Ely hesitated in the doorway, both of them reluctant to venture farther. His reluctance was fueled by packs of clear liquid that lay scattered on the tables. He'd seen those before. In the Greco-Roman museum that first night.

Two bodies lay on the floor. One an emaciated woman in a bathrobe, the other an enormous man in dark clothes. Both had been shot.

"According to Lyndsey," Ely said, "Vincenti was holding the flash drive when Zovastina killed him."

They needed to finish this. So he stepped carefully around the tables and stared down at the dead man. Three hundred pounds, at least. The body lay on one side, an arm outstretched, as if he'd tried to rise. Four bullet holes in the chest. One hand lay open, near a table leg, the other fist closed. He used the rifle barrel to pry open the fingers.

"That's it," Ely said with anticipation, as he knelt and removed the flash drive.

The younger man reminded Malone of Cai Thorvaldsen, though he'd only seen that face once, in Mexico City, when his life first intersected with Henrik Thorvaldsen's. The two younger men would be about the same age. Easy to see why Thorvaldsen had been drawn to Ely.

"This place is primed to burn," he said.

Ely stood. "I made a bad mistake trusting Zovastina. But she was so enthusiastic. She seemed to really appreciate the past."

"She does. For what she can learn from it."

Ely motioned to his clothes. "I have that stuff all over me."

"Been there. Done that."

"Zovastina's a lunatic. A murderer."

He agreed. "Since we have what we came for, how about you and I not become one of her victims?" He paused. "Besides, Cassiopeia will have my ass if anything happens to you."

NINETY-THREE

ZOVASTINA BOARDED THE CHOPPER. LYNDSEY WAS already strapped into the compartment, handcuffed to the bulkhead.

"Minister, I won't be a problem. I swear. I'll do whatever you need. I assure you. It's not necessary to confine me. Please, Minister—"

"If you don't shut up," she calmly said, "I'll have you shot right now."

The scientist seemed to sense that silence would be better and hushed.

"Don't open your mouth again."

She inspected the spacious compartment, which usually accommodated a dozen armed men. Vincenti's computers and the two spare robots were lashed tight. Cassiopeia Vitt lay still on the ground and the prisoners were being guarded by the four soldiers.

Viktor stood outside the compartment.

"You've done well," she said to him. "Once I'm gone, detonate the house and kill all of these people. I'm trusting you to keep this location secure. I'll dispatch additional men when I return to Samarkand. This is now a Federation site."

She stared toward the mansion, its top floors fully ablaze. Soon, it would be nothing but rubble. She already envisioned the Asian palace she'd construct here. Whether Alexander's tomb would be revealed to the world remained to be seen. She needed to consider all the possibilities, and since she alone controlled its location, that decision would be hers.

She faced Viktor, stared hard into his eyes, and said, "Thank you, my friend." She saw the momentary shock on his face as her words of appreciation registered. "No, I don't ever say it. I expect you to do your job. But, here, you did exceptionally well."

She took one last look at Cassiopeia Vitt, Stephanie Nelle, and Henrik Thorvaldsen. Problems that would soon be a thing of the past. Cotton Malone and Ely Lund were still in the house. If not already dead, they would be in a few minutes.

"I'll see you at the palace," she said to Viktor, as the compartment door slid shut.

VIKTOR LISTENED AS THE TURBINE FIRED AND THE chopper blades twirled. The engine revved to full power. Dust swirled from the dry earth and the helicopter rose into the late-afternoon sky.

He quickly moved toward his men and ordered two of them to head for the estate's main gate and control ingress. He told the final two to keep watch over Nelle and Thorvaldsen.

He stepped over to Cassiopeia. Vitt's face was bruised, her nose bloodied. Sweat streamed down leaving furrows of grime.

Her eyes flashed opened and she clamped hard onto his arm.

"Come to finish?" she asked.

His left hand held a pistol, his right hand the controller for the turtles. He calmly laid the signaling device on the ground beside her. "That's exactly what I came to do."

The helicopter with Zovastina leveled off overhead

and headed east, back toward the house and the valley beyond.

"While you fought her," he told Vitt, "I activated the turtles inside the chopper. They're now programmed to detonate when the ones inside the house are told to explode." He motioned. "That controller will make that happen."

She scooped it from the ground.

But he quickly brought his gun to her head. "Careful."

CASSIOPEIA GLARED AT VIKTOR, HER FINGER ON THE controller button. Could she push it before he shot her? Perhaps he was wondering the same thing?

"You need to choose," he said. "Your Ely and Malone may still be in the house. Killing Zovastina could also kill them."

She had to trust that Malone had the situation in hand. But she also realized something else. "How could anyone possibly know when to trust you? You've played every side."

"My job was to end this. That's what *we're* about to do."

"Killing Zovastina might not be the answer."

"It's the only answer. She won't stop otherwise."

She considered his statement. He was right.

"I was going to do it myself," he said. "But I thought you'd like the honor."

"The gun in my face for show?" she quietly asked.

"The guards can't see your hand."

"How do I know, when I do this, you won't shoot me in the face."

He answered her honestly. "You don't."

The chopper was beyond the house, out over the grassy meadow, maybe a thousand feet high.

"If you wait any longer," he said, "the signal will not reach."

She shrugged. "Never thought I'd make old age anyway."

And she pressed the button.

STEPHANIE WATCHED FROM THIRTY FEET AWAY AS VIK-tor aimed his gun at Cassiopeia. She'd seen him lay something on the ground, but Cassiopeia faced away and it was impossible to know what was happening.

The helicopter became a flying fireball.

No explosion. Just brilliant light erupting from all sides, like a supernova, its volatile fuel quickly joining the mélange in a destruction that thundered across the valley. Flaming chunks of debris propelled outward, then rained down in a fiery cascade. At the same instant, windows on the mansion's ground floor shattered outward, the frames filled with a raging blaze.

Cassiopeia rose, with Viktor's aid.

"Seems he is a help," Thorvaldsen said, noticing, too.

Viktor pointed at the two guards and barked out orders in what she thought was Russian.

The men dashed away.

Cassiopeia fled toward the house.

They followed.

MALONE TOPPED THE STAIRS BEHIND ELY AND REEN-tered the library. Thumps echoed from somewhere inside the house and he immediately noticed a change in temperature.

"Those things have been activated."

Outside the library door fire sprang to life. More thumps. Closer. Plenty of heat. Building. He bolted to the door and glanced both ways. The corridor at each end was impassable, flames were consuming the floor and headed his way. He recalled what Ely had said. *I have that stuff all over me.* He turned and studied the towering windows. Maybe ten feet by eight feet. Beyond, in the valley, he noticed something burning in the distance. There would only be a few more seconds before the fire arrived.

"Give me a hand."

He saw Ely stuff the flash drive into his pocket and grab one end of a small settee. Malone grasped the other. Together they tossed it through the windows. Glass shattered as the sofa propelled outward, clearing a path, but too many shards remained for them to leap through.

"Use the chairs," he yelled.

Fire wrapped itself inside the doorway and started its assault of the library walls. Books and shelves erupted. Malone gripped a chair and rammed it through what remained of the window. Ely used another chair to scrape away jagged remnants.

The floor started to burn.

Everything basted with Greek fire quickly identified itself.

No more time.

They both leaped through the window.

CASSIOPEIA HEARD GLASS BREAK AS SHE, VIKTOR, THORvaldsen, and Stephanie ran closer to the destruction. She saw a settee fly out and crash to the ground. She'd taken a chance killing Zovastina, with Malone and Ely still inside, but, like Malone would say, *Whether right or wrong, just do something.*

Another chair flew out the window.

Then Malone and Ely leaped out as the room behind them filled with waves of bright orange.

Malone's exit was not as graceful as it had been in Copenhagen. His right shoulder slammed to the grass and he tumbled. Ely, too, hit hard, rolled a few times, his arms shielding his head.

Cassiopeia ran to them. Ely stared up at her. She smiled and said, "You having fun?"

"About as much as you. What happened to your face?"

"Got the crap beat out of me. But I had the last laugh."

She helped him to his feet and they hugged.

"You stink," she noted.

"Greek fire. The latest fragrance."

"What about me?" Malone grunted, as he stood and brushed himself off. "No 'how are you?' Good to see that you're not a crispy critter?"

She shook her head and hugged him, too.

"How many buses ran you over?" Malone asked, noticing her face.

"Just one."

"You two know each other?" Ely asked.

"We're acquainted."

She saw Malone's face sour as he spotted Viktor. "What's he doing here?"

"Believe it or not," she said, "he's on our side. I think."

Stephanie pointed to fires in the distance and men running toward them. "Zovastina's dead."

"Terrible thing," Viktor said. "Tragic helicopter crash. Witnessed by four of her militia. She'll be given a glorious funeral."

"And Daniels will have to make sure that the next Supreme Minister of the Central Asian Federation is more friendly," Stephanie said.

Cassiopeia spotted dots in the western sky growing larger. "We've got company."

They watched as the aircraft drew closer.

"They're ours," Malone said. "Apache AH64s and a Blackhawk."

The American gunships swooped in. One of the Apache's compartment doors swung open and Malone spotted a familiar face.

Edwin Davis.

"Troops from Afghanistan," Viktor said. "Davis told me they'd be nearby, monitoring things, ready when needed."

"You know," Stephanie said to them. "Killing Zovastina that way may not have been smart."

Cassiopeia sensed the resignation in her friend's tone. "What is it?"

Thorvaldsen stepped forward. "Vincenti's computers and Lyndsey were on that chopper. You don't know this, but Vincenti found the cure for AIDS. He and Lyndsey developed it, and all of the data was on those computers. There was a flash drive, which Vincenti had when he died. But, unfortunately"—the Dane motioned to the burning house—"that's surely gone."

Cassiopeia saw a wicked look form on Malone's dirty face. She also noticed Ely smiling. Both men looked exhausted, but their feeling of triumph seemed infectious.

Ely reached into his pocket and held out his open palm.

A flash drive.

"What's that?" she asked, hoping.

"Life," Malone said.

NINETY-FOUR

MALONE ADMIRED ALEXANDER THE GREAT'S TOMB. After Edwin Davis arrived, an army special forces unit had quickly taken control of the estate, disarming the four remaining troops without a fight. President Daniels authorized the incursion, Davis saying he doubted there'd be any official resistance from the Federation.

Zovastina was dead. A new day was coming.

Once the estate was secure, as darkness began to claim the mountains, they'd all climbed to the pools and dove into the tawny eye. Even Thorvaldsen, who wanted desperately to see the grave. Malone had helped him through the tunnel and the Dane, for his age and deformity, was a surprisingly strong swimmer.

They brought flashlights and additional lights from the Apaches, the tomb now ablaze with electric illumination. He stared in wonder at a wall of glazed bricks, their blues, yellows, oranges, and blacks still vibrant after two millennia.

Ely was examining three lion motifs formed with great skill from the colorful tiles. "Something similar to this lined the ancient Babylon's processional way. We have remnants. But here's one totally intact."

Edwin Davis had swum through with them. He, too, had wanted to see what Zovastina had coveted. Malone felt better knowing that the other side of the pool was being guarded by a team operations sergeant and three U.S. Army soldiers armed with M-4 carbines. He and

Stephanie had briefed Davis on what happened and he was beginning to warm to the deputy national security adviser, especially after he'd anticipated their need for backup and had been ready to move.

Ely stood beside the two sarcophagi. On the side of one was chiseled a single word. ΑΛΕΞΑΝΔΡΟΣ. More letters adorned its other side.

ΑΙΕΝ ΑΡΙΣΤΕΥΕΙΝ ΚΑΙ
ΥΠΕΙΡΟΧΟΝ ΕΜΜΕΝΑΙ ΑΛΛΩΝ

"This one is Alexander's," Ely said. "The longer inscription is from the *Iliad. Always to be the best and to be superior to the rest.* Homer's expression of the heroic ideal. Alexander would have lived by that. Zovastina loved that quote, too. She used it many times. The people who put him here chose his epitaph well."

Ely motioned to the other coffin, its inscription simpler.

ΗΦΑΙΣΤΙΩΝ
ΦΙΛΟΣ ΑΛΕΞΑΝΔΡΟΥ

" 'Hephaestion. Friend of Alexander.' Lover did not do justice to their relationship. To be called 'friend' was the supreme compliment of a Greek, reserved for only the most dear."

Malone noticed how dust and debris had been cleared from the image of a horse on Alexander's coffin.

"Zovastina did that when she and I were here," Viktor said. "She was mesmerized by the image."

"It's Bucephalas," Ely said. "Has to be. Alexander's horse. He worshipped the animal. The horse died during the Asian campaign and was buried somewhere in the mountains, not far from here."

"Zovastina named her favorite horse that, too," Viktor noted.

Malone scanned the room. Ely pointed out ritual buckets, a silver perfume container, a drinking horn shaped as a deer's head, even gilded bronze greaves with bits of leather still remaining that once protected a warrior's calves. "It's breathtaking," Stephanie said.

He agreed.

Cassiopeia stood near one of the coffins, its lid slid open.

"Zovastina snuck a look," Viktor said.

Their lights shone inside at a mummy.

"Unusual that it's not in a cartonnage," Ely said. "But they may not have had the skill or time to make one."

Gold sheets covered the body from neck to feet, each the size of a sheet of paper, more lay scattered inside the coffin. The right arm was bent at the elbow and lay across the abdomen. The left arm stretched straight, the forearm detached from the upper. Bandages wrapped most of the corpse in a tight embrace and on the partially exposed chest lay three gold disks.

"The Macedonian star," Ely said. "Alexander's coat of arms. Impressive ones, too. Beautiful specimens."

"How did they get all of this in here?" Stephanie asked. "These coffins are huge."

Ely motioned at the room. "Twenty-three hundred years ago, the topography was surely different. I'd wager there was another way in. Maybe the pools were not as high, the tunnel more accessible and not underwater. Who knows?"

"But the letters in the pool," Malone said. "How did *they* get there? Surely the people who fashioned this tomb didn't do it. That's like a neon sign to alert people."

"My guess is Ptolemy did that. Part of his riddle. Two Greek letters at the bottom of two dark pools. His way, I assume, of marking the spot."

A golden mask covered Alexander's face. No one had yet touched it. Finally, Malone said, "Why don't you, Ely? Let's see what a king of the world looks like."

He saw the look of anticipation in the younger man's eyes. He'd studied Alexander the Great from afar, learned what he could from the scant information that had survived. Now he could be the first in two thousand years to actually touch him.

Ely slowly removed the mask.

What skin remained cast a blackish tint and was bone dry and brittle. Death seemed to have agreed with Alexander's countenance, the half-closed eyes conveying a strange expression of curiosity. The mouth ran from one side of the cheek to the other, open, as if to shout. Time had frozen everything. The head was devoid of hair, the brain, which more than anything else accounted for Alexander's success, gone.

They all stared in silence.

Finally, Cassiopeia shined her light across the room, past an equestrian figure on horseback clad only in a long cloak slung over one shoulder, at a striking bronze bust. The powerful oblong face showed confidence and featured steady narrowed eyes, gazing off into the distance. The hair sprang back from the forehead in a classic style and dropped midlength in irregular curls. The neck rose straight and high, the bearing and look of a man who utterly controlled his world.

Alexander the Great.

Such a contrast to the face of death in the coffin.

"All of the busts I've ever seen of Alexander," Ely said, "his nose, lips, brow, and hair were usually restored with plaster. Few survived the ages. But there's an image, from his time, in perfect condition."

"And here he is," Malone said, "in the flesh."

Cassiopeia moved to the adjacent coffin and wrestled open its lid enough for them to peek inside. Another mummy, not fully adorned in gold, but masked, lay in similar condition.

"Alexander and Hephaestion," Thorvaldsen said. "Here they've rested for so long."

"Will they stay?" Malone asked.

Ely shrugged. "This is an important archaeological find. It would be a tragedy not to learn from it."

Malone noticed that Viktor's attention had shifted to a gold chest that lay close to the wall. The rock above was incised with a tangle of engravings showing battles, chariots, horses, and men with swords. Atop the chest a golden Macedonian star had been molded. Rosettes with petals of blue glass dotted its center. Similar rosettes wrapped a central band around the chest. Viktor grasped both sides and, before Ely could stop him, lifted the lid.

Edwin Davis shined a light inside.

A gold wreath of oak leaves and acorns, rich in stunning detail, came into view.

"A royal crown," Ely said.

Viktor smirked. "That's what Zovastina wanted. This would have been her crown. She would have used all of this to fuel herself."

Malone shrugged. "Too bad her helicopter crashed."

They all stood in the chamber, soaking wet from the swim but relieved that the ordeal was over. The rest involved politics, and that didn't concern Malone.

"Viktor," Stephanie said. "If you ever get tired of free-lancing and want a job, let me know."

"I'll keep the offer in mind."

"You let me best you when we were here before," Malone said. "Didn't you?"

Viktor nodded. "I thought it better you leave, so I gave you the chance. I'm not that easy, Malone."

He grinned. "I'll keep *that* in mind." He pointed at the tombs. "What about these?"

"They've been waiting here a long time," Ely said. "They can rest a little longer. Right now, there's something else we have to do."

CASSIOPEIA WAS THE LAST TO CLIMB FROM THE TAWNY pool, back into the first chamber.

"Lyndsey said the bacteria in the green pool could be swallowed," Ely said. "They're harmless to us, but destroy HIV."

"We don't know if any of that is true," Stephanie said.

Ely seemed convinced. "It is. That man's ass was on the line. He was using what he had to save his skin."

"We have the disk," Thorvaldsen said. "I can have the best scientists in the world get us an answer immediately."

Ely shook his head. "Alexander the Great had no scientists. He trusted his world."

Cassiopeia admired his courage. She'd been infected for over a decade, always wondering when the disease would finally manifest itself. To have a time bomb ticking away inside, waiting for the day when your immune system finally failed, that changed your life. She knew Ely suffered from the same anxiety, clutched at every hope. And they were the lucky ones. They could afford the drugs that kept the virus at bay. Millions of others could not.

She stared into the tawny pool, at the Greek letter Z

that lay at its bottom. She recalled what she'd read in one of the manuscripts. *Eumenes revealed the resting place, far away, in the mountains, where the Scythians taught Alexander about life.* She walked to the green pool and again admired the H at its bottom.

Life.

What a lovely promise.

Ely grasped her hand. "Ready?"

She nodded.

They dropped to their knees and drank.

NINETY-FIVE

MALONE SAT ON THE SECOND FLOOR OF THE CAFÉ NORden and enjoyed more of the tomato bisque soup. Still the best he'd ever eaten. Thorvaldsen sat across from him. The second-floor windows were flung open, allowing a lovely late-spring evening to wash over them. Copenhagen's weather this time of year was nearly perfect, another one of the many reasons why he so enjoyed living here.

"I heard from Ely today," Thorvaldsen said.

He'd wondered what was happening in central Asia. They'd returned home six weeks ago and he'd been busy selling books. That was the thing about being a field agent. You did your job, then moved on. No postanalysis or follow-up. That task was always left to others.

"He's excavating Alexander's tomb. The new Federation government is cooperating with the Greeks."

He knew that Ely had taken a position in Athens with the Museum of Antiquities, thanks to Thorvaldsen's intervention. Of course, knowing the location of Alexander the Great's grave certainly fueled the museum's enthusiasm.

Zovastina had been succeeded by a moderate deputy minister who, according to the Federation constitution, temporarily assumed power until elections could be held. Washington had quietly ensured that all of the Federation's biological stockpiles were destroyed and Samarkand had been given a choice. Cooperate or the Federation's neighbors would learn what Zovastina and her generals had planned, and then nature could take its course. Luckily, moderation prevailed and the United States sent a team to oversee the viral extermination. Of course, with the West holding the antiagent, there'd been no choice. The Federation could start killing, but they could not stop it. The uneasy alliance between Zovastina and Vincenti had been replaced with one between two distrusting nations.

"Ely has full control of the tomb and is quietly working it," Thorvaldsen said. "He says a lot of history may have to be rewritten. Lots of inscriptions inside. Artwork. Even a map or two. Incredible stuff."

"And how are Edwin Davis and Danny Daniels?" he asked. "Satisfied?"

Thorvaldsen smiled. "I spoke with Edwin a couple of days ago. Daniels is grateful for all we did. He especially liked Cassiopeia blowing up that helicopter. Not a lot of sympathy from that man. He's a tough one."

"Glad we could help the president out one more time." He paused. "What about the Venetian League?"

Thorvaldsen shrugged. "Faded into the woodwork. It didn't do anything that can be proven."

"Except kill Naomi Johns."

"Vincenti did that, and I believe he paid."

That was true. "You know, it'd be nice if Daniels could, for once, just ask for my help."

"Not going to happen."

"Like with you?"

His friend nodded. "Like with me."

He finished his soup and stared down at Højbro Plads. The square was lively with people enjoying a warm evening, which were few and far between in Copenhagen. His bookshop across the plaza was closed. Business had been great lately and he was planning a buying trip to London the following week, before Gary arrived for his yearly summer visit. He was looking forward to seeing his fifteen-year-old.

But he was also melancholy. He'd been that way ever since returning home. He and Thorvaldsen ate dinner together at least once a week, but never had they discussed what was really on his mind. Some places need not be trod.

Unless allowed.

So he asked, "How's Cassiopeia?"

"I was wondering when you'd inquire."

"You're the one who got me into all that."

"All I did was tell you she needed help."

"I'd like to think she'd help me, if needed."

"She would. But, to answer your question, both she and Ely are virus free. Edwin tells me scientists have also verified the bacteria's effectiveness. Daniels will announce the cure shortly and the United States government will control its distribution. The president has ordered that it be available to all at minimal cost."

"A lot of people will be affected by that."

"Thanks to you. You solved the riddle and found the grave."

He didn't want to hear that. "We all did our job. And, by the way, I heard you're a gun-toting fool. Stephanie said you were hell in that house."

"I'm not helpless."

Thorvaldsen had told him about Stephanie and the shooting. He'd spoken to her about it before they left Asia and had called her again last week.

"Stephanie's realizing it's tough out in the field," he said.

"I spoke to her myself a few days ago."

"You two becoming buddies?"

His friend smiled. "We're a lot alike, though neither one of us would admit that to the other."

"Killing is never easy. No matter what the reason."

"I killed three men myself in that house. You're right. It's never easy."

He still had not received an answer to his initial question, and Thorvaldsen seemed to sense what he truly wanted to know.

"I haven't spoke with Cassiopeia much since we left the Federation. She went home to France. I don't know about she and Ely—the two of them. She offers little." Thorvaldsen shook his head. "You'll have to ask her."

He decided to take a walk. He liked roaming the Strøget. He asked Thorvaldsen if he wanted to join him but his friend declined.

He stood.

Thorvaldsen tossed some folded papers across the table. "The deed to that property by the sound, where the house burned. I have no use for it."

He unfolded the sheets and saw his name on the grantee line.

"I want you to have it."

"That property is worth a lot of money. It's ocean-front. I can't take that."

"Rebuild the house. Enjoy it. Call it compensation for me bringing you into the middle of all this."

"You knew I'd help."

"This way, my conscience, what little of it there is, will be satisfied."

From their two years together he'd learned that when Henrik Thorvaldsen made up his mind, that was it. So he stuffed the deed into his pocket and descended the stairs.

He pushed through the main doors into the warm touch of a Danish evening. People and conversations greeted him from occupied tables that sprawled out from the café.

"Hey, Malone."

He turned.

Sitting at one of the tables was Cassiopeia.

She stood and walked his way.

She wore a navy canvas jacket and matching canvas pants. A leather shoulder bag draped one shoulder and T-strap sandals accented her feet. The dark hair hung in thick curls. He could still see her in the mountain. Tight leather pants and a sports bra, as she swam with him into the tomb. And those few minutes when they both were down to their underwear.

"What are you doing in town?" he asked.

She shrugged. "You're always telling me how good the food is at this café, so I came to eat dinner."

He smiled. "Long way for a meal."

"Not if you can't cook."

"I hear you're cured. I'm glad."

"Does take a few things off your mind. Wondering if today is the day you start to die."

He recalled her preoccupation that first night in Copenhagen, when she aided his escape from the Greco-Roman museum. All the melancholy seemed gone.

"Where you headed?" she asked.

He stared out across the square. "Just for a walk."

"Want some company?"

He glanced back at the café, up to the second story, and the window table where he and Thorvaldsen had been sitting. His friend gazed out the open frame, smiling. He should have known.

He faced her and said, "Are you two always up to something?"

"You haven't answered my question about the walk."

What the hell. "Sure. I'd love some company."

She slid her arm into his and led him forward.

He had to ask. "What about you and Ely? I thought—"

"Malone."

He knew what was coming, so he saved her the trouble.

"I know. Just shut up and walk."

WRITER'S NOTE

Time to separate fact from fiction.

The style of execution described in the prologue was utilized during the time of Alexander the Great. The physician who treated Hephaestion was ordered killed by Alexander, but not in the manner depicted. Hanging is what most chronicles mention.

The relationship between Alexander and Hephaestion was complex. Friend, confidant, lover—all would apply. Alexander's deep distress at Hephaestion's untimely death is documented, as is Hephaestion's elaborate funeral, which some say may be the most expensive in history. Of course, the embalming and secreting away of Hephaestion's body (Chapter 24) is fictional.

Greek fire (Chapter 5) is real. The formula was indeed held personally by Byzantine emperors and was lost when that empire fell. To this day, its chemical composition remains a mystery. As to any salt water vulnerability, that is my invention—actual Greek fire was used offensively against ships at sea.

The game of *buzkashi* (Chapter 7) is both ancient and violent and continues to be played across central Asia. The rules, dress, and equipment, as detailed, are correct, as is the fact that players die routinely.

The Central Asian Federation is fictional, but the political and economic details outlined in Chapter 27, of this region of the world, are accurate. Unfortunately, that land has always been a convenient battleground, and the region's governments remain riddled with corruption.

Frank Holt's book, *Alexander the Great and the Mystery of the Elephant Medallions,* taught me about these unusual objects. Herein, their existence was narrowed to eight—many more than that still exist. Their description (Chapters 8–9) is faithful, save for the microletters—ZH—which are my addition. Amazingly, utilizing crude lenses, ancient engravers actually possessed the ability to microengrave.

With regard to the use of ZH, the literal translation of that word in Old Greek is the verb "to live." The noun "life" is more accurately ΣΦΠ. Some liberty was taken with the translation for the sake of the story. As for the description of Greek language throughout the story, the term "Old Greek" was employed, though some would say the more accurate term would be "ancient Greek."

The Sacred Band that guards Irina Zovastina (Chapter 12) is adapted from ancient Greece's fiercest fighting unit. One hundred and fifty male couples, from the city of Thebes, slaughtered to a man by Philip II and his son, Alexander the Great, in 338 BCE. A funerary monument to their courage still stands in Greece at Chaeronea.

The draught that appears throughout the story is fictional, as is the account of its discovery in Chapter 14. Archaea bacteria (Chapter 62), though, do exist and some bacteria and viruses do, in fact, prey on one another. My use of archaea in that way is pure invention.

As to Venice, the locales are accurate. The inside of St. Mark's Basilica is stunning and the tomb of St. Mark (Chapter 42), along with its history, is accurately described. On Torcello, the museum, two churches, bell tower, and restaurant are there. The island's geography and history (Chapter 34) are likewise retold faithfully. The Venetian League is not real. However, during its long history, the Venetian republic did periodically form alliances with other city-states in what were then called leagues.

X-ray fluorescence (Chapter 11) is a recent scientific breakthrough that is being used to study ancient parchments. I'm indebted to the talented novelist Christopher Reich for sending me an article on the concept.

The History of Hieronymus of Cardia (Chapter 24) is purely fictional as is Ptolemy's riddle, though all of Ptolemy's actions in relation to Alexander's funeral cortege and his dominance of Egypt are historically correct. The appropriation of St. Mark's body from Alexandria by Venetian merchants in 828 CE (Chapters 29 and 45) happened as related, and the body did indeed disappear, in Venice, for long periods of time. The story of its reappearance in 1094 (Chapter 45) is proudly retold daily by Venetians.

Unfortunately, zoonoses (Chapter 31) exist and periodically wreak havoc with human health. The search for these natural toxins and their adaptation for offensive uses (Chapter 54) is nothing new. Mankind has toyed with biological war for centuries and my fictional Irina Zovastina is just another example.

The statistics detailed in Chapter 32 reflect accurately the growing problem of HIV. Africa and Southeast Asia are indeed its favorite haunts. The biology of the virus described in Chapter 51, and how HIV may have moved from monkeys to humans (Chapter 60), is correct. The idea of someone discovering the cure for HIV, then holding it while the market built (Chapter 64), is simply part of this story. But the politics of HIV, as well as the insufficient global response to this threatening pandemic, are all too real.

Vozrozhdeniya Island is where the Soviets produced many of their biological weapons and the dilemma caused by its abandonment (Chapter 33) actually happened. The disappearing Aral Sea (Chapter 33), precipitated by the insane Soviet divergence of its main water source, is generally regarded as one of the worst ecological disasters in history. Unfortunately, no happy resolution to this catastrophe has occurred in real life.

The heart amulet (Chapter 59) is actual, though my inclusion of a gold coil inside is fictional. Scytales (Chapter 61) were used in Alexander the Great's time for sending coded messages. One is on display at the International Spy Museum, in Washington, D.C., and I could not resist its inclusion. The Scythians (Chapter 75) existed and their history is correctly retold, except that there is no indication they buried their kings in anything other than mounds.

Now to Alexander the Great.

The story of his death (Chapter 8) is a composite of several accounts. Lots of contradictions in those. The three versions of what Alexander said in answer to the question *Who do you leave your kingdom to?* are mine. The generally accepted answer is *to the strongest,* but a different response fit better here. Historians have long pondered Alexander's death, its suddenness and inexplicable nature, suggesting foul play (Chapter 14), but no proof exists.

Alexander's embalming with honey, what happened to his funeral cortege, and his ultimate Egyptian tomb in Alexandria are all taken from historical accounts. The possibility that the remains of St. Mark in Venice may actually be those of Alexander the Great is not mine. Andrew Michael Chugg in his excellent *The Lost Tomb of Alexander the Great* postulated the theory. It is fact, though, that early Christians routinely appropriated pagan artifacts (Chapter 74), and the body of Alexander the Great did disappear from Alexandria at about the same time that the body of St. Mark reappeared (Chapter 45). Further, the political debate over the return of all or some of the remains located in St. Mark's Basilica to

Egypt continues and the Vatican did, in fact, hand over a few small relics to Alexandria in 1968.

Alexander's tomb being located in central Asia is purely fictional, but the items described therein (Chapter 94) were adapted from the tomb of Alexander's father, Philip II, which was supposedly located by archaeologists in 1977. Recently, though, doubt has been cast on the identity of that tomb's occupant.

Alexander's political and historical legacy continues to be a matter of intense debate. Was he a wise visionary or a reckless, bloody conqueror? Malone and Cassiopeia's discussion in Chapter 10 mirrors the two sides. Many books have been written on this subject, but the best is Peter Green's *Alexander of Macedon, A Historical Biography*. Green's thoughtful study makes clear that Alexander spent his entire life, with legendary success, in pursuit of nothing but personal glory. And though the empire he fought so hard to create collapsed the moment he was gone, his legend lives on. Proof of this immortality can be seen in the belief he has long inspired in others. Sometimes good, other times (as with Irina Zovastina) detrimental. To Peter Green, Alexander is an enigma, whose greatness simply defies any final judgment. He personifies an archetype, restless and perennial, the embodiment of an eternal quest, a personality that has grown greater than the measurable sum of his impressive works.

In the end, Alexander himself said it best.

Toil and risk are the price of glory, but it is a lovely thing to live with courage and die leaving an everlasting fame.

Read on for an excerpt of
Steve Berry's newest thriller

THE CHARLEMAGNE PURSUIT

Published by Ballantine Books

ONE

GARMISCH, GERMANY
TUESDAY, DECEMBER 11, THE PRESENT
1:40 PM

COTTON MALONE HATED ENCLOSED SPACES.

His current unease was amplified by a packed cable car. Most of the passengers were on vacation, dressed in colorful garb, shouldering poles and skis. He sensed a variety of nationalities. Some Italians, a few Swiss, a handful of French, but mainly Germans. He'd been one of the first to climb aboard and, to relieve his discomfort, he'd made his way close to one of the frosty windows. Ten thousand feet above and closing, the Zugspitze stood silhouetted against a steel-blue sky, the imposing gray summit draped in a late-autumn snow.

Not smart, agreeing to this location.

The car continued its giddy ascent, passing one of several steel trestles that rose from the rocky crags.

He was unnerved, and not simply from the crowded ascent. Ghosts awaited him atop Germany's highest peak. He'd avoided this rendezvous for nearly four decades. People like him, who buried their past so determinedly, should not help it from the grave so easily.

Yet here he was, doing exactly that.

Vibrations slowed as the car entered, then stopped at the summit station.

Skiers flooded off toward another lift that would take them down to a high-altitude corrie, where a chalet and slopes waited. He didn't ski, never had, never wanted to.

He made his way through the visitor center, identified by a yellow placard as Müncher Haus. A restaurant dominated one half of the building; the rest housed a theater, a snack bar, an observatory, souvenir shops, and a weather station.

He pushed through thick glass doors and stepped out onto a railed terrace. Bracing Alpine air stung his lips. According to Stephanie Nelle his contact should be waiting on the observation deck. One thing was obvious. Ten thousand feet in the high Alps certainly added a heightened measure of privacy to their meeting.

The Zugspitze lay on the border. A succession of snowy crags rose south toward Austria. To the north spanned a soup-bowl valley ringed by rock-ribbed peaks. A gauze of frosty mist shielded the German village of Garmisch and its companion, Partenkirchen. Both were sports meccas, and the region catered not only to skiing but also bobsledding, skating, and curling.

More sports he'd avoided.

The observation deck was deserted save for an elderly couple and a few skiers who'd apparently paused to enjoy the view. He'd come to solve a mystery, one that had preyed on his mind ever since that day when the men in uniforms came to tell his mother that her husband was dead.

"Contact was lost with the submarine forty-eight hours ago. We dispatched search and rescue ships to the

*North Atlantic, which have combed the last known po-
sition. Wreckage was found six hours ago. We waited to
tell the families until we were sure there was no chance
of survivors."*

His mother had never cried. Not her way. But that
didn't mean she wasn't devastated. Years passed before
questions formed in his teenage mind. The government
offered little explanation beyond official releases. When
he'd first joined the navy he'd tried to access the court of
inquiry's investigative report on the sub's sinking, but
learned it was classified. He'd tried again after becoming
a Justice Department agent, possessed of a high security
clearance. No luck. When Gary, his fifteen-year-old, visited over the summer, he'd faced new questions. Gary
had never known his grandfather, but the boy had
wanted to know more about him and, especially, how he
died. The press had covered the sinking of the USS
Blazek in November 1971, so they'd read many of the
old accounts on the Internet. Their talk had rekindled
his own doubts—enough that he'd finally done something about them.

He plunged balled fists into his parka and wandered
the terrace.

Telescopes dotted the railing. At one stood a woman,
her dark hair tied in an unflattering bun. She was
dressed in a bright outfit, skis and poles propped beside
her, studying the valley below.

He casually walked over. One rule he'd learned long
ago. Never hurry. It only bred trouble.

"Quite a scene," he said.

She turned. "Certainly is."

Her face was the color of cinnamon which, combined
with what he regarded as Egyptian features in her
mouth, nose, and eyes signaled some Middle Eastern an-
cestry.

"I'm Cotton Malone."

"How did you know I was the one who came to meet you?"

He motioned at the brown envelope lying at the base of the telescope. "Apparently this is not a high-pressure mission." He smiled. "Just running an errand?"

"Something like that. I was coming to ski. A week off, finally. Always wanted to do it. Stephanie asked if I could bring"—she motioned at the envelope—"that along." She went back to her viewing. "You mind if I finish this? It cost a euro and I want to see what's down there."

She revolved the telescope, studying the German valley that stretched for miles below.

"You have a name?" he asked.

"Jessica," she said, her eyes still to the eyepiece.

He reached for the envelope.

Her boot blocked the way. "Not yet. Stephanie said to make sure you understand that the two of you are even."

Last year he'd helped out his old boss in France. She'd told him then that she owed him a favor and that he should use it wisely.

And he had.

"Agreed. Debt paid."

She turned from the telescope. Wind reddened her cheeks. "I've heard about you at the Magellan Billet. A bit of a legend. One of the original twelve agents."

"I didn't realize I was so popular."

"Stephanie said you were modest, too."

He wasn't in the mood for compliments. The past awaited him. "Could I have the file?"

Her eyes sparked. "Sure."

He retrieved the envelope. The first thought that flashed through his mind was how something so thin might answer so many questions.

"That must be important," she said.

Another lesson. Ignore what you don't want to answer. "You been with the Billet long?"

"Couple of years." She stepped from the telescope mount. "Don't like it, though. I'm thinking about getting out. I hear you got out early, too."

As carelessly as she handled herself, quitting seemed like a good career move. During his twelve years he'd taken only three vacations, during which he'd stayed on constant guard. Paranoia was one of many occupational hazards that came with being an agent, and two years of voluntary retirement had yet to cure the malady.

"Enjoy the skiing," he said to her.

Tomorrow he'd fly back to Copenhagen. Today he was going to make a few stops at the rare-book shops in the area—an occupational hazard of his new profession. Bookseller.

She threw him a glare as she grabbed her skis and poles. "I plan to."

They left the terrace and walked back through the nearly deserted visitor center. Jessica headed for the lift that would take her down in the corrie. He headed for the cable car that would drop him ten thousand feet back to ground level.

He stepped into the empty car, holding the envelope. He liked the fact that no one was aboard. But just before the doors closed, a man and woman rushed on, hand in hand. The attendant slammed the doors shut from the outside and the car eased from the station.

He stared out the forward windows.

Enclosed spaces were one thing. Cramped, enclosed spaces were another. He wasn't claustrophobic. More a sense of freedom denied. He'd tolerated it in the past—having found himself underground on more than one occasion—but his discomfort was one reason why, years ago, when he joined the navy, unlike his father, he hadn't opted for submarines.

"Mr. Malone."

He turned.

The woman stood, holding a gun.

"I'll take that envelope."